THE STONE MASTERS

A VAMPIRE'S RISE

BOOK I

V.M.K. FEWINGS

ZOVA **Books**
Los Angeles

ZOVA BOOKS

This book is a work of fiction. References to real people, events, establishments, organizations, or locales are intended only to provide a sense of authenticity and are used fictitiously. All other characters, and all incidents and dialogue are drawn from the author's imagination and are not to be construed as real.

First ZOVA Books edition 2011.

A VAMPIRE'S RISE. Copyright © 2011 by V.M.K. Fewings

All rights reserved.

Printed in the United States of America.

No part of this book may be used or reproduced in any manner whatsoever without written permission except in the case of brief quotations embodied in critical articles and reviews.

For information or permission contact:

ZOVA Books
P.O. Box 21833, Long Beach, California 90801
www.zovabooks.com

ISBN 13: 9780984035007
ISBN 10: 0984035001

Cover Design ©Matthew Pizzo

For Kim

The Stone Masters Vampire Series

A Vampire's Rise (Book I)

A Vampire's Reckoning (Book II)

A Vampire's Dominion (Book III)

PROLOGUE

⊕pium.

The perfume wafts. I breathe it in . . .

Intoxicating.

This is the closest scent to her that I can find. With care, I place the bottle down, dropping the delicate stopper back into position, pushing it aside. An inner tide sweeps me up as nostalgia saturates my senses.

Deep in thought, I recapture her, bewitched, lost to reason, hoping that this impassioned fever breaks, dissipating these emotions. Freedom from such has eluded me thus far. Of course I've taken lovers since, but they've come and gone like seasons, unworthy of memory.

The darkest hour draws near.

And I find myself predictably alone in my London residence. Comfortably ensconced in my shadowy sanctum, I rather enjoy my own company. I'm assured solitude.

Despite the minimal décor, the room is homey, with time-honored furniture that captures the classic style. Leaning against the arched window frame, I trace the tumbling leaves. A howling wind blindly forges on, weaving its way amongst the lamp-lit streets. Taking in the dramatic nightscape, it's easy to become entranced by the grey city skyline. Little evidence is left of its former silhouette.

Rain batters the window. I've left it ajar in hope of airing this neglected room, and some drops find their way through, settling below the ledge, pooling on the stone floor. Turning away, I take a seat at the oak writing desk, resting in the high-backed chair. An all too precious moment taken to reminisce, inspired by thoughts of missives once written here, others received, the waxed seal crumbling as the envelope was ripped open and the letter read.

And read again.

Elm beams run along a low ceiling, holding the warmth. An open fire crackles in the hearth, casting out the occasional spark. The wooden mantelpiece is engraved with a fleur-de-lis. Scratches surrounding the design reveal someone took a dislike to the decorative symbol. The carved iris, though blemished, remains recognizable, suggesting that the culprit became bored and moved on. The carpenter's choice of mahogany saved the design.

There are symbols like this throughout, hidden motifs incorporated into every room, their purpose lost in time. Another secret of this mansion that I'm privy to, a clandestine doorway behind a contemporary painting hanging on the far wall, a discreet exit should one be needed, another of many intrigues, its past is as rich as its thickly lined, black velvet drapes.

I sip from the crystal glass of red and savor the taste. The candlewick burns, but I don't require it. The stillness would be eerie if it weren't for my refined senses, an evolved heightened awareness enabling the detection of the smallest movement or the slightest sound—a supernatural advantage.

I long gave up sleeping by night. These dark hours, I now own.

When your heartbeat ceases, it's fatal, though for my kind it's just the beginning, an endless pathway strewn with the remarkable. Myth unravels as we, the immortals, linger in the underworld and, when the mood takes us, integrate with the living. I don't consider myself the walking dead, for I'm very much alive.

The fresh breeze clears my mind and my thoughts wander back over centuries to the year 1745. I'm lying naked on a rug before a fireplace, entwined with my lover. We're savoring what is left of dusk, sensual delights beyond imagination. She'd captivated me long ago and I'd become obsessed with her. Over time, I've come to appreciate the words she'd spoken that winter night as I caressed her soft skin and kissed her.

"Orpheus, why do you refuse to talk about the past?" she asked.

"Some memories, I choose to forget." I sighed.

"The pain fades."

"What if I don't want it to?"

She shifted in my arms. "So you hold onto the pain and forget the cause?"

I pushed her away. *"Whatever it takes."*

"To survive eternity?" she whispered.

"To exist."

She dressed and withdrew, leaving me to consider our conversation. Finding no benefit in sentimentality, I ignored her.

Her face is fading.

My beloved had changed everything, the woman who'd saved me time and time again, patiently guiding.

Now I understand. It's time to write it down. For her, I'll document all that I know, everything that I remember. If I capture those moments, she'll come back to me. I'll feel her near, hear her voice, and sense her touch.

I refuse to let her go.

With a glance at the crimson glass, I'm reminded that it wasn't always this way, though history is invariably distorted, skewed prose, old-fashioned perspectives deteriorating in unread books.

I, however, am a walking historian.

Once, I desired death but feared to drink from its cup. Such reticence has since waned.

I just noticed the candle's gone dark, leaving a wisp of curling smoke. I'm too easily distracted and drawn into the drama of the past as I remember the defining moment, the event that changed everything . . .

PART ONE

I

Spain 1471

OUT OF THE DARKNESS, I saw it.

More alarming, it saw me, too. Even at the age of nine, I knew well enough to remain still.

The bull would be attracted to movement.

I sucked in air, trying to fill my lungs, yet no breath remained. Orange flames flickered from the few fire torches positioned around the empty arena.

He trotted toward me and then broke into a gallop. The ground shook and time slowed, forcing a dreamy sense of reality. Hoofs skidded to a stop, spraying up a cloud of dust. Sweat evaporated off his hide and a pungent aroma reached my nostrils.

Our eyes locked.

I bit down on my lip, fists clenched, fingernails digging into my palms, though I barely felt them.

He snorted, sniffed, and tilted sharp, devilish horns. My heart pounded, racing ever faster, and my hands shook as I rose to my full height and pulled my shirt over my head, hating those vulnerable seconds, careful to minimize my movements.

He pawed the dirt.

"Control with composure." My brother's words spoken to me long ago, conveying his poise as a seasoned bullfighter.

The bull flicked his tail and snarled. I judged which horn he favored, indicating the direction he'd go.

He thundered toward me, his hoofs rhythmically striking the ground, and I raised my make-shift cape. It brushed over his horns as he galloped past, and swerved left, snorting stale breath that left a putrid taste buried deep in the back of my throat. Lumbering, he turned to face me again, inclining his enormous head. My dry tongue cleaved to the roof of my mouth and I tried to gulp my fear. Taking short breaths, unable to remember my last, I suppressed a whimper.

Large nostrils sniffed the air again. I steadied my hands and flicked the garment as he lurched under my left arm, spraying up soil.

I backed up.

Head down, he followed.

My back struck the arena wall, betraying my escape, trapping me between it and him. His stare met mine and went on through. In a state of dread, those terrifying seconds seemed more like hours as they took my breath with them. I struggled to recall which saint could be rallied.

The ground vibrated, bringing with it a sea of black as a billowing dust cloud arose. I threw my shirt over his head and then dived to the right of him. The material blinded him and he plunged into the stone, horns scraping and grinding. He bellowed and shook his head.

I leaped to my feet and bolted along and over the enclosure, landing on the gravel, scraping my hands and knees. Still tasting the dirt he'd sprayed up, I turned awkwardly and peered back. The bull's eyes bulged, his tail hung low between his legs as he trotted, searching. I sighed, almost forgetting my stinging, bloodied knees.

Whack!

Thrown forward by the crack that struck my head, pain exploded in my skull. Through a bleary stare, I lay looking up at three men, their shadowy figures looming over me, handkerchiefs pulled up to obscure their faces. The tallest of the three tapped his fingers against his thigh. In his other hand, he grasped a wooden cudgel.

After the third strike, I blacked out.

11

THE FAINT SCENT OF ROSES.
 Blackness.
 I awoke to sobs and realized they were mine. I squinted in the darkness at the four dirty grey walls of a small room. An aching head hindered my ability to focus. Moonlight seeped in beneath the door.
 Hands bound in front of me, tied with coarse rope, I rolled onto my side and used my elbow to prop myself up to better see. Shirtless, the cold caught up.
 Not just any room.
 Resting firmly in the center lay an intricately carved, white marble sarcophagus. Afraid to move, I hoped my heart would stay in my chest and not beat its way out. I struggled to pull up my legs and then realized that my ankles had been bound together and tied to the iron leg of a corner bench. Struggling to free myself, the rope chafed my wrists. Despite the burning, I continued tugging, almost freeing one hand.
 I had no idea how I'd come to be in here.
 Or how long.
 Less than a year ago, my friends had dared me to enter a tomb much like this one, but I couldn't even look inside, fearful of their stories of rotting corpses stacked high, the stench so bad that it would choke me. Their tales had convinced me I'd made the right decision. Now, laying just inches away from such a tomb, I wondered how many corpses lay within. Even though I couldn't see them, I knew they were in there. My sobs pushed away the silence.
 Make it go away.
 Engravings along the sides portrayed ancient Roman battles. Years had worn away some of the dramatic images, but not all. With my struggles came the tearing of my flesh. I gnawed at the rope, frustrated that nothing gave. I fell back and stared up at the ceiling. Then back at the tomb.
 Dried scarlet petals were scattered nearby, a few strewn upon the marble coffin lid, fallen from a bouquet, seemingly abandoned in the corner. Mourners had long forgotten this place.
 Numbness in my limbs thwarted my movements, and my lips were so dry that they stung when I grimaced. The ground felt rough against

my bare back.

The walls closed in.

An awful thought struck me that I might die alone in here. My body would be discovered by the visitors who'd eventually come back to pay their respects, maybe in a week, maybe in a year.

I needed to get out.

I had a faint recollection of scrambling down the rough vines that straddled our house and sneaking out to the amphitheater—an awful feeling that I'd done the unthinkable, and broken the golden rule of bullfighting. The bulls received minimal human interaction, never experiencing a man on foot before entering the arena. To do so would mean they'd know to charge the matador instead of his cape.

But I'd done just that, barely surviving and leaving behind a bull dangerously conditioned. With Fiesta Brava scheduled for that night, set to begin in a few hours, the bull would now be deadly to anyone who approached. And my brother, a seasoned matador, was expected to fight. The fire torches had been lit by someone on purpose, perhaps the very same man who'd worked the bull so hard that a vapor had risen off his hide.

Cobwebs weaved along the sides of the sarcophagus and dangled. Fear of the spiders that had spun them caused near panic. I heard a sound from outside, branches crunching underfoot, and I took a deep breath ready to call out for help.

I froze.

Something was moving in here as well, and though I didn't like the idea of a rodent scurrying around inside the sarcophagus, it was easily preferable to the notion that I'd awoken the dead. My face itched and I reached up, slightly thwarted by the restraints, and scratched my chin. Something had caked on my face and it crumbled beneath my touch. Dried blood wedged under my fingernails.

I had to get out.

A gust of warmth blew as the door creaked open and a man-shaped silhouette appeared in the entryway. He burst in and stomped toward me, as though expecting to find me. Beads of sweat spotted his brow.

My words came out but had no meaning. I squeezed my eyes shut, afraid of his menacing scowl.

Quiet.

His foot tapped my thigh.

I peeked at the gnarly club poised above me, trying to make out the features of the stranger who clutched it. His thick black eyebrows almost met, and the cleft in his chin was barely obscured by his morning shadow. He wore a sinister glare that declared he was ready to strike at any moment. I feared this was my punishment for the bullfight that I'd unwittingly stepped into, a dance with death that should never have happened. I wanted to explain that I had no idea the bull would be in there.

His knuckles whitened as he raised the weapon high.

The lid of the coffin scraped open. I couldn't bear to look. He could use that cudgel on the thing. Something heavy landed on my thigh. He'd dropped the club. Peeking through one blurry eye, I saw a young woman standing by the tomb, and felt an inner quickening, a strange tingling in my chest. My gasp echoed off the walls and found its way back to me.

She wore a long, white gown made from the finest linen. Her porcelain complexion was flawless, her features exquisite, and she sauntered as though floating as she approached. Straight raven hair fell over her shoulders and flowed down her back. Gold trinkets on her wrists jangled. Her startling turquoise gaze darted between the man and me.

I shifted. "Don't hurt me."

His foot struck my mouth and I winced in pain.

The deepest sigh, or something like one.

I opened my eyes.

He'd gone.

I stared out through the open doorway and saw no sign of him. Just the woman sliding the tomb lid closed. Several dry rose petals fluttered to the ground, one of them resting on the abandoned cudgel.

She knelt close and traced my bruises with her cold fingers. "It's over now," she said.

"Who are you?"

"Suna."

I glanced at the tomb. "I have to get home."

"You can't." She untied me.

I ran my fingers through my sticky, matted hair and shivered with the thought that it might be blood. I scrambled to my feet.

Her fingers wrapped around my forearm and tugged me back. "It's not safe."

Alarmed, I considered her warning, and turned toward the doorway.

She gazed out at the twilight. My footing gave and she caught me. I pulled away and bolted out, met by the welcome warmth of freedom, and glanced up at the stark white cross atop the steeple of the nearby church, heartened by the familiar landmark that would guide me home. I glanced back and saw Suna vanish amongst the shadows.

Out of sight of the mausoleum, I urinated a dark yellow stream against a sorry looking hedge, then, in spite of my aching limbs, I scampered through the graveyard, following the few village lights that guided me into town and, just beyond that, the bullring.

On my arrival, I lingered at the arena edge.

Empty seats indicated that the bullfight had come and gone. Short of breath, overcome with a stomach ache, my heart pounded and my hands shook with fear. I ran home ignoring my suffering body, hoping to wash off this blood before my mother caught sight of me. My thoughts carried back to the mausoleum. I tried to understand what had happened and was so relieved that the dead had remained hidden.

The señorita had come out of nowhere, but more alarming was that awful cudgel that man had tried to kill me with, and the dread that he'd try it again. My brother would know what to do.

I stared up at my shut bedroom window.

Sleep would not come easily tonight.

I'd have to enter via the back door that was usually left open. I was shocked by the sight of chaos within the kitchen — sporadically placed unwashed dishes, half-eaten food, and a table left untouched from supper. Not the usual tidiness my mother insisted upon. A basket of clean clothes lay next to the kitchen table. I gulped warm cup of water after warm cup of water, trying to quench a thirst that refused to relent.

In the back room, I leaned over the wash bowl and poured water over my matted hair. I disposed of the pinky-red water before someone saw it. The throbbing in my head caused more waves of nausea. All I wanted was to sleep off the rest of the day.

Hushed voices carried down from the upper rooms. With deliberate footsteps, I ascended the stairs, avoiding the floorboards that creaked, memorized over time. A warm breeze brushed past billowing the curtain of an open window. Through the keyhole, I made out the shape of my grandfather lying upon my mother's bed.

With a deep breath, I opened the door. My mother rested on the bedside with my grandfather's hand in hers. Although she turned to face me, she didn't look at me. My grandmother sat in an armchair and she too avoided my stare.

Roelle Bastillion loomed in the corner, the twenty-three-year-old owner of the ranch where my brother worked. He glanced at me sideways.

I hesitated to explain where I'd been, fearful of worsening my mother's disappointed demeanor, not only for the fact that I'd gone missing, but also because I'd gotten into such trouble.

Grandfather coughed. The left side of his face hung lower than his right in an unfamiliar grimace and his left arm was twisted beneath him.

"He'll be well taken care of," Roelle said. "Discipline won't put it right, but he'll gather the magnitude."

At my mother's feet lay my bloody shirt. I struggled to speak. Bile rose in my throat and threatened to spew.

Roelle reached for me and clutched my arm. "I know it seems harsh," he said. "Better to come with me than to the *bastille* to hang." His fingers squeezed over a cut near my elbow, and it started bleeding again.

The more I wriggled, the firmer he held me. My grandfather seemed for a moment to recognize me. Mother still wouldn't look at me.

Roelle dragged me out of the room, shoving me along the corridor and down the stairs. Unable to escape his ironclad grip, and despite my heels digging in, he hauled me outside.

"Your brother's dead," he said.

III

THE BARE, DANK, DARK cell smelt of musty, stale wine.

With my head buried in my hands, I tried to grasp Ricardo's death. My mind scrambled to comprehend. Roelle confirmed my worst fear, that my brother had died in the bull ring.

Minimal access to light made it impossible to determine the passing of time. The unrelenting cold chilled my bones. The pain burrowed in. Discarded hessian sacks that I wrapped around me prevented me from freezing.

My arrival at Roelle's estate went unnoticed. I'd been locked up in the cellars before any of the staff had gotten a look at me.

Nothing but quiet.

Chaotic thoughts took advantage of the silence.

In the stone walls, I made out patterns, and distorted faces emerged. I counted the exposed bricks until memorized, then changed positions to alter the view.

Recalling the way my bedroom had looked, I closed my eyes and pretended I was back there. I imagined the chair I sat in at breakfast, the way the pot in the hearth swung after my mother had stirred the broth, and my mother's face, the way her top lip curled when she smiled. She'd forgive me, come back for me.

Save me.

Fourteen bricks across and twenty down. Paint still covered the last few I counted. I used my hands to judge how many there were before they reached the ground. After counting the bricks, I kicked them, twisting my ankle and sending brown dust into the air. I didn't try it again.

I developed a love-hate relationship with the bucket in the corner, grateful that I had it, but hateful when its stench overwhelmed me.

Despite protesting that I didn't know anything about his friend Aaron, who'd mysteriously disappeared, Roelle used his fists to force my recollection. His knuckles struck my flesh, punching old bruises and making new ones. Curled up, I tucked my knees beneath me, using my hands to protect my face. With each strike came his worsening frustration.

"If I knew, I'd tell you," I cried.

He stormed out.

My sobs caused a rift in the stillness.

Guilt for my brother's death eased during the long days when a visit from Roelle distracted me. Physical and mental torture became frequent. Fretful to learn the fate of his best friend, Aaron, he interrogated me. I tried to convince him that I knew nothing.

Sleep was my only refuge. My mind turned to thoughts of the señorita as I tried to recall her face, haunted by her. "*Suna*," was the name she'd told me. *Sunaria*, I called her now, my phantom savoir who'd warned me.

I yearned for home, for my mother's love, her forgiveness. I surrendered to the despair and embraced the void. With such pain, there's no hope, and with that no chance of disappointment. When darkness engulfs, there's no fear of losing one's way.

One is already lost.

The news that I'd acclimated the bullfight that killed my brother caused terrible anguish. My thoughts spiraled again and again, never finding their way out of the rut of confusion. I had no choice but to relinquish all memories of him as a way to suppress the twisted agony that wrenched at my small, weak frame.

Start anew.

To survive this, I had to win Roelle's approval. Though his visits had lessened, when he did impose himself into my dark prison, I presented the air of a boy humbled but strong, respectful and yet resilient.

His brow furrowed as he considered me with an oddly conflicted gaze.

I chose my words carefully. "Sir, I can fix that."

About to head out the door, he glared back.

"Your jacket pocket," I said. "My grandfather's a tailor. He taught me—"

He left and slammed the door shut.

Within two hours, I'd been provided with a needle and a fine thread, and given the opportunity to mend Roelle's jacket. Kneeling in the corner next to my all too precious, near fading candle, I sewed the finest stitches.

When Roelle returned, he brought bread and cheese, and I gulped the cup of milk he offered. He examined his neatly sewn jacket, with a thoughtful expression.

* * * *

After several weeks, Roelle freed me from the cellar.

But he warned that if I attempted to run away, he'd personally deliver me to the jail. To prove his point, the day before my release, he made a noose out of coarse rope and hung it around my neck.

Understanding came quickly.

With decisive steps, unable to speak, I followed Roelle up and out of the dark.

Daylight appeared different.

Within the interior of the mansion, ostentatious decor hindered homeliness. The house seemed more of a statement of power than a family residence. Enough opulence to make any visitor unwelcome.

I couldn't fathom why a part of me missed my small, dark cell.

Roelle appointed me as his personal manservant, his way to keep me close. He provided a damp, empty room close to his, though I rarely slept there due to Roelle's insistence that I sleep in the corner of his bedroom, perhaps to allay his loneliness.

As master of the Bastillion empire, Roelle ruled the household with fierce intimidation and no one challenged him. His abuse on the small boy, who cleaned his matador apparel and carried out other chores, went unnoticed. If anything, the staff admired his courage in taking on the unruly son of the Velde family.

I clung to Roelle and gradually found an eerie comfort in his presence and strived to perform my errands well.

That cell still threatened to eat me up again.

Within his office, I set to work sorting out his desk and, as instructed, not disrupting any further his already disorganized filing. My thoughts drifted back to that beautiful señorita in the mausoleum, then dared to wander back further.

I'd shamed my family.

My father, the ultimate hero, had fought in England's battle of Blore Heath. I'd overheard him telling Ricardo that many Lancastrians perished during the battle that they eventually lost. The defeated leaders fled the country and my father too had found wisdom in placing distance between himself and the land he'd never called home. The scars went deeper than his war torn limbs. A few days before my sixth birthday, he'd died.

As the eldest, Ricardo had been tasked with supporting our family.

Ricardo stood in the kitchen doorway, his expression strange as he glanced down at the object he held in his right hand. Alicia, our six-year-old sister, a year older than me, clapped her hands with excitement as Ricardo slapped the bloody bull's ear onto the table, its tendrils hanging. My sister went quiet and I knew that this moment was meant for me, this precious gift that represented a matador's bravery, bestowed from the bullfighter himself, and I felt unworthy to touch it. Sensing my reticence, Ricardo winked at me. Our mother regarded the specimen with a glint of pride, though the quiver of her lips exposed her fear, and she yelled that it would leave a stain.

And it did.

Roelle and I had never spoken about the events that led to my brother's death, though on several occasions I'd felt compelled to open up to him and try to shed light, find the truth. Doubt sealed my silence.

Somewhere far off in the house, Roelle could be heard shouting at a servant. Thoughtful, trying to retrieve even more from my shaky memory, I stole into the well-stocked library.

* * * *

Eventually, I slept in the servant's quarters. The firm, musty bed felt like luxury.

Once a week, Roelle arranged for one of the city's finest teachers to visit. Señor Machon provided much of my early education and under his strict tutelage, I studied hard. Such an indulgence was an unusual occurrence for a lowly servant, though the gossiping staff soon became accustomed to my schooling. Roelle reassured them that he had every intention of putting my education to use as his office boy. He hated dealing with the boring details of running the estate and thought it a fantastic idea that he could educate me to do it.

I looked forward to my lessons. Eager to present to my teacher numerous questions, I hauled large books borrowed from the library down the corridor. Machon patiently answered. He shared his belief that the world, previously considered to be flat, had been proven to be round. He presented ancient Greek texts that supported this theory. Sworn to secrecy, he warned me that such thinking brought accusations of heresy.

Wide-eyed, I nodded and although I'd hesitated to question the meaning of heresy, I fully understood that I'd been entrusted with something very special. Señor Machon reported to Roelle that he considered me his best student.

I found the courage to request a visit home, after all. Cook had told me my village could be reached in half a day.

"Maybe," Roelle said.

I looked out beyond the estate wondering if my mother would ever visit. Jealousy seeped in when I thought of my sister nestling in my mother's arms, and I wondered if they'd forgotten me.

My new life absorbed my time, the passing of which softened the faces of my past.

IV

AT EIGHTEEN YEARS OLD, I towered over Roelle.

At just over six feet, wearing the clothes he'd purchased for me, I presented the very image of a young gentleman. Although my quiet demeanor disconcerted the staff, my dark locks, hazel eyes, and sharp features easily enamored them. Head down, I engaged in my duties, often avoiding interacting.

For my birthday, Roelle presented me with one of the estate's best stallions. He personally taught me how to ride. With boredom rose his wickedness. He'd strike the horse's rump, causing the animal to rear up. As I hit the ground with a thud, I could hear his laughter.

I had my revenge while cleaning Roelle's office. I'd rummage through his private papers, eager to discover something that might embarrass him. I soon found where he hid the key to a secret compartment in his desk. Inside, he'd stashed letters.

Reading one of them by candlelight, it became clear that my progress had been followed by a Felipe Grenaldi. Puzzled, I replaced my find, wondering why this man would be interested in me.

Shoved behind a stack of wooden boxes, half-hidden, rested an upside-down artist's canvas. I'd never noticed it before. I eased it out, turned it over, and laid it on the desk, pondering on the portrait of four men standing closely together, all dressed in matador apparel. One of them was my brother, Ricardo, his likeness masterfully portrayed. My stomach wrenched and my throat tightened.

In the picture, Roelle had flung his arm affectionately around the shoulders of a man whose face had been blacked out with what looked like ink.

On hearing someone approaching, I quickly put the painting back.

* * * *

Despite my seeming promotion, Roelle never let me forget my place and often provided chores that would easily remind me. One wrong move could result in a threat of returning to that cellar. Therefore, I strived for perfection, very often going over tasks I'd already completed.

One late evening while I was tidying Roelle's bedchamber, he entered carrying matador apparel. I recognized the embellished gold braid that swept up the breast of the jacket and along the shoulders. The small, black buttons had been fastened with fine, scarlet ribbon. This suit had been my brother's. Roelle slid it into the wardrobe.

I reached for Roelle's black leather shoes and polished them.

He relayed with a smile, "In your mother's letter, she insisted I take it." He studied me. "Not sure who to give it to yet."

Discreetly watching him preen, I steadied my hands and swallowed hard, unsettled by a wave of uneasiness. In the newly shined reflection, my brother stared back. It was my own image. A quick glance confirmed Roelle hadn't noticed my reaction. He sauntered out.

I faced the mirror, placed my hand upon the glass, then traced my reflection. My stone-faced expression concealed so much, even from me.

A creak caused me to spin round.

Roelle leaned against the doorframe. "What's going on in that head of yours?" He approached, grabbed my arm, and dragged me over to his closet. "Get in."

I resisted.

Roelle opened the door and shoved me in. He turned the lock and removed the key. I'd never liked the dark, or confined spaces. I started to perspire.

"I'm not angry with you, Daumia." He pressed up against the closet door. "This is your best vantage point."

He disappeared.

With my shoulder against the door, I gave it a shove and cracked the wood. Just as I went to give it another thrust, I heard voices. Roelle had returned with someone. I peered through the keyhole.

The blacksmith's daughter allowed Roelle to undress her and as he did so she giggled nervously. Despite the fascination, this felt wrong. Roelle threw her playfully onto his bed.

Her plump legs wrapped around Roelle's hips and her fleshy arms pulled him closer. His trousers were halfway down.

I felt used. Something in the tone of his voice as he spoke, the way she whimpered in response, sent shivers up my spine.

Roelle glanced in my direction.

My sweat-soaked shirt stuck to my skin.

Fourteen bricks across and twenty down. Paint covering the last few . . .

Roelle had put me in there and kept me in there.

At that moment, I knew that I had more honor than him and my pride arose. The headboard banged against the wall. With my hands over my ears, I tried to block out that noise, as well as their groans.

I thought back to the books I'd read and the ideas they'd inspired— that painting and my brother's happy expression, and the mystery of the obscured face. I considered the rest of my chores yet to be completed.

The closet door opened and a smug Roelle held a silver goblet of red wine and offered it to me. The girl had gone.

Sitting on the end of his bed, keeping some distance from him, I stared into my empty cup. Roelle topped it up again. I drank and he talked. Not really listening to his self-important droll, I phased out. The drink tasted good, if not bitter, the warmth of the liquor a welcome sensation. It softened my mood and as I took another sip, it made me desire more.

That painting could very well be my last chance of capturing Ricardo. I leaped up, but my legs failed me and I slumped to the floor. The drink slipped from my grasp and bounced along, stopping at the edge of the worn rug. Roelle's laughter almost impeded his ability to get me back onto the bed. From the rim of the goblet, the last few droplets of wine trickled out onto the corner of the rug's tasseled fringe.

I fell asleep.

* * * *

I heaved over the bedside, grateful that Roelle had provided a chamber pot. I wondered if he also had a head that pounded. The rug's red stain was the only trace of last night's weirdness.

Roelle sat up. "Your mother's dead."

I used my sleeve to wipe the vomit from my mouth. My voice broke as I asked, "When?"

"What does it matter?"

My jaw gaped.

"A week ago," he said.

"And my grandparents?"

"What about them?" He looked surprised. "They died years ago."

The empty wine bottle rested on the side table. A cruel trick of its contents to lie like that, soften one's feelings yet later produce such ghastly symptoms. And yet Roelle seemed unaffected.

"Go and help Miguel in the stable," he said. "He needs a hand."

I headed for the door.

"Daumia," he called after me.

I faced him, wondering if this dragging pain in my chest would ever let up.

"I'm sorry about your mother," he said.

I imagined what it would feel like to smash the empty bottle over his head.

"You're doing that thing," he said. "Where you stare off and waste time. My time." Roelle slipped into the shoes I'd just polished.

Black wax stained my hands, polish ingrained under my fingernails.

Halfway down the stairs, I stared back up at Roelle's bedroom. That painting had been defaced and yet he'd kept it.

Back in the office, I went straight for the portrait. I turned it over and studied it more closely. In the left-hand corner, in small scratchy handwriting, the subjects' names were written on the back: *Ricardo Velde, Felipe Grenaldi, Roelle Bastillion, and Aaron Luis.*

I turned the painting over again and scraped the smudge that obscured the mystery man's face, exposing black eyebrows too close together, a familiar dark expression, and a cleft in his chin.

That awful cudgel.

Lightheaded, I made my way to the servants' quarters.

On finding a bath prepared for someone else, I climbed in. Scrubbing my skin, trying to wash away this unclean feeling, the memories flooded and so did the agony of losing my mother. I'd never explained the truth to her. Biting my hand to quiet my sobs, I slid beneath the surface and water whooshed over the sides of the tub, soaking the floor.

This time, someone else could clean up the mess.

V

LYING ON MY BED, staring up at the dirty, white ceiling, my thoughts raced.

Roelle had been a good friend of Aaron's, good enough to be painted together. Aaron may not have acted alone. Felipe Grenaldi had requested updates from Roelle on my progress. What had inspired his interest? Those fire torches lit up around the arena had proven that someone else had been there that night, probably the same man who let the bull loose in the ring. The bullfight that killed my brother had been rigged.

Three men.

The coldest shiver slithered down my spine.

Italy beckoned, my father's homeland. I resisted the urge to bolt. Time spent in Rome would rekindle my Italian. I'd pass off as a merchant. If assumed dead, freedom would be possible. As my plan came together, my mood lifted, and for the first time, I felt hope. With my decision made, it wouldn't be easy to stay any longer than necessary.

My room felt less stifling. Staring out of the window, my gaze followed puffs of clouds gliding over the half-moon, caressing its grayish orb.

Sleep did not visit me that night.

Before sunrise, I took up my new chores working with Miguel, a fifty-year-old, seasoned horse breeder. His tanned, lined face reflected a lifetime of labor carried out under a scorching sun, his passion for taking good care of the livestock, an inspiration. Had my thoughts not been on greater matters, I may have paid more attention. The mind numbing duties assigned ensured time to think.

To scheme.

That same afternoon, Roelle had taken one of his regular visits out of town. With him away, there seemed a palpable sense of relief amongst the staff. As the sun beat down, I found some pleasure in working an untamed horse in the paddock. Nearby, two stable hands discussed Roelle's dinner party planned for that night and I eavesdropped, hearing that Felipe Grenaldi would be guest of honor. Felipe had apparently followed in his father's footsteps and become a senator. I also gleaned from their conversation that Felipe had found favor with royalty.

Over the years, Felipe had occasionally visited Roelle. During his social calls, I found myself confined to the servants' quarters.

And I suspected why.

From the kitchen, I gathered leftover portions of bread and cheese and wrapped them in a small sack, stashing the stolen items under my pillow, ready for the following afternoon when I'd make my escape.

In Roelle's study, I found a few loose coins in the bottom drawer of his writing desk, enough doubloons to get me to the port. I buried the money under the root of one of the garden's oak trees and marked the spot with three stones. In the library, I searched out a book of maps and tore out one of the pages. The chart would guide me out of Spain.

Having organized Roelle's bedroom closet, and taken care of his clothes for years, I knew he wouldn't miss a jacket. I removed one and held it up to myself, checking its fit. Smarter attire would arouse less suspicion. A well-dressed man is often offered assistance and quickly gains respect. The jacket was just slightly short in the sleeves, but it would do.

The hairs on the back of my neck stood up. Roelle lingered in the doorway.

I slid the suit back, resisting the urge to bite my lip. "Señor, your suit needs tailoring."

"I'm told that you're doing well." Roelle entered. "Miguel tells me that sleeping with the animals earns their trust."

I glanced out of the window and saw Miguel in the paddock, training a skittish horse. His patience was paying off.

Roelle approached me and followed my stare. "We think it will be good for you to sleep in the stables for now."

I swallowed my reaction.

"I haven't decided for how long yet," he said.

Dusty earth sprayed up around the horse.

"Do you want that jacket?" he said.

Miguel had subdued the horse in record time.

I'd read in one of Señor Machon's books that an artist of extraordinary talent, who resided in Italy, had found favor with the Roman Catholic Church.

"Daumia?" Roelle's voice seemed far off.

If Giovanni Bellini agreed to hire me as his assistant, he might take me with him to the Vatican, and there I could receive an audience with the Pope and my sins would be absolved. My mother would have found solace in that.

Roelle sighed.

Miguel caressed the horse's muzzle, lulling him.

Roelle brushed past me and sat on the bed. "The good news is that you won't be alone anymore. Your sister's joining us."

I snapped back into the room.

"I've accepted her as one of my housemaids," he said.

I bit the inside of my cheek.

"I'm sure we'll find lots for her to do." He patted the bed sheet.

Before me sat the man whose authority had been the benchmark by which I'd measured all things. His morality had shaped my own. Roelle had allowed me in and provided full access, and such was my advantage.

VI

ENTRANCED, HOLDING THE map over a candle flame, I watched it burn, sending a grayish spiral of smoke toward the open window, escaping into the night. I considered whether I'd recognize Alicia. I felt ready to forgive her, though for what I wasn't sure.

Miguel had expected me in the barn hours ago, but I still hoped Roelle would change his mind.

I crept downstairs into the basement, avoiding that terrible cell, the dark dwelling where I'd been held captive. I continued on into the fully-stocked wine cellar. Using my teeth, I uncorked one of the better vintages. The first, fruity gulps stung my taste buds and the cold liquid quenched the thirst I didn't know I had, and then it came . . . that exquisite flush, that rush of warmth.

Recalling my previous hangover, I didn't finish it but shoved the half-empty bottle into the corner where the others had been stacked. Strolling back along the corridor, I considered peering into *the* cell. I didn't do it, though.

Heady with the liquor, with one foot on the first stair leading up to my room, I paused, and then turned to look at Roelle's office door.

Inside, I settled comfortably at his writing desk and rummaged through his papers. Within moments, I'd located his will, embossed with the Bastillion family crest. I found a perfect match to the paper that his legal document had been scribed on. With Roelle's feathered fountain pen dipped in fresh ink, I scribed in his handwriting. Within an hour, the Bastillion legacy had become my own, the house and all its contents bequeathed to me. I admired my handiwork.

Felipe had witnessed the will. His signature took longer. I pressed the official Bastillion stamp into the thick, red, liquefied wax and sealed the document. I destroyed the original.

This boy had truly proven himself to be Roelle's protégé. I placed the dispatch, addressed to Roelle's legal counsel, in the master's out tray and headed back up the stairs, taking two at a time. When I reached the landing, I almost yelped. My pulse raced so fast, I feared my voice would fail me.

Roelle had returned earlier than expected. A slender woman stood facing him. Straight raven locks fell down her back.

Alicia?

"You still up?" Roelle eyed me suspiciously.

The woman turned and fixed her turquoise gaze on me. Her jaw-dropping beauty was dazzling, just as I remembered her.

Roelle glared. "Are you just going to gawp or are you going to say hello to your sister?"

He'd never met Alicia, so he'd have no idea that this woman, the one from the mausoleum, wasn't her. More surprising still, despite my maturing, she hadn't altered.

"You'll have to forgive your brother," Roelle said, "he's not one for words."

Her bracelets jangled.

A long white tomb inside a deserted mausoleum.

As though reading my mind, she offered me a smile. Roelle guided her away, down the corridor, and although I knew I should quietly amble off in the opposite direction so as not to arouse suspicion, I found myself staring at her, captivated by her womanly form swaying as she strolled beside him, her fine, black linen gown trailing behind her.

Roelle shooed me away and they turned the corner.

This woman had prevented Aaron from bludgeoning me, the lady who'd warned me not to return home. Trying to work out the reason for her being here, and what she'd told Roelle, I pressed my ear against the door.

Miguel appeared at the end of the hallway. "There you are," he said.

I pretended to be straightening a nearby mirror.

With squeaky shoes, he approached. "I know it takes some getting used to."

"What?"

"Sleeping in the stables."

"I'm just finishing off some errands."

Miguel raised an eyebrow. "I can see that." He gestured to Roelle's door. "Your sister?"

I stayed quiet.

"Come on." He wrapped his arm around my shoulder. "Life isn't meant to be easy."

* * * *

It wasn't only the noisy animals that made it impossible to sleep. My life teetered on the edge of change and I was eager to see it through. I obsessed over the mysterious woman, Alicia's imposter, the last person to see Aaron. This woman had willingly entered the Bastillion residence, fully aware that I could give her identity away. I'd looked forward to seeing Alicia but felt relief that it wasn't her who now lay in his bed, though the thought of my Sunaria there evoked jealousy.

My plan to leave, with its real promise of freedom, was rekindled. I bit down onto my hand when I remembered that I'd burnt the map and buried my teeth even further when I recalled forging Roelle's will. It would still be in the out tray.

Find it and destroy it.

There were small dent marks where I'd bitten into my hand. Mouth dry, I climbed off my straw-stuffed bed and dashed for the exit, still taken by the line upon line of stabled horses and their ability to sleep on their feet.

I stopped in my tracks.

Miguel sat by the entrance with an open book resting on his lap, the upside-down title unreadable. He looked up as though he'd been expecting me and said, "Can't sleep either, uh?"

I stared at the house. "I just have to—"

"You read and write, I hear?"

I nodded, half-distracted.

"I'd like you to teach me," he said.

"Now?"

Miguel stared at me for a long time. "Who is that woman with Roelle?"

My gaze fell away from his all-seeing eyes and lingered on his book.

"She's not from around here, is she?" His lined face softened with the raise of his grey, bushy eyebrows. "You chose not to tell Roelle that she's not your sister?"

"I wasn't sure—"

"How he'd react?"

"Perhaps I should check on her?"

Miguel tut-tutted his disapproval.

"What are you reading?" I said as my stomach twisted.

"I have no idea. I don't read, remember?" He closed the book.

"You have no interest in learning, do you?"

Miguel turned and gazed up at Roelle's window. "Now that we know it's not Alicia, we can sleep." He winked. "Get some rest. Tomorrow will be a long day."

"Here, it's always a long day."

"Life is fluid. It changes. That's one of life's guarantees."

"In my experience, there are no guarantees."

Miguel sighed. "So young to be so jaded."

"What they say about me, about what happened to my brother, it's not true."

"I know."

"How do you know?"

"The animals trust you, which means you trust yourself."

"How do you know that?"

"I don't know what happened that night, but I do know that Roelle carries with him a tremendous guilt. I see it in his eyes when he looks at you. He treats you as a son and yet punishes you for things you do not do. He's punishing himself."

I stared down at my worn shoes.

"I may not read words," he said, "but that doesn't mean I can't read people."

I returned my gaze to him. "You wanted me out of the house? You advised Roelle to have me come in here?"

"I choose to sleep near my animals. I wouldn't expect such dedication of another unless—"

"You thought I might be safer?" I wanted to believe this. For the first time, I'd find someone who glimpsed the good that I'd always hoped was in me.

"Go to bed." He dropped the book and it landed silently on the straw-covered ground.

I went to express my disapproval of treating a book like that, but my tongue found itself wedged between my teeth. I wondered where he'd gotten that book from. Miguel's quiet forced me to return to my makeshift bed.

The smell of the animals was fading.

* * * *

At dawn, my stare lingered on the maple out tray, as though Roelle's forged will would magically reappear if I gazed at it long enough. Heart pounding, taking three stairs at a time, I headed up the stairs.

Roelle was still in bed, sitting with his back against the headboard. A servant girl laid his breakfast tray by his side - an assortment of breads, eggs, and a small pot of milk.

With my hands behind my back, I hid their tremor. One hint from Roelle that he knew what I'd done and I'd bolt.

I blamed my reckless behavior on the liquor I'd consumed last night, foolish to have thought I could get away with it.

"Can't the chef be more imaginative?" Roelle glanced at the food and then his irritated frown settled on me. "What?"

"Alicia?" My voice was quiet.

Roelle's expression turned to confusion. "I have no idea who you are talking about." He rubbed his neck as he watched the maid draw the curtains, allowing the sun to flood in, casting white rays that quickly banished even the sneakiest of shadows.

I was amazed he'd forgotten Sunaria so soon, but reasoned he just didn't want to talk, not with me, anyway.

Roelle's fumbling fingers clumsily stroked his hairy thigh. "My skin's crawling." He scratched, digging his nails into his flesh, throwing off the bed sheets and kicking at them. His head slumped back onto the pillow, his body jerking, spasming. His jaw slackened and his contorted lips formed into a cry, out of which came a terrible throaty gurgling, and then a screech escaped his over stretched mouth, spittle bursting out and trickling, wetting his chin.

Roelle thrashed.

The maid, pale now and shaking, reached for the milk pot as it tipped, its contents pouring onto the floor, leaving a trail of creamy-white liquid snaking its way beneath the bed, as though fleeing in terror.

Roelle's skin blistered, and his eyes bulged. He fell off the bed and the tray crashed with him, spilling the rest of its contents. A flash of flames, his hair alight, his flesh melting, as he crawled along, his crazed stare searching, as he lurched for me, arms flailing.

I grabbed the water jug and threw it over him, ready to jump out of his way if he turned. Roelle rose up and bashed against the window frame, catching the curtain on fire. I seized the maid's hand and yanked her out of her horrified trance, and out the door, leaving behind that dreadful wailing. We scurried along the corridor and ran for the stairs.

The breath left my lungs when I saw Roelle staggering behind us, his arms outstretched as he almost caught up, a monstrous human inferno trailing close. The girl tripped and I yanked her up and pulled her with me down the steps. Several of the staff, their faces full of fright, stared past us and up at Roelle, who crashed against the velvet backdrop hanging from the ceiling. Dancing flames leaped from him and onto the drapes, raging ever skyward, spreading wildly.

The heat pushed us back.

Roelle's face was dissolving, unrecognizable. With that awful glow of yellow, orange, and fleeting red, quivering and clinging to him, he tumbled toward us, his grotesque scream now a primal cry.

VII

THE SMOKE HAD FORCED us out.

Only when the last horse had been secured did I allow myself the indulgence of looking back. My throat felt scratchy and dry. A member of the staff handed out water, but looking at my empty cup, I couldn't remember drinking mine.

That painting with my brother's face had gone. As only fire can, it gutted the house, leaving mounds of grey ash in its wake. As I stared up at where the estate had once stood, I felt free.

Although I'd hoped God had in some way intercepted, something told me Sunaria held the answer. I searched for her face in the crowd, but saw only tired workers, their worried expressions fading into exhaustion. Although everyone but Roelle had survived, their livelihood had gone up in smoke along with their master.

Rumors circulated that a candle had fallen onto the bed and caused the fire. The maid's incomprehensible ramblings didn't help, either. With Miguel's testament that I'd slept in the stables and the girl as witness to my innocence, I avoided any blame. With no house to run, the staff disbursed, though the horses still needed tending.

Miguel persuaded me to assist. "At least until the animals are sold," he said.

The stables had been left intact. After cleaning the ashes that had blown into their stalls, it was safe for the horses to return. They grazed on the estate's grassy fields so we could ration the leftover hay.

Taking my time grooming one of the more startled horses, trying to calm him, I knew that I delayed the inevitable. Nothing stopped me from going home now. Yet, as the days rolled by, one after another, I tried to push from mind the reality that since my arrival here, I'd never set foot off the ranch.

Miguel lay on the grassy bank, his hat covering his face, taking his usual afternoon siesta. Making sure I was out of his line of sight, I dug up the coins I'd previously buried.

I then saddled the fastest horse, which seemed to take longer than usual. The stallion sensed something was wrong and acted skittishly.

Only one way to do it, gallop out of the ranch so fast that turning back would risk me falling off.

Where there had once been vast areas of land, cottages were now lined here and there along the route, the church tower off in the distance the only landmark. A busy marketplace had sprung up in the old town.

No one recognized me and I recognized no one.

Upon arrival at the place I'd once called home, I dismounted. There, up high to the left of the house, was an open bedroom window that had been mine. The property had been maintained well, so much so that time seemed to have stood still. I wondered how much the house had changed inside. I'd run out of this front door more times than I could count, taken for granted the warm meals and my mother's hugs that I'd squirmed my way out of, the bedroom where my brother Ricardo had sat beside me, recounting tales of his adventures, inspiring the most daring of dreams, that one day I too might hear the cheer of the crowds, as I entered the bullring as a matador.

Full of excitement, I'd climbed down those vines that still straddled the house.

I wanted to tell that small, naïve boy that was me to go back. I pushed such thoughts away and knocked on the front door. A young girl answered, her weary-looking mother soon came up behind her. Agitated, my mind tried to keep up with the words the woman spoke, that the Veldes had all passed away, other than their daughter Alicia, who'd moved, her forwarding address unknown.

My past had been stolen from me.

The happiest memories were bullied out by the worst ones. Freedom had arrived too late. I mounted my horse and galloped off, tears streaming. Facing my fears, with jaw clenched and motivated by hunger, I headed back into town.

VIII

TURN BACK BEFORE it's too late.

Head high, I entered the law office. The front reception seemed surprisingly disorganized, papers scattered here and there, and piles of documents stacked high. On one of the heaps of files lay a curled up tabby cat. Upon the mantle, a candle dripped wax. It trickled to the edge and poured over, plopping onto the floor, its red splashes hardening into shiny circles. A seeming inability to keep up with the client's affairs presented an advantage.

Señor Teofilo, Roelle's solicitor, greeted me. As the minutes unfolded, so did his eagerness to rid himself of all dealings with the house of Bastillion. Teofilo had once had his share of disagreements with Roelle, it seemed.

We headed to his private office and settled at an old bay table. I studied his expression for any sign that would indicate his suspicion of a tampered will. He recited in monotone Roelle's wishes. His methodical demeanor almost made up for the disarray.

During the reading, I feigned surprise that I'd inherited the estate. Although the property had been destroyed, his fortune, banked with the house of Refair, had been substantial. Certainly more than I'd anticipated. Roelle's penchant for wearing tatty suits had fooled everyone.

I could only wonder how Felipe would react when he learned of the fortune being handed down to Ricardo's youngest brother. Grenaldi had been bequeathed in the old will, but removed completely from the new. With a flicker of the fountain pen, I signed the official papers and the name Bastillion changed to Velde on the legal possessorship. Although no amount of money could ever make up for all that I'd lost, it did offer some comfort that I would never know hunger again.

The cat's gaze stayed on me as I headed out.

With the large advance, petty cash from the estate, I purchased new clothes for both Miguel and myself. I also returned with fresh food purchased from the expensive stalls that I'd stuck my nose up against as a boy, peering eagerly at the delicious assortments, though denied a taste.

Riding home, I scoffed thick pieces of bread, closely followed by a large chunk of cheese, then chomped on the largest piece of ham I'd ever seen, followed by several sweet cakes, hardly tasting them. Relief came when my stomach ache wore off and I marveled at my ability not to throw up.

When I'd fully recovered from my gorge, I kicked my horse and galloped the rest of the way home.

I'd pulled it off. The real challenge would be when I told Miguel. I found him in the paddock, exercising a young mare.

"It's time you took a day off," I said.

"Where have you been?" he asked.

"In town."

Miguel pulled on the horse's reins. "You can't handle them on your own, and besides I don't consider this work."

"We can hire staff."

He let the mare loose, allowing her to have the run of the paddock and she flicked her long, grey-white mane, cantering free. He climbed over the gate.

"Hungry?" I said.

His hand disappeared into the linen bag that I'd tied to the saddle. "Where did you get the money?"

"It was left to me by Roelle."

"That's where you've been?"

"Yes."

"With Roelle's lawyer?"

"Yes."

"Why didn't you tell me?"

"It was last minute."

Miguel pulled out a piece of ham and bit into it. "How much?"

"More than enough food to last a week."

"I meant how much money?"

"Quite a sum."

His bushy eyebrows rose in surprise.

"Life is fluid, it frequently changes," I quoted him.

"What happened?"

"Just chatted with Roelle's lawyer."

"That's not what I meant."

I stared off.

"What happened that night?" Miguel asked. "How did the fire start?"

The breakfast delivered but uneaten, the maid tending to her duties. Roelle thrashing.

"Before he died, I'd considered running away," I said.

"No one blames you for his death," Miguel said. "We just want to know how it happened."

A lump caught in my throat. What happened that night would remain a mystery, like Aaron's disappearance.

Miguel patted my back. "His reasons for leaving you something are taken with him to the grave."

"You disapprove of his decision?"

"He cared about you, but considering you enough in this manner, it does surprise me, yes."

"I was a loyal servant."

His eyes glistened. "Roelle has influential friends."

"Had."

"What if they come looking for you wanting answers?"

"Are you telling me not to accept the money?"

"Just give it some thought, that's all."

"We're on the verge of starvation."

Miguel peeked back into the linen bag and reached in. "Perhaps I should stop asking questions?"

"Perhaps."

"I hope you know what you're doing."

"I'm taking back my life. And in the process, I plan on clearing my name."

"Daumia, no one remembers that now—"

"I remember."

"Then you're destined to be like Roelle."

"I want people to know that I'm innocent."

"Your inability to forgive—"

"This is forgiveness." I pointed to where the house had stood. "This is retribution. The house of Velde will pale the house of Bastillion."

"Exactly how much did you inherit?"

"Why?"

He stared off at the mounds of ash. "It just goes to prove that people often do things out of character."

"Do you mean him or me?"

Miguel raised his arms up in exasperation.

I leaned against the gate. "We start rebuilding tomorrow."

"Much responsibly comes with such a position."

"So does power."

He shook his head. "What kind of bread did you get?"

"I don't know . . . bread."

He pulled out a loaf, broke some off, and handed me a piece. "We break bread together for the last time."

"It will never be that way between us?"

"Perhaps I may suggest a new barn. The horses deserve better."

"Once the house is built, you'll sleep inside?"

Miguel jumped over the gate. "Look up."

I followed his gaze skyward at the stars.

"That's my view," he said. "Now why would I want to stare up at a ceiling?"

IX

THE HOUSE OF VELDE rose up out of the ashes.

Taking the advice of Señor Teofilo, I hired British architect Harold Ferring to design the new house. Ferring's reputation preceded him, and the fact that his services were affordable convinced me I'd made the best choice. Local men worked tirelessly to rebuild under Ferring's watchful eye.

Teofilo inferred that Ferring's reason for leaving England was unfortunate, but assured me that he would complete the work in a timely manner. He had, after all, designed the grandest of country homes for Richard III, the king's newly built Wensleydale estate in Yorkshire.

Ferring liked to drink and, not wanting to imbibe alone, he persuaded me to partake with him. During those long evenings, when I encouraged him to talk and I stayed quiet, he regaled me with the most fascinating of tales. I discovered that Ferring had completed his royal appointment, fulfilling his duty by designing the finest home in the North. When he failed to receive payment, he mentioned the matter to the king's executive secretary, and it didn't go down well. His continued request for payment resulted in their threats.

Miguel kept his distance from the man he called 'the wayward Englishman.'

I insisted on no part of the original manor being replicated. My vision for the house went askew as the structure manifested. The façade had appeared relatively simple on paper, though when it materialized, the house possessed an aura of supremacy. We easily went over the budget I'd initially set. The work continued inside the towering walls. The downstairs rooms were deliberately spacious with high ceilings and low hung chandeliers, wondrously invoking a gracious atmosphere that ventured to be stately, yet at the same time, homey. The bedrooms counted twenty in number.

Ferring stocked the wine cellar and at times would disappear for hours, sampling the vintages. He outlined what would become two secret rooms, one behind the bookshelf in my office and the other actually constructed beneath the four poster bed in the front master bedroom. I tried to reason with him that I'd never need them, but to allay his high-pitched insistence, I relented.

For the library, I purchased a considerable collection of books, many of them scribed in several languages. I took pleasure in placing them in order along the tall shelves. The task took me longer than expected as I'd open a book and become lost in it.

With the work almost complete, and having received payment, Ferring disappeared. Relief that I could take over and make the finishing touches on my own without Ferring's eccentric influence flooded me. My taste inclined toward a more simple style, and with him gone, I could decorate modestly.

* * * *

Later, I discovered through Teofilo that a royal warrant had been issued for Ferring's arrest. I hoped that Ferring had escaped the British authorities. As I strolled along the sweeping corridors of my new home, I often thought of him. He'd also been wronged by those wielding power. That much, we had in common.

Spending many an evening reading in my favorite room, the library, my confidence flourished, the promise of happiness ever present.

I often considered the woman who'd made it all possible. Although I had no real proof that Sunaria had taken Roelle's life, I had a nagging feeling she had. She'd appeared like an exquisite phantom, only to disappear once again into the night. Thoughts of her faded as the day to day challenges of running the estate drew my attention.

I hired new staff, ensuring fresh faces around the manor. I strived to reinvent myself, take on the convincing role of master, a man to be respected, revered even.

The cook provided meals with good portions for the staff, helping to maintain morale. A delicious fare is a boon to a hard worker. Pascal, my discreet butler, oversaw the employees, including several maids, a gardener, an ageing handyman I'd taken pity on, and several young horse hands to assist Miguel. I still couldn't persuade him to take a room inside the house. He said he'd be miserable indoors. Even during the long winters, he prevailed.

However, when designing the stables, I'd taken into consideration his penchant for fresh air and constructed a thick walled building to keep him warm in winter and cool in summer, a comfortable apartment where all his needs were met, as well as his desire to be close to the horses. A safe dwelling where he could rest up after a hard day's work, knowing that he was deeply valued. And from where he lay, he'd still see the stars.

Housing the employees in cottages on the estate ensured that they had their privacy and I had mine. At night, with everyone banished, I paced the many rooms, marveling at what I'd accomplished and not taking any of it for granted. I learned more of the horse breeding business from Miguel, studying under the master. I had every intention of establishing a business that would enable the house to turn a profit and ensure my future.

Miguel and I often dined alfresco. We enjoyed watching the horses running free in the enclosure. Despite Miguel's initial hesitation, he soon relented to my insistence that we eat off the finest plates and drink from silver goblets. The cook prepared flavorsome dishes and delighted us with his exotic recipes, a luxury we both appreciated. During one of those long, warm evenings, after several bottles of wine, Miguel revealed his dream of working with Andalusians.

He leaned forward with fire in his eyes. "Andalusians have an exceptional temperament," he said, "and a tranquil presence. Perfect mount for a picador."

I found his description appealing, and his portrait of the horse, with its generous frame, arched neck, and sculptured beauty, convinced me he might just be onto something.

X

THE OLD BUTLER told me to wait.

It had seemed more like an order. The central iron chandelier hung low in the unfamiliar grand foyer.

Considering whether accepting Señor Moran's invitation had been a mistake, I knew my chance to go home had been lost.

Aged twenty-four years, I'd reinvented myself, reflecting nothing of the boy. Even my walk appeared different. I took longer strides with my head held high. My gait reflected pride and my manner confidence.

Miguel's vision had became my own. We'd established ourselves as Spain's most successful Andalusian horse breeders. Spellbound, Miguel and I would linger at the paddock gate, admiring the ethereal vision of our cantering Andalusians, enchanted by their extraordinary sense of balance, natural grace, and astonishing ability to learn quickly, proving them invaluable in the bullring.

Our success had aggrandized the house of Velde, the very reason why an invitation to tonight's soirée from such a renowned family brought no surprise.

The estate had been built on royal land, and the home's varied history was reflected in its structure. Although in need of repair, its character remained and white washed walls loomed. Here in the entrance, glorious broad pillars rose up, providing a Romanesque air.

Music carried.

Señor Moran greeted me and with pride he relayed that his youngest son, Salvador, had just returned from a military excursion to the Canary Islands, on a mission to vanquish the native Guanche uprising.

With a convincing nod, I appeared interested when he conveyed that the Vespers were renowned for their thuggish tactics. Apparently, the fight had been bloody.

My intrigue into his son's achievements earned me approval. We strolled down the longest corridor I'd ever seen. How easily brick and mortar can intimidate.

Having access to skillful tailors ensured I blended in. Fine clothes have always made the man and I was grateful for this. Although eager to impress upon my host the advantage of replacing his entire stock with Spain's finest horses, I'd have to parley into the subject naturally. Mention it too soon and I'd appear desperate, bring it up too late and the moment could be lost.

The grand ballroom opened up before us. Two hundred or so guests mingled. An extensive gathering of family and friends shared in the festivities. The décor reflected a homey philosophy, simple but comfortable.

My unease relented when Señor Moran's wife, Renee, hugged me warmly. She introduced me to Cornelius, her eldest son, and then her youngest, the man of the moment, Salvador. Wearing his captain's uniform, Salvador cut a striking figure. Both brothers had inherited their mother's appealing features, not their father's. Something they both must have been grateful for.

Despite Salvador remaining seated, his majestic height was clearly evidenced by his long legs, one of them crossed over the other, his left foot resting on the lower rung of his brother's chair. He was bestowed with rugged good looks, and by the way he raised an eyebrow during our introduction, Salvador knew it. But the playful smile with which he greeted me made up for his spirited loftiness.

He directed me to sit beside him and I accepted the large goblet of plum wine he handed me. His air of confidence would have thrown me if it weren't for my belief that I belonged.

This dashing captain appeared to be the quintessential man's man. I found myself staring at him and in return he stared back, until his intense brown-eyed gaze forced me to look away.

My attention turned to his mother, Señora Renee. Sipping my third glass of wine, I easily conversed with her. All the Morans had an easy charm, it seemed. Her kindheartedness reminded me of my own mother. Fearful of spiraling into melancholy, my attention turned back on Salvador. Something about him fascinated me. His unassuming demeanor reflected wisdom.

A tap on my shoulder caused me to turn.

Señor Moran smiled. "Señor Velde, may I introduce a dear friend."

I rose up, biting hard on my inner cheek. I knew this face, though I'd never met the man.

Senator Felipe Grenaldi's likeness to his image in the portrait was uncanny. The artist had captured his crooked mouth and his receding hair line. He'd aged well, easily hiding his fifty-years. When we shook hands, I felt moisture on his palm. Felipe gave a smile that quickly faded.

Señor Moran patted my arm. "The senator's interested in purchasing an Andalusian," he said.

I nodded, my stare not leaving Felipe's.

"Business should never be discussed in front of a lady." He turned to face me. "Shall we?" He gestured to the garden.

As Felipe led me away from the table, he said, "They've certainly picked a good evening for their party."

Stone-faced, I concentrated on keeping my jaw relaxed, not wanting to give away any tension. In a single night, I'd mastered his signature and used the skill to deprive this stranger of his inheritance, and I wondered if he knew.

Beads of perspiration appeared on his forehead. I glanced up indicating I'd noticed.

The gardens were sprawling. Two gentlemen passed by heading back into the house.

"How's the ranch?" Felipe asked appearing casual.

"Good."

"Affluence agrees with you," he said.

"I have a good stallion for you. He's temperamental but nevertheless fast."

"Señor Moran misspoke."

"I'm sorry. I thought he suggested—"

"I have a proposition," he said. "I'd like to invest in your ranch. Help establish your business."

"It's a generous offer, but—"

"I could further your reputation."

Something about the way he favored his right leg, flicked the fingers of his right hand against his thigh—an impatient trait—seemed familiar and yet the painting had been the only time I'd ever seen him.

"A royal seal will advance your success," he said.

I turned to go. "Let me know if you change your mind about that horse."

"Roelle had a tendency to be unruly, but you know that."

I faced him again.

"Such a long time ago," he said. "But I haven't forgotten him."

I didn't want to say that I had. No happy memories there, none worth their time, anyway.

Felipe slid both hands into his pockets. "Roelle was the only one to die in the fire."

I nodded.

Felipe squinted. "I still believe it was foul play."

"Have you known Señor Moran long?" I asked.

"Long enough. You were there that night?"

"Where's this heading?"

"Have you forgotten who you're speaking with?"

I shrugged.

"I never got answers," he said.

"We were all devastated."

He gave a look of surprise.

"If you'll excuse me," I said.

"Roelle planned to leave me an inheritance in his will."

"Did he?"

"You know the answer to that."

"I take it that's a *no*."

"Take the offer," Felipe said.

"As you can see, my business is doing well."

"But it could do better."

"What is it you really want?"

"Roelle educated you. He tried to liberate you from your peasant background."

"You know nothing of my family's history."

He gave a subtle smile. "At least consider the offer."

My stare gave my answer.

"Don't cross me, Daumia. I'll bring you down. My power reaches all the way to the crown."

"I'll never be beholden to you."

His eyes widened. "You tampered with the will."

"Is such a thing even possible?"

He shifted uncomfortably. "What happened to Aaron?"

"I was nine when he disappeared, remember?"

We both stared off in the direction of the rustling leaves. A bird hopped out from the greenery and flew off.

"You're naïve." Felipe ran his fingers over his jaw.

"Stay off my ranch."

"And if I don't?"

"I have nothing to lose," I said. "You, however, risk money, status, and power. Your future lies in my hands."

"And your sister lies in mine."

I reacted before I could stop myself.

"That's right. You kept the money and I kept your sister," he said. "Perhaps you'd like to exchange?"

"Where is she?"

"Vigo. The way I see it, you're benefiting from this transaction."

"I want to see her."

"Perhaps."

I tried to conceal my panic.

"I warned Roelle, but he wouldn't listen. I told him you were trouble."

"He was a coward, as are you."

"I'll see to it that Alicia's given to the soldiers."

I thrust him against the wall.

His head struck the masonry. "If anything happens to me . . ."

I pulled back.

He straightened his jacket. A little way off Cornelius appeared in the doorway and signaled to us.

I gestured to Cornelius that we'd seen him. "We're finished."

"Then you agree to my terms?" Felipe said.

Cornelius motioned for us to hurry. "You've been summoned by Father," he shouted. "The entertainment's about to begin."

Felipe turned to me and whispered, "A dispatch from the king will be sent to you."

I felt cornered.

Felipe seemed to sense this. "I'll have my lawyer draw up the papers that secure my share in Roelle's ranch." He walked away and followed

Cornelius back into the house. "As I recall," he shouted over to him, "you promised me the girl after the dance."

"Come see your prize," Cornelius said.

* * * *

I remained by the large double doors of the ballroom.

Leaning against it, grateful for the cool evening breeze, my hands shook.

I lifted one of the drinks offered from a tray and gulped the wine. Responding to my gesture, the waiter paused, allowing me to drop the empty glass and immediately take another. I felt a nudge and turned to see Salvador.

"Happy with your transaction?" he said.

My guess had been right. He stood an inch taller than me.

"What?" I said.

"The senator's horse?"

"We're still negotiating." I forced a smile.

"Must be some horse."

I grimaced at the thought of Felipe touching Alicia. My reaction had apparently gone unnoticed.

"My intention is to work for the senator when I retire," Salvador said. "I have one more year as a captain."

"Politics?"

He nodded.

More guests lingered at the ballroom's edge and the orchestra struck up.

"Change is what this country needs." Salvador raised his voice over the music. "I have no interest in business." He flinched. "Sorry I didn't mean—"

"You'd make a fine politician."

Upon Salvador's breasted jacket hung a gold medal engraved with a military emblem. I wondered how many men he'd had to kill to get it.

I followed his gaze.

"Isn't she gorgeous?" he said.

I sucked in my breath, entranced. At the center of the ballroom there stood a beautiful flamenco dancer, sixteen in years, or so, but her dramatic make-up made it difficult to guess.

Staccato handclapping arose from the crowd.

Waiting, she tilted her head, as though listening to the rhythm of the chanting. The fingers of her left hand struck the right, slapping the perfectly formed hollow. She threw back her head and lush, dark curls cascaded over her face. She snapped her fingers again and clicked her heels in an explosion of passion as she twisted the frills of her red dress. It swayed and whipped around her. She conveyed a tortured expression, exposing a broken heart, shattered into a thousand pieces and then flicked up her lace fan to cover her face and peered over it.

Our gazes met.
I wanted to know her.
I closed my mouth. "When does the senator return home?"
"Tonight," Salvador said. "He has to be back in Vigo by the morning."
"How far away is Vigo?"
"It's a two-day journey."
I studied the faces of the other guests. They too were captivated with the girl.
"Look at the senator. He's virtually drooling," Salvador said.
Salvador's stare held mine, then his gaze drifted onto my mouth. The moment caught me off guard.
He gestured to a waiter and placed my empty glass on the man's tray, lifted a full drink off it, and handed it back to me. He took one for himself. "To new acquaintances that become close friends." His hand brushed against the lower arch of my back.
I felt a sudden thrill.
Unfazed, I raised my glass and clinked it against his, and then glanced back at the girl.

XI

THE SPINNING SLOWED.

Salvador and I lay on the lush lawn of his parent's home admiring the low hung moon. Wine flowed through my veins taking the edge off.

There had to be a way to ensure my sister's safety and extricate Felipe from our lives.

The guests withdrew, discussing the flamenco dancer who'd taken their breaths away. I was spellbound with her. Falling into this beautiful stranger's arms held the promise of forgetting and I found myself smiling when I thought of her.

Salvador unbuttoned his jacket, revealing his white shirt, pulled taut over his chest. The way the corner of his mouth turned up revealed he'd caught me staring. The night sky bestowed an array of silver stars. Alcohol enhanced their mystery, causing them to dance like fireflies. The mood had taken a pensive turn when Salvador recounted his experiences in battle. Absorbed in his description, I could smell the gunpowder.

"Sleep deprivation allows a man to see who he really is," Salvador said.

"Was it worth it?" I asked.

"Of course. We overran the skirmish."

"You're a better man than I." Although fascinated, I felt no such loyalty. Royalty only existed to control the people and tax them well. My opinion would remain my own. I pointed to his medal. "Why did they give you that?"

He glanced down at the dangling metal that resembled a coin. "My regiment ambushed the enemy's camp." He peeled back his shirt to show me a scar on his chest. "A memento."

"How did you get that?"

"Their king resisted arrest." Salvador sighed. "War is not how you imagine it. Rules that I learned as a junior officer didn't apply in battle."

"Life is already so short."

"And if heaven does exit," Salvador said, "I'm not sure I'd get in."

I burst into laughter.

His smile widened into a grin. "Now that I'm home, I'm going to make the most of every moment." He gave me an affectionate nudge. "What do you want?"

My gaze fell to his lips.
He fell back and laughed.
I rested my head on my hands. "What do *you* want?"
"I think . . ."
"Careful what you ask for."
"You know I'd do anything for you."
"And we've only just met."
He turned to face me. "Some people are more likable than others."
"I might just put that to the test."
"Try me."
"Bring me the girl."
Salvador sat up.
I leaned in close to his ear. "Bring her to me."
"I believe she's with the senator."
"Then you'd better move fast."
Salvador leaped to his feet and stared at me.

I had nothing to lose. I'd soon be reunited with Alicia, my last link to my family. All this time, she'd been with Felipe who'd poisoned her mind, no doubt. When I found her, I'd explain everything. The promise of vindication was real.

* * * *

Salvador headed fast toward me. When I saw that he was alone, I felt disappointment.
"I've been on some dangerous missions," he said, "but this one beats them all."
"What happened?"
"We were just in time," he said. "Felipe had her taken to his guest quarters. She's terrified. You do realize if he ever found out—"
"Take me to her."
Disappointment danced in his eyes.
I rested my thumb on his lower lip and his mouth parted. An uncommon arousal stirred as Salvador's pout met mine and our tongues brushed. He opened his mouth wider to deepen our kiss, and there came a passionate surge so fervent that it seized my breath.
I broke away.
Salvador looked disconcerted.
We ascended the stairs, quickly reaching Salvador's bedroom. He opened the door and signaled for me to enter. Silhouetted at the window stood the beautiful flamenco dancer.
"It's tradition to spoil our guests." He gave me a wink and then closed the door as he withdrew.
The dancer backed away toward the bed.
"You're safer going in the other direction," I said.
Her cheeks blushed.
"What's your name?" I asked.

"Annabelle."

Her hands scrunched the material of her dress, lifting it slightly off the floor.

"You're safe now," I said. "Will you dance for me?"

She hesitated.

I gestured, "Please," and then settled upon the edge of the bed.

Her demeanor changed.

Where there had stood a virgin, now an exotic creature struck a graceful pose. Her chin pointed down with desire. A flurry of evocative steps, a señorita's yearning, she tapped into her emotions and translated them into movement, twisting and turning, stomping and then stepping delicately with pointed toes, a wondrous performance.

Though no words passed between us, we spoke. With all my will, I resisted the urge to pull her into my arms. Annabelle was once again a young girl. She broke into ripples of laughter.

"You move like a goddess." I sighed.

She gave a coy smile.

"You don't say much, do you?" I folded my arms.

She fluttered long eyelashes.

"Well?" I said.

"They ordered me to wait."

"For the senator?"

From her expression, I could see she didn't like the idea, either.

"I won't let him touch you," I said.

Her shoulders dropped their tension. Her clenched fingers relaxed.

"Where are you from?" I asked.

"Seville."

"You look Spanish, but something else—"

"My grandfather was Egyptian."

Such lineage had bestowed an exotic mix, delicate, noble features, and a petite dancer's frame.

"You're beautiful," I said.

A noise outside startled her.

"The senator doesn't know you're here," I said.

She ran to me and buried her head into my chest. A hint of lilies wafted. Even though she held me, I was the one who felt safe. I marveled at her serenity as she snuggled into me. Time ceased at that very moment, and I was unable to recall the last time I'd experienced such affection. A few maids had bestowed relief over the years, but none of them had captured me like her.

"You can't stay here. Look." I led her over to the window and pointed. "Head for that house. Give this note to the butler." I scribed quickly.

She accepted the folded paper.

"That's my home," I said. "Stay for as long as you like."

She stared off at the great manor.

"You'll be safe there, I promise."

She hugged me again.

"Now go. A warm meal and soft bed awaits you."

With her fingers wrapped around the door handle, she turned and smiled.

Something internal melted. She'd penetrated my very core, by passing my life-long wall, and I didn't even know her.

She was gone.

I hoped to be the one to win her over. But a more pressing matter tormented me, Alicia. A terrible feeling came with the knowledge that Felipe had used her to get to me.

Alicia, I'm coming for you.

From the window, I watched Annabelle run along the garden pathway, making her way north toward the estate. The full moon guided her steps. I sighed as I left the room, captivated with the idea that I'd stolen her away, and I offered a quiet prayer that she'd make it.

Staff were reluctant to divulge Salvador's whereabouts, but I wouldn't take *no* for an answer. They relented and pointed in the direction of the servant's quarters.

From outside, noises in the room hinted at a tussle. Unable to resist, I opened the door ajar and saw Salvador, completely naked, embracing a male servant. The inner rush caused me to freeze. Taking pleasure from the moment, I enjoyed the view. I slid through and lingered in a shadowy corner. I'd trespassed into a risqué rendezvous. It felt wrong, but it felt good, too. I considered that my kiss had alighted such passion and here now unfolded the result of my flirting.

Once hidden beneath a dashing uniform, Salvador's muscular physique was now exposed.

I turned to go.

A long groan drew me back. The man leaned forward with outstretched arms against the wall, supporting both he and Salvador, his fingernails digging into the granite.

And that could have been me.

Salvador, this dashing conquistador, still a virtual stranger, and yet we'd connected immediately and our rapport had fired our imaginations, kindling something impossible to ignore, impossible to turn away from.

Beads of perspiration shimmered over both of them. Candlewick flickered, throwing dancing shadows. I exhaled, unsure of when I'd taken my last breath, hoping that they'd not heard my sigh.

The sublime affection they shared was stirring to watch.

Salvador regained his composure. And then he saw me.

"Out," he directed his servant.

The man grabbed his clothes and ran past me, avoiding eye contact. I opened the door for him.

Salvador cringed. "I thought you were with the girl."

I smiled. "If you're going to tell me this is not what it seems . . ."

"Like to watch, do you?"

"You'll have to make your indiscretion up to me."

Salvador nibbled on a fingernail. This man had faced the most ferocious of armies and yet with me, he yielded.

"Don't you ever knock?" He reached for his trousers.

I snatched them out of his hand. "And spoil your fun?"

He rested his hands on his hips and faced me. "I'm so embarrassed."

"Why?" I said. "You of all people deserve anything you desire."

He gave me a long stare.

"I have to go," I said.

"I'll make it up to you, Daumia."

"I do believe you will."

He buried his face in his hands and I tortured him with the protracted silence. Outside, leaves dangled from a crooked branch and tapped against the window.

I handed his trousers back. "Get dressed." I beamed at him then turned and headed out.

XII

FELIPE'S APPOINTED GUEST room was easy to find.

The bed hadn't been slept in and an unopened bottle of white wine rested on the mantelpiece. Beside it, a candle had burned to the wick. A fresh bowl of water had been provided. I leaned over it and splashed my face to wake up, and then used the nearby towel.

Felipe could have the house. We would take the horses and rebuild elsewhere. Start over, and make a new life for ourselves. Sobering up, my head cleared, the decision obvious. My family had been virtually wiped out, and I wasn't prepared to lose Alicia on account of my pride.

Looking around for Felipe's personal items, I noticed there weren't any and doubted he'd even been here, or perhaps the servant who'd pointed to this room had been mistaken.

Outside, hoofs clipped along, pulling a rumbling carriage. I peered out of the window and saw Felipe climbing in, ignoring the butler who closed the coach door behind him. With the crack of a whip, the carriage jerked and sped off. I flew out of the door and along the balcony, down the stairs and through the house. Dodging staff, I bolted through the kitchen and came face to face with the man I'd caught Salvador with. He was dressed as a chef. I threw him a wide smile and he beamed back. With a leap in my step, I headed outside.

Within minutes, I'd found the stables and saddled my stallion. I threw a coin to the groom who'd taken care of him and galloped out of the barn. The small amount of money I had would have to be enough to feed both my horse and me.

Fear of losing sight of Felipe's carriage ensured my focus.

* * * *

I lived up to my reputation of being reckless.

The unforgiving rain poured. It was impossible to remember ever being dry.

Within two days, I was in Vigo. The harsh climate was a contrast to Santiago De Compostela, the town somewhat larger, busier.

Fatigue set in. I needed a place to rest. Having ridden my horse too far for too long, I'd sealed his fate. I'd pressed him on past his pain, and I was well past mine.

Limbs aching, I rallied the remnants of my fading strength. From a little way off, keeping a safe distance, I observed Felipe enter a well-guarded manor. Searching the windows, I wondered which room Alicia might be in.

I turned my weary horse and followed the tattered sign back into town. Concerned stares from passersby pointing at my stallion's rear left hoof forced me to choose the nearest tavern.

The innkeeper's wife escorted me to my room. Nausea welled as I entered. The stale odor of the previous tenant lingered, but exhaustion forced me to stay. With a thrust, I secured the bed against the door. Despite the nasty bedding, fatigue pulled me down and I fell asleep. Nightmares and dreamscapes, disconnected memories and fears came and went. Carried away, impossible to escape, I cycled through terror.

Caught in the grip of a nightmare, I was a boy again, standing in the pitch dark, and out of nowhere a large bull thundered toward me, gnashing white teeth, and snarling.

I sprang up.

Stifled by the lack of air, I climbed out of bed. It was impossible to judge how long I'd slept. Dust puffed off the tatty curtains as I peeked outside. It was dark.

The tavern entertained a few locals eating supper. At a corner table, I inhaled the scent of stale bread, boiled chicken, and gulped cups of warm water. Stroking my chin that hadn't felt a razor in days, my thoughts drifted once more to Annabelle. Although I'd heard of the flamenco, this had been the first time I'd ever seen the exotic dance that gypsies had brought from the Mediterranean to Spaniards desirous of a rich expression of love. Annabelle's performance had bewitched all the guests, including me. Still shaken from Felipe's threat, though, I'd not been able to truly appreciate her.

This indulgence wasted time.

I had just enough money left to pay for my stay. Much to the tavern owner's concern, I removed my horse and despite his insistence, refused to destroy the animal. My horse had benefited from the rest, but he still limped.

Brute force ensured my entry into the local tailors. Row upon row of clothes awaited their turn. In the corner, I found what I'd come for—officer's uniforms—and after finding one that looked about my size, I stripped.

The corner mirror would have reflected a dashing Army Captain if the trouser legs weren't two inches too short. I found another. This time, Spain's finest stared back in the warped mirror, despite my stubble. In the back of the store, I found what I needed to shave. I left my old clothes and withdrew.

My horse trotted bravely.

I steadied my nerves and marked the direction in which the stable boy led my stallion, and ignored his comment about the horse's 'gammy leg.'

Tilting my heavily braided cap, I ascended the stone steps. Several passable salutes later, I strolled on into the senatorial residence.

* * * *

I'd spent a lifetime wondering about my sister.

I leaned up against the door, *her door*, and listened, marveling at the influence of a dashing officer, the uniform having gotten me in. I'd found the staff's quarters and used my affable nature to cajole the female cook to get information. Wiping her powdered hands on her apron, feeling sorry for the young officer newly returned from active service, she told me that she'd just delivered warm milk to Señorita Alicia's boy in the south wing. With a wave of her pointed finger and her lowered tone, she showed her disapproval. The senator was after all married, but not to Alicia. I attempted to remain stone-faced, despite the heaviness in my chest. Felipe had fathered Alicia's son, the scandal, a closely guarded secret amongst his innermost circle. Felipe had lied. He had no intention of freeing my sister.

I became that nine-year-old boy again, struggling for the right words and unable to find them.

Alicia, the only family I had left, and I was seconds from seeing her. With a turn of the handle, I entered. She lay asleep upon a large bed. Dark flowing locks spilled over white linen, our similarity startling. Beside her slept her child, a one-year-old boy. I removed my braided jacket and flung it over the back of a corner rocking chair. Careful not to make a noise, I sat in it.

Seeing her again stirred once buried memories.

Alicia's look of horror when Ricardo had slapped down that bull's ear onto the kitchen table, or the way she clung to our mother when she thought I might win one of our fights, and the endless days we'd played by the river, both of us lost in our own imaginary worlds, and sometimes crossing into each other's.

Dusk promised to arrive at any moment. I wiped the perspiration from my brow with my sleeve.

The child stirred.

Alicia awoke and sleepily swept a few stray hairs away from her face. She bolted upright. "Daumia?"

I rose out of the chair. "It's so good to see you."

She pulled her son closer to her.

"He's sweet." I forced a smile, though I could see Felipe in him.

"What do you want?" Her eyes narrowed.

"I've come to get you out."

"Don't hurt us."

"Never!" I glanced at the door.

She stared past me at the officer's jacket that had slipped off the chair and lay crumpled on the floor. "Guards," she yelled.

"Whatever Felipe's told you is a lie."

"Get out!"

"I've come to take you home."

"I am home," she screamed.

The door burst open, but I didn't wait to see who entered.

With my throat tightening with panic, I peered out of the window and down at a drop that would kill me. I leaped up onto the ledge, leaning out, grabbing hold of a handful of vines.

And then I jumped.

Dangling, I pulled myself along. I slipped and struggled to hold on as the twisting vines tore into my palms. Clutching at an open window, I hauled myself up and clambered in.

Descending the central staircase too fast, I tripped and tumbled over marble steps. My right shoulder bashed against the iron banister, shooting searing pain down my arm. Three guards closed in on me, their swords pointed.

I scrambled through the front door and out as something behind me, cold and sharp, sliced into my left ear, burning it fiercely and streaming a warm gush down my neck. Unable to catch my breath, I descended four steps at a time, startling a flock of crows. They flew up and around me, flapping their black feathered wings in my face as I dashed into the center of the courtyard.

A horse-drawn carriage swerved, just missing me by a hair, and I felt myself being grabbed hold of and dragged into the careening vehicle.

* * * *

Carved oak bedposts came into focus.

"You're safe now." A husky female voice whispered in the dark.

"Alicia?" Not recognizing anything, I froze.

I was lying on a bed with no idea how long I'd been there. Several flickering candles threw dark forms over thick, drawn drapes and plush furniture that denoted expensive taste. A female's silhouette loomed.

With fumbling fingers, I explored the material used as a bandage, wrapped around my head, covering my left ear. As she stepped into the light, shadows danced across her, revealing those familiar, striking turquoise eyes that lit up when she smiled.

"I know you." I sat up.

She raised an eyebrow.

"*Sunaria?*" I tried to focus.

She gave a nod and then a gesture that I'd almost got it right. "Your ear's fine."

"How long have I been here?"

"Not long."

"I have to get to my sister. Wait . . . you're . . ."

"Hush."

I could make it to the door in about ten steps. The idea of a woman being any kind of threat felt ridiculous, and yet she conveyed an unearthly presence and that stare of hers elicited a visceral response, a sense that she had within her the power to entrap, to seduce completely, enslave.

This arousal could have been better timed. I shook it off. "That carriage, it was yours?"

"Yes."

"You saved my life?"

"You're reckless."

"That's the first time anyone's ever made that remark about me." I climbed out of bed. "Roelle, what the hell happened to him?"

She wrapped her pale, delicate fingers around the bedpost and hugged it.

I gestured. "Please don't come any closer."

"Daumia, lay back down."

I placed my feet firmly on the floor. Those long, red fingernails of hers would leave a mark, scratching a man's back until he came.

My back.

Not arousal, I'd confused it with the excitement stirred by danger.

"You've lost a lot of blood." Her heavy-lidded gaze held mine.

There were no marks on my hands from the vines. I turned to face the vanity and peered into the mirror. I peeled back the bandage and to my astonishment my ear had healed. "How long have I been here?" Blood on my collar was the only suggestion of an injury. I remembered the sword slicing through, shivered and spun round, lifting my shirt and checking my back. Again no laceration where I thought I'd been stabbed, caused me to question my judgment.

Her curious expression faded. "How much do you remember?"

"Everything."

She stepped toward me. "Then we have a problem."

XIII

A COLD CUP PRESSED against my lips.

I shoved it away and scrambled up, leaning back against the headboard.

"Steady." Miguel sat on the edge of the bed, frowning.

I welcomed the familiarity of my four poster bed, enshrined within the long, sweeping net that kept the mosquitoes at bay in summer and shrouded me against the maid's inquisitive gape on mornings when I craved privacy.

"How long have I been asleep?" I asked.

"Try to settle down." He gave me the cup.

"How long?"

"A day."

"How long was I away for?"

"A week."

"What happened?"

"I was going to ask you that."

"What time is it?" I gulped the rest of the water.

"Seven."

"Morning or evening?"

"Evening." His tone was anxious.

"Everything seems so foggy."

"We've checked you over. You have no injuries." He pulled open the curtains.

"Close them." I motioned to the long, white drapes.

"We found you collapsed by the front door."

I examined my left ear, but it felt normal. "Please, close the curtains."

Miguel lifted the window latch and opened it. "And you need fresh air."

I flopped back down onto the pillow.

"You're home now." He rested beside me. "Where did you go?"

"To see Alicia."

He folded his arms. "How did you find her?"

"She doesn't want to see me."

"She'll come round."

"She has a son."

"That's wonderful."

I pulled the bed sheet up and over me. "Senator Grenaldi's the father."

"She married well."

"She's not his wife."

Miguel flinched.

"Why can't I remember anything?" I wiped sweat from my brow.

"The shock of seeing Alicia after all this time was too much perhaps?"

I had a vague memory of Alicia's awful grimace when she saw me for the first time in years, and the emptiness of her stare, sorely reminding me of the distance festering between us. I cursed my inability to rescue her.

He patted my shoulder. "Why don't you write to her?"

"I don't think the letter would reach her."

"I'll hand deliver it."

I stared at him to make my point. "I don't want you anywhere near Vigo."

"Is that where you went?"

The warm breeze billowed the curtains.

He topped up my cup. "The Romany performers asked a high price for their main act?"

"Annabelle? She's still here?"

"She is."

I slid down the headboard and stared up at the ceiling.

"She's done nothing but talk about you since she's been here." His eyes lit up.

I smiled.

"You have two letters." He handed me an envelope. "This one came two days after you left."

I ripped it open.

Velde,
My lawyers are scribing the deeds of ownership to your estate. The papers will arrive shortly. See that you sign them.
FDG

Miguel studied my reaction. "Everything all right?"

The coward hadn't even signed his name. "There were two?" I tucked Felipe's letter back into the envelope.

"This one has the Royal Seal of King Ferdinand V." He gave me the second dispatch.

The luxurious parchment and royal crest illustrated its noble source. Peeling back the adhered seal, I eased out and unraveled the scroll.

He leaned in. "What does it say?"

"I've been knighted."

"Is this one of your jokes?"

"I can't accept it."

Miguel peeked at the official parchment. "Is it real?"

I nodded.

He lowered himself down onto one knee.

"Please don't." I gestured for him to stand. "I didn't earn it."

"Well, the king doesn't bestow such an honor unless—"

"Evidently he does."

"Well, you did give him our best horse. Only you would consider refusing a royal command. You don't get to decline." He withdrew.

I wondered if it was heresy to tear it up.

* * * *

My mind raced to unravel the chaos.

Although my memory had fractured, I recalled being at the senator's residence. Those injuries had seemed so real. I'd lost a week and hated the feeling.

Annabelle appeared at the doorway, a vision of loveliness. Light from the corridor illuminated her.

"Daumia, how are you?" She came closer, reached for my hand, and kissed it. "Thank you for letting me stay here." She picked up the cup from the bedside table and gave it to me.

"How long have you been a dancer?" I tried to work out her age.

She lifted the net out of her way and sat beside me. "My father sold me to the Romany. I've danced for them ever since."

I was about to ask her to dance for me again, but couldn't now, not after hearing that.

She gazed about, as if taking in the room.

"It wasn't always this way for me." I caught myself staring at her.

"This wasn't your family's home?"

"No."

"Then how did you end up as master?"

I raised myself up onto my elbows. "A mixture of luck and," I scratched my head, "hard work."

"Miguel told me it's because you work alongside the ranch hands that the staff admire you."

I drank the rest of the water.

"How long can I stay here?" she asked.

She bestowed the very image of innocence. Having stolen her away, I was no different than her father who'd betrayed her trust, or the men he'd sold her to. No different than Felipe who'd laid a claim to her.

I reached for her but quickly withdrew my hand.

I'd closed my heart before. This time would be no exception. I had to let Annabelle go.

XIV

THE LAST TIME I'D seen Salvador, it had been sans clothes.

I now sat next to him at the Moran's dinner table, both of us acting as though nothing had passed between us.

The other guests, three in number, were all nobility. I perused them one by one and gauged their characters from the little they revealed of themselves.

General Hernandez, the stocky gentleman who sat beside me, was Salvador's commanding officer. Hernandez's rugged features indicated a man who'd seen many a battle and wasn't shy of getting down and dirty with the troops, thus earning their respect. Yet Hernandez's unsteady eye indicated his need for approval. Perhaps such insecurity had been a catalyst for his desire for promotion into the highest ranks.

Countess Miranda Ebro, with her painted face and tight bodice, her attractiveness enhanced by her confidence, was a lady in her thirties. A widow no doubt, revealed by the sadness in her eyes and the way she sighed deep in thought throughout the evening.

Lady Rosalie Ambrith, with her hooked nose and small mouth, had a fixed expression of disapproval. A lady eager to offer criticism, her way of making the world a better place, ensured her strict, moral legacy continued unabated. Even I couldn't win her over.

All the guests warranted a good stare.

And Salvador, with his dashing good looks and captivating smile, his bravery warranted the title I held—a fine officer who showed a deep respect for his men, and a willingness to hear both sides of a story before sharing his opinion. When he focused on me, arousal soon followed.

Señor Moran proposed a toast to Spain's new knight of the realm. I accepted the honor, hoping to convince them I'd earned it. As the alcohol flowed, so did the camaraderie.

Salvador enthralled me. I found it difficult to define the cause of the numerous fissions, the fine wine or Salvador's firm hand brushing my thigh.

He leaned in close and whispered, "Rumor has it that the flamenco dancer is a guest at your estate."

"And what else do the rumors say?" I asked.

"That you've found favor with the king with your Andalusians."

"His highness has acquired several of our horses."

"Pleased to hear it."

"I've selected yours from my finest stock."

Salvador beamed.

I sipped my wine, forcing my confidence. "Tell me what you know of Senator Grenaldi."

"He's ambitious." Salvador's gaze held mine as if to exaggerate his point. "A man not to be crossed."

"In what way?"

"He uses questionable tactics."

"He likes to win?"

Salvador raised his eyebrows. "He does."

"And you want to work for him?"

"He gets things done."

"What about his wife?" I looked away briefly.

"The king's cousin. That's a marriage of alliances."

"To further his political career?"

"Felipe blatantly keeps a lover."

I nodded casually. "Doesn't his wife complain to the king?"

Salvador topped up my glass, shooing away a waiter. "The king has more mistresses than you can count."

"So Felipe's wife is powerless?"

"But she knows that affair won't last." Salvador shrugged. "Felipe believed his wife to be barren, so he took a mistress and fathered a bastard."

"A son?"

Salvador nodded. "Felipe's wife is pregnant."

Alicia and her child's days under Felipe's roof were numbered. Though not knowing why I fretted, Salvador offered a reassuring smile. I followed his gaze.

"The countess is very wealthy," he whispered. "She's declined many an offer of marriage."

"The widow?"

"Yes. Have you met her?"

"No, never."

"Well, you're spot on. She's good friends with the senator. Insatiable appetite."

I raised an eyebrow.

"Not me, her." He burst into laughter.

My thoughts wandered to Annabelle, her sweetness, her innocence, how long she might stay.

The countess blinked her long lashes at me.

I reeled with dread as I considered Salvador's words, and found no amusement in the countess' subtle flirting.

* * * *

Salvador and I found the opportunity to withdraw from the other visitors. We sauntered outside into the cool evening air. The stuffy dinner party wasn't my scene, and by the way Salvador loosened his necktie, it wasn't his, either. The garden possessed a lush assortment of greenery and the well-tended flowers sprung up around us. I avoided treading on them as we crossed the stony pathway and leaned against an ivy covered wall.

"You seem pensive." Salvador gave me a quizzical look. "I think you know me well enough to trust my discretion."

I turned to face him. "Perception is reality."

"For some, yes."

"The Pope has received a royal warrant to purify the kingdom of Spain."

He nodded. "The Church has sanctioned an inquisition."

"What are your thoughts?"

"The king's word is final."

"I'm happy to hear that. I knew you were a royalist."

Salvador gestured for us to continue walking. "Your knighthood, it has something to do with this?"

I followed him further into the garden. "We have reason to believe that we have a heretic amongst us." I gazed off at the dramatic landscaping.

"You found evidence of his dissent?"

"But we need more."

"Which I'm qualified for."

"We plan to infiltrate his estate."

"Send in a spy." He gestured he wanted in.

I liked Salvador, but I loved my sister and with every passing day the threat that loomed over her worsened. And there was now the matter of her son.

"Come for dinner tomorrow night." I leaned against the wall. "And bring the countess."

XV

ON MY ARRIVAL HOME, a dispatch awaited me.

A lump caught in my throat and I hesitated to open the envelope.

Ferring had insisted on using a rich plaster design to line the ceiling. The focal point was an overly ornate fireplace, the hearth still burning. All this sumptuousness was too flamboyant for my taste. I rarely visited what had been intended as a living room, easily more drawn to the modest, quiet corners, where I could sit and think clearly, undistracted by garish décor. No one would disturb me in here.

I read the document.

If signed, it would transfer half of my estate to Felipe. The fist of fate punched me hard and I threw the letter into the flames, watching it flare, then disintegrate.

As I ascended the stairway to my room, I knew I had no choice but to go through with encouraging Salvador to take up residence at Felipe's manor. I'd never convince Alicia to leave Felipe, and he wasn't just interested in investing in the business I'd built from the ground up. His demeanor had implied a more sinister scheme, that of full ownership.

I'd grown fond of Salvador, and my plan involved risking his safety. More thought needed to go into my scheme.

My mind teetered on the very edge of reason. My strategy thrust Salvador right into the center of Felipe's world, and I hated myself for throwing him into the lion's den. Even though Salvador had expressed his ambition to work for the senator, I was drowning in guilt.

I hesitated at my bedroom door. Through the netting, I could see that someone had crawled into my bed, the rumpled covers pulled up and over them. I grabbed the bed linen and pulled it off, and caught my breath.

Annabelle, wearing only a chemise, shyly reached for the sheet and pulled it back over her. "This house is so big." She yawned. "I can't sleep."

"You get used to it." I averted my gaze.

"Please stay."

The corner chair was an uncomfortable option. Annabelle patted the bed with insistence. Fully clothed, and too tired to argue, I slid in next to her. I reached for the cup of water on the bedside table and took a sip. Picking up the nearby book, I opened it and peered down at the last page I'd read. Even her perfume imbued the exotic.

I pretended to read.

Annabelle prized the book from my hands and pushed it off the side of the bed and her laughter rippled. She leaned in, planting kiss upon kiss upon my cheek.

You have the dancer in your bed, came the restless voice of my conscience that I tried to ignore.

Returning her kiss, tasting her sweetness, her soft lips pressing against mine. With my hands on either side of her face I held her there, firmly captured, an explosion of passion. Instinctively, I slipped my hand beneath her chemise and then quickly pulled away, trying to think of something else, somewhere else. I leaned over and reached for my book. Impossible to stay here with her, fearful that I'd take advantage, I found myself in the position of no going back.

I'd lost my page.

She grabbed the book from me again and threw her head back with laughter. As though controlled by a force outside my will, my hand was drawn by some mystical charm.

She arched her back and sighed.

Within me was the desire to protect her, even from myself. At the same time, I couldn't deny her.

I pulled her chemise up and off her.

I gazed at her beauty, beholden by her perfect olive skin, endowing a flawless complexion, ringlets cascading over slender shoulders.

On and on pleasuring her, I responded to her gasps that begged me to continue, both of us ascending closer to euphoria.

Her affection for me gave me the confidence to find mine, look inside that once scary place and touch the serene. Feeling the purest devotion, I cherished her.

She was lost, gone from me, possessed, shaking her head, whipping dark locks from side to side.

Annabelle's expressions reflected her vulnerability twinned with joy. Her long lashes fluttered. Her rosebud lips pouted.

To think I'd left her to find her own way from the Moran's to my house and risked her getting lost, even worse, the thought of Felipe finding her and stealing her away.

We tumbled over and over until we slid off the end of the bed, laughing all the way. In Annabelle's arms I felt safe and knew that she did in mine. A foreign emotion seized me completely and I knew it could only be love.

* * * *

Trying to wipe off my ridiculous grin, I set about checking that evening's arrangements. The table had been set with luxurious settings, our finest plates. The chef prepared lamb, accompanied by flavored vegetables, tasty pastries, and a wine selection from our best vintages. I instructed the waiters that Salvador's glass must remain topped up.

Pacing, I replayed my plan.

Within hours, the countess' imaginary outline had been realized. She sat next to me, on my right. Salvador, who sat to my left, held his hand over the rim of his glass, gesturing to the waiter he'd had enough. I reached over and filled his glass myself.

The evening flowed as did the Bordeaux. Countess Miranda charmed us with tales of her late husband's business endeavors. The count had been a successful merchant, traveling to London on several occasions. She'd accompanied him on many of his trips abroad. Salvador and I were intrigued when Miranda recounted reports on life in merry old England. We roared with laughter when told how little the English bathed.

We were enthralled with her morbid tales. Apparently, London's undertakers frequently dug up caskets for lack of room, and often found markings on the inside of the coffin lids. The undead had tried to scratch their way out. Some of those who'd been laid to rest had not actually been dead, not at their burial anyway.

Salvador howled at my expression. Apparently, my mouth had been gaping.

"Remind me never to step foot on that godforsaken island." I laughed.

"Oh, but they also have the most wonderful artists." Miranda turned to face me. "Many of Europe's greatest works find their way to the capital."

"Still not convinced." I cringed at the thought of falling down drunk and finding myself buried alive.

A discreet waiter served us dessert.

I knew how to play Miranda. She'd be used to men fawning over her. This woman had everything—money, power, and beauty. The alcohol loosened her nerve and she let down her guard. Her husband had died at forty, falling ill after a trip to France. He'd left her childless. Now one of Spain's wealthiest widows, with nothing but time for pleasure, she failed to conceal her desire for excitement, from me anyway.

I ignored her and concentrated on Salvador. When Miranda fidgeted, I fed her sugared almonds, wooing her all over again, pushing and pulling her into a state.

"There's nothing more interesting than a woman who's well traveled." I sighed, my thoughts drifting to Annabelle.

Miranda gave a crooked smile. "Or a man with a mysterious past."

"Daumia is certainly indefinable." Salvador downed his wine.

I raised my glass in a toast. "To defining the indefinable."

They laughed.

"We want to know more about you," Miranda said boldly.

Salvador leaned forward and broke the silence. "Well, I know one thing, he's certainly honorable."

I took a sip. Such regard for myself slipped away. A war between Felipe and I raged just beneath the service. No room for procrastination and no time for cold feet.

"But he's so coy about revealing anything." Miranda ran her fingertip around the rim of her glass.

I topped up her wine. "What do you want to know?"

"How you came to live in such a great home?" she asked.

I held her gaze. "Fate dealt me a kind hand."

"This was once the Bastillion estate?" She patted her lips with her serviette.

My back stiffened. "Right up until the house burnt to the ground."

"And Roelle Bastillion?" Miranda gave a long stare.

I placed my fork on my plate, my appetite now dulled.

"Such a terrible way to die," she continued. "No kind hand for Roelle."

I hated where this was going. "You have French heritage?"

Miranda appeared surprised. "Most people don't notice, Daumia. And what's your heritage?"

"Italian father, mother, Spanish."

"You were born in Santiago de Compostela?"

"Yes. Near the Romanesque Cathedral."

The butler entered. Never had I been so happy to see the man who'd unwittingly enabled me to change the subject.

"Tell me more about England." I gestured to the waiters to leave.

"They're very progressive," Miranda replied. "Take their architecture for example . . ."

Her words faded as thoughts of Harold Ferring came to mind. After he'd left, I'd come to realize his talent. He'd designed the house so that when the sun rose, it flooded the servants' quarters and breakfast room. At sunset, the light lingered in my office, the library, and the bedrooms. Masterful, the genius was captured in the details.

With dinner over, Miranda excused herself, withdrawing to powder her nose.

"She's quite taken with you," Salvador slurred, and gave a grin that quickly faded.

"Come and sit with me." I gestured to the couch.

Once seated, his fingers traced the braid on his uniform's jacket pocket. *Don't go through with it.*

"The man who needs watching is Felipe." I glanced away.

Salvador's arm stretched out along the back of the sofa. "I can't believe it."

"And you were already planning on taking up residence at the senator's?"

"He'd not suspect anything."

I was conflicted, but Alicia's life hung in the balance.

There had to be another way.

"Daumia?" Salvador shifted closer.

Desire surged through me and dragged me with it, possessing me with the thrill of his lips almost touching mine.

The door handle turned.

Miranda entered, barely missing our brush with lust, and Salvador slumped back.

"This . . . conversation will continue," I said at last.

Salvador sighed.

I rose and filled their half-empty glasses and handed their refreshed drinks back to them, then poured myself my second drink of the evening.

Miranda's soft flush of cleavage disappeared beneath the lace of her corset. When she caught my stare, she blushed. Salvador had imbibed so much wine that he fell comatose on my couch. The opportune moment was not lost on Miranda, who insisted she accompany me when I mentioned taking an evening stroll.

Halfway across the courtyard, just before reaching the stables, I sensed someone watching us. Annabelle's silhouette lingered at an upper window. I wanted to signal to her and reassure her, but couldn't risk Miranda seeing.

I sent the grooms away and led Miranda down the long line of stables, stopping before one of my most treasured stallions.

"He's beautiful." She patted his dappled neck, running her fingers through his thick, white mane. "I can see why nobility favors them." She caressed the horse's muzzle. "Salvador will be overjoyed."

I checked his hind leg. "He caught a stone in his shoe earlier." I lowered his hoof. "No harm done."

I caught Miranda staring. She quickly turned and patted the horse again.

An edgy, creeping sensation worked its way into my stomach. "I hear that you're a good friend of the senator's?"

"More of an acquaintance. I own a summer retreat in Vigo, but I rarely go there since my husband, George, died."

I nodded my understanding. "Salvador's been appointed to the senators. I'm concerned."

"Felipe's ways are a little heavy handed."

"You know him?"

"George," she glanced at me as if to check my reaction, "didn't really trust him."

"From what I hear, your husband had good judgment."

She nodded, but with a distant stare, as though lost in thought. "I have friends in the senate who'll watch out for him."

"I'm in your debt." I strolled behind her.

She was breathing faster now, her embroidered laced bodice appeared so confining, designed to restrict her desires, it seemed. I imagined that as each ribbon loosened, so would her passion.

"I'm going to walk away now," I whispered. "Forgive me, but you know why." Barely touching, aware of the tension, I lingered.

I reached up and caressed the fine, blond hairs on her nape, and she shivered beneath my touch. Although the evening was unfolding as planned, I recognized the illusion of this inner stillness. The rippling sensations of pleasure tried to convince me to take her.

She gave the deepest sigh.

I sauntered away.

XVI

THE MORAN'S BUTLER ASKED me to wait in the foyer.

I ignored him and headed up the staircase to look for Salvador myself. Several months had passed since my dinner party and Salvador had returned the favor and extended an invitation to dine at his father's home. With his family out of town, our privacy was assured. He'd taken up his appointment as Aide-de-camp at the senatorial residence, and I looked forward to questioning him. This visit promised to be interesting on all levels.

The great house had been restored to its former glory. A recent royal visit inspired a refurbishment. Whitewashed walls loomed resplendent.

I caught the butler's disapproving glare from the base of the stairs and threw him a big smile. He quick footed it out of sight.

Salvador greeted me halfway along the passageway. His expression was difficult to read.

"You never told me you had a sister." He frowned playfully.

"How is she?"

"Why don't you ask her yourself?" He pointed to a door.

I hesitated.

"She's been looking forward to seeing you," he said.

I clutched Salvador's arm and guided him along the corridor. "What's she doing here?"

"I had to get her out." He rested his hand over his heart. "She's not going back."

"What happened?"

"Felipe was beating her."

I stared off down the hallway.

He reached out, closing the space between us and held my arm. "What's wrong?"

"You're both in danger. Felipe will come after you."

"Maybe."

"You can't stay here."

"I know."

I looked past him, trying to ignore my badgering conscience warning me to keep my mouth shut. "There's something I have to tell you."

"Go on."

"I lied to you." I turned to face him. "That stuff about the inquisition." I gestured my apology.

"Shit!"

"I needed someone I trusted to watch over Alicia."

"I didn't remove her because of Felipe's heresy. I fell in love with her and wanted her safe."

I let out an uneasy laugh, but as the idea settled, so did my relief.

"Felipe is a complete bastard," he muttered.

"Will you ever forgive me? She had to be protected by any means possible."

"You were very convincing."

I cringed.

He shook his head and gave a wry grin.

"I'm forever indebted to you," I said. "I owe you so much."

"Just give me your blessing."

"Are you sure she wants to see me?"

"Yes."

I sighed. "When Felipe finds out—"

"We're going to Italy. She wouldn't leave without seeing you." Salvador patted my shoulder. "Come on."

* * * *

Still wary from our last interaction, I gestured my affection for Alicia from the doorway. She'd lost weight, evidence of her mistreatment.

Alicia caught a sob. "I thought you'd fallen from the ledge."

"I'm pretty fast, you know that." The lump in my throat refused to let up.

Alicia ran to me and I hugged her.

"You tried to warn me." Tears stained her cheeks.

"All that's forgotten now." I breathed in her familiar scent, reminding me so much of our mother's.

Salvador was smiling.

Alicia pulled back. "You've grown into such a handsome man."

"I've missed you."

"You look well," her voice faded. "Felipe—"

"I'm glad you're out of there."

She grasped my hands and held them to her face.

A flurry of crows and a rocking carriage.

I glimpsed something forgotten and tried to grasp it.

She closed her fingers around mine. "It's so good to see you."

"Salvador's told me about you both."

"We're so happy." She smiled his way.

"And that makes me happy." I nodded toward Salvador to make sure he knew it.

Alicia squeezed my hand. "Felipe told me you were dangerous, that's why I . . ."

"I understand."

"But I almost got you killed."

"No, you didn't."

"Grandpa became sick, and you disappeared, and Mama wouldn't talk about it." She inclined her head, as though trying to make sense of it all.

I feared that with my words, tears would fall.

"You were so young, how could you have known about the bull?" she reasoned.

"There were men there that night." I spoke calmly, my tone void of emotion. "I was shoved into the arena with a bull that had been worked hard for hours."

She gasped. "That's why you were taken away, so that you wouldn't tell anyone?"

I shrugged. "Perhaps."

From Salvador's expression, he knew that I was protecting Alicia.

"How is your son?" I asked.

"He's in the garden." She pointed out of the window at the one-year-old child playing on the lawn, watched over by a maid.

Knowing they were all safe allowed me a moment to breathe. "What's his name?"

"Ricardo." She watched my reaction.

I stared at the boy named after our eldest brother and resisted biting my lip.

"Felipe chose his name." She whispered it.

I glanced at Salvador.

He turned away, unable to look at me.

* * * *

After a fine meal at the Moran's dinner table, we spent the rest of the evening and well into the early hours conversing, never wanting it to end. Alicia stirred long lost memories that I'd once suppressed. Nothing could make up for a lifetime of being apart, but the precious moments we shared during that time proved somewhat cathartic.

Alicia held me for the longest time as we lingered before the horse drawn carriage. It pained me to have spent such little time with her.

With all that had passed between Salvador and I, our closeness had never wavered. Even now when he knew the truth of how I'd misled him, Salvador gave me that same look of affection with that illuminating smile of his.

The carriage lumbered off.

Alicia, her son, and Salvador headed for the road out of Spain. The sun arose and an array of orange burst over the horizon. With a new day arriving came a new life for them.

My smile faded.

My home would be the first place that Felipe searched.

XVII

THE SENATORIAL CARRIAGE EMERGED on the horizon.
And I'd just been thinking what a perfect day it was. A Sunday, and Miguel and I had been training one of the stallions in the paddock.

I ordered the staff to send Annabelle into the safe room. Harold Ferring's foresight of constructing a clandestine room beneath our bed and not just in my office had proven to be a godsend. As Felipe approached, I really appreciated the value of Ferring's experience.

Miguel guided the horse back to the stables. Without speaking, he'd conveyed, *Use caution*, with a glance.

Felipe stomped toward me.

Two weeks had passed since Alicia and Salvador had left for Italy. I assumed they'd be halfway there by now.

Casually, I strolled to meet him. "Good morning."

"Fuck the niceties," Felipe snapped. "Where are they?"

"Alicia?"

"I want my son."

"They're not here." I'd long ago mastered the art of deception. Now more than ever, I needed those skills—a calm demeanor, a steady hand, and an innocent stare that held his.

"If I find out you're lying . . ." Felipe turned to his men. "Go!"

They headed for the house.

A thin line of sweat trickled from his brow. "My lawyers report that you failed to sign our agreement."

"I was meant to sign it?"

"Search every room," he shouted, his fingers familiarly tapping his thigh.

I swallowed hard. "Aren't there laws against trespassing?"

"I am the law."

"I thought your wife bore you a son."

He glared at me. "When you see Salvador, tell him he's dead."

"Your wife, she bore you a daughter?"

His fist struck my jaw with a crack and I staggered back, though made a quick recovery. So much for Miguel's advice to use sound judgment, though I doubted it would have changed the way I handled this. My hate for Felipe made it nearly impossible to remain civil.

Felipe stared up at the house, searching the windows. "Tell me where my son is and I'll spare Alicia."

A chill ran through me.

His eyes burned with loathing. "Your title doesn't protect you."

"And neither does yours."

"I gave you your knighthood. I can take it away."

"I never did care for it. You're the one into power."

"I'll see you hang, Velde."

"If you ever set foot on my land again, it will be the last time you do so."

"Threaten the senator and you threaten the king."

"Hiding behind the crown now?"

"Your luck is running out."

My gaze settled on his agitated hand. "Leave my property."

"This is Roelle's house." His fingers stilled.

"His house burned to the ground, remember? This one was built on the ashes."

"This land is mine."

"As I recall, Roelle didn't actually like you."

"Where is she?"

"Now why would Alicia suddenly turn up on my doorstep and want to be all cozy?" I shrugged.

"You owe me."

"For what?"

"You're here because I allow it."

"You desecrated my family."

He shrank back. "I have no idea what you're talking about."

His men reappeared at the door and one of them signaled to Felipe they'd found nothing.

"Your political career is hanging by a thread," I said.

His jaw muscles tightened. "And how do you reckon that?"

"I know your dirty little secret."

Perspiration settled on his upper lip. "I do what has to be done."

"In whose name?"

"The king's."

"He'd be interested to know that murder comes easily to you."

"Peasants must be ruled with a firm hand, or like you they get ideas."

"If you mean that they desire their freedom . . ."

"Don't debate with me. You set yourself up for failure."

"Like that kind of failure." I pointed to the house.

"Roelle should never have educated you. I warned him."

I eased up on the smile. "He told me he found no value in your opinion."

Felipe turned and headed back to his carriage.

"Would you like to know where Aaron's remains are?" I called after him.

Felipe stopped in his tracks and spun round to face me.

I drew a deep breath. "If that's what a nine-year-old boy can do, imagine what I'm capable of now."

He twitched. "Don't sleep, Daumia."

XVIII

STARING DOWN AT THE gooey mess, I knew I had to go through with it.

Although I'd considered how to get out of eating the baked biscuit prepared by Eduardo, my five-year-old, his hopeful gaze melted my heart. Annabelle, my wife, balanced Jacob our one-year-old on her hip, as she suppressed a laugh. The cook also held a grin but diverted her gaze.

Although I disapproved of my oldest doing anything in the kitchen, Annabelle insisted that he loved nothing more than to play with dough and flour. Eduardo's penchant for making a mess could be best achieved in here, apparently.

The biscuit tasted how it looked. I feigned my delight and Eduardo's face lit up. He ran into my arms, insisting I finish it.

And I did.

Annabelle gave a nod of approval. Cook offered me another with that familiar smirk. I gestured to Eduardo that I was full.

I still had to pinch myself with the realization of such fulfillment. As his small hands clutched at my shirt, and he snuggled to my chest, I knew the responsibility of keeping him safe.

Keeping them all safe.

I followed Annabelle and the children along the corridor and we made our way out onto the back porch. This once shell of a house had become a home thanks only to the presence of my family. My children had redefined my world and, as only the young can, they helped me to perceive all things through an innocent perspective.

Annabelle headed further into the garden, carrying Jacob with Eduardo trailing close behind. I leaned against the doorframe. I loved these summer evenings. Our children's bedtime routine played out night after night as Annabelle, the perfect mother, used up the last of their energy.

Annabelle strolled over the lush lawn and placed Jacob on the blanket. She grasped Eduardo's hands and spun him round and round, much to his squealing delight.

Annabelle was the free spirit that the house of Velde needed. This was normalcy now and I loved it. Eduardo and Jacob were in every way their father's sons. Eduardo the mischievous one, taking after me, off exploring at every opportunity, and Jacob who took after Annabelle, with his dark complexion and large brown eyes, a calm, sweet soul. Even aged one year, his kind temperament was evident.

Annabelle turned, picked up her skirts, and ran away from the house with little Eduardo running after her. I strolled over to Jacob and picked him up.

Sublime innocence.

Giving my boys a happy childhood did in many ways make up for the loss of mine. Through them, I found myself reliving all that I'd missed out on.

Jacob stared up at me with that mischievous grin of his and then vomited onto my shirt. Annabelle's laughter rippled around the garden and Jacob giggled and Eduardo screamed. I too saw the funny side. Annabelle offered to take Jacob, but I gestured I was fine, and planted kisses onto his soft cheek and to the top of his head.

The stickiness soaked through to my skin. Jacob stared at the gooey mess and giggled again.

"Have I no power in this house?" I winked.

In an hour, the boys would be in bed and I'd steal precious time with the woman who'd taught me how to trust and how to love.

I welcomed the happiness in.

* * * *

Later that evening, I read the dispatch from Señor Teofilo's office.

The letter from Salvador and Alicia had originated in Italy, routed via the attorney's office, and even then written in code. After reading the letter, I memorized the words, the tone, then threw it into the fire.

A small price to pay for the peace of mind that Felipe wouldn't find them. Ever wary, I ordered my workers to take turns in guarding our residence. I fired three men I found napping during their watch before they took my paranoia seriously.

Smoke spiraled up and into the chimney. I heard a knock on the study door and Annabelle entered.

She wrapped her arms around me and we both watched the flames burst up, taking with them more than just words.

"How would you feel if I gave Eduardo his first riding lesson?" I asked.

She scrunched up her face. "On those big horses of yours?"

"We'll get him a pony."

"Perhaps when he's a year older?"

I nudged her. "They'll grow up one day, you know." I smiled. "Talking of babies, Alicia's pregnant."

"How far?"

"Five months."

"And Salvador?"

"He's well. Ricardo, too."

"Perhaps we'll be blessed with another child."

I hugged her. "What would you say to us moving?"

"But I love it here."

"We can rebuild."

Annabelle squeezed me tighter. "This is our home. I won't let that man run us out of it." She gazed up at me. "He's forgotten all of that now."

I knew that's what she wanted to believe, and so did I, but Felipe had proven himself to be vicious.

"What could he do to you now?" Her eyes widened, as though she'd read my mind.

Some part of me knew, despite the five years that had passed since I'd last seen him, Felipe still held a grudge. His thirst for power paled in comparison to his desire for wealth. We lived on the very land he believed should be his. Yet Annabelle was right, we had been left alone. No dispatches from his lawyers and no more threats.

"I have something to show you." Annabelle placed her small hand in mine and guided me out of the study.

"Where are we going?" I pulled her toward me and stole a kiss.

"You'll see."

I followed her out onto the lawn that crushed beneath our feet, above us a clear night sky.

I cringed. "Oh, God, I haven't forgotten our anniversary, have I?"

"Silly." She pointed to a row of small shrubs. "This is the best place for them."

I stared down at the twigs sprouting out of the ground.

She beamed with pride. "Rose bushes."

"What color?"

"Red."

I pretended to find joy in this moment, even though disconcerting memories were stirred by the scent of a rose. I studied the barest shrubs and considered the wisdom of staying here to see them grow.

"There's plenty of sun here." I knelt to examine more closely one of the buds. My fingertip caught on a thorn, and the puncture went deep. I sucked on the oozing drop of blood, quietly alarmed that coupled with the sharp sting, it brought with it a terrible omen.

XIX

AN AUGUST EVENING FILLED the air with the scent of jasmine, and the cool summer breeze carried with it the faint chirping of cicadas.

Taking my usual seat on the front porch, I topped up my glass of white wine, the fermented grapes cultivated on this very land.

The sunset flooded the landscape.

The years had unfolded, seamlessly shifting from one glorious month to another. The relief from suffering sustained during my former years bestowed a visceral gratitude not easily forgotten, as it seeped into the present.

But as I glanced up at the horizon, I was gripped with a wave of terror that the peace I'd come to cherish was about to end.

Salvador's father galloped toward the estate. I put down my drink and leaped to my feet.

Señor Moran dismounted. "He has them." His color was ashen.

"Dear God." My voice broke.

"I don't know how he found them. They were in Italy." His eyes were sick with fear. "By the time I receive an appointment with his highness, it will be too late."

"Ready my best horse," I shouted to the stable boys. "Now!"

Moran was shaking violently. "He accuses Alicia of witchcraft."

No. The ground became unsteady.

Miguel quickly joined us.

"I'm going to Vigo," I blurted, my mouth dry.

Miguel grabbed the horse's harness from the stable boy. "Felipe?"

I nodded and quickly mounted. "Tell Annabelle . . ."

"I know." Miguel tightened the reins. "I'll tell her."

XX

BLOOD STAINED MY HANDS.

My horse collapsed just outside Vigo. Unable to bear seeing him suffer any further, I unsheathed my knife and with an unsteady grip, slit his throat. After it was done, I retched on an empty stomach.

I washed off the blood in a trough outside a deserted cottage. Still trembling, I used the same knife that I'd slaughtered my horse with to shave off my stubble. Thieves were not unusual in wealthy neighborhoods and I didn't want to be confused for one.

Staring up at the senator's residence, exhaustion lingered beneath my terror.

Several service carts rumbled along, pulled by mules, following the road up to the great house. I ignored the first two and leaped onto the third, scrambling beneath the hessian material covering the mound of vegetables. I reached for a carrot and munched on the orange stick, despite the taste of soil. The cart rolled to a stop outside the deliveryman's door.

With no real plan, only a sense of urgency to get my sister and Salvador out, I willed myself to find courage. I wiped the dirt from my mouth, straightened my hair, and slid out from beneath the material.

Inside the kitchen, I strolled through, looking like I belonged, nodding in greeting to servants who scurried about, busy with their chores. Carrying a tray of food, I walked through the doorway that led into the foyer.

Three guards stood talking nearby and glanced my way, but I kept going, ready to reach for my concealed knife. With a confident air that I didn't feel, I headed for the cellars.

I'd half-listened as Ferring had explained long ago that it was typical to keep supplies in the cold vaults, and apparently it was the best place for the prisoners.

A maid believed my story that I was new, and guided me to the top of the stairwell and pointed to the basement. As I descended, the dank prison smell brought back stark memories, and I tried to push the dark nostalgia away.

Alicia lay asleep in the corner of a squalid chamber. I'd not expected to see her down here, rather Salvador incarcerated in these terrible conditions. But after checking the few cells, I only found her. I was surprised to find the door unlocked. Careful not to startle her, I knelt close.

Alicia opened her eyes and sighed when she saw me.

"I'm going to get you out," I mouthed.

"Salvador?" she asked.

"I haven't seen him." I glanced out of the cell and turned back to face Alicia with a puzzled stare.

She staggered to her feet. "Felipe told me he'd kill Ricardo if I left here."

"I'll find him." I wrapped my arm around her waist to support her.

Through the dungeon, we made our way up and out, and then lingered at the top of the stairwell, waiting for our pathway to clear.

"I can't leave without them." She trembled.

"I'll come back." My gut wrenched when I realized Alicia didn't look pregnant.

Gaunt, she became distant and tears soaked her pale cheeks. Then, as though coming round a few seconds later, she murmured, "Felipe sent his men to arrest us." Her hand lay on her belly. "I lost the baby."

I felt an awful, twisting grief and couldn't imagine what she endured. "How did he know you were in Italy?"

"Felipe told me he intercepted a letter from Salvador's mother." She grasped my sleeve.

I let out a slow breath. "I'll come back for them."

When we reached the stables, I found what looked like a fast horse and bridled him. I patted his neck, trying to earn his trust as I slid on the saddle and then secured the girth around his chest.

I turned to Alicia. "Promise me," I held her arm to make sure she listened, "you won't stop until you get to Miranda's home."

Alicia nodded. "I remember it."

With my assistance, Alicia grasped the reins and mounted.

"Neither of you can stay there." With caution I led the stallion out. "Felipe may come looking for you."

Alicia sobbed. "I can't leave."

"It's getting dark. They won't be able to catch you. Hold on tight." I slapped the horse's rump.

Alicia galloped off and I continued to watch her, making sure she didn't turn the horse around. She rode well and was light in the saddle. I prayed she'd make it.

Two guards came from out of nowhere. A fist struck my jaw and an unseen foot kicked me forward into the dirt.

I spat out soil and then came an awful pressure of a man kneeling on my back, and hands choking me.

Muffled orders were shouted our way. The knee lifting its weight, the hands easing their grip, I sucked in air . . . and yelled my rage.

* * * *

A lone soldier was ordered to guard me. His gruff expression was all I needed to find something else to look at in the office.

My throat hurt so bad, I had trouble swallowing.

An oversized mahogany writing desk was positioned in the center, and pretentious leather-bound books furnished the shelves. Upon the wall behind the desk hung a painting, a portrayal of the biblical tale of Belshazzar's Feast.

Prince Belshazzar's morbid expression matched my own. He'd made the mistake of insulting God. He, his wives, concubines, and other cohorts had tasted from the sacred vessels stolen from Solomon's temple. The prince glared back at a disembodied hand that reached out of a cloud of nowhere.

The guard coughed and I caught him wiping his brow.

I turned my attention back to the painting where God scribed in Aramaic that Belshazzar's days were numbered.

The door opened and several men entered, closely followed by Felipe.

Salvador was somewhere within these walls, held prisoner, at Felipe's mercy. I had to persuade Felipe to let him go.

Felipe followed my gaze. "You're unable to appreciate the significance of such a portrait."

A lump in my throat, I swallowed hard. "Where's Salvador?"

Felipe neared the canvas. "God's reckoning with an arrogant man," he leaned in close, "Belshazzar believes himself greater than his creator. Sound familiar?"

"God destroys Belshazzar's seat of power," I said. "Sound familiar?"

"My men have gone after Alicia."

Belshazzar's eyes bulged and the petrified expressions of his guests reflected the horror of my own drama. I steadied myself.

"No reaction?" Felipe looked amused.

His men patted down my jacket and found my knife.

"Was that for me?" Felipe drew near. "I can add conspirator to your list of crimes."

"Where's Ricardo?" I asked.

"Home." Felipe picked up a parchment from his desk and handed it to me. "I assumed you'd pay a visit, so I had this prepared."

The lawyer's scrawl was familiar, as was the content. I reached for the quill on his desk and signed it.

Felipe snatched the paper back. "Well, that was easy."

Having just signed over my entire estate, I tried to keep focused and tell myself that such things were unimportant.

"I'm afraid the news isn't good." Felipe seemingly paused for effect and then said, "Any act of treason is punishable by death."

"But I signed—"

"Everything you own over to me."

The air was stifling and a wave of nausea hit me hard.

"Out," he ordered the guards, and then waited until we were alone. "I want the dancer."

"What?"

"I take that as a *no*."

"Senator—"

"Salvador's alliance with you seals his fate."

"But you're friends with his father."

Felipe glared. "Meddling in my affairs has consequences." His fingers tapped against his leg in that familiar frenetic rhythm.

Stunned, I searched for words. "Wait . . . listen . . ."

Felipe opened the door and with a thin smile, he turned and shrugged. "Your widow will become my whore."

He was gone before I could get to him.

* * * *

The guards dragged me across the foyer close behind Felipe, past the startled gazes of servants, to the edge of a courtyard where a large crowd had gathered.

I panicked.

There in the center, Salvador was in man-to-man combat with three soldiers and judging by his wounds and blood stained clothes, they'd been sparring for some time. Steal blades clanged. A whiff of sweat and blood carried. My legs almost gave way.

"Hold back," Felipe ordered his men.

These were seasoned swordsmen, well-fed and rested. Salvador had no advantage and his balance was affected. I grappled with the guards to get free, but they tightened their grip. Salvador caught the scuffle and peered up and staggered. With a sweaty palm, he struggled to grasp the weapon's hilt.

"This is not the way a gentleman defends his honor," I shouted at Felipe.

"He has no honor," Felipe said.

"Let me fight with him."

"And ruin the entertainment value?" Felipe nodded to a six-year-old boy who watched from nearby.

Ricardo, the child with my brother's name and my sister's eyes, ran to Felipe, clutching a small sword fashioned just for him.

Having lived with Salvador for the majority of his early years, I wondered how Ricardo would react. Salvador had adopted him, caring for him as his own. The child didn't understand and, wielding his sword, he stabbed at an invisible opponent.

"Ricardo." Felipe signaled to the boy. "Should your uncle fight?"

"Say yes," I pleaded.

Ricardo frowned.

Felipe laughed and turned to his soldiers. "Continue."

They beleaguered Salvador, thrusting their swords at him. One man closed in, while the other two stalked him from behind.

"Don't make the boy watch this." I stumbled.

A guard punched my stomach, winding me.

Salvador caught one of his attackers and struck his arm. Blood poured from the man's wound and his opponents forged ahead, inflicting viscous strikes. Salvador's sword fell. They strode around him, closing in like animals.

Felipe's grin didn't reach his eyes. "I've outmaneuvered you both."

"Spare him."

"Your life for his?"

"Yes."

"How noble."

Salvador brought his hand to his chest in a gesture of affection for me.

"Salvador, raise your sword," I shouted.

His stare glazed over as a rapier sliced into his back, and he sunk to his knees, burying his face in the dirt.

With a nod from Felipe, his men let me go and I sprinted into the center of the courtyard, skidded on my knees, and pulled Salvador into my arms. Blood poured from his wounds. I pressed against them, trying to cease the flow. Several of his fingernails were gone. They'd tortured him first.

"Alicia?" Salvador rasped.

"She's safe."

"I told him nothing," Salvador whispered.

I glared at Felipe, full of hate.

A scarlet line trickled from Salvador's mouth and onto his chin, his breathing labored.

My vision blurred with tears. "I've always loved you."

Salvador forced a smile and then his head fell against my chest, his eyelids half-closed.

I rocked him into death.

Salvador was ripped from me and the soldiers pulled his body to the edge of the courtyard. A sword landed near my feet.

Everything felt surreal.

Standing now, my shirt soaked with sweat and Salvador's blood, I judged my assailants carefully. If I took out one man at a time, I could live through this.

Taking the first attacker by surprise, my weapon slashed his thigh and he collapsed, badly wounded. Turning awkwardly, facing the man behind me, I defended his lunge, clashing metal against metal. A thrust and I had the other one down. One man remained.

Two more soldiers stepped into the courtyard. A dreadful wave of futility caused my throat to constrict.

A perfect life awaited me, but I'd thrown it away. Annabelle would be left vulnerable and my boys threatened.

Felipe smiled.

I was attacked from every angle. A blade cut into my side, knocking me off-balance, and I landed heavily. Dust sprayed up and was kicked into my eyes. Through gritty vision, my assailants gathered. I sprang to my feet and leaped back, ensuring distance between us. I hurled forward, swiftly striking another man who swayed to my right. The tip of my weapon sliced his forearm. A sharp stab tore into my lower back and another thrust into my right shoulder. Acute pain radiated. Another fierce strike to the back of my head threw me forward. Face down, taking small gasps, ignoring the torment of each breath, I tried to hold on. Desperate to save my sister and get back to my family, I fought unconsciousness.

And lost.

* * * *

Bound to a large pillar positioned at the edge of the courtyard, I was unable to move. Sweat stung my eyes. My limbs were numb. A few torches provided some light, but not enough. The sword I'd used lay a few feet away and beside it stood Ricardo. He waved his own in the air.

"I didn't want you to miss this, Velde." Felipe's fingernails dug into my jaw and he raised my chin. "The handling of fine weaponry runs in the family. Your nephew shows great swordsmanship." He motioned to Ricardo. "Provide your uncle with a demonstration."

Through bleary eyes, I focused in on the child's sword and my chest muscles tightened, forcing air from my lungs. It was impossible to struggle.

"Straight through the heart, boy." Felipe stepped aside. "Swift and sure."

Ricardo hurtled toward me.

Stupefied, I watched the silver tip penetrate my stomach and continue on through, searing, blinding agony as the point struck my spine.

Somewhere far off, I heard the sound of cheers.

"I shall have words with your teachers, boy." Felipe's voice was distant. "Their lessons in anatomy are lacking."

I prized open my eyes to see my blood gushing and staining the earth at my feet. Terrible numbness . . .

Bound again in the mausoleum, a small, abandoned boy lay waste. I laughed with Annabelle. Heard Eduardo and Jacob but couldn't see them.

I craved one more embrace with them.

An Andalusian cantered past.

Dizziness. Blindness. Deafness. Drifting close to fatality, its spiraling momentum caught up, dragging me into nothingness.

PART TWO

XXI

QUIETNESS LOOMED IN the deserted courtyard.
　My tongue cleaved to the roof of my mouth. I'd lost all sense of time. The scent of sweat mixed with blood permeated the air, and something else too, something intoxicating.
　"Do you choose life?" It was a woman's voice, like a soft purr.
　She exuded that familiar fragrance, stirring remnants of a long ago desire.
　"You're not real." I sighed. At least I thought I did.
　Sunaria stood close and she was unchanged, flawless.
　I struggled to breathe.
　"I offer you a life beyond this one. Say *yes* and I'll bring you over."
　"I'm dying."
　"I can bring you back."
　A gnawing pain shot through me. I cried out.
　"What do you choose?" she asked.
　"Don't leave . . ."
　"What do *you* want?"
　"Life."
　She nuzzled in and I welcomed her softness, her comforting, a sharp sting at my neck and the feel of her kissing me there.
　Too weak to flinch, I strained against my bindings. "I can't breathe."
　She pulled away. "It will feel worse," she whispered, "before it feels better."
　I tried desperately to break free. Had to find my way out of here—*and find my way home.*
　The tickling sensation of her nuzzling in again and lapping there made me wince.
　Her wrist pressed firmly against my mouth, which opened wider to receive the warm taste of the finest claret. Even though I knew my actions were depraved, an unspeakable act, the arousing sweetness was too thirst quenching to refuse. My dry tongue licked and suckled. I hoped this could save me, whatever this was.
　A boy again, full of excitement, climbing out my bedroom window. Near the far wall on the other side of the arena stood Roelle and Aaron, only this time I observed them with a man's insight. Felipe's rough hands nudged me into the

bullring.

I choked on a sob.

Despite their covered faces, I knew it was them and recognized the cudgel that Felipe raised into the air.

It was a dying man's realization, or something else, something shown to me by her, a mystical revelation of what had truly happened that night. My suffering dissipated and, with the wafting of her perfume, my torment crept shamefully away, like a nightmare that had done its worst.

"I have you now." Sunaria's words lingered. "You're safe."

Transfiguring, I gazed skyward, as a pulsing surged along my arms and down through my thighs and calves, eliciting a thrilling vibration, a quickening of mind, body, and soul.

A sensuous imagining . . .

Sunaria astride me, a fantasy so real, guiding my imagination, luring me, and holding my gaze. Dark locks spilling over naked shoulders. My hands found her small waist, controlling the rhythm. Yearning for her, my body drenched in a wet heat.

"Not really happening."

In all this time, I'd not once looked at another woman. Annabelle was my one true love who'd freed me from myself, the wife who waited for me even now.

Her chilling whisper, *"Surrender."*

I desired nothing more than to hold onto this feeling, then realized that my restraints remained and my hands were still bound behind me and secured to the post, restricting me from moving.

Rocking together, sharing these visions, exquisite pleasure carried us along. Sunaria mastered me, dominating every nuance.

Spellbound, I exhaled for what felt like the first time. Sighing, she guided me on.

Solace.

"Avoid daylight." Sunaria's voice came seemingly distant.

Shuddering, I passed through Death's dark veil.

* * * *

Night.

I awoke to find myself slumped against the post in a deserted courtyard, untied.

No sign of Sunaria.

Had she even been here?

My clothes were blood soaked. I poked around my abdomen, searching for wounds that weren't there. No pain. No scars. Just blood.

At my feet, a monstrous vision of a dead soldier, his skin pale and leathery, his mouth open in a silent scream. I looked away, all the while removing the knife from his belt. My vision was sharp, lines more defined, and despite the dark, colors vibrant.

No time for madness.

A lump caught in my throat. Salvador's body lay at the end of the courtyard. A strange memory of Ricardo's sword tearing into me, it had seemed so real. I traced my tongue along the crimson smudges on my fingertips and headed into the house.

Searching Felipe's desk, I found the warrant that transferred my estate into his name. I held it over a candle and it flared brightly, and then disintegrated. A flame caught my thumb and I sucked on the burn, trying to cool it. When I reexamined my hand, there was no redness and no blister.

I approached the painting of Belshazzar's feast. With a rip, the canvass tore out of its frame. Taking a moment, I studied the rich strokes of Belshazzar's golden coat. The portrait's meaning: the writing was on the wall, obscurely highlighting the fact I should have known Felipe's cruelty would find me again.

Felipe had lied about everything. I'd exposed not only myself to danger but also my family.

I returned to the courtyard and hooked the canvas onto a nail that protruded from the top of the pillar where I'd been tied, piercing it in the center.

For a moment, I considered searching for Ricardo, but my usual sensitivity eluded me. Feelings that had once come easily, now dissolved. Recollecting metal striking my spine sent a sliver of pain radiating up my back. Such a strike would be deadly.

I'd come back for him.

In a trance-like state, I lifted Salvador and carried him through the desolate house, not surprised to find a dead guard lying at the front door. Stranger things had befallen me tonight.

I stepped over him and disappeared into the night.

* * * *

I found an abandoned shovel leaning up against a tilting grave. The peacefulness of the churchyard was tranquil enough, but Salvador deserved better, an honorable tombstone to mark a life well-spent.

As I poured the last few handfuls of soil over him, I swore revenge. My hands were filthy and, engrained beneath my fingernails, the blackest dirt. I wanted to wash it off, wash away this pain. The heavy mound of earth was all wrong, and the thought of Salvador waking to find himself beneath layers of dirt made me fling myself at his grave and dig. When I reached his cold hand, I groped for his wrist, fumbling for a pulse.

Nothing.

I held his mottled palm, planting kisses there, staining my lips with soil. Weeping, refusing to let him go, my cries echoed, releasing a wellspring of grief.

Misery, I know thee.

On the horizon, the glint of dawn approached and an uncommon fear persuaded me to tuck Salvador's hand back. A burning sensation crawled over my flesh as darkness faded, and an irrational terror gripped me as sure as the impending daylight. Searching for somewhere to shelter, I ran past row upon row of slanted gravestones, the names of the departed as worn away as their memory.

At the center of the cemetery, larger tombstones lined the pathway. The wealthy had a monopoly even in death.

Morbid inner ramblings that made no sense held my thoughts hostage, making it nearly impossible to think straight.

A burst of cold, dusty air hit me as I entered a rundown crypt. Wooden shutters blocked out some daylight, but not enough.

This place was hauntingly familiar, similar to the mausoleum I'd been trapped in as a boy. A sunray caught my hand and blisters bubbled. I flew into a panic as red welts tracked up my arm, stinging as they spread. I shoved the stone lid and stared at the rotting casket inside. Reconsidering sharing the space with a corpse, I glanced at the garish sunrays.

A hellish nightmare.

I leaped in, lay down and slid back the stone. A sudden drop in temperature helped me to focus. Spitting a sticky mass of cobwebs, I hacked the rest out, cringing at the thought of being trapped. Leaning over, I heaved stale blood and it trickled along the edge of the coffin, and dripped. I wiped my mouth with my sleeve.

The dust settled. It was so uncomfortable that I considered climbing out, but the incessant stinging persuaded me otherwise. I could see even though there was no light. I tried to focus, and struggled to find reason.

Trembling, I replayed the day's events.

Miguel had once told me that shock could trick the mind into all sorts of things. Thoughts of seeing him and the boys again, and holding Annabelle, offered some comfort.

By the time I awoke, things would be normal again, I'd feel normal again.

I begged sleep to find me.

* * * *

I chastised myself for delaying my journey.

Darkness welcomed me when I withdrew. Staring back at the tomb, I marveled that I'd slept there.

Alicia would have reached Miranda's by now. I hated the thought of telling her about Salvador and even worse, I'd failed her by not going back for her son.

I craved meat, yet the thought of eating anything sickened me. I had an uncontrollable urge to suckle, draw from an animal's veins.

The pathway to madness, my mind lost its grip, as I struggled for clues to explain what had happened over the last few hours.

Sunaria had nestled into my neck and suckled. My imagination groped to comprehend, realizing that I'd seen something similar happen to Roelle. He'd been fine until daylight flooded in.

What the fuck was going on?

Rumors of nightwalkers came to mind. Creatures that stalked the night. Staff had retold tales about the once disappeared who'd staggered back into town with crazed expressions and fang marks, unintelligent talk from uneducated peasants.

The shock of seeing Salvador's murder had sent me over the edge.

* * * *

I lingered outside a deserted house.

The sensation of a hot orb boring through my eyes persuaded me to scramble on in. Rubbing my eyes, I prayed that the damage wasn't permanent. My crawling flesh subsided and my vision returned. I would try again tomorrow. I must be tired, weary from my journey, but not the usual weariness. *This was different.*

Finding the darkness inadequate, I descended into the basement and caught a whiff of a human presence. The entwined couple slept soundly in the corner. With a sense of excitement, I knelt beside them, watching their chests rise and fall. Their pink flesh offered up a bright illumination, my reaction to the pair uncharacteristic. A corporeal desire to embrace them both confounded me. Unable to resist the urge, I moved closer.

He stirred.

Questioning my behavior subsided as the sensation of my tongue tracing his neck brought a wave of exhilaration. I marveled at how easy it was to pierce his skin and then suckled.

My mind followed him down corridors, through golden wheat fields and into lovers' beds. His memories rolled on, making no sense. Through his eyes, his world unfolded. I lived his life—men he'd seduced, woman he'd taken regardless of their consent, children he'd fathered and then denied were his own, fights he'd won and lost, and the lives he'd torn apart.

The woman awoke and glanced at her lover, and then stared wide-eyed at me. Her screams shocked me back into the room. I scooted toward the wall. The vein on her neck was a tease difficult to resist.

My thumb grazed along my upper teeth, and I flinched when I touched the sharp point of what felt like a fang.

I found my voice and rasped, "Run." My fingernails dug into the dirt, resisting my own will.

She glanced back at her lifeless lover.

"Run!"

* * * *

I'd stripped the dead man and now wore his clothes, replacing my blood soaked shirt. His trousers were a little short, but they'd do. I reassured myself that this would never happen again. Whatever disease plagued me, if I could just make it home, I knew I'd recover. Once reunited with my family, I'd find a way to overcome this hysteria.

The two sharp teeth that I thought I'd felt had now gone. My imagination spiraled.

Better never to speak of it again and deny it ever happened. Yet, as I recalled how I'd hunted down that sweet girl, and what followed when I'd caught her—sensuous sensations that I'd never experienced before—I wondered if I'd break my own promise.

I had to get a grip.

Upon my arrival at Miranda's house, I flew into a panic. Her home had been ransacked. Each room was in disarray, the work of angry men. Overturned tables, upside down chairs, and smashed glass everywhere, paintings ripped from the walls, their portraits slashed through, and from her empty jewelry boxes, evidence of looting.

Running from room to room, searching for a coded message left to reveal where they'd gone, it was more than obvious that it was impossible to find anything amongst this mess. And from the look of it, they'd failed to find what they came for, just as I had.

I'd lost Alicia again.

XXII

WHEN I REACHED Santiago De Compostela, the air was still.

Lingering on the steps, I took a moment to gather my thoughts. I turned to face the reek of decay and my breath left me. Three slaughtered horses lay rigid in the paddock, their eyes bulging.

I bolted into the house and up, ascending the staircase with dizzying speed.

Miguel lay face down outside my bedroom door, and a knife emblazoned with the senatorial crest protruded from his back. The man who'd treated me like a son was now dead. At the doorway, I teetered on collapse and tears bleared my vision. Upon the bed lay Annabelle and our eldest son, Eduardo.

I settled beside their motionless bodies, their skin mottled. I looked around for Jacob but couldn't see him, and feared finding his small body like this.

I hugged Annabelle. She lay like a rag doll in my arms. I ran my fingers through her spiraling curls. I reached for my son, and then pulled back, unable to go through with touching a cold, lifeless hand. I leaned over him and my tears dropped onto his pale cheek.

Shaking, I tried to make sense of what I saw and what I felt. I wanted to turn back the clock. I'd gone to save my sister and Salvador and left my family here, vulnerable.

I removed Annabelle's necklace and opened the dangling locket. Inside, our portraits were captured perfectly. My breath left me as the ache in my chest wrenched so badly that I felt it could kill me.

I wanted it to.

On the bedside table rested an open book and an empty cup. The window was open and the lace curtains billowed.

* * * *

Staring back at the house, my mind splintered. Numbness severed the pain. A breeze whirled dead leaves around me and they settled at my feet. I couldn't remember what I'd been doing out here, lingering before a mound of earth, my fingernails filthy.

My mind fractured.

Whatever had tried to entangle me over the last two days found its way in. Surrender brought little relief. My sense of smell heightened, enhancing my awareness, sharpening my perception. My vision cleared. I honed in on the nature around me. Emotions scattered.

Voices carried and I followed the ruckus, meandering back the way I'd come.

Twenty soldiers or so sat talking around the kitchen table, before them, plates stacked high with food and numerous empty bottles of wine. The murderers were having a midnight feast.

Again that terrible chatter of voices, the strange illusion that more men spoke than were here, and for a fleeting moment, a diabolical notion that I wasn't only hearing their conversations but also their thoughts, as voices crossed over, clashed with each other, and made no sense.

Movement in the corner caught my eye.

Jacob, my one-year-old son, played on the floor and he was filthy. I had to get to him before the madness got to me. Strolling past the soldiers, I headed for him, vaguely aware that they leaped to their feet and drew their swords. I planted a kiss onto Jacob's forehead and carried him over to the pantry where I plopped him in and shut the door.

And then I turned to face the men.

* * * *

The claret tasted off.

I sat back, resting my feet on the kitchen table, taking a moment to consider if the grapes had soured before the wine had been corked, or if the fermenting process had gone askew. The wine's consistency was too thick and its flavor unlike any vintage I'd ever had.

Sunaria sat opposite to me, wearing a long, black gown that gathered at her waist and clung to her figure. Her revealing dress was overlaid by a sweeping, hooded cloak, pulled back, the lining a burgundy velvet.

Jacob played at my feet with milk-stained lips. He crashed a cup onto the floor and then smiled up at me, proud of the noise, and then did it all over again.

The drink refreshed me nevertheless. "Sure you don't want one?" I grinned. "Perhaps white would be better?"

Her lashes fluttered, but she didn't blink. "Take a breath, Daumia."

I took another sip. "When did you come in?"

"Do you know what day it is?"

I beamed at her. "Your beauty, it mocks me."

She smiled down at Jacob, who was tugging on my shoe laces. I focused in on him and my gaze caught the scarlet circle of dried blood on the floor nearby.

Slaughtered men were everywhere.

This is not wine that I'm drinking.

I bolted up.

Flashes of images came to mind, a sense of sharing their secrets, the darkest intimacies, and a dusky memory of attacking each man, like a crazed animal. The glass slipped from my fingers and smashed, splattering remnants of blood that mingled with the glass splinters. I struggled to slow my breathing, control my panic, and hold back my cry.

Stifled by the putrid air, I heaved in. "All of them?"

She nodded.

"But how?"

"You know you're in denial."

"What happened?"

She raised her hand to quiet me.

I fought back panic. "What's wrong with me?"

"Nothing."

"Clearly there is."

"I'll take care of it."

"Dear God, Jacob." I picked him up, and carried him down the corridor, covering his eyes as we passed another dead soldier. The man had bolted and I'd caught him.

Sunaria followed us into the living room. Here, some normalcy, though it offered no comfort. I placed Jacob down and allowed him to crawl.

"If we're leaving, then it will have to be soon." Sunaria glanced at the window.

"You think more soldiers will come?"

"If there are any left, yes." She drew the curtains and turned to face me. *You're more magnificent than I imagined you'd be.*

A wave of dismay, realizing her thoughts seeped into mine. "Your voice is in my head."

"It's the mind gift."

"What the hell does that mean?"

"We can hear each other's thoughts."

If it were true, it would explain the awful babbling of the soldiers. *I don't understand.*

She gave what looked like a practiced smile. "In time, you will."

"What's happening?"

"You're adjusting."

"I've gone mad?"

"No."

I ran my fingers through my hair and paced. "Is there a cure?"

She gave me an incredulous stare.

I tried to keep up with my racing thoughts. "This fogginess—"

"It's different for everyone. For you, some memory loss."

"I feel drunk."

"It'll pass."

"You're the daughter of the woman from the mausoleum?"

"I *am* the woman from the mausoleum."

"That's not possible."

"My name's Suna."

"*Sunaria*," I whispered.

She gave a smile.

"Then it was you who rescued me in that carriage outside the senator's?" I searched her face for the truth.

She nodded.

"I don't believe you."

She shrugged, or at least I thought she did.

"Why don't you age?" I brushed my fingertips across my smooth jaw, where stubble should be.

She peeked out of the window. "You have the potential to live for eternity."

I arched an eyebrow. "Right."

"Unless the sun—"

"How long before I can face it?"

Her gaze lowered and she knelt close to Jacob and offered him a stuffed toy rabbit that she'd found on the floor. It had been Eduardo's.

I held back tears. "Can you bring my son back? My wife?"

"It doesn't work like that." She waved the floppy, well-loved rabbit before Jacob.

"Don't."

"But he likes it."

"I'm not asking you. Now step back."

"I saved you."

"Is that what you call this?"

"You're here because of me."

"But not my family."

"I was watching over you." She turned away.

"Why didn't you show yourself?"

She sighed. "I can't interfere with your first steps."

"You're not making any sense."

She sat down on the couch, her movement so sleek that it verged on supernatural.

"I don't want this," I murmured.

"Then you'd be dead."

"Turn me back."

She stared at me for a long time with a painful brightness in her eyes. "I can't." She stretched out her arms along the back of the couch. "Once a vampire—"

"Don't call me that." I glanced at my stained shirt. "What if I can't control it?" And then I stared at Jacob, fearing he'd one day recall seeing his father covered in blood, or worse, the bloodbath.

"I'll teach you." She swept her hand up in a casual gesture.

It was as though she'd reached out and touched me, even though she still sat a few feet away.

"You have all the answers, don't you?" I fought my desire.

Come to me willingly, she seemed to say and then broke the silence with that purr of her voice. "I'll show you the way." She rose so effortlessly that even Jacob stopped what he was doing and looked up.

"Dear God." I leaned against the back of a chair.

"He can't help you."

"Maybe he can."

"Think about it. Already you have an aversion to holy artifacts." Sunaria pointed to the Bible resting on a side table.

I approached the book and placed my hand on the time-worn cover. Anxiousness twined with guilt, but nothing else.

Sunaria's stare held me intently. "Perhaps you're one of the few."

"How convenient."

"Myth tells of those of our kind who are drawn to the Church, even serve it."

"You contradict yourself." I stepped back. "How can I trust you?"

"I'm here to help you."

"Hell has been unleashed under this roof and I wasn't here to stop it."

Her gaze burned through me as though something possessed her. "Don't look at me like that. I had nothing to do with this."

Whatever it was, it threatened to take me, too. "Convenient though," I tried to shake it off, "my family dead. You've been pursuing me."

"Watching over you."

"Stalking me."

"You're a hard man to keep track of."

"Why are you here?"

"Because you're out of control."

"No, something else."

"You were destined to die young. A free will existence that was faulty from the beginning."

"You offered no guidance," I shouted. "No advice."

"Your stubborn ways—"

"Your demonic ways."

"Don't talk to me like that." Her hands rested on her hips.

"You're crazy."

She came closer, close enough to touch, and her gaze lingered on my lips. I found myself staring at hers. My breathing was so fast, I feared my ability to control myself, and act out of character in a way that felt carnal, as her scent stirred a desire which was out of place. I had to will myself not to punish her with a kiss and I fought the strongest urge to drag her out into the corridor and take her by force.

Her fingertips traced over my lips, as though she dared me to do it.

"Get out," I snapped.

"I risked everything for you."

"I don't want you near me or my son."

"I saved your life."

I stepped back. "That's what you call this?"

Her fists clenched in anger.

My rage welled, and I struggled to contain it. "Looks like we're both mad."

She slapped me and the force of her assault jolted my head back. Jacob looked stunned.

"This thing was done to me." Her voice cold and controlled. "No one asked me."

"I don't recall a conversation with you asking for this."

"You agreed to this."

"Half-dead, hanging by a thread!"

"You said *yes*."

"Well, perhaps if I'd have known what was actually being asked of me, I wouldn't have."

"And what of him?" She pointed to Jacob. "I could have turned you sooner. But I waited, let you have a life."

"How considerate."

"You have no idea what I've risked in turning you."

"What are you talking about?"

"I'm being hunted."

"Can't imagine why."

"By my own kind."

"You best get going then."

She held her head high, her gait proud.

"Close the door on the way out," I rasped.

Jacob wailed.

"How am I supposed to take care of him?" I whispered.

"Like a father." Sunaria dropped a small object at Jacob's feet.

He stopped crying.

I sighed. "I have to get to my sister."

"She's safe."

"You know where she is?"

"I'll show you."

I dismissed the idea with a wave.

"She gave me something to give to you that will prove she's safe."

"Why should I believe you?"

Sunaria stepped closer. "Because you belong to me."

"The hell I do." I stared into those perfect, almond shaped eyes of hers, so very close to surrendering to the spell she'd cast. "When your elders come for you . . ." I neared her. "I'll tell them where you are."

"I've watched over you all your life."

I pointed to the door.

"This is not how I saw it. You were to run into my arms, tell me that I've haunted your dreams."

"Those would be nightmares. I want my life back!"

"But I love you."

"Don't be ridiculous."

Sunaria stormed out.

Jacob was enthralled with the metal box. I eased it out of his hands and prized it open, immediately recognizing Salvador's medal, the crest of his old regiment emblazoned upon it.

My thoughts turned to Alicia.

I'd just sabotaged any chance of finding her.

I approached the mirror hanging above the fireplace. The terrified moan escaped my lips before I could stop it.

XXIII

DARKNESS IMMERSED the manor.
After searching for answers in almost every book I owned, I braved the mirror again. With my hand tracing where my reflection should be, I kept expecting the view to change. Unable to shake off the dread, I smashed the mirror with my fist without thinking.
Jacob wailed.
I brushed off glass fragments from my hand and licked at the small cuts.
Jacob frowned up at me and his cries worsened.
I calmed him down, having successfully hidden my own terror from him, and returned to the kitchen, leaving him outside.
I tried to keep my eyes off the massacre. The stench forced me to breathe through my mouth. Jacob's cries grew more insistent, so I quickly grabbed what I needed for him and withdrew.
Denial came easily. After all, no one man could take on so many soldiers and live. Examining my hands, I was amazed to see the cuts had gone, yet blood stained the edge of my cuff.
Loneliness had me by the throat.
Talking words of comfort to Jacob, I was really trying to draw strength from my own voice, but even that sounded altered, the tone deeper, bestowing an enticing quality.
I was just tired.
After gulping his third cup of milk, Jacob fell asleep in my arms. I found us both fresh clothes and then carried him through the house into what had once been the nursery. Unaware of the horrors that had unfolded, Jacob beamed up at me with that sweet smile of his. Lying beside him, I tucked my feet beneath me to fit his bed and hoped to find peace in the presence of sleep.
Despite all that had happened, I had Jacob to think of. I drew strength from his unwavering affection and as he snuggled to me, I was consoled by his breathing, a sure rhythm against my chest.

* * * *

I awoke, stirred by a presence in the house, and leaped off the bed.

The door burst open and I was immediately faced with a sword pointed directly at my face. The tip neared my right eye. Jacob was still waking up. A guard had him and I could do nothing about it. More men rushed in and, just behind them, strolled Felipe.

He stared at me, aghast. "Impossible."

I was trapped.

"One wrong move and he dies." Felipe leaned in, his stale breath too close. "Bury him, alive."

I wanted to grab Jacob and run, but we'd never make it out the door. The men restrained me and dragged me outside. The knife in my back that persuaded me to comply, cut into my flesh.

Wanting to fight back, wanting to tear into all of them, I feared what would happen to Jacob if I showed any resistance.

With a shove, I tumbled into the deepest hole.

My hands were bound together, and I struggled to free myself as crushing soil pressed against my chest, oppressing me.

Thrashing, terrified, I cursed myself for not leaving the house. I'd outdone myself with my arrogance. The rope wrapped around my wrists gave, but even more mounds of earth were being shoveled over me.

Encased, the dirt poured into my nostrils. With my mouth prized shut, soil blocked my airway. I shook my head from side to side until the weight of the resistance held me still, a last ditch effort to claw my way out.

Suffocating, or so I thought, I willed Sunaria to save Jacob.

And yet, despite the lack of air, I didn't lose consciousness. My chest rose and fell as though I were breathing.

"Jacob!"

Sunaria, save my son.

I gagged and choked, angry that I'd allowed Annabelle to persuade us to stay, believed as she had done once, that we were free from Felipe's intimidation. Though if I faced the truth, it was me who hadn't wanted to leave the home I'd built. This place was more than just bricks and mortar. But my pride yet again ravaged everything in its wake and now I'd risked Jacob's life since I'd not thought it through. Felipe had not found my corpse where he'd left it, and I suspected that was what brought him here.

Sunaria, I need you.

Above me, Jacob's faint cries were eaten up by the night.

My whole life had been one mistake after another. Everyone close to me was now dead, or missing.

Sunaria!

* * * *

Trapped.

Nights came and went.

Another valuable lesson was Sunaria's stubbornness.

"*Whatever you want,*" I relayed to her. "*Whatever you want me to be to you, I will.*"

Buried deep within the earth, I unraveled. My initial hyper-arousal settled. Despite resisting introspection, I had nowhere else to go but within, into unfamiliar territory. The first few days, I had only sleep to be grateful for and when awake, denial eluded me.

After the fifth day, I yielded.

Like a fleeting shadow, Sunaria's presence swept over me, offering a moment of solace. News that she had Jacob caused me to sob pitifully. I relayed my thanks, but feared that she might disappear with him. I begged her not to.

Jacob, I'll find you.

Quiet again.

Terrified of earthly creatures munching on my flesh, I dreaded my mind disintegrating. Madness lingered but soon scurried off, lurking not far enough away. Deep within my burial ground, I knew Sunaria's true punishment. She haunted my waking hours as well as my dreams.

And then silence.

I let go, a sublimely surrendering to the isolation, and gradually what had been a suffocating trap became a safe dwelling. All that I'd known slipped away. Rules no longer applied down here, *in here*. Thoughts that had served me well in the past had no use now. A new way of seeing my world begged for discovery.

Sunaria offered me hope, dependence impossible to deny.

"Forgive me," I conveyed.

She came to me in thought, utterly possessing me, and I gave myself over to her.

* * * *

Sunaria deemed me ready.

I ascended out of my dark grave and, as though I needed it, I sucked in the fresh air.

Sunaria's hair was pulled up behind her head. A few trailing strands fell over her face. She stared through me with those almond eyes of hers, pouting with full red lips, exotic features that I'd once tried to disregard. Now though, I realized her devastating beauty and felt beholden to her.

Unable to make eye contact, hesitant to view her austere expression, I fell to my knees.

I panicked when I didn't see Jacob.

Sunaria stared down at me with her arms folded. "Jacob's safe with your sister."

These were the words that I needed to hear more than anything.

"Alicia and Miranda are safe in Nuevo Portil, near Palos," she continued.

I wanted to ask why she'd waited this long to tell me this, but I didn't want to remind her of my arrogance.

She sent me a mind message, a vision of Jacob safe with Alicia, proof that Sunaria told the truth. I marveled at this ability to convey without words.

She stared off. "If you ever displease me, I'll personally put you back in the ground." She tugged on my locks, insisting I stand. I was slightly taller than she. Despite her closeness, I wanted her closer. Thoughts of her enslaving me were exhilarating. Never before had I been dominated and never before had I desired subjugation. Yet here, now, I yearned for it and craved to please her, pleasure her. The shudder came and went, confirming the wisdom of relinquishing. The tone of her voice was stunning.

Glancing back at the hole in the earth, I dissociated with the man who'd been buried there, my new life reflecting nothing of the old.

Leaving behind all resistance, I followed.

She commanded me to keep up with her and as my confidence increased, so did my ability to run with a mind-blowing, lightning speed. The land opened up to reveal a vast nightscape and I pursed my lips, afraid to swallow something other than air.

"*Imagine yourself already there,*" she said.

Though I had no idea where 'there' was, I followed her direction nevertheless, trying to free my mind of preconceptions of how fast I believed I could actually sprint, bewildered with the pace which she maintained. We raced across land, over hills, and through valleys, my teeth chattering from the excitement.

Within minutes of arriving at a creek, I stood dazed from our supernatural trek, sans clothes, grateful for the thick forest, surrounded by dense trees, their leaves hanging low.

A moment of calm brushed over me.

I shuddered from the rush, hesitant whether this ability to move so fast could be considered a benefit. Sunaria took a moment to admire my naked physique, her gaze lowering and then settling. For the first time, I allowed myself to envision how those lips would taste, or what I could get away with doing to her.

She shoved me head first into the shallow stream.

* * * *

I knew the mausoleum she led me into, the very tomb where I'd first seen her, the eerie place stirring terrifying memories, though here with her now, I sensed that new ones would replace the old. Even the cobwebs had gone.

Fresh clothes awaited me, a gentleman's attire. She'd even gotten my size right. Sunaria had removed the coffin and replaced it with reams of material, rich silks and soft velvets that softened our bedding, luxuriating our place of rest.

She climbed in first.

With a nod from her, I slid the stone lid over us and hugged her into me. Despite the dark, her turquoise-eyed gaze pierced mine. Her beauty extraordinary, a resplendent vision, I traced the tattoo of an ancient design on her left arm. "What does it mean?" I asked.

She softened into me.

"You're beautiful," I whispered.

She nuzzled into my chest and I conveyed gratitude for being here with her, thankful that I didn't have to go through this on my own, whatever this was. Sunaria's expression was still. She'd been like a phantom floating in and out of my life, and now she lay in my arms, this moment devoid of all understanding.

A preternatural awakening, an epiphany of what had befallen me, hinted that I might even cheat death, lessening my sadness and absorbing my attention, and providing the courage to turn inward. I drew comfort from this mysterious woman, captivated by her alluring timelessness.

The promise of this woman like a sublime rite of passage from my world to hers.

With her nod of permission I made love to her, worshipping her, demanding nothing less With a glance at her half-lidded gaze and the soft sound of her sighs, I confirmed that she approved. With her fingers wrapped around locks of my hair, tugging, I felt beholden for the chance to serve her.

Not so long ago, deep underground, I'd allowed my imagination to run to this moment. How I'd ever disrespected her, I don't know, couldn't comprehend that I'd once allowed her to walk away. My thoughts obsessed over her, and even this close there was the need to be closer, and for this fierce intimacy never to end.

I didn't want to ever cease, responding to the arch of her back and her soft moans, subtle movements that clued me in on her unspoken words. I wanted to punish her this way for making me so indebted, provoke her to scream in ecstasy as I continued on, refusing to relent until she commanded me to.

Sunaria's domination of me was a bewitchment of extraordinary tenor.

XXIV

LYING IN SUNARIA'S ARMS within the mausoleum, we waited for the sun to set.

Strange how I'd developed an aversion to daylight, more alarming the very idea that I might draw blood as sustenance and indeed find pleasure in it. It scared me to my core, and I tried to hide my fear of damnation. Yet at the same time, I fantasized about the act. The most fiendish of desires burned within.

Still wary of staring directly into Sunaria's eyes, I avoided her gaze. Instead, my fingertips traced the outline of her tattoo.

"It's the symbol of a master's ownership," she said softly.

"You were a slave?"

"Once."

I followed the curve of the design.

"I was sold to a Roman. As a child."

She sent me a mind image – a twenty-three-year-old female slave ending the bond with her master.

Her turquoise eyes glistened. "I loved him."

"But you killed him?"

"I did."

"How old are you?"

With delicate fingers, she stroked my face and kissed my cheek and with that very movement, she conveyed she didn't want to talk about it. She guided my chin up so that she held my gaze. As I stared into that unending blueness, I sensed the last remnants of daylight slipping away, an internal awareness, a natural connection to the night.

A chill reached my bones. "Help me to understand."

"I will."

"We're being followed?"

She sighed. "They're easy to evade."

"Who are they?"

"The elders."

"Are they like us?"

"Yes."

"Why are they following you?"

"There are statutes that we must follow."

"And you broke one of their rules?"

She stilled and moments fell away, then she let out the deepest sigh, like a dark whisper. "I turned you."

I gestured for her to continue.

"Elders rule our kind." She twisted her delicate fingers in my hair. "Or try to. They deem who is to be turned. Who is worthy."

"I wasn't considered worthy?"

"It's complicated."

"How many of us are there?"

"Impossible to keep track of. Wayward nightwalkers are turning people all the time."

"What would they do to you?"

She sighed as though bored with my questions.

I didn't like the idea that we were being hunted. An internal coercion ignited my senses, the promise of what the night might offer. "I need to see my son."

"And you have unfinished business." Her gaze left mine. "To have any chance of surviving, you must see it through."

I acknowledged Sunaria's command and slid the tomb lid open. I offered my hand to assist her. When we withdrew, I had a strange feeling that we were being watched and discreetly studied Sunaria to see if she also detected it. She didn't seem to.

Within several minutes, we arrived at the edge of the graveyard where a horse-drawn carriage was parked. The horseman's face was half-hidden by a low tipped hat.

"He works for you?" I asked as I climbed in after Sunaria.

"Tonight, he does."

"You feel safe like that?"

"One thing you'll learn, Daumia, and this is imperative for your sanity, we easily mingle."

"Does he know we just slept in a mausoleum?"

"Of course not. But he knows he's paid well."

The carriage lumbered forward and we were off.

She folded her arms. "We don't need to hide in the shadows."

"Are we being followed?" I tried to shake off the feeling.

"The only enemies we have are those who consider themselves superior to us."

"Well, that pretty much includes everyone in Vigo," I muttered, not sparing the sarcasm, and stared out of the window. "Am I condemned to hell?"

"You're condemned to a lifetime of sensuous pleasures and luxuries most never get to enjoy."

As she reminisced, I sensed she'd tasted such pleasures beyond my wildest imagination and she turned her head slightly. Staring at me, her bright red pout seemingly promised that I would, too.

We rode out of Santiago De Compostela, our carriage rocking along the well-worn pathway.

I wondered if I'd ever return to the city of my birth. *"I'm so afraid."*

* * * *

Conflicted, I yearned for Sunaria, yet at the same time my independence.

Her hold on me was due to my fear and she knew it. With little knowledge of what I'd become, I conveyed gratitude for her continued guidance. My confidence in making the right decisions was lacking. I'd arrogantly judged those whom history had deemed satanic—Prince Belshazzar, Julius Cesar, and Judas Iscariot came to mind. I couldn't find any difference between them and me, and believed that my sins now equaled theirs.

I shook off the melancholy, fascinated with my ability to feel less. Nature's way of lulling the guilt, I assumed.

My courage to hold Sunaria's gaze increased and with such an exquisite vision sitting opposite me, I was comforted. Fantasizing about her was a delightful distraction to more terrifying thoughts.

She smiled, having picked up on my musing.

Sensing that she heard my every thought, I tried to control them. She'd haunted me as a boy, a mysterious apparition, appearing and then withdrawing, altering life's course. Sunaria had saved me on numerous occasions and, more recently, she'd saved my son.

I reached for her.

Sunaria raised her long leg and pressed her foot against my chest, pushing me back into my seat. Her shoe traced down, lingering between my legs. Nervous of her heel and yet enjoying myself, I bit my lip.

She lowered her foot and crossed her legs with an imperious stare. With her head held high, she gazed out of the window.

I let out the deepest sigh.

From the familiar countryside, we were getting close. Far off, a deer galloped across a grassy ridge and over. Estimating its distance, it appeared at least four miles away. I marveled at my new ability to see with remarkable sharpness, but it also alarmed me.

I missed Annabelle.

* * * *

With no time to grieve, I pushed the ache away.

No part of what I saw around me, or experienced now, reminded me of my old life. It had passed so quickly, and at no time had I considered that it would one day become a memory.

The carriage came to a stop.

Sunaria stroked my leg with a comforting gesture. "I'll follow you." She paid the driver several coins and we watched the horseman drive it away out of sight.

"Find us somewhere to sleep," she commanded in that husky way of hers. "And it better not be a graveyard."

The thought of having to find shelter and delay our visit made me wary, but we had no choice. I relented, agreeing that it was actually better to face Vigo with a clear head.

Sparrows burst into song, announcing the imminent daybreak.

With minutes before sunrise, I surveyed the well kept cemetery, trying to ignore Sunaria's disapproval. The grand mausoleum was a slight improvement over the one we'd slept in the day before.

I read the inscription of who lay within: *Thomas A. Haywood, aged 37,* and rubbed away the dust to read the epitaph.

Sunaria yanked on my sleeve. "Now that's creepy."

I raised my eyebrows only to quickly lower them again when the idea of being buried alive came to mind. A soft bed beckoned, a luxury I'd once taken for granted. The next time I got to lie on sheets, I promised myself I'd savor every second.

Despite that, as we settled into the mausoleum, I drew comfort from lying with her. We fell asleep in each other's arms. Nightmares came and went, providing a myriad of images, a restless sleep. I'd been fighting an invisible force, held in some continuously revolving bad dream.

I awoke with a jolt and found myself alone.

Sunaria had left my side without waking me. My breath left me and I was gripped with fear. I slid open the stone slab and climbed out.

Sunaria had reassured me that she'd placed Jacob with my sister.

What if she'd lied?

Outside, I turned around and around, trying to get my bearings. Leaves and twigs rustled as small creatures scurried away, and then voices carried. I followed them down a grassy bank. The gravestones were smaller here, many of them sunken and tilted.

Sunaria was in conversation with a young man dressed in a well-cut suit. I tried to hide my panic. Sunaria flirted with him, stirring my jealousy.

"What do you think?" She glanced at me.

"About what?" I kicked up yellow, dry leaves.

She gestured to the stranger and he approached me, conveying nervousness intermingled with excitement.

She smiled at him. "Arnold, isn't he everything I told you he'd be?"

He nodded.

I cringed. "What?"

His smile dropped.

Sunaria threw her arms around him and he leaned into her and grinned. My glare made him let go.

Sunaria pointed to Arnold again. "His clothes will fit me."

"What are you talking about?" His mouth gaped.

Sunaria's tongue traced her upper lip. "Thirsty?"

"I am a little, yes." He glanced from her to me.

"Daumia?" Sunaria smiled.

I knew to refuse would displease her, but I hesitated. Despite my recent attack on the soldiers, this was wrong, cruel even. Trying to get my head around the situation, I sensed her growing impatience.

My gaze locked with his and he seemed to catch the subtle change in me, as I focused in on him, the mark of a hunter.

He bolted.

Sunaria's hands rested on her hips. "Well?"

I shrugged.

She sent a pulse of anger my way.

I tracked Arnold through the graveyard and into the woods, and with a shove, I had him down and flipped him over. Sunaria ran her fingers through my hair and then her pressure increased, as she held me there.

Arnold struggled beneath me. A familiar rush as his blood tingled in my mouth. All became familiar and knowledge flowed as he drifted. I rocked, grateful for both the sustenance and the information. Tracing his steps through time, he unwittingly introduced me to people he'd known, adventures he'd taken, cities he'd visited, and the books he'd read.

Arnold the architect. Amongst the scattered designs within his mind, we settled upon one of the plans he'd drawn, followed the ink upon the page as it manifested into structure. I recognized these corridors, bedrooms, and staff rooms, and as we passed through the courtyard, I dug deeper, willing him to go on ahead as I lingered, taking my time in Felipe's senatorial office.

XXV

WE STOOD FIFTY FEET or so outside the senatorial residence. Sunaria had stripped our architect and now wore his clothes. Arnold's jacket concealed her curves.

"Easier to get about." Sunaria twisted her hair and poked it beneath her cap.

I'd dragged Arnold's body into the mausoleum where we'd slept, petitioning *Thomas A. Haywood, aged 37,* to watch over him.

I tried to fathom how taking his life was so natural, like how I'd imagine an animal might feel after a kill, as though we were privileged to choose who lived and who died, gifted with the ability to be another's undoing.

Or cursed.

Such a cruel trick for Sunaria to appear so alluring, so exquisitely bewitching, the moonlight reflecting off her dark locks, shimmering off her pale skin, lulling everyone, including me.

"After what Ricardo did to you," she said, "you still want to rescue him?"

I studied the windows of the great house. "He had no idea what he was doing."

"Still."

"He's my nephew."

She pursed her lips. "Let's deal with the senator first."

"He's my unfinished business."

She squeezed my shoulder. "And now you have the layout in your head."

I turned to her. "You think you'll pass as a man?"

"I've done it before."

Her attire convinced me, but her demeanor would have to change.

"I'm ready." I nodded, trying to persuade myself that I was.

"Stick to the plan."

That had sounded like an order. I questioned whether I could. Within moments, we landed on the senatorial roof. I peeked over the edge at the sheer drop, astounded that I'd just scaled a building. We pried open the loft door and entered.

"Felipe's office, go," she whispered.

I hesitated.

She frowned. "I'll be fine."

Stepping mindfully over the rafters, I proceeded ahead and quickly found the room, but when I turned to show Sunaria, she was gone.

She was going through with it.

Peering down, I had a good view of Felipe's office, and saw him sitting at his desk, scribing away. With all my will, I resisted the urge to descend and strangle him.

The painting had been replaced by a smaller, less significant portrait. He must have panicked when he'd discovered me gone and his decimated Belshazzar's Feast there.

Sunaria entered with a member of staff who introduced her to Felipe as a royal representative. With the shake of their hands, Felipe welcomed her. Sunaria's voice was a tone deeper, her mannerisms masterfully imitating that of a man, an effeminate one at that.

Felipe bowed. "How is the king?"

"He sends his deepest regards." Sunaria tilted her head in greeting.

I closed my gaping mouth.

"To what do I owe the pleasure of such an unexpected visit?" Felipe gestured to a chair. "My staff will prepare a room for you."

"I won't be staying." She sat down. "This is the king's time, therefore, I must be brief."

"What brings you here?"

She frowned. "Propaganda is devised to mask the truth."

"I quite agree."

"The Church must keep its ministerial throne secure in these times of unrest."

Felipe showed impatience. "Go on."

"As you know, I have served the king for many years."

This he didn't know, but he hid it well.

"His highness," she continued, "has chosen well . . ."

Felipe's intrigue was palpable.

"In you," she emphasized with a long stare.

Felipe nodded.

"Intelligence reports indicate that there is a plot against the throne."

Felipe sat back.

"The king needs evidence." Sunaria leaned forward. "Proof before he convicts the queen's favorite courtier."

"Does her majesty know?"

"He wishes to protect her, just in case the information is—"

"False?"

She smiled and loftily raised her chin.

"What is required of me?" Felipe asked.

"Travel to Palos—"

"When?"

"Now."

"Tonight?"

"Yes. The queen's ship is due to set sail."

His brow furrowed. "The *Santa María*?"

"Yes."

"But I—"

"At seven o'clock tomorrow night, you must be in The Captain's Table Inn. Wait for further instructions."

"I don't think I can make the port, even if I leave right this minute."

"What shall I tell the king?" Sunaria rose.

Felipe flinched. "There must be some mistake."

"This is your message to his majesty?"

Felipe's stare searched the room. "Tell his highness that my utmost discretion is assured."

She gave a deep bow. "The throne expects nothing less."

* * * *

"You think he fell for that?" I kept my voice low.

"Yes."

"It can't be that easy."

She grasped my chin with long fingers, and then she softened, tracing my cheek gently.

I avoided her insistent stare. "I think it's this way. I hate being back here."

"I can only imagine."

Within minutes, we'd found the nursery. With ease of step, I followed Sunaria in. Six-year-old Ricardo slept in a corner bed and appeared well cared for. In the other corner, his nanny snored lightly, a young girl of twenty years or so. On the floor, near the foot of Ricardo's bed, lay a wooden, broken soldier splayed out. Someone had tried to rip its head off. Ricardo's penchant for violence left no object safe.

Sunaria nudged me toward him and, with one hand over his mouth, I picked him up, and he squirmed and bit me.

The nanny stirred.

"Go," Sunaria whispered.

With Ricardo in my arms, I flew out of the window and landed on the lawn behind the far wall and knelt beside him, trying to calm his wails. My hand pressed against his mouth. "I'm taking you to your mother."

He calmed a little.

I eased my hand off, ready to ram it back if needed.

"Mama's dead," Ricardo sobbed.

"Why do you say that?"

"Papa told me."

"Well, she's not. She asked me to bring you to her."

Ricardo made me unbearably uncomfortable. If it weren't for the fact I adored my sister, I'd have shoved him back into the house. Sunaria came up behind us several minutes later.

There was immediate relief to see her. "What happened?"

"The nanny won't remember," she whispered. "I gave her a 'little drink.'"

After a brief pause, I said, "What?"

Sunaria stared down at Ricardo. From her expression, she didn't like the boy, either.

"Can nanny come?" Ricardo asked.

Sunaria sighed. "Nanny's too busy writhing in ecstasy."

I tapped Sunaria's arm in disapproval.

By the way Ricardo clutched my hand, Sunaria had scared him. Hoofs clopped along a gravel pathway. We sidled along the wall until we reached the front of the manor.

Sunaria peeked around. "Felipe's getting in."

Despite the fact that Ricardo's teeth gnawed into my hand, I smiled.

* * * *

Aware that Ricardo would soon be in his mother's arms and out of mine, inspired more speed. The thought of seeing Jacob consumed my thoughts.

We reached the Ocean View Manor by ten in the evening. It was a perfect sanctuary. Sunaria had memorized Miranda's instructions on how to reach their residence. We arranged to meet afterward, just before sunrise, as Sunaria being with me would invoke even more questions. A cross-examination I wasn't prepared for. Despite having covered Ricardo's eyes, the events of the night, which included throwing myself out the window with him in my arms, would have to be explained away if he brought it up.

We passed through an avenue of tall cedars that led to the front of the house. Sunaria rose on her toes and planted a kiss upon my cheek. She knew what lay ahead for me and, through her gesture, assured her support.

Ricardo remained uncharacteristically quiet, not surprising considering the last two hours we'd spent flying through the air at great speed. I'd held him toward me, his face tucked into my jacket to protect him from the wind chill, and the remarkable view.

Lingering at the door, I took a moment to gather my racing thoughts.

The moderately sized house possessed a simple charm. Although not able to see the ocean from the house, the fresh air and occasional seagull that flew overhead revealed we were close. Inland, the property would be safe from the weather, yet close enough to access the beach if one desired the trek down the winding pathway.

I couldn't fathom why it had been called The Ocean View Manor if it lacked one. A title to impress those who'd never see it, I supposed.

Ricardo tugged on my trouser leg.

When Alicia opened the door, my heart soared. I willed myself not to burst out all that had happened. Sunaria had known I'd face this very challenge. Alicia's suffering had been great. My woes could not be added to them. Ricardo ran into her arms. A little further in stood Miranda holding Jacob. His face lit up when he saw me. I entered, wary of revealing anything by my movement, and took Jacob from Miranda, nuzzling into his hair, and smelling his familiar baby scent.

Oak logs crackled in the hearth in a nearby room.

The aroma of lamb cooking on the stove, the perfume of soapy lavender imbued from Miranda's bedroom and rose petals from Alicia's, and the faint scent of dying lilies, all flooded my senses, mercilessly reminding me that I was now different. They'd been playing cards, and although I didn't see the deck on the table in the living room, I heard one of the cards tossed up, caught by a breeze from an open window, and then flip over onto the floor.

I closed my mind to Alicia and Miranda's internal dialogue, respecting their privacy, but also not wanting to know what they really thought about me. My own demons raged within. I didn't feel ready to face what they might imagine mine were. I wasn't ready to defend things I had or hadn't done.

Strangely, I missed Sunaria, her strength, her domineering presence that gave me the time I needed to regroup.

Alicia gave my arm a reassuring squeeze. "It's over now."

She looked too happy for me to tell her that it wasn't.

Sparse furniture decorated the interior. This aristocratic retreat was not meant for permanent living but merely a summer retreat. Here in the great house, they had no servants, the ultimate sacrifice for living in secret. They'd exchanged luxury for safety.

Alicia leaned in and hugged me. "Annabelle?" she asked.

I shook my head. "We'll talk later."

Alicia's hand covered her sob. "What happened?"

My mind wandered, trying to guess how close to Palos Felipe's carriage might be.

Miranda drew in her breath. "You must be hungry."

The thought of food made me cringe.

Alicia stroked my arm. "You're tired?"

"He's been through a lot." Miranda sounded nervous. "How did you get Ricardo out?"

I shrugged. "I walked into his nursery and took him."

A shadow of doubt flashed over her. "And no one stopped you?"

"Evidently." I stared down at Ricardo.

Alicia wrapped her arm in mine and we strolled into the drawing room. Two large couches were placed opposite each other and upon them over-stuffed pillows. I leaned back onto one of them, and despite the lumpiness, I was grateful for the rest, and comforted by the ordinary setting.

"Felipe didn't have a guard watching Ricardo?" Miranda asked.

I shook my head *no*.

"You look so pale." Alicia studied me, as though trying to figure out what was different.

"Tired, that's all." I gave a reassuring smile.

Ricardo ran around the room screaming, waving an imaginary

sword.

With my jaw clenched, I signaled to him. "Please don't do that."

He lunged his sword into an invisible opponent.

"Stop," I shouted.

Ricardo stood stock-still and stared at me. I'd startled Alicia and Miranda, too.

I rubbed my forehead, easing the tension. "Take him to bed. He's exhausted."

Alicia grabbed Ricardo's hand.

"Alicia, I'm sorry I . . ."

She gave a comforting smile and then took Jacob from me and rested him on her hip.

Just like Annabelle used to do.

"I'll put them to bed." She ruffled Ricardo's hair.

"I'm so very proud of you."

"Not as proud as I am of you." Alicia smiled and headed out with the children.

I hoped Ricardo wouldn't mention his leap out of the nursery window, though I'd ensured he'd seen nothing.

Miranda picked up the bottle resting on the table before us and poured two glasses of white wine and offered me one. "Here, you look like you need it."

I gestured I didn't.

Miranda settled on the couch close to me. "That woman Sunaria warned us before Felipe's guards came." She leaned toward me. "She saved our lives."

I bowed my head. "We owe her our gratitude."

"How do you know her?"

"I just do."

"How did she know we were in danger?"

"We were all in danger."

"Rumors carry, Daumia."

"What do you mean?"

"While at the senator's, you were mortally injured." Her inflection deepened. "I have my spies, remember?"

"Rumors are just that, rumors."

"The way you look at Ricardo, one would think he caused you some terrible grief."

"I'm tired, that's all. I keep thinking of Salvador."

"He didn't make it and yet you did?"

"Whatever your spies thought they saw, they were wrong."

"Ricardo ran his sword into your gut!"

I stared off. "Then I'd be dead." I rose and headed for the door.

"Where are you going?"

"To put my son to bed." I headed after Alicia.

Within the small bedroom, I tucked Jacob in and stroked his hair. He tried so hard to keep his eyelids open, full of excitement over seeing me again. He clutched my hand and I kissed his forehead, my perfect child, so much like his mother. Jacob's love for me was a much needed boon—innocent, pure affection.

I recalled Eduardo, the way he smiled when I ate a biscuit or his expression when I first sat him in the saddle of one of my smaller, placid horses. Then the awful vision of him lying dead in his mother's arms, my son gone from me forever. I wiped away a tear, though more fell. I'd been present at his birth, but not at his death. Fathers should die before their sons.

The first night I'd met Salvador, we'd lain on the grassy bank together staring up at the stars, such a perfect moment of intimacy. Salvador had the kindest nature, the ability to say the right thing at the right time and always see the best in people. He'd be the one person who'd know what to do in this situation.

Jacob closed his eyes. With my head in my hands, I let go and sobbed. I missed Annabelle's touch.

I want my life back.

I tried to disengage from these thoughts, this terrible wave of grief. Strange how my emotions were different, muted, and yet ever present, a constant reminder that I was no longer human. I shook off the melancholy, couldn't alert Miranda or Alicia that anything was wrong, had to act as though everything was fine and that we might again revisit the contentment we'd once known.

I returned downstairs to join them for supper in the kitchen. The candelabra at the center of the table threw shadows. A homey, rustic décor, a welcoming haven, afforded by the domestic order, suggesting the children might once again feel safe. Though offered food, I declined, but accepted the glass of blackberry wine, the fruity scent wafting beneath my nose. It dawned on me that I may never taste food again. The smell of lamb made me nauseous. Miranda's cheeks blushed, the liquor apparently warming her.

My attention turned to Alicia. "You've hardly eaten."

Alicia looked up at me. "I was just thinking the same about you."

Miranda's stare locked with mine.

Alicia placed her fork down. "I hate Felipe, but he's the father of my son."

I rested the rim of my glass on my lower lip and almost sipped.

The sweet taste of revenge.

My imagination spiraled, offering up the darkest fantasy of how it would feel when Felipe looked into my eyes as I stole his life. I'd make him suffer before I let him know death.

"You brought Ricardo home to me." Alicia lowered her shoulders, relaxing a little. "My son's home."

"He's safe now." I shifted my gaze to Miranda. "You all are."

"Salvador?" Alicia's voice was quiet.

I pushed my chair back, strolled around the table, and sat beside her and held her hands in mine. "He fought bravely." I removed Salvador's medal from my jacket pocket and lay it on her palm.

She closed her fingers around it. "I knew you'd understand that it meant we were safe. Sunaria promised to give it to you."

And Sunaria had gone through with that vow, a softer side to her nature only hinted at, making it easier to trust her.

Alicia pressed her fingers to her lips. "She told you we were here?"

I nodded.

"Who is she?" Alicia asked.

I shifted in my seat. "A friend."

A vampire who has me so seduced that even now I can't stop thinking of her.

"Where is she now?" Alicia said.

I straightened up. "I'm more interested in how you're doing."

"You were with Salvador when he died?"

I nodded. "His last thoughts and words were of you."

Tears rolled over her flushed cheeks. "Why wouldn't Felipe let us be?"

I looked away.

"What happened to Annabelle?" Alicia asked.

I swallowed. "Felipe sent his guards."

"Eduardo?"

I nodded.

Her lips quivered. "Dear God."

"They murdered everyone." I stared at her as though she might help me find the answer to why.

"I'm so sorry," Miranda barely whispered.

Alicia's hands covered her face. "This was my entire fault."

"No, Alicia." I shook my head. "Felipe did this."

"When will it be over?" Miranda exchanged a look with Alicia.

My fists tightened. "One last detail to take care of."

"You're going to kill Felipe," Miranda said.

I topped up her glass and then Alicia's.

Alicia reached for her drink and took a sip, and then another. "How do you go on?"

I placed the bottle down. "I have you."

Her eyes glazed over. "I want peace."

"He'll never come near you again." I wanted to reach inside her and ease the hurt.

"What are you going to do?" she asked.

"End it."

"Please be careful, Daumia. I couldn't bear it if anything—"

"It's almost over." I leaned forward and stroked her cheek, wiping away a tear.

A creak outside the door gave away the person who'd been listening there.

Alicia sprang to her feet. "Ricardo, what are you doing up?"

A wave of anxiety overwhelmed me that he'd overheard us, and caught our entire conversation. He ran to Alicia and nestled into her bosom, and she carried him out, back to his room.

I reached for my glass and then thought better of it. Staring at the claret, I yearned for its taste.

Or something like it, something forbidden.

Miranda arose. "Ricardo's unruly like his father."

Unable to lower my gaze, I stared at her pale neck, the pulsing of her perfect veins that begged to be known.

"After everything you've been through?" She sat down on my lap, her bosom lingering close to eye level.

On the table, the ruby liquid caught the candlelight.

Miranda's intense stare locked on me. "Go on have a sip."

"I've had enough."

"But you haven't had any."

"Have you been watching me drink?"

"Actually, watching you *not* drink. Which is so unlike you."

"Strange that you'd find that interesting."

"I know what you are," she whispered.

My shirt collar was stifling. I loosened the top button.

She nuzzled into me. "You even smell different."

The promise of those blue veins, a fine, perfect flow that glistened, profoundly beckoned me to taste from that alluring, delicate stream.

"I have no idea what you're talking about." I gave a half-smile.

"You were impaled. It was a mortal strike."

"I'm here, aren't I?"

"Felipe left you in the courtyard to bleed out."

I gestured. "And yet." The room was suffocating. "It's been a long day."

She leaned into my ear. "I was there."

"You're wrong."

She slid her finger into my mouth and rested the tip on an incisor.

I pushed her hand away. "What you saw, or what you thought you saw—"

"I wanted to stop him," she said. "I couldn't believe Felipe's cruelty."

"That makes two of us."

"Had I done anything, he'd have killed me."

"I'm sorry that you had to see Salvador's murder. And my torture."

"Your murder."

"No one comes back from death." I raised my hand to exaggerate my point.

I read Miranda's mind and swore to extract every thought from now on, to reach into the very core of every human interaction, shake off this guilty feeling of trespassing. Self-preservation took precedence. Miranda may have watched my attack, but she'd not witnessed my rebirth.

"I need fresh air." I tried to gently ease her off.

She wrapped her arms around my neck. "I couldn't do anything to save you," she sobbed, "I was so afraid."

"Please don't."

"Scared of what Felipe would do to me."

"You did the right thing."

"What are you?"

"Miranda, you have nothing to base any of this on."

She lifted a small, golden rimmed hand mirror and held it up. I gazed into the glass and saw Miranda's reflection, but not mine. I'd never get used to that.

Miranda lowered the mirror. "She did this to you?"

"Who?"

"Sunaria."

Frustrated, I pinched the bridge of my nose. "She saved your life."

"And changed yours. It explains how she knew Felipe's men were coming." She gripped my wrist, pulling my fingers away. "She moves in a certain way. Like you do, now."

I avoided her stare.

"Where is she?" Miranda asked.

Outside, I heard the sound of leaves and bracken swirling and then settling.

"What does it feel like?" She clutched my hand, bringing it up to her cheek.

"Everything got out of control." I sighed.

"You should have killed Felipe when you had the chance."

I tried to ignore her alluring scent.

Just a sip of her blood. Do it for her.

I tried to resist the lie of my own desire.

Miranda blinked long lashes. "What does it feel like to be immortal?"

"I don't actually believe that part."

"Do you know how seductive you've become?"

"I've not had much time to think about it." I laughed at her ridiculous statement.

"Make me into what you are."

"This is a curse."

"Turn me."

"This thing, whatever it is, has made me do terrible things."

"What like?"

"Being like this, it's not what you think."

"But you're perfect now."

I smiled. "I was perfect before."

"You'll live forever."

"I don't think so."

"You'll never grow old."

"How do you know all this?"

"My husband traveled to Transylvania." Her eyes widened. "He brought back documented evidence..."

"Show it to me."

"And you'll turn me?"

"Don't ask me that."

"How is it done?"

I'm not staying like this. I will find a cure.

"I'm childless. I'm ageing." Her voice softened.

"Never discuss this with my sister, do you understand?"

"I've thought it through."

"You've always been so kind to me and to my family."

"Then repay me." She flicked strands of hair away from her neck and with her hand on the back of my head, guided me, and my lips rested against her soft skin, my fangs grazed her. My thumb brushed along the lace of her bodice, lingering over the material, eliciting the very moan from her that I needed to hear.

Miranda's fingernails dug into my back.

With willpower that I didn't know I had, I pulled away and whispered, "Soon."

XXVI

A BALMY AUGUST NIGHT, the fullest moon suspended low, hauntingly illuminated the night sky.

Alone, I lingered on the Palos boardwalk, staring up at the largest ship docked in the harbor, the *Santa María*. A few sailors scurried about, making their way back to their ships from land leave.

Last night, it had been difficult to pull myself away from Jacob. The evening had been fraught with emotion. Later, I'd described my evening to Sunaria.

She listened quietly and then cast a stern glare. "You'll turn no one."

I wondered how it was even done. When I felt Sunaria's gaze, I turned my thoughts to the task at hand.

Safe in the shadows, blending in with the other tourists, I considered the famous ship. The crown had paid for the *Santa María's* refurbishment, ensuring an extraordinary, custom-made 100 foot long, sea worthy vessel. The sails were undergoing their last minute adjustments.

Under the command of its captain, Christopher Columbus, the *Santa María* would undertake the expedition to locate new territory. Columbus had been sanctioned by the crown, sponsored by Isabella I Queen of Castile. He would become viceroy of all territories he located. The land would be taken in the name of Spain, by the queen's trusted courtier, her finest diplomat.

The *Santa María*, scheduled to set sail later that night, would be escorted by the *Pinta* and the *Niña*, the two smaller caravels commanded by the Pinzon brothers, Alonzo and Vincent Yanez, both reputed to be successful fishermen, and master navigators. The two boats floated close to the *Santa María*.

As though out of nothing, Sunaria appeared by my side. Having just fed, she was lulled a little. My hunger would not be sated. I wanted to stay sharp.

Her gaze fell on the small rowboat that bobbed close to the ships. The two sailors aboard gestured to the crew of the *Pinta*. Within minutes, they'd loaded a good supply of ale and rum aboard. The sailors then steered their boat toward the *Santa María*. Eager sailors leaned over the balustrades, calling out for their free booty. The boat made its last delivery to the *Niña*.

I glanced at Sunaria. "A gift from you?"
She gave a sly smile.
Twenty young girls, the prettiest harlots, gathered near the pier and then dispersed, a few to each vessel.
"That's what you meant by a distraction?" I asked her.
She nodded.
On all three boats, the girls were met by gleeful soldiers with open arms.
I smiled. "Nice."

* * * *

Two hours later, I boarded the *Santa María*.
Columbus dined on land having his last fresh meal, unaware that his sailors partied hard.
With the utmost stealth, I made my way unseen to his stateroom. Columbus kept an organized office. A broken compass lay on the navigational table, along with several rolled up maps. The compass had sentimental value no doubt.
Whispers carried into Columbus' private quarters. From his officer's conversations, I picked up that they trusted his navigation, though from the crew below deck came grumblings of their master's stubbornness. He'd gotten them lost on several occasions. Last minute jitters, perhaps, before setting out to prove that the world was indeed round. The fact that they may also arrive in hostile lands had them rattled. If they set eyes on the broken compass, they'd probably leave the ship.
He had extensive maps of islands in the Bahamas, crisply revealing their newness. Despite my fascination, I had to pull myself away. I folded them up and placed them back in their original position.
All accept one.
Columbus' working compass rested on a side table next to his bunk. Beside it lay a small collection of Bibles. I peeked inside the most ornate one, and read. *"God's speed."* Her Majesty Queen Ferdinand had signed and dated it, *August 1492*.
Remembering Sunaria's warning of how religious artifacts could affect us, I dropped it back onto the table.
Checking that the way was clear, I headed out.
Unbearable heat in the ship's galley and a lingering odor of sweat, salt, and something indeterminable, made me gag. I wondered how the sailors could stand both that and the cramped conditions. There, in the corner, was the chain that secured the anchor. After half an hour, I'd made a fine incision, invisible to the human eye.
Voices alerted me to someone heading in my direction. A young sailor had invited one of the harlots down into the galley. I waited until they were in the throes of passion then slid away, unseen and unheard, having completed my mission.
Once onboard the *Niña*, a boat even rowdier than the *Santa María*,

despite being the smallest of the three vessels, I hid for a moment in the shadows. With the pathway clear, I climbed to the top sail and withdrew the knife and began to saw. Within minutes, I had cut a third of the way through the mast. I had no time to admire my handiwork, which all the way up there wouldn't be noticed.

With that accomplished, I returned to The Captain's Table Inn where Sunaria awaited me. I joined her in the corner. Sitting opposite, I reached for her hand. She pulled away. She was, after all, still dressed as a man. My gesture had gone unnoticed.

"It's done," I said.

"You have the map?" Sunaria asked.

I nodded.

She gave me that long stare of hers, her almond eyes taking me in. She melted and beamed at me, shaking her head.

"What?" I tried to read her.

Her smile faded. "He's here."

I turned in my chair to see Felipe in the doorway, and I rose and disappeared into the horde of rowdy sailors. Leaning on the bar near the door, I had a good view.

Haunted by memories of what Felipe had done, I tried to calm my rage, all the while trying to mingle in. When a sailor bumped my arm, I pretended I hadn't noticed.

Felipe took the chair opposite Sunaria.

"You're late." Her gaze never left him.

"Is there a road I'm unfamiliar with?" Felipe crossed one leg over another.

"We don't have much time." She gestured for two ales.

Felipe pulled out a handkerchief and wiped his brow.

She sighed in frustration. "Try not to look out of place."

Felipe pursed his lips, annoyed.

"As you're aware," Sunaria lowered her voice, "Columbus has been commissioned to administer the teachings of the Holy Testament when he discovers new lands."

"What of it?"

"Calm down. I need you focused."

He gestured he was.

"Columbus is permitted to claim any country he encounters," she continued.

Felipe cleared his throat. "He's been granted one tenth of all precious metals that he finds."

"His part of the bargain. But Columbus has other intentions."

Felipe took a gulp from his ale. "Like?" He wiped away the moustache of froth.

She frowned. "When he finds land, he intends to not only claim it, but rule it."

"Are you sure?"

She leaned back and folded her arms.

"But that's heresy." Felipe looked confused. "Columbus has no intention of spreading Christianity?"

"He's a heretic."

"He must be stopped."

"We're on the same page." Sunaria feigned a sip.

"And the king wants me to prevent the ship from leaving?"

"Not exactly."

He looked astonished. "The ship is to still set sail?"

"It is."

"You're not suggesting that . . . ?"

Sunaria pushed her cup to the side. "The king's orders are clear. You're to board the *Niña*."

"But—"

"Spy on Columbus."

"There must be someone more qualified."

She dismissed his reply with a gesture. "The king trusts you."

"I have duties to attend to back in Vigo."

Sunaria tilted her head.

Felipe squirmed. "But I've never sailed before."

"I must report back to his majesty."

Felipe wiped his brow again.

"I understand that what is being asked of you is somewhat difficult." She nodded knowingly.

"I'll commission one of my men."

"His majesty wants you and no one else. Vincente Pinzon, Captain of the *Niña*, will welcome you. The ship sets sail in an hour."

"What shall I tell Vincente Pinzon?"

"That you're on the king's business. Hand him this."

"What is it?"

"A royal warrant permitting you to board." Sunaria gave him the forged document.

Beads of perspiration spotted Felipe's upper lip.

Sunaria glanced around and then locked her stare back on him. "The king requested proof that I had accomplished my mission."

"Which was?"

"Proof of your loyalty."

"I'm their highnesses' obedient servant."

"As I am yours, Senator." Sunaria pulled out a blank parchment and laid it on the table.

"What's that for?"

"His majesty requests evidence." Sunaria leaned forward and lowered her voice. "Dissent is everywhere." She reached under the table. "For your journey, from his majesty."

Felipe glanced at the bundle she offered and hesitated.

"Take it." She gave a thin smile of reassurance.

He accepted the parcel of doubloons and shoved it into his coat pocket.

"No expense has been spared," she said.

"That's a lot of money."

"You may use it for bribes, or whatever else. Your safety is the king's priority." She offered him a feathered pen and then glided a small pot of ink across the table.

Felipe stared at the paper. "I'm not going." He leaned back. "I'm not qualified."

"Per contra, you speak Spanish, French, and more importantly Italian. The language of the crew. And you have the king's favor. He trusts you."

"I need to speak with his majesty."

"Turn around."

Felipe followed Sunaria's gaze that fell upon an unsuspecting, well-dressed businessman sipping on his ale at the bar.

"He's here to ensure I do my bit and you do yours," she said.

The man frowned, uncomfortable with Felipe's critical stare.

Felipe spun round to face Sunaria again. "What will happen if I don't get on that ship?"

"I'm not willing to put that to the test. Are you?" She slid the parchment closer to him. "In your note to his highness, clarity is important."

Felipe glanced at the blank piece of paper.

"You'll need this." Sunaria offered him a velvet wrapped object.

Felipe eyed it suspiciously.

"For your protection." Her voice was low, somber.

He peeled back a corner of the material and gawped at the tip of the small knife.

* * * *

A fresh sea breeze blew through the dock.

Within the hour, Sunaria and I lingered in the shadowy doorway of an inn that had long closed.

"Having friends ensconced at the royal palace pays off," Sunaria said.

I shook my head. "Remind me never to piss you off."

She snuggled into me.

"Seriously," I hesitated and then continued. "You make a dangerous enemy."

She peered up at me. "This was your idea."

"So it was. Still, you're executing it so well and yet you have the face of an angel."

Our lips met and I kissed her leisurely. A man passed by and gave us a wary stare. He thought he'd caught two men at it. I burst into laughter, couldn't remember the last time I'd laughed like that.

We turned our attention back onto the Santa María, escorted by the *Pinta* and the *Niña*, as all three vessels set sail. Hundreds of spectators had gathered to watch the caravels launch. Columbus waved from the bridge. He cut a fine figure with his striking white beard and his traditional admiral's coat. His intelligent blue eyes scanned the harbor and I wondered how a man of the sea could appear so light in complexion. His aquiline features provided an air of sophistication that reflected his Italian heritage.

A crew of ninety or so navigated through the harbor. Under the moonlit sky, the fleet reeled out its sails to full mast. Columbus wasn't the only well-dressed man who offered a wave to the crowd. Felipe also bid the spectators goodbye from the bridge of the *Niña*.

Sunaria handed me the parchment on which Felipe had written his letter to the king. I smiled and tucked it into my coat pocket. Sunaria pressed her ear up against the inn's door.

"What do you hear?" I asked.

"Nothing." She worked the lock until it gave.

Stale beer mixed in with sweat permeated the air and candles had burned down to the wick, leaving waxy stains. During the day, this place would be buzzing, now though it passed for a dreary hiding place for us.

With my arms folded, I browsed the long oak bar. "We're not staying, are we?"

"I owe you."

"An apology?" I asked.

"A punishment." Sunaria shoved me back against the wooden panel and flipped me up and onto the bar.

I caught my breath as I stared up at the beer mugs lined above my head. Sunaria leaped onto the bar and straddled me. She grabbed my wrists, pressing my hands down on either side of my head.

I smiled up at her.

"No more talking." She held my wrists with one hand and pressed a long finger against my lips. "Punishments come in many forms."

I opened my mouth to reply but knew better. I tugged my wrist from out of hers and reached for her.

The sting of her slap across my face caused me to flinch. I placed my hand back beside the other, returning to a captive pose. Her calm expression never wavered. I tried to work her out, recall how the evening had unfolded, remember if at any time my behavior had been out of line, but I sensed that this might be another way that Sunaria expressed her power over me.

With a rip, my shirt came open. The bite came without warning

Silence challenged me to a duel and I knew the inevitability of losing. My jaw tensed as I envisioned where she might take this. Again a moment of nothing, only stillness, cruel anticipation and then that familiar sensation, bedazzled me, sending me closer to the edge each time.

I bit down on my lip in order to stay quiet, hoping not to fail her.

I reached for her again.

Sunaria's stare caused me to cross one wrist over the other again, silently swearing not to move until permitted. I wanted to ask if I'd insulted her, but as the pleasure increased and my reward for submitting spiraled, I doubted my own judgment. I counted the bronze cups on the ceiling, trying to prevent myself from ending this evening earlier than she or I desired.

Sunaria paused.

She slid off me and stood close, arms folded, a disapproving gaze.

The silence made me squirm and the minutes ticked past with her staring at me.

Sunaria hunted those weaker than herself and she took her prey swiftly. As I lay vulnerable, I wondered if I too would be numbered amongst her victims and for some warped reason that idea sent a thrill of excitement up my spine.

I grinned. A chance, but I felt willing to take it, had nothing to lose. My dignity was already compromised.

"Close your eyes." Her voice quiet, reassuring even, but her stern presence revealed a fierce determination.

My grin was my answer that her request was out of the question and I turned my head away.

"I'll not ask you again." She spoke slowly, emphasizing her authority.

Remaining still now seemed like the next best option, until I had time at least to think. I may very well need to talk my way out of this. Surprisingly, the only part of me that seemed not to understand this threat was between my legs.

And as Sunaria settled back on top of me I found no choice but to relent.

This was the very image that I'd seen the day she'd turned me. When I'd followed that pathway, the choice that led to what I was now, she'd taken me this way, eased my transformation and I'd welcomed it, as I welcomed her now.

Quickened with the thought that my obsession with her would find its way back to me, I caught my breath and I chased after my brilliant bliss. And as the last ripples made their way through me, I felt beholden to her.

XXVII

STROLLING ALONG ONE of the darker corridors within the senatorial residence, I wondered if Felipe had developed his sea legs yet. Although only a day had passed since he'd set sail, I imagined he regretted ever getting on that boat.

I rubbed my wrists. The stark memory of those chains that Sunaria used sent a thrill, and thoughts of her caused my hardness to swell.

But I had work to do.

Felipe's desk remained the same as when he'd left it. Papers were strewn across the table, and a half-written letter lay abandoned. Remembering what the architect had conveyed, I shoved the bookcase back and found the secret doorway, eager to discover what lay on the other side.

Standing within the dark chamber, I reached into my coat pocket and withdrew the forged waxed stamp, with King Ferdinand's royal seal engraved in the silver base. I placed it upon a worn table and beside it I lay a parchment strewn with the same signature practiced over and over again, proof that someone had studied hard the flick of the wrist of the flamboyant F of Ferdinand.

I examined several of the wooden boxes stacked high against the far wall. Inside one of them was a collection of coins, an embellished cross, and a Catholic communion chalice. Shoved in with them was a warrant stating that failure to pay taxes would result in even more items being confiscated.

In another of the boxes was a collection of tatty documents. Felipe had not only taken possessions from the Church, but also local residents' legal rights to their property. Those who'd struggled to pay tariffs to the crown had been evicted from their homes. The victims would know better than to complain.

Even the local bishop had not escaped Felipe's greed. A ledger written in scratchy ink indicated that Felipe had taken fifty percent of the Church's donations.

I withdrew and pushed the bookcase back.

I froze.

The door handle turned and a young soldier entered. With my hands and feet firmly wedged in between the ceiling's ornate molding, I held my breath.

* * * *

"But I've become rather accustomed to mausoleums." I gave Sunaria a wry smile.

"Those places are for emergencies only." She flicked a stray hair away from her face.

Inside the modest house, I felt relaxed for the first time in weeks. This home, built on the outskirts of town, provided an austere air, the dark furniture and simple décor extraordinarily formal. No feminine touch here. I strolled through the lower rooms getting my bearings, enjoying the opportunity to spy on another's life. So much was revealed by the extreme tidiness. On the maple desk, the feather pen had been aligned perfectly with the paper, proving the owner's penchant for orderliness, even the way the logs had been stacked neatly in the hearth verged on pedantic.

"Where's the owner?" I asked.

"Out of town on business." Sunaria was dressed in a long, red gown, accentuating her curves. A perfect, erotic vision, and yet even with her back to me, I knew she was regarding my response. She seemingly warmed her hands in front of the fireplace.

I admired her from the doorway.

We were minutes from Miranda's place, and knowing that we were close to Jacob provided some comfort. I'd declined the invitation to stay with her and Alicia, especially with my nocturnal lifestyle being what it was, and keeping Sunaria away from Miranda was a wise decision.

Sunaria peered back at me. A reflection from the orange flames danced over her. So much had happened that I'd found little time to consider my life until now. Thoughts of Jacob kept me focused. I couldn't go back, but I had hope for the future, my son's future, and the elusive promise of his happiness.

Having not fed in awhile, fatigue was setting in and my hands shook slightly. The guilt after each kill weighed so heavily upon my conscience that I wondered if I'd ever get used to it. Hunger seemed a good alternative to the dread that followed the act of satiating it. I'd never want this for Miranda.

Sunaria's long, black hair tumbled over her shoulders. "You were thinking of her." She turned to face me.

"Miranda? Not in that way."

"Remember I hear your every thought."

"Then you know I'm honest." I neared her and concentrated on shutting her out.

"What are you doing?" She faced the hearth again.

I slid my hands down her arms and grasped her wrists, clutching them behind her back and tightening my grip. "Don't be angry with me for wanting privacy."

She leaned back into me.

"For the first time, I'll be able to understand how a woman really thinks." I chuckled to myself.

"You don't get to hear mine."

"Ah." I let her go and massaged her shoulders. "This vampire order, is it safe to assume they've lost track of you?"

"No."

I wrapped my arm around her waist and hugged her.

"As your elder, I have a right to your mind," she said.

Silence, the best answer.

"If you obey me," she continued, "you'll escape punishment and will be well rewarded."

The thought of her rummaging around my mind made me uncomfortable.

"Like the reward I have for you upstairs." She turned to face me.

Her mind was inaccessible as she grasped my hand and led me out. Her expression was full of excitement.

We ascended the slender stairway.

When we reached the top, she lifted herself up onto her toes and leaned in to kiss me, pressing her red, full lips against mine. She tasted lusciously sweet, like cinnamon.

We burst into the room.

There, wearing nothing but a jeweled choker, lay a young, pale blonde on the chaise lounge.

Above the fireplace hung a portrait of an older gentleman and this very girl, who now wrapped an arm around Sunaria and softened into her.

The banker had married her youth, and she his money it seemed, and now she lay in Sunaria's arms. I wondered if business had really taken her husband out of town. Sunaria gestured she wanted me to join them.

Twenty or so plush, tasseled burgundy pillows were strewn over the carpet. This room had been prepared.

But I wasn't.

"Daumia," Sunaria beckoned.

"I've never liked surprises," I muttered.

Sunaria's smile faded.

Whatever Sunaria had told the girl, it wasn't the truth. So lulled by what had been done to her before I'd arrived, she seemed exceptionally passive.

I gave Sunaria a long stare, then turned and walked out.

* * * *

Imagining what they were up to, I lay on the living room rug staring up at the ceiling.

A lifetime lay ahead of trapping and devouring and it caused an awful dread. There had to be another way, a cure even. As an eternal being, I had the unending possibility of finding a way back. Fear of what I didn't know scared me. I'd become the myth.

The legend, documented by those who'd encountered our kind and lived.

And I yearned to learn everything about what I'd become. Never had I needed anyone like I needed Sunaria. Perhaps that's why, uncharacteristically, I'd left the hunter alone with the victim.

After several minutes, Sunaria rejoined me.

"I wasn't sure whether you wanted me to fuck her or drink from her," I snapped.

Sunaria lay down beside me.

I frowned. "How old is she, for God's sake?"

"What does it matter?"

I couldn't look at her. "This is not who I am."

"Get used to it."

"Never."

"Says he who fed on twenty men back in Santiago."

I turned away from her.

She grabbed my arm. "You have to let go of your past."

"The past is who I am."

"No, it holds you back. Remember it, but don't clutch at it."

"What of my humanity?" I pulled away from her.

"You're not human now."

"What happened to her husband?"

"He's away."

"Don't lie to me."

"Don't speak to me like that."

"What are we, Sunaria? Lovers?"

"We are not equals." With a superior expression, she reached up to my face and her long nails dug into my chin. "You dare to defy me."

I shoved away her hand. "You left me under the earth for days."

"And if you don't shut up, I'll put you back there."

"I'm done." I leaped to my feet.

"I own you. I control you."

"I'm leaving."

I reached for the door handle, but a strange sense of powerlessness ensued, and I knew it was Sunaria's hypnotic power that held me. I struggled against her. "Please—" Impossible to resist her. "*No.*" I slumped to my knees.

Locks of Sunaria's hair fell over my face. Her lips met mine in a smoldering kiss and passion exploded. A desire like nothing I'd ever experienced. Her thoughts were inside my mind. She controlled me, and held me down. Sending panicked thoughts, I begged her to release me. Her will, not mine, forcing my obedience, intermingled with my anger, a desire for this powerful union. Confusion interfused with moments of clarity.

"Now," her expression changed from seductress to mistress, "go back upstairs."

* * * *

Back in the bedroom with the pallid, naked girl, I felt strangely controlled by Sunaria, as I whisked our sleeping victim up into my arms, my touch stirring her. She stared up in a daze that turned quickly to panic. There was an initial struggle until fear stilled her. The sweet taste of cinnamon, as she flooded my mouth, was quickly followed by a tingling in my throat.

Arms folded, Sunaria watched.

Too fired up to pull away, wanting nothing more than to drain her, to save her, I peered up.

Sunaria gave a nod that I must finish it, and the girl's arms flopped by her sides and her breaths grew shallow. When I found her true self deep within her, I chose to proceed after her, and in doing so, lost myself. All compassion dissolved and I couldn't follow where she headed. As the final patter of her heart ceased to beat, I knew the true horror of what I'd done.

I clambered off the bed and flew at Sunaria. With a shove, I had her pinned against the door. "I'm a monster!"

She tried to push me away, but I thrust her back, and grabbed her wrists to control her. Another kiss, this time deeper, punishing her, conveyed my anger for this violation. I pulled away. "You did this to me." I ripped at Sunaria's dress.

She scratched at my face.

I spun her around, pushed her down, and bent her over several of the pillows, not caring if I hurt her or not, assuming she could take it.

Sunaria fought against me.

"Hands by your head," I demanded.

She reached back and scraped my forearms, drawing blood. I spanked her so hard that she sucked in her breath and froze.

"Do it," I snapped.

Slowly, Sunaria brought her hands up in front of her, holding one hand with another.

I followed the arch of her back, brushing my fingernails over her and digging them in and along. Sunaria's raven locks tumbled over her shoulders and she softened, her sighs revealing a lifetime of yearning for this very moment.

With a firm grip on both of her arms, I guided her so her forehead rested upon the black rug, her long hair spilling over it.

"Don't move." I rose and strolled past the dead girl, avoiding her vacant stare, and picked up one of the tall, red candles. It had burned halfway but still had some use, and its flame flickered as I carried it back.

Sunaria had obediently remained still. I stood before her, staring down, and savored having her subjugated at my feet, exhilarated that I'd become her master. Sunaria's taut stomach muscles flexed, as though she threatened to spring up in defiance.

"Do it and you'll regret it." I tilted the dancing flame and dropped hot red wax onto her spine.

She gasped with each splash and dared to lift her head. Another sharp smack to her derriere persuaded her to resume her pose

With another tilt, red wax trickled onto her upper back, snaking its way, circling and hardening, leaving fine, red lines and scarlet welts that soon dissipated. She was shaking uncontrollably.

For a long time, I waited and watched, enjoying having conquered her, savoring the sense that I now had her. Empowered, I luxuriated in the frissons that pulsed from my solar plexus, lingered there, and then surged downward. The more I resisted the urge to finish this quickly, the more delectable it felt.

Sunaria's nails clawed the rug, revealing her need, her fingers splaying out, and then curling again. With the candle still burning, I positioned it close by.

I taught Sunaria her lesson . . .

Sunsets and sunrises were lost to me, the finest meals, the best wines, but not this last pleasure. This one rapturous thrill could never be stolen from me.

From us.

The dead girl's eyes were open and her jaw slack, her expression calm, our only audience, our perfect, naked witness.

I drove Sunaria on, feeling her surrendering.

And then I paused. I yanked Sunaria up and whispered, "If you ever do that to me again, I'll never take you like this again."

She sobbed with pleasure.

"Understand?" I resumed, taking her to the edge of pleasure and sending her over.

She caught her breath and leaned back against me.

I enfolded her in my arms and whispered, "We *are* equals."

XXVIII

NINE O'CLOCK AND I FELT more than ready for my confession.

Sunaria and I had stopped off at Vigo's old parish church, a slight detour on our way back to Palos.

I'd be seeing Jacob soon.

Sunaria insisted on waiting in our carriage. I noticed a subtle change in her demeanor, a slight shift in her manner, and her affection more evident than previously, a refreshing change to her usual austere presence.

It felt good to take back my authority.

I carried with me the small wooden box, the one I'd found in Felipe's secret chamber.

Inside, there was a rich aroma of incense and a severe chill. Churches are cold, a detail I'd forgotten. Their stone walls omit warmth, designed this way perhaps to keep the congregation awake during boring sermons.

Putting myth to the test, I took a moment to linger before the large wooden cross hanging behind the ornately decorated altar, and then waited for hell to be unleashed.

I gave a shrug, bored but pleased that there was still no aversion to religious artifacts, not for me anyway. Maybe that also meant I could find a way to face the daylight. Yellow light flickered over white washed walls and peeling paint. Felipe had stolen the money for the church's restoration.

Taking long strides, I made my way to the back of the church and slid the box into the confessional booth entrance and then entered the confessor's side. The red, drawn curtain hinted at authority and equaled its sense of mystery.

I wanted to see Bishop Bonaire's expression, the man on the other side of the curtain.

"These items belong to the Church," I said. "And I trust that you'll return the documents to their rightful owners."

"Where did you find this?" Bonaire lifted out the communion chalice.

"At the senator's residence."

He shuffled through the papers. "It belongs to Senator Grenaldi."

"Did."

The bishop fidgeted. "Did he ask you to return them?"

"Not exactly."

Bonaire pulled the curtain back. His heavily lined face revealed a lifetime of worry, though I detected a strong faith, a dedicated man of God, and a comforting presence.

"Is there something you wish to confess?" he asked.

"I don't actually have that much time."

He frowned.

"I have something for you." I held up a crisp scroll.

He opened the rusty grate.

"This belonged to Columbus." I passed it through.

He unraveled the map. "Where did you find this?"

"In the box I just handed to you," I lied. "It's evidence of a plot against the king."

"Senator Grenaldi?"

"He's at its center."

"But he's the king's closest ally." Tension rose in his voice.

"Felipe wanted us to think that. It's time to restore power to the Church."

"How does this map prove the senator's heresy?"

I handed Bonaire the letter that Felipe had scribed before Sunaria in The Captain's Table Inn.

Bonaire fidgeted. "He wrote this?"

"Felipe's handwriting and *his* signature."

"Has he gone mad?" Bonaire's jowl shook with surprise.

"Felipe is after the precious metals that Columbus is currently searching for."

"But why write a letter to the king?"

"As a warning? Perhaps we will never know."

"He threatens Columbus?"

"When Columbus finds land, Grenaldi plans to claim it."

"He *is* mad." Bonaire rolled up the letter. "When this gets into the king's hands—"

"You will be free to take care of your parish."

He peeked again at the contents of the box.

"One more thing," I said. "Behind the bookcase in Grenaldi's office is a chamber, in case the authorities need more evidence."

In order for me to appear as a convincing religious zealot, I lingered for a moment or two, kneeling before the altar. I genuflected and then headed out, passing the font full to the brim of holy water.

Something in the receptacle caught my eye. I approached and, careful to avoid contact with what could apparently burn me, I glimpsed in.

After I caught my breath, I took another look. My refection stared back. Although I recognized a little of the old Daumia, there were real changes in my appearance, my hazel eyes were luminous and my chiseled bone structure was striking.

And my hair was sticking up.

* * * *

I gave a nod to our horseman that we were ready for our journey to Palos and climbed in, sitting opposite Sunaria. With a crack of the whip and a jolt, the horses trotted off, pulling our carriage along. We rocked as the wheels rolled over the worn cobblestones of the churchyard.

"Nice church." I flattened my hair with my palm.

Sunaria gazed out of the window. "Will you ever forgive me for bringing you over?"

I rested my feet on the seat opposite. "I never took you for one who'd ask for forgiveness."

"You have time with your son."

"And time with you."

Moonlight shimmered off her dark locks, her perfect, porcelain complexion enhancing her beauty, and her infinite, blue-green irises intensified when her mood darkened, like it did now.

I held her hand and kissed it. "Let me in."

She sighed.

"Never leave me," I whispered.

"Do I detect a moment of weakness from my dark lord?"

"Is that what you're calling me now?"

"A new life deserves a new name."

A thrill coursed down my spine that she'd allowed me access to her thoughts, even though it was fleeting. "Lord of the underworld?" I repeated her silent words.

"My immortal beloved," she said, *"My Orpheus."*

XXIX

SET THE PROVERBIAL FIRE and step back.
Observe the destruction of Felipe Grenaldi's political career and his impending downfall. I pondered how our plan unfolded upon the high seas, impatient for it to be over with.

Sunaria, however, had remarkable patience, a hint of her longevity. She'd found us a residence near the Ocean View Manor. I delighted in her find and had been more than pleased to take refuge in luxury.

I was done with cobwebs.

The great house was nestled within a naturally formed alcove. Inside, the décor paid homage to decadence. The previous residents had adored all things French, their expensive tastes evident in the fine furnishings. It was the consummate hiding place.

Sunaria and I continued to bond and my dependence on her was transforming into an intense love. She bewitched not only me, but everyone who came into contact with her. Elegantly, she conversed with strangers in their own language. She'd even mastered Welsh. Her worldly knowledge and the ease with which she faced each night also reflected in her maturity. Other women seemed sheltered compared to her.

Sunaria couldn't shake off her old ways, much to my delight. Up until the moment she'd slaughtered her master she'd been a perfect slave. By the time she reached adulthood, she'd been groomed to satisfy every one of her master's needs. She thought first of her lover's desires before her own. A natural nurturer, she delighted in spoiling me.

I'd find myself standing naked in a hot tub of water, leisurely bathed by her, or she'd present a victim, still surprised by my squirming. Confliction still came easily for me.

Sunaria's talents as a lover left me breathless. Her easy access to my thoughts ensured awareness at the deepest level of my psyche, thus she understood me. She calmed my fears and satisfied my yearnings.

I'd wake to find my clothes laid out on the end of our bed. She chose the most distinguished of outfits for me to wear. I delighted in the rare books she left for me on the bedside table and I devoured them all.

I was obsessed with her.

With my passion came a desire to fulfill her every need. Perfect lovers, unchanging, we tumbled through time, two inseparable nightwalkers drunk on their desire for each other. We'd mingle with high society, enjoying hunting amongst the privileged. Women offered themselves to me willingly and men would surrender all too easily. I had to tame my ability to cause havoc in rooms full of mortals, not only could I walk on consecrated ground, I could also seduce anyone. I'd stand in the center of a room and marvel at the crowd that gathered, all eager for play. Sunaria insisted that her royal blood had bestowed my unique gifts.

Here in our lavish bedroom, I lay on the four-poster bed and watched her dress, a dark goddess of the night. I savored her voluptuous figure moving dreamily before me. Again, as on so many occasions before, she disappeared into the night. Her habitual leaving me alone seemed to be her way of intensifying my fixation. I'd lay back, staring up at the ceiling, fantasizing about what I'd do to Sunaria upon her return, and then lure her back with my erotic imaginings.

Our endless infatuation with each other heightened our mutual dependence—my new life balanced precariously with my old one.

Not ready to face my sister with the whole truth, for fear of her rejection and dread of losing Jacob, I kept up the façade.

Miranda hovered close, a constant reminder of a promise I'd once made. I'd managed to delay her request, but wasn't sure how long I could hold her off. Expensive gifts and a great deal of flirting seemed to placate her, but I knew it would only be a matter of time before she demanded my dark kiss.

By October, Miranda and Alicia had settled into their new life.

Although still in hiding, we all had a sense of impending freedom. They both trusted my ability to deal with Felipe and, though the details were rarely discussed, they showed remarkable faith in my handling our affairs.

During my frequent visits to their house, I savored spending time with Jacob. We hired distinguished tutors for the boys. Their lessons promised to establish them into high society. Alicia would very often complain that I kept Jacob up late. I'd smile and shrug, avoiding Miranda's critical stare.

Ricardo's unruly temperament became troublesome and I often had to pull him off Jacob, his jealousy a frequent cause of the fights. Although I tried not to show Jacob favor, this wasn't easy. Ricardo, a troubled child, needed a father's discipline. Where I could, I tried to help Alicia raise him, but Ricardo reminded me of my past and I'd not yet forgiven him. Having experienced firsthand Ricardo's swordsmanship, weapons were banned. Of course Ricardo had no memory of impaling his uncle. For me however, it was impossible to forget.

Lessons in horsemanship were permitted. With my heart in my throat, I'd watch proudly as Jacob steered his pony over the small gates. I secretly spoiled him, taking him out for long walks and delighting in our precious time together. I found solace in seeing Annabelle in his character. Even Jacob's patience reminded me of her. Very often, I'd marvel at his ability to grasp ideas quickly and his kindness extended to those in need. He'd stop and offer a coin to a beggar, not thinking twice about offering a word of comfort or a kind smile.

Ricardo, however, would often be found outside play acting sword fighting, taking on an invisible opponent, stabbing yet another victim to death.

I would watch Jacob sleep, and at times had to be dragged away by Sunaria, who had snuck into the house to get me, minutes before daylight. The next evening, I'd be back again, witnessing my son flourish, wanting him to have everything that I never had.

One late evening, I found the strength to tell Jacob about his mother. He gazed down at Annabelle's image rendered perfectly in the left side of the locket that I'd removed from her neck soon after her death, the silver chain dangling.

"You can keep it if you like." I closed the clasp and tucked the memento into the palm of his small hand.

Jacob squeezed his fingers around it and silently mouthed a prayer for the mother he'd never known.

Through him glimmered the hope of my salvation.

✗ ✗ ✗

ON DECEMBER 6TH 1493, the *Niña* clashed with disaster.

Its mast snapped in two and the vessel almost sank. Experienced sailors managed to salvage what was left of the damaged mast and the ship continued on, but as a result of the delay, it became separated from the two other vessels.

Two days before, Felipe had requested a transfer from the *Niña* to the *Santa María*, and tragedy soon followed. The shipwrecking of the *Santa María*, just off the Caribbean, was more evidence of sabotage.

Three months later, on March 15th, Columbus returned to Palos on the *Niña*, with its fixed mast. Felipe Grenaldi, also aboard, waved to the crowds, happy to have survived. His expression of delight to see his homeland soon faded when the king's guards arrested him on his disembarkation and charged him with mutiny.

Columbus was shocked to hear that the man he'd befriended had been accused of treachery.

A late evening trial enabled Sunaria and I to attend. We sat at the back of the courtroom, hidden by the crowd that clamored for a good view. Dumbstruck, Felipe had no idea who'd set him up. The journey halfway across the world had aged him and he'd lost weight. New worry lines had appeared and the old ones were more defined.

Vincente Yanez Pinzon testified that Felipe had joined them at the last minute, insisting that he represented the king. Although Pinzon had initially felt suspicion, the royal warrant given to him by Felipe was stamped with the official crest of his majesty, and King Ferdinand had personally signed it. The document, meticulously forged by myself, was now presented by Pinzon to the court.

During the voyage, Felipe had requested he leave the *Niña* and join Columbus on the *Santa María*. Felipe had claimed that he had important information for Columbus and the transfer had been permitted by Vincent Pinzon.

Felipe boarded the *Santa María* a mile from Haiti, or as Columbus preferred, Hispaniola.

Soon after, the *Niña*'s mast snapped, causing no real issue for the ship, other than a rattled crew. Suspicions arose, but the journey took precedence, and with no time for an investigation, the expedition continued on. Despite

Felipe's protestation of innocence and his previous alliance with the king, the court case proceeded and more evidence came to light.

Firstly, the letter addressed to the king was examined and confirmed to be written in Felipe's handwriting. Next, the knife found on him was the size of the very one used to saw through the mast of the *Niña*. The king's investigators had discovered Felipe's secret room, tipped off by a local source. Other papers were discovered. More condemning still was evidence that Felipe had practiced the King's signature and had in his possession a forged royal stamp, which was undeniable proof of treason.

Felipe's once tanned complexion now paled as the judge proclaimed that the evidence decided his fate.

It was done.

* * * *

Back in the living room of our French styled home, I stared out of the window. Melancholy, my new acquaintance, was brought on by my inability to find any kind of relief in Felipe's undoing.

My thoughts had been so consumed with revenge, that I'd given little thought to our future. So caught up in the drama, I'd avoided the real challenges ahead.

I considered that my altered emotions resulted from my transformation. My capacity to love had not changed, for I felt the same for my son as I always had. I'd also developed a deep affection for Sunaria, but this ability to murder and feel less guilt than before surprised me. I even feared myself, or should I say feared what I could become. Felipe had led me here. These were the consequences that followed that night in the bull ring, my last night of innocence.

I hoped that Sunaria would remain by my side and together we'd face the future, the ultimate unknown.

Sunaria allowed me the illusion of control.

Looking out at the impending dawn, I wondered if I'd ever accept not seeing a sunrise again. Until now, I'd never given much thought to the profoundness of daylight, the colors that only a sun could sustain, exquisite hues now lost to me.

"Carpe Noctum," Sunaria's voice came from the corridor.

I turned. "Seize the night?"

She lingered by the door. "You may lose the day but gain so much in return."

"Like?"

"Always looking young."

I laughed bitterly.

"I don't like seeing you like this." She wrapped her arms around me.

"Why don't I feel some kind of vindication?"

"Because you need answers."

"It's incredible that Felipe fell for our ruse."

"He believed what he wanted to."

After a long sigh, I said, "How do I move on?"
"You prevent the inner ghosts from getting to you."
"And how do I do that?"
"You face your demons."
"My demon is lying in a prison."
"I know you better than you know yourself."
I spun round.

With my heart in my throat, I followed her, ascending the stairs. We headed for the rear bedroom and, sensing something was off, I trailed after Sunaria, glancing at her expression.

I had an uneasy feeling as I turned the corner and entered the room.

Felipe was crouched low, unshaven and bedraggled, his once white shirt now crumbled and filthy. He was chained to the fireplace.

I leaned against the wall. "He was to be hanged tomorrow!"

Felipe's hollow stare tried to focus. "Impossible."

He seemed such an unlikely enemy, and yet this man had decimated my world.

"But . . . they . . . buried you." Felipe's voice was flooded with fear.

I almost smiled at his reaction. "Most unpleasant."

Felipe shook. "Impossible to survive that."

"How *was* your trip?" I neared him.

"You set me up." He yanked at the metal cuff and pointed to Sunaria. "I should have known you'd have something to do with this.'

"She makes a fine gentleman, don't you think?" I scowled. "Consider this your confession."

"Where's my son?" His voice broke.

I folded my arms. "Whose idea was it to kill my brother?"

"I'll take that to my grave."

"It was you, wasn't it?" I said.

He stared from Sunaria to me. "Witchcraft?"

I shook my head. "*No.*"

"I've lost everything because of you." His voice broke.

"Why thank you."

He grimaced. "But my men buried you."

"I'm pretty resilient."

"No, you're something demonic."

"Time to take responsibility for what you created."

"Unchain me."

I trespassed into his thoughts. "Start talking."

"Not until—"

"Talk!"

He flinched. "Ricardo caused a rift between Roelle and his father."

"Go on."

"Not until you promise to let me go."

"I promise to wrap that chain around your neck."

"Señor Bastillion wanted to adopt your brother, give him what belonged to Roelle."

"Was the bull your idea?"
Felipe's smile was defiant.
"You named your son Ricardo, why?" I asked.
"Ricardo was a brilliant bull fighter, the best."
"And yet you murdered him."
"So you say."
My fists tightened.

"Your brother stood to inherit money from the Bastillion legacy," he said. "He threatened Roelle's birthright. His father favored Ricardo, he saw his potential. Your brother reminded Señor Bastillion of the old days when he'd once been crowned as Spain's greatest bull fighter. Roelle paled in comparison to Ricardo's talents."

"What did that have to do with you?"
"Roelle promised to fund my political career."
"My brother threatened that?"
Felipe glanced at Sunaria and then back at me.
My stare forced him to look away. "And Aaron?"
"Aaron was misguided."
"You sent him to kill me?"
Felipe tugged, trying to pull his wrist out of the metal cuff.
"And Roelle?" I said.
"Roelle wanted to keep you quiet."
"You wanted him to kill me?"
"Then why didn't he?"
"That's what you couldn't understand."
He turned to look out of the window. I could smell his fear.
I followed his gaze. "I imagine they're searching for you, yes?"
He shrugged.

I tried to subdue my hatred, fearful that I'd kill him too soon. "It was you who planned Ricardo's death?"
He yanked at the shackle. "Where's my son?"
"Have your political achievements been worth it?"
"And what do you have to show for your life? A mere horse breeder?"
"Ask me in a millennium."
His eyes widened.
I smiled. "Yes, I am."
He barely formed the words.
"Forever and ever, amen." I bowed.
He stared at Sunaria then back at me. "*Vampires*."
"And capable of more love than you can imagine," I said wistfully.
"A weak emotion."
"You love your son."
"He has yet to earn it."
I glanced at Sunaria. "And I'm called cold blooded."
"Your soul is damned." He spat at me.
"Just like yours."
"You're not going to kill me." Felipe leaned back against the fireplace.

I tilted my head and felt a sense of calm.

He cowered. "I'm Ricardo's father."

"Were."

"Is it money you want?"

"I remember everything." I nodded. "The night before the bull fight."

"What?"

"You were holding the cudgel."

He looked horrified.

Sunaria approached Felipe. "Or we can offer you something else." Her fingers traced his unshaven face and then moved lower and hovered at his neck, lingering there.

"Make me into what you are?" His eyes were full of terror.

Sunaria gazed coquettishly at him. Filled with envy, I stepped forward, but her hand shot up and she gestured I was to stay put, and then she turned to face him again.

Felipe had caught our interaction.

Rip out his throat.

With a pointed fingernail, Sunaria stabbed Felipe's neck, striking an artery. He flinched as the warmth snaked its way down and he stared aghast at his shirt, which was fast turning red. He slumped to his knees, pressing against the hemorrhage, though blood seeped beneath his trembling hand.

Sunaria dipped a finger into the flow and sucked on the tip, causing Felipe to whimper.

She stepped back and gestured for me to approach. Ready for the truth, I leaned in and followed the scarlet trail to its source, biting hard, cringing at Felipe's wails. He thrashed, but I held him still.

Raping his mind, I trespassed into his streaming thoughts, and a dreamy haze unfolded back over time. With the coursing of his life source came the images of faces, conversations, and decisions, an argument: *Roelle and Felipe discussing my brother, silent words flowed and delivered a torrent of truths. Felipe had decided Ricardo's fate, and then he'd persuaded the others to join him.*

For my brother, I kill you, for Annabelle, Eduardo, for Miguel, for what you did to Salvador. My sister's pain . . . for desecrating my life.

Felipe's jaw went slack.

Sunaria tugged at my shirt, but I ignored her and continued to drink. *For every life you've destroyed.*

Again she yanked at my sleeve.

I pulled away. "What?"

Sunaria shoved me aside and bit into her wrist, and then thrust it firmly against Felipe's mouth.

"*No!*" I shouted in disbelief.

She crushed his lips with her wrist and Felipe's mouth gaped as he tried to catch his breath and find air, and in a daze his tongue lapped at the bloody slash on her arm.

Sunaria tilted her head and smiled at me.

Felipe sucked, enjoying the drink, seemingly aware that salvation came with this very act. Pulling on his restraints, he thirsted for more, mouth wide open, gorging on her.

Filled with jealousy, I wanted to rip out his heart.

What are you doing?

Felipe convulsed, fighting the impossible, a violent transformation as his age softened and he writhed in ecstasy. I wondered if the expression on his face had been similar to mine, upon my turning.

Fear tore a yell from him so primal that I backed away. Hating this moment, I tried to find the words to tell Sunaria that she'd made a mistake.

She neared me and whispered, "Then you admit that this gift is only for the worthy?"

I held her stare for the longest time as that dark gaze of hers reached deep within me, until she got the answer she wanted.

Felipe was studying us with a mad expression. "I feel strange," he murmured.

Sunaria assisted him to his feet. "It'll pass," she said, her tone comforting.

He glanced at her half in terror, half in awe, and Sunaria guided him toward the window.

"Look," she pointed outside, "see how perfect the world is now."

Felipe's eyes bulged and his thin lips slid into a smile. Silhouetted at the window stood my lover and her new fledgling.

My jealously was so fierce that it burned me up from the inside, and, as though hearing my inner screams, Sunaria's attention turned to me, her stare so shocking that it silenced them. But something about the way her mouth curled and then pouted and the glint in her eye as she arched a brow, in that very gesture she gave me her permission.

A long sigh, not sure if it was mine or hers, but it elicited an inner calm.

Felipe examined his hands fascinated with their appearance. "I am immortal."

"That's the good news." I bolted forward and shoved him.

Felipe tumbled out through the window.

We both leaned over the sill and peered down to see Felipe clambering to his feet, seemingly impressed with himself that he'd survived the fall. He stared back up at us with a crooked smile.

Sunaria pulled the curtain closed and we leaped back.

Silence followed, as those perfect seconds dissolved and the air stilled with nature poised ready, just moments before the arrival of daybreak.

Felipe's wails carried.

"And that'll be the bad news," I said.

XXXI

FELIPE'S WAILS FOLLOWED us down the back stairs.

Sunaria threw her head back and laughed. "Did you see his face?"

I opened my arms to her and she softened into me. I thanked her, silently showing my gratitude that she'd delivered closure. We lay in the dark corner, snuggled up together, and for the first time since I'd been turned, sleep came easily.

Upon awaking, I strolled out into the night and glanced up at the window ledge that Felipe had tumbled from. Scooping his ashes, I let them slip between my fingers and the grey dust disbursed.

Our new life beckoned.

Sunaria's unpredictable nature promised eternity would not be boring and, despite my desire for independence, I found comfort in her presence.

I craved excitement and Sunaria satisfied that very need. She'd enter a room and all would gaze at her. Though her demeanor reflected that of an innocent woman, she was the worst kind of hunter, easily mingling with her prey. We passed for aristocracy, wooing guests at parties or lavish functions, finding no trouble in seducing those whom we chose to satisfy our primal needs.

It seemed to be getting easier.

I wanted it all—luxury, indulgence and the most exquisite of comforts. My dark desires manifested before me as Sunaria created a home for us, ensuring fulfillment of our every craving. She found us a large villa, deep in the countryside, and made sure that we had no curious neighbors to bother us. The Ocean View Manor could be seen from our bedroom window.

Frequent visits enabled me to steal precious time with Jacob, and evenings in his presence ensured my somewhat shaky grasp on my humanity. Watching him flourish gave me such pleasure. A precious reminder of another life, now fast faded, though the memories still selfishly guarded.

His strength gave me mine.

XXXII

SEASONS CAME AND WENT, unfolding irrevocably before me.

My sophisticated style revealed itself. During the days that followed, my true nature arose. No longer hindered by my former life, I felt free to self-examine, still calculating, though now with an intuitive streak that gave me the ability to predict a victim's weakness, a striking intensity that for the most part I was unaware of. This gift, I know no other way to describe it, had provided me with the ability to seduce anyone, a supernatural capacity to entrance. It refined my abilities, enabling me to possess anything that I coveted, and control anyone.

But I craved normality too, and found it at the Ocean View Manor. Evenings were uneventful. Here I could feel like my old self, that is until Miranda would search me out and kindly point out that I lived a lie.

Like she did now.

With Alicia and the boys asleep upstairs, Miranda had cornered me yet again.

"What more is there for me to know?" Miranda stood before me with her arms folded.

I peered up from my book, Chaucer's *The Canterbury Tales*, pressing a finger against the page so as not to lose my place. Miranda had brought the book back from London years ago. I'd found it in the lounge.

"Don't ignore me." Miranda curled her fingers into fists.

Over the last seven years, I'd always managed to placate her, but not today. Her expression conveyed she wasn't going to let me change the subject this time.

I stared back down at my book.

"I've thought about it." She sighed. "Changed my mind and changed it back again."

"Doubt is your heart telling you *no*."

"You haven't aged."

I gestured exasperation. "I don't want this life for you."

"Who are you to decide what is right for me?"

"Your friend."

"You can't hide it from Alicia anymore." She sat in the chair next to mine. "In a week, I turn forty."

"We'll throw a party."

"Funny."
I glanced up briefly. "Face it, this is never going to happen."
Her hand rested on my knee. "But you promised—"
"Please don't ask this of me." I glanced at her hand moving up my thigh.
"I've done everything you have ever asked."
I lifted her hand off. "For that, I'm grateful."
"Why are you being difficult?"
"You have no idea what it is that you're asking."
"You promised."
"To talk about it, in hope of talking you out of it." I looked away.
"Why won't you tell us what happened to Felipe?"
"Please don't go there."
"He escaped from prison and yet you were unaffected by such news."
"Just know this. You are safe."
"Did you kill him?"
I turned a page.
Miranda sighed. "Take me with you when you go out tonight."
"Out of the question."
I will tell your sister. Miranda's thoughts carried.
"Another night."
Miranda headed for the door. I jumped up and grasped her arm.
A long silence ensued.
"Change your dress," I snapped. "Wear something dark."
She smiled.
I tightened my hold. "This is a dangerous game you're playing."
She kissed my cheek. "You won't regret this."
"I already do."

* * * *

In the lavish courtyard, the party thrived.

The sparsely lit enclosure ensured a good view of the starlit sky and the thumbnail moon. The stone fountain spewed out water from its center and more from within that. Our hosts were Venetians and they'd decorated accordingly. Fifty or so guests chatted. Wine flowed.

Miranda and I lingered in a corner. She'd dressed in her finest blue gown and looked exquisite. Dreaming of this moment, she'd prepared for this very night, down to the finest details.

But her expression was vexed. "You want me to choose?"

"Yes." I gestured with a nod to the mingling guests.

A waiter passed by carrying a tray of wine glasses. Miranda waved him away and then changed her mind and grabbed one. The remaining glasses clinked. The startled waiter moved on.

"That's how it works," I said dryly. "You find the ones you like, and then you seduce them."

Her hands trembled. "You know nothing of who they are?"

"It's easier that way," I lied.

Miranda looked conflicted.

"Take your time." I watched her.

A nervous rash spread down her neck, disappearing beneath the line of her black lace bustier.

I rested my hand in the arch of her back. "Let's go home, sweetheart."

"No, I can do this." Miranda pressed her hand against her chest.

I blew a puff of cold air onto her throat.

"That's not actually helping," she said.

I stroked her arm. "You come to terms with the fact that they love and are loved."

"Don't."

"Or the fact that when you do take them, their fear is overwhelming."

"I know what you're doing." She was breathless.

"And of course, disposing of their . . . corpses." I perused the courtyard. "During the act, their thoughts feel as though they're yours. If they've made plans for tomorrow, you'll know them."

Miranda's eyes watered.

"And you'll also know," I stared at her, "that they'll never realize those plans."

"You choose." She looked away. "Make it quick."

"Very well." I strolled into the crowd and smoothly interjected conversation with a small gathering. I discreetly pointed to a pretty young man.

Miranda shook head no.

Of course, I'd chosen the youngest guest who wore an expression of wonderment and conveyed a zest for life. I worked my way around, taking my time to find the most alluring, yet innocent guests.

After ten minutes, I returned to Miranda's side. "None of them?"

She squinted. "I need more time."

An uncomfortable silence.

"Him." Miranda stared off into the crowd.

She'd chosen a rotund, middle-aged aristocrat. He munched on a pastry and crumbs fell out of his mouth and sprinkled onto his shirt.

"To be your first?" I asked gently.

"Does it matter?"

"Consider this, your first kiss, your first glass of wine, your first—"

"All right, all right."

"Or your first lover?"

Miranda stormed away from me, past the fountain, and headed out.

* * * *

A crack of the whip and our carriage rumbled over uneven ground. With Miranda's hand in mine, I kissed it. She pulled away.

"To survive, you have to do that *every* night," I said.

She wiped away a tear.

I stared out of the window. "I miss daylight."

She kicked me.

We rocked over the dirt roads, speeding past overgrown fields. The trees hung low, their branches bashing the window.

Miranda looked puzzled. "Where are we going?"

"A detour."

Within minutes, we'd pulled up outside a graveyard. I assisted Miranda out of the carriage and guided her along the worn trail. Out of sight of the horseman, we stopped before a tall mausoleum.

Miranda read the inscription on the tomb entrance. "Carmen Casimiro?"

"But Carmen does not lie alone," I said.

"What do you mean?"

"She has company."

Miranda's gaze settled on the bouquet of rotting flowers.

"Sometimes, when a person is transformed . . ."

"Yes?"

I turned to face her. "It goes wrong."

"What?"

"I appear normal to you. Able to pass for ordinary. Or may I say extraordinary."

"Handsome."

"Dashing even." I winked. "A romantic idea of what it is to be immortal."

"And I want that."

"I know you do, my love." I lowered my voice. "But there are risks."

"What kind?"

"I thought that before we take that leap into the realm of the not going back, I should show you Deloris."

"Deloris?"

I stared at the mausoleum entrance.

"She's in there?" Miranda asked, whispering now.

"As we speak."

"Does she know we're out here?"

"Of course."

"She's a—"

"Immortality is just too much to bear for some."

"What?"

"I thought I'd wake her so that you could get an idea." I leaned against the door and listened.

"Wait!"

"She's quite harmless, just a little—" I gestured that Deloris was crazy.

"Are you saying that could happen to me?"

"That's *one* of the risks, yes."

"What's another?"

"That it doesn't take."

"What does that mean?"

"That when I turn you, I take too much."

"You're lying. There's no one in there."

I wrinkled my nose. "This takes me back."

Miranda glared.

I tried the handle. "Locked from the inside."

"You bastard."

"Soon after I was turned, I slept in one of these."

"Whatever for?"

"If you stray too far from home, you can get caught unawares by the morning."

"Then I won't."

"And who will you feed upon, your neighbors?"

She bit down on her lower lip.

"Talk about bringing attention to yourself, Miranda." I knocked. "Waking the undead usually pisses them off. Good thing for us I'm a good talker."

Miranda lifted the hem of her gown and sprinted off. I followed her back to the carriage.

The horseman cracked his whip and we headed home. *Deloris.* Surely I could've come up with a better name.

Had I turned Miranda prior to our evening soiree, her natural desire to find a victim would have facilitated the act. There was no remorse on my part for ensuring that my friend would not be joining the ranks of the undead.

I kissed her forehead. "I adore you."

She gazed at me for the longest time and then broke into a smile.

"You're perfect the way you are," I said, with a sense of relief that I'd done the right thing.

"I'll always love you, you know that?" She reached for my hand and squeezed it with affection.

"When you get up tomorrow, I want you to do something for me."

"Anything."

I stared out of the window. "Watch the sunrise for me."

XXXIII

"WE'VE SEARCHED EVERYWHERE." Miranda sobbed, tears staining her cheeks.

With my heart in my throat, I stared down at thirteen-year-old Ricardo, who leaned over a warm bowl of chicken soup.

"Where is he?" I demanded. "You were with him last."

Ricardo shrugged and dipped a piece of bread into his soup.

I half expected Jacob, barely six years old, to burst in through the kitchen door and shout about his adventures – the tree he'd climbed, the castle he'd defended, or the imaginary army he'd taken on and won.

"Ricardo, you must tell us," Alicia said.

Something about his uneasy smile, the way his eyes reflected nothing, it was as though he tried to hide something. He was his father's son.

He shifted in his seat. "Jacob ran away."

I slumped next to him and drew upon my last remnants of patience. "What are you talking about?"

I caught visions from Ricardo's wandering mind and grabbed his wrist.

"He was frightened." Ricardo fixed his gaze on his spoon.

"Of what?"

"You." He yanked his wrist away.

I reached for the bowl and threw it against the wall. Soup splattered.

"You scared him," Ricardo said.

My fingernails dug into my palms.

"He was terrified." His tone was strangely even, reflecting nothing of the moment.

"And yet you remained behind?"

"I'm not frightened of you."

"You're lying." I caught a sob. "Where is he?" I tried to stay calm, but I could feel the tingle of my fangs.

Ricardo's expression portrayed innocence. "I don't know."

Lines of brown soup trickled down the wall and met the floor.

"Tell me," I snapped.

"Ricardo!" Miranda said, her voice firm.

When I glanced at my palms, there were beads of blood. I'd punctured my own flesh with my fingernails. I leaped from my chair.

Ricardo flinched. "Jacob knew that you killed my father."

Alicia sat beside him. "What are you talking about?"

"We overheard you." Ricardo glared up at me. "You admitted murdering my father to Aunt Miranda."

"Dear God." Alicia sighed.

Ricardo rose. "You lied to Mama that Papa fled Spain."

"Those were not my words." I glanced at Alicia.

"What has this got to do with Jacob?" Alicia asked.

Ricardo glanced at a discarded knife on the table. "What did you tell my father before you killed him?"

Alicia looked horrified.

"My father was a good man," Ricardo muttered. "A fine politician. He would never want for us to live in this squalor."

Another wave of anxiety, a terrible sense of despair at not seeing this coming, I scoured Ricardo's thoughts. "*No!*"

"What?" Alicia gasped. "You're scaring me."

"He sold him," I said in disbelief.

"*How could you know that?*" Ricardo's thoughts carried.

* * * *

I turned the hourglass over.

Sunaria convinced me of the wisdom of remaining composed and staying focused on getting Jacob back. Together, we'd flown to the docks, the place where Ricardo admitted having taken Jacob.

We scoured the port and soon confirmed that Jacob had been seen with a lone sailor. Ricardo had sold Jacob to him for pennies. More money had changed hands here in the admiral's office.

Glaring at the portly, middle-aged man, I stared him down as sand trickled through the narrow timer, pooling into the base.

"By the time it's empty," I pointed to it, "you'll have told me where the boy is."

The admiral coughed. "As I've already told you, I have no idea where the boy is."

My gaze fell onto the hourglass.

"You're mistaken." He shifted his stare to Sunaria.

Meager maritime furnishings revealed the gentleman's profession. Beads of perspiration spotted his brow. Fire roared in the hearth and flames lapped in the grate.

I turned the hourglass over. "This time when it's empty, I'll kill you."

Hooves clipped below just outside the window. Foreign accents drifted in from the sailors working late into the night. This was business as usual for the bustling dock.

But not in here.

From where I stood, I could see the vast, white sails of *The Pride* unraveling as it sailed out of the harbor.

He bolted for the door.

With my teeth buried in his neck, I tried to extract the information, but I was so full of panic, I had trouble grasping anything. A mishmash of images, though nothing definitive, and nothing to grab hold of.

The mariner slumped to the ground. "What the hell are you?"

"Which ship is he on?" I yelled.

"Why should I tell you?"

"Because our next stop is at your home."

"The Pride," he mumbled.

Sunaria loomed close. "Where's it heading?"

Taking short breaths, saliva trickled down his chin. "Portsmouth."

She knelt beside him and grasped his head with both hands firmly positioned on either side, and, with a crack, she snapped his neck.

* * * *

Sunaria knew the wisdom of saying nothing.

Aboard the British vessel *Godisgrace,* we leaned against the balustrade and stared out at the port of Palos. Sunaria wrapped her arm through mine and rested her head upon my shoulder. From the port side, we had a good view of the other passengers boarding.

I broke the silence. "Please tell me we'll find him."

"I'm certain of it," she said.

"I should never have let Jacob out of my sight. This is my fault entirely."

"How could we have known?"

I followed her gaze to the crew preparing for our launch.

Sunaria sensed my anxiety. "First class tickets ensure our privacy."

"We won't appear suspicious?"

The wind caught in her hair and she swept strands out of her face. "You maybe, but not me." She squeezed my arm.

The last few pieces of luggage were carried aboard. Our two large trunks were amongst them.

Farther down the dock heading for the boat were three men, their hoods pulled well over their heads, obscuring their faces. *Not men.*

Sunaria clutched my sleeve. "Creda!"

"The elders?" I asked.

They were disguised as mortals. They neared eerily fast.

My heart raced. "What will they do if they catch us?"

Her fingers grasped the balustrade.

Her fear reached me. "Can you swim?" I asked.

Two crew members reeled in the ropes that secured the ship to the dock.

"We have to jump." I grabbed Sunaria's arm, ready to take her with me.

With a jolt, the ship launched.

I let her go. "Talk about timing."

The three vampires lingered on the edge of the dock, their hollow stares locked on us. For a brief moment, I thought they'd dive in and answer my question about whether vampires could swim. The ship rocked, sailing off through the harbor.

"Why do I have a sense that there's more going on with your wily friends than you've previously let on?" I muttered.

A merchant officer signaled to us.

"Our cabin's ready." She turned to me. "And they're not my friends."

We strolled after the officer tasked with escorting us to our quarters. Nostalgia hit hard. Up until now, Alicia and Miranda had been reliant on me. Although they had access to finances, I felt terrible leaving with no word.

Once in our cabin, I paced the small space, trying to calm down, miserably eyeing the two wooden trunks pushed up against the far corner. I climbed into one of them to try it out. No matter what position I got in, it was uncomfortable. I closed my eyes and tried to imagine a week of sleeping in it. Thoughts of Jacob's terror caused me to strike the inside of the trunk. He'd have no idea what was happening or why. A jealous cousin's betrayal would never even cross his mind.

Strange thoughts wandered and took me to a place where my hands were wrapped around Ricardo's throat, strangling him, squeezing out his last breaths. My fists clenched with the idea.

Sunaria lifted the lid and peered down at me.

"I refuse to sleep in this," I said.

She raised her eyebrows and let go of the lid and it slammed, just missing my head.

I climbed out. "How long have they been chasing you?"

She peeked out of the port hole.

"Sunaria?" I pushed.

"Awhile."

"And remind me again why?"

"I left without permission." She turned away. "The Creda owned me."

"You were sold to them?"

"I was given to them."

"By whom? The one that turned you?"

"No, I killed him, remember?"

I gestured for her to continue.

She looked grim. "The vampire that turned my master heard what I'd done."

"Why have you never talked about this before?"

"I want to forget."

"What happened?"

"After several years of fighting in the coliseum—"

"Roman coliseum?"

"Yes."

God, you are old, teetered on the tip of my tongue. I was grateful it stayed there.

"When I refused to fight anymore, he punished me."

"You hated your master for what he made you do?"

"He drew me in with the promise of a glorious life. Immortality."

"And the fact that you never died, the audience, they didn't catch on?" She reminisced. I wondered if she could still hear the cries of the crowd.

"And when you killed your master?" I finally said, breaking her trance.

"I had, after all, been taught to fight bloody."

"The Creda gave you that tattoo?"

She nodded.

"It's a mark of ownership?" I asked.

"It's meant to be a mark of distinction. An honor to serve them, but I've never really been one for following orders."

"I'll talk with them."

"They don't negotiate."

"I'll buy you off them."

"It doesn't work like that."

"Everyone has their price."

"The Creda don't care about money."

"So you're meant to go back to them and—"

"Serve."

"Is there something you're not telling me?"

"Like what?" She avoided eye contact.

I tried to read her, reach into her mind and extract the truth.

She peered up. "I belong to you now."

"We belong to each other."

She approached her trunk, opened the lid, and peered inside.

"What did it feel like fighting in the coliseum?" I said.

"You mean apart from the blood, gore, and endless death?"

"Why didn't you run away?"

"Why do you ask so many questions?"

"You could have broken the chains, escaped. What did they have over you?"

Her expression changed as she daydreamed, she was somewhere else, somewhere far off.

"I love you." I tried to smile. "And no matter what happens, I'll protect you."

"And I promise you that we'll find Jacob." She held my gaze for the longest time.

PART THREE

XXXIV

ENGLAND WAS A FORMIDABLE contrast to Spain.

The weather felt colder, much colder, and the sweeping landscapes bleaker. A round tower greeted us at the mouth of Portsmouth Harbor. We sailed beneath it, passing several British Navy galleys heading in the opposite direction, out of the port. Trade ships vied with us for prime dock space. Our captain's experience paired with his connections won out, and we were soon on dry land again.

I assumed I wasn't the only one amongst the passengers who considered kissing the ground. People scurried about, their faces full of worry. A horrid chaos with no promise of resolution, we edged our way into the center of the frantic crowd, all moving as one, trying to get out.

Our journey had been eventful. We'd endured a storm, barely outsailing a tropical hurricane, and the ship became water logged. For us though, there was temporary respite from the elements as we lay within our wooden chests, self-imposed prisoners, willing the voyage to end, and hating every second of it. And there were the strange circumstances of the disappearance of several of the passengers. We were reassured by our captain that this was unusual, and we were more than welcome to return to Spain as guests upon his ship. Although not responsible for the weather, the same could not be said of the other.

We soon found *The Pride.*

I parted with the last of our money by paying the ship's sailors for information. They admitted to us that several boys had been aboard, the youngest matching Jacob's description. After some coaxing, we ascertained that he'd been quiet during the journey, complaining little, but begging to be taken home. On their arrival, all four boys had been bundled into a horse-drawn carriage.

Struggling to remain calm while hearing all of this bordered on cruel, though my desire to slaughter everyone in our path was crueler. Sunaria's grip on my arm was a constant reminder not to arouse suspicion and put us in harm's way. These men were merely the messengers, witnessing the kidnapping and not partaking in it. As such, they got to see another day.

Portsmouth and London were connected by only the one road. Our carriage wheel came loose causing further delays. We didn't wait for them to attach a new one. We headed out on foot. There seemed to be an ever growing distance between us and the carriage that Jacob traveled in.

I looked forward to ripping out the throats of the men who'd played any part. I wondered how Sunaria could bare to be this close to me. I pushed her away and, if such a thing were possible, at the same time clung to her.

London had swallowed up Jacob's carriage.

Climbing out of ours, we were met by a maze of white-washed, half-timbered houses that lined twisting, filthy lanes. The air was thick, the smell verging on unbearable. It inspired an underlying threat of mayhem. A contrast from my homeland, I was struck by a heavy yearning to return. There seemed to be something about the city's grayness that reflected back onto its populace, who, scurrying about, all seemed eager to buy or sell something, or as we noted on more than one occasion, steal something.

The spire of St Paul's Cathedral rose up out of the skyline, a fervent reminder of the Catholic Church's ironclad rule. People barged past, not wanting to engage.

A foul stench lingered. "Don't people here wash?" I covered my nose, though it didn't make much difference. "That'll be a *no*."

"We need to slow down," Sunaria said.

"What!"

"We'll find him." Sunaria faced me and rested her hands on my shoulders. "Look at me. He's here."

Old wooden homes overlooked narrow drain channels. Sewage flowed nearby. We were in the center of a rundown market. Poverty was everywhere and the difference between the wealthy and poor was easily evident. Those few with money dressed in fine linen, riding on horseback or within plush carriages. In stark contrast, the poor wore homemade, knitted outfits, some donning tatty leather shoes, others even barefoot.

"No one looks more than thirty." I looked at her for answers.

"There's disease here," she said. "That also means few night walkers. Those who do linger are not the sort you want to associate with."

Panic hit me and I heaved in my fear. "When do we start?"

"Tomorrow."

I cursed the daylight, but it was futile to resist. We had to find a safe place for shelter—and soon.

* * * *

The Strand, a street in the City of Westminster, served our needs.

We handed over the first week's rent to a half-blind night porter. Despite his disability, he had no problem counting our money. We insisted that a tour of the apartments was not required.

"Just show us our room," I said. *And make it fast.*

He led us up a winding staircase to the top floor.

Once inside, we took in the modest décor—a medium sized bed, a tatty old side-table, and a chair that I didn't trust to sit in. But the heavy-lined drapes on the only window and the working lock convinced us to stay.

"Better than a mausoleum," I reasoned.

"It'll do," Sunaria said.

Our room overlooked the River Thames. In different circumstances, I'd have admired the vista, but viewing the sprawling city, sweeping miles upon miles of territory, I felt only desperation. When Jacob surfaced, we'd be asleep, and when we emerged, he'd be inside again.

I pulled the curtains, turned, and slid down the wall. With my head in my hands, I sobbed.

* * * *

With despair so terrible, I found it difficult to focus.

Within a week, we'd searched virtually every workhouse in London. Many of them were matchmaking factories. Our third factory of the night was nestled in a rundown neighborhood that verged on the edge of Westminster Abbey. We made our way to the manager's office.

We strolled past child after child, all of them bending over their wooden work benches, laboring away. I searched each face and saw Jacob in all of them. Heads rose in a moment of interest. Big, sunken eyes stared back, and then they returned once again to their tasks at hand. These children would work well into the night and start early again tomorrow.

At the rear of the bleak factory, just off to the right, old straw beds lay stacked up against the far wall. They lived here and slept here, trapped in a cycle of deprivation. Such a sorrowful existence.

But for the chosen few, for those children blessed with health and good bones, an alternative offered hope. A reasonable profit could be made from wealthy family members who, unable to bear children of their own, would seek to adopt. They'd pluck out a child, paying whatever was asked of them. The thought of unscrupulous buyers crossed my mind.

I wanted to open the doors to the factory and yell at the children to run. Though if they did escape, a new threat awaited them. If caught, they'd sustain a severe punishment. The threat of execution was very real, a brutal and undeserving death. More surprising still, this building, along with two thirds of London, belonged to the Church.

The numbness within had for a moment lifted and provided such inner turmoil that I feared my ability to restrain my temper. I took a moment to compose myself.

Easily passing for wealthy aristocrats eager to adopt, we presented ourselves to the owner's wife. The hard-faced woman, Mrs. Amesbury, who wore a permanent scowl, greeted us with a suspicious eye. A harsh task mistress, no doubt.

"We want to pass the child off as ours," Sunaria explained.

"Do I detect Spanish in the gentleman's accent?" Mrs. Amesbury asked.

I gave a nod, trying to suppress any visible disdain.

"Oh, dear, had you come on Wednesday, you might have beaten the other couple to it."

I tried to remain calm.

"We did have a Spanish boy," she spoke slowly. "Didn't say much, though."

"His name?" I asked.

"I can't remember that now." She shook her head. "We have so many boys."

Every sinew in my body felt on edge.

"May we inquire as to the boy's new address?" Sunaria asked.

Mrs. Amesbury smiled through pursed lips. "We never divulge such information. Discretion is so important in this business."

"As it is in ours." My fake demeanor of courtesy fell away.

As Sunaria closed in on her, Mrs. Amesbury's smile faded.

* * * *

Many of the streets were named after the trades practiced there, like Threadneedle Street, the aptly named Tailor's District, or Baker Street, where locals bought their bread. Here in Fleet Street, the wealthy resided—the aristocracy, rich merchants, architects, and men of law.

At the east end of Fleet Street, London's walls rose high, the dark waters of the Fleet River flowed by. One building miraculously untouched by the constant surge—saved, it seemed, by sturdy white brickwork along the riverside—was the Bradbury's residence. Their large town house towered three stories high. Long black timbers split along the front, enhancing its sturdiness.

Mr. and Mrs. Bradbury and their staff had retired to bed.

Kitchen shelves were stacked with dark colored breads, vegetables, and assorted cheeses, their scents permeating the air. Several dead rabbits hung upside-down from the back wall, their eyes frozen in fear. The more savory view was the numerous pots of honey lined along a thin shelf. Jacob enjoyed dipping his finger in the tubs of honey at home. I wondered if he'd been allowed to do that here.

The home extended well back from the street. Its size was larger than it had first appeared.

The thought of seeing Jacob overwhelmed me.

A discarded wooden toy boat lying just outside one of the bedrooms signaled that it may serve as the nursery.

In the corner, a child slept and with a gentle tap on his shoulder, the boy stirred.

My heart sank when I saw that it wasn't my son.

"Jacob?" I whispered. "Is he here?"

The door opened and a woman's silhouette appeared. She carried with her a bronze candleholder. A breeze extinguished the flame.

I assumed I'd just met Lady Bradbury, but ignored her and spun round to face the boy again.

He rubbed his eyes. "He ran off."

Lady Bradbury shrieked.

Sunaria grabbed my arm and, like mere phantoms, we flew out of the window, with a terrible scream trailing behind us.

I landed just beneath the window, inconsolable. I'd lost my son to London.

XXXV

LONDON OFFERED EVERYTHING a man could want.

But all I wanted was Jacob. I scoured the city, searching night after night, ignoring my own needs. With no trace of him, I thought I'd lose my mind. The loss felt unbearable, the emptiness, agony. I blamed myself for not seeing Ricardo's jealousy, should have predicted he'd be as wayward as his father. So many times, I'd showered Jacob with affection, but ignored Ricardo. By spoiling my son, I'd put him in danger. How he'd spied on me without detection, I couldn't work out.

After another agonizing night, I climbed the spiraling steps to our room, cursing my ineptitude.

Once inside, I fell to my knees. "I just want him back," I sobbed. "I just want him back." Tears soaked my shirt.

I crawled into my coffin and the darkness closed in. Horror violated my dreams, transmuting them into nightmares.

* * * *

Sunaria caught up with me. I'd taken a moment to peer over London Bridge to watch my victim's body float down the Thames.

"Oops." I smiled.

She flashed an angry glare. "You think that's funny."

"I assumed he'd sink."

"A month in the city and you're infamous."

"It took me that long?"

"You kill and you don't look back."

"I've been a little distracted."

"They burned our building down."

"What?" I turned to face her.

"Burned to the ground."

"Who?"

"Don't fake interest."

"How do you know it's because of me? Perhaps a candle fell over—"

"I'm assuming it wasn't you who left the rose on my casket this morning?" She glanced at the bobbing corpse. "All you think of is you."

"I was just about to ask about our blind landlord."

"Half-blind."

"Did he get out?"

"So now you pretend to care about someone else."

"Did he?"

"Yes."

I gazed at the city skyline. "Jacob is out there right now, alone."

"You've brought attention to our kind. They don't like that."

"I'll be more careful."

"I'm done cleaning up after your nightly escapades."

"You should be out there searching for him." I stared at the city's nightscape. "Not wasting your time."

"Keeping us alive is not wasting time."

I turned back. "I'm going to find my son and then we're leaving this godforsaken city."

"Are you even listening to me?"

"What do you want me to say?"

"That you'll use discretion," she sighed. "Follow the rules."

I glided up onto the bridge wall. "It's time we came out of the shadows."

"That attitude will get us killed."

With my arms out, I shouted, "Hello, London!"

"Get down."

"Check out the view."

"Get down now!"

I sat on the wall. "It's time the world knew that we're not myth."

"Have you lost your mind?" She joined me up on the ledge and wrapped her arms around my waist. "Please shake out of this."

"I miss Spain."

"I've lost you."

"No."

"Come back to me."

"I'm sorry I put you in harm's way." I kissed her forehead.

"Have you considered that he may have left London?"

"Shit," I said. "Look."

The body caught on the left side of the riverbank.

"Did you hear me?" she continued, impatiently.

Within seconds, it bobbed off again.

"What do you want me to do," I said. "Run between Spain and here?"

"It's just that I wonder if he's trying to find his way home."

"I feel him," I whispered. "He's out there somewhere. Why can't I hear his thoughts?"

"I believe it's because he's so young."

"So unfair."

"What if the Creda left the rose as a warning?" she whispered.

"You're just paranoid."

"I think they're following me."

"Yep, that defines paranoid. It's your imagination."

She hugged me tighter. "I'm worried about you."

"I'm fine, just distracted, that's all."

"I've planned something for you tonight." She leaned against me. "It'll do you good."

I pulled away. "Not interested."

"We'll have dinner together. I've arranged a little something that'll take your mind off London."

The body sank.

"Thank fuck for that." I pulled my knees up and hugged them.

"You need a break." Her words sounded rehearsed. "Lately, you've been backtracking over old ground."

"Whatever it is, I'm not going."

* * * *

Sunaria's persuasion had been impossible to oppose.

Within the Globe Theatre, sitting comfortably in our private box up to the right of the auditorium, we had a good view of both the apron-style stage, and the audience. I finally agreed to attend, half out of guilt for neglecting Sunaria, and half hoping that she might be right, that this evening's diversion might actually be good for me. Maybe it would even silence the internal chatter, if only for an hour or two.

The dialogue-heavy play was ordinary enough, the company of actors portraying a day in the life of a Tudor family. The theme emphasized the moral attitude of supporting a stable government.

Weekly shows were a popular social gathering for the aristocracy. Even the fashions contrasted Spaniards. The women wore such high hats that I wondered how the audience members behind them could see. Many of the men wore what was considered the latest fashion, heavy tunics over their woolen shirts, and breeches. Textures had advanced and enriched color pallets reflected a fresher style, conveying privilege.

Sunaria's clasp tightened. I assumed my fidgeting annoyed her, until I followed her gaze over to one of the other burgundy draped boxes, high up to the left of the stage, and caught sight of Lady Bradbury. Her pale blue glazed stare revealed her boredom. She seemed to sense someone staring at her and our gazes met. Although she'd seen us only for a moment, our dramatic exit from her bedroom window had left an impression.

Her face flushed brightly as she offered her apologies to the three other women who shared her booth. Almost tripping on the hem of her dress, she withdrew.

Through sheer determination, and the reminder from Sunaria's grip, I maneuvered at a laborious pace, not wanting to arouse suspicion. We ran out through the theatre front doors. Lady Bradbury climbed into her horse drawn carriage.

We followed.

The carriage rumbled over cobblestones, past her home, and continued on. Within half an hour, we were flying through a forest, heading for the outskirts of London.

Converging dense woods surrounded a lone house. Lady Bradbury climbed out of the carriage with the horseman's assistance, and headed for the front door. She slammed the brass doorknob and checked behind her.

We sneaked around the back and sidled along the rear wall of the building. I peered into the study. Lady Bradbury conversed with a young man who tried to calm her. I considered that she must have sought out this place soon after our shocking appearance and mysterious disappearance. We had, after all, been two floors up. In order to unravel the truth behind such a marvel, her search had obviously brought her here. And by the way she argued with the man, this was not her first visit.

A tug at my trouser leg made me look down. I flinched in horror at the large dog gnawing through my flesh, sending searing pain into my ankle. Four more hounds turned the corner. I shook off the dog and flew after Sunaria, up and onto the roof. The dogs barked and growled at us, their teeth bared.

Even now, under these circumstances, it was easy to become distracted by the way my torn skin healed, the edges shrinking rapidly. The only evidence from my scrap with the animal was my blood soaked trouser leg.

Sunaria reached for my hand and grasped it. "We have to get out of here."

"Who are they?"

She caught her breath. "Stone Masters."

XXXVI

MY FIRST RUN-IN with our one true enemy, the Stone Masters, left me unimpressed.

They were no more than a handful of men with little sign of leadership, evidenced by their lack of security. An amateur's collection of do-gooders that women like Lady Bradbury sought out for help, only to leave without resolution, failed by men unable to grasp the true extent of London's underworld. These were aristocrats who were awarded responsibility, but lacked the power to effectively alleviate what they saw as a threat. Though I had to admit, the same could not be said for their dogs.

We checked into The Fountain Hotel—one of London's larger hotels—just off the Strand. Guests could come and go with some assurance of privacy, and business and pleasure agreeably mixed. A temporary residence until we found something more suitable.

Sunaria and I had gone our separate ways at my insistence. I reasoned that we'd cover more ground if we split up. Despite her protests, I'd given her no choice.

Bad weather, sleet, and hail, cleared London's streets like nothing else. No one would brave such elements, other than me of course. When eventually the rain did let up, it left a welcome freshness and the air became tolerable, at least for an hour.

I recognized nothing. I'd flown along the darkest streets to the farthest outskirts and dawn threatened to break at any moment. Sparrows broke into song.

I'd run out of time to make it home.

Westminster Abbey welcomed me with its familiar perpendicular style—simple lines and minimal artifacts. I strolled down the aisle tempting daylight, passing under wide arches and admiring the stonework and half-finished stained glass windows—some relaying biblical narratives, others perfectly crafted images of serene saints captured in their moment of martyrdom.

I made my way through the nave then down into the cathedral's lower tenements. With the drop in temperature came the promise of darkness. I peeked into one of the few doors along the corridor and found a burial chamber. Hoping for something more suitable, I trekked on, checking out my temporary dwelling.

I reached a dead end.

My foot splashed into a shallow puddle and I traced its origin. A trickle of water leaked from the roof and trailed under the end wall. I studied the lower bricks.

I ran my fingers up and along until I found the lone brick that jutted out just a little more than the others. I heaved open the doorway and was hit by a burst of cold air and a puff of dust. Excited by my find, I entered and strolled down a long tunnel. Within a few minutes, I had arrived at the end of the passageway and found another door. My skin tingled—nature's way of alerting the undead. Unable to resist, I peeked through a keyhole.

Light!

I flinched and staggered back. A stupid idea to take such a risk. Searing pain settled in my right eye and I bit into my hand to stop me from yelling. Rubbing it, trying to ease the searing stab, blinking several times and willing normal sight to return, I headed back. Once through, I gave the wall a shove and secured the passageway.

The burial chamber would have to do.

I banged the door shut. The air felt clean and the chill actually quite refreshing. Nearby, water dripped. Already, it irritated the hell out of me. When my sight returned, I viewed line upon line of caskets, the scent surprisingly pleasant. From the ornate brickwork and craftsmanship on the dark wood shelving, this place was reserved for the privileged.

A rat scurried around at the back of the chamber. And something else too. *A Vampire.*

"Good evening." I bowed.

Luminescent eyes glared from beneath his hood, which he'd pulled forward, making it difficult to read his expression. Hidden from view, but detectable, a woman lay just around the corner.

I gestured to the door. "As soon as it's dark, I'll leave."

"Who are you?" he asked with a cockney accent.

"Daumia. And you are?"

"Why are you here?"

He had a tall, slender build, not as tall as me, but almost.

"Did Count Delacroix send you?" His hood flopped back and revealed an eighteen-year-old face.

"Who?"

"To take us back?"

"No."

He eyed me suspiciously.

I gave a wry smile. "Nice place you have here."

"Piss off."

"If we're going to spend the night, we might as well be cordial."

"Get out."

"You know quite well that's not possible."

"Turn around and leave."

I shrugged.

He looked puzzled.

"Your name?" I asked.

"Get out!"

As I studied his mind, a stream of confused thoughts flowed. He had no idea that he'd been turned.

He closed his mind, an interesting skill for a fledgling and an ability I still had to master.

"What's wrong with the girl?" I asked, softly.

He glanced in her direction. "You knew we were down here?"

"Well, now I do."

"Don't hurt her."

"Of course not. How long have you been here?" This threatened to be a long night. "Are you a Londoner?"

"Why?"

"I'm just making conversation."

He stared at the door behind me. "I'm Benjamin."

"So this Delacroix . . . ?"

"You really don't know him?"

"Never met him." I stepped closer to the girl.

"Don't!" Benjamin's eyes widened.

"All right, all right. She's not well. I was just—"

"We don't need your help."

"So I can see."

He stumbled, quickly finding his feet again. "I feel . . . kind of . . ."

"How long have you felt like this?"

"A couple of nights. I'm sick."

"Well, you're definitely afflicted."

"You've seen this illness before?"

"You could say that."

"Can you help us?"

I held my patience. "Sure."

"What's wrong with me?" Benjamin's face reddened.

"May I take a look at your friend?"

"Sister."

I turned the corner and there on the floor lay a young girl, sixteen or so, her hair a vibrant titian. I knelt beside her.

"Can you help her?" He looked woeful, as though already aware of the answer.

"What's her name?"

"Rachel."

"She's very pale." I felt a wave of sadness. In his confusion, Benjamin had drank from her, leaving her close to death.

"Does she have what I have?" he asked.

"How did you come to be down here?"

Benjamin settled beside me, his face sallow. "Rachel got a job as a housekeeper and I as a servant at Delacroix's."

"Go on."

"The count found favor with her."

Delacroix had also found favor with Benjamin, but I didn't push it. Again, Benjamin closed his mind to me, providing only controlled glimpses, allowing me just enough to make assumptions.

Benjamin sighed. "The count's behavior was so strange."

"I get the idea."

"No, I don't think you do."

Rachel's bodice was tight. I wanted to loosen it to aid her breathing, but knew how it would appear.

"Is she dying?" he asked.

"I think she is, yes."

Benjamin's anxiety was increasing.

Rachel had not been turned, but if it wasn't done soon, she wouldn't last another night.

"Tell me something," I said, "have you bitten your sister?

"He did send you!"

I strolled under the stone archway and laid down on one of the coffins. I rested my hands behind my head and crossed one leg over the other. Uncomfortable, but I'd known worse.

"You're going to wait until I fall asleep." Benjamin's face contorted in fear. "Then you're going to kill me."

"A moment ago, I was taking you back to the count."

There'd be no rest today. The last thing I needed was to fall asleep while trapped with a crazed teenager.

I retraced my steps through London, rethought my strategy for finding Jacob. With nothing to distract me, my mind raced. I liked to stay busy, the only way to keep my inner ghosts at bay. I glanced over at Benjamin. His deranged stare was all I needed to look away.

Hours passed . . .

I tried to convey the cathedral to Sunaria, though she'd probably be asleep by now. My gaze wandered over to the exit.

"You can't go out, either?" Benjamin broke the silence. "You have what we have?"

I loosened my shirt collar.

"How do I know," he heaved the deepest sigh, "that we can trust you?"

I stared off.

"Well?" he asked.

"My actions."

Benjamin fell quiet. Rachel's fevered dreams caused her to sob. Her sighs echoed.

"How come she has red hair and you don't?" I studied him.

"Don't know."

The ceiling's paint peeled. The painter had done a shoddy job trying to cover up the cracks. Probably, like me, he'd not wanted to hang out in here any longer than necessary.

Benjamin's sense of melancholy reminded me of my own at his age. Occasionally, he tended to his sister, unable to bear to see her fading. He didn't stay beside her for long. At one point, I caught him sucking on the back of his hand.

I remembered that feeling.

The drip, drip, drip that broke the silence really pissed me off. Despite my better judgment, I dozed off.

I jolted awake. Benjamin's face loomed over me. I eased him away.

"Is it true that we can live forever?" he said.

"The count told you that?"

"Yes."

"So you have some idea of what happened to you then?"

"Is it true?"

I shrugged.

He frowned. "You don't trust me."

"Don't take it personally."

"The count told me he was over six hundred years old."

"Interesting."

Whoever had turned Benjamin had left him for dead, though Sunaria insisted that this taught a newly turned vampire how to survive. I'd take my protégés under my wing and nurture them. The perfect patriarch honored the responsibly from their first night, and stayed with them until they'd adjusted.

Glancing at Benjamin again, I questioned the sanity of turning anyone, especially if his sister had his annoying traits. The thought of Benjamin hanging around caused me to cringe. The old ways certainly encouraged the survival instinct to take over. It was better to respect my elders and do as they did. My guilt lifted.

Thank fuck for that.

Until now, I'd not wanted to turn anyone. I still needed time to come to terms with my own transformation, though if neither of us helped his sister soon, do the dark deed, she'd be dead. In my hands, I held the key to eternal life. If I went through with it, she'd be my first. And my last.

No time for such indulgence or unselfish acts of kindness of which Sunaria would never approve. This place closed in and I badly wanted out. A sense of relief came as my preternatural inner rhythm hinted that day had faded.

Benjamin squinted my way. "How do I know you aren't tricking me?"

Because in half-an-hour, I'll be gone.

Rachel stirred.

"If you don't help her, she'll die," he whispered.

I gave a sympathetic smile and my gaze roamed the chamber.

"Please help us." Benjamin shifted closer.

"How do you want me to help you?"

"To understand."

I slid off the coffin.

"These cravings," he murmured.

Soon, I'd be outside and the night air would be cool. Even though an unpleasant city aroma would greet me, I'd welcome it. Thoughts of relief came with the idea that I'd soon be out of there, and this place would be an annoying memory.

His stare was vacant now. "I'm so hungry."

I reached into my pocket. "Here." I offered him several coins.

"What's that for?"

"Get your sister to a doctor." As I handed over the money, it dawned on me that if a physician examined either of them, a stake through the heart might be the treatment of choice.

"My thirst is driving me to do terrible things," he confessed.

"Control it."

Benjamin fell to his knees. "I'm craving rats."

"Think of something else."

"Like what?"

"Your future."

"See, you can help me, you know what this thing is." Benjamin threw himself at my feet and wrapped his arms around my legs.

I regained my balance.

"I'm so afraid," he sobbed.

"Please let go." I pushed him away. "Just stay clear of daylight."

"Don't leave us like this."

I sat back on the edge of a casket.

"Can you help us?" He grasped his hands in prayer.

"Look, just give her some of your blood."

"What?"

"You're special now."

"I'm damned."

"Come here." I ran my fingers over his face. He'd been transformed unshaven and he'd remain that way.

Benjamin softened.

"I was also confused," I said, "when I was first turned. Like you, I struggled to understand my desires."

He leaned into my chest.

I embraced him. "Benjamin, there's no going back. You must come to terms with what you are." I kissed his matted hair. My teeth pierced my wrist and blood trickled. Benjamin leaned in and followed the scarlet trail, pressing his lips up against the gash.

Thoughts of Jacob came to mind, how I'd enjoyed taking care of him. Now I bestowed a different kind of nurturing. After all that had unraveled in my life, I'd managed to hold onto the last remnants of kindness, bestowing it now to this sweet, frightened boy.

He let go and stared at me in awe, his mouth and chin covered in red smudges.

"Feel better?" I asked.

He gave a nod. I ran my fingers through his hair and Benjamin swooned.

I pulled away from him. "Let me give some to Rachel."

"It's all my fault."

"Life takes us down roads that we are unprepared for."

"Your son?"

Despite trying to lock him out, he'd glimpsed images. "You'll need to feed like that once every night," I said. "Take criminals. It'll be easier. Just take a few sips and let them drink a little back and they'll remember nothing."

"But you've not done that for awhile?"

He'd done more than glimpse. "Just don't get caught." I emphasized the importance of that statement with a pointed finger.

There was truth in his words, that I'd far from taken my own advice. Over the last few weeks, I'd been so crazed that they'd been no small drinks, rather a sucking dry. "I need to go back to my old ways."

Even though I'd taken thieves and murderers, I couldn't shake the guilt and, when least expected, the memory of their faces revisited me.

As though full of wonder, his eyes widened. "Such a life you've had."

An unfamiliar sense of affection filled me. I'd been so distracted lately that I'd forgotten how kindness felt. As soon as I saw Sunaria, I'd remind her how much she meant to me. Her patience had been extraordinary. Despite the fact that I'd pushed her away, she'd stayed. I missed her.

"Perhaps you should turn away." I encouraged him.

"What are you going to do?"

"Save her." I pulled Rachel into my arms. Her soft, spiraling curls tumbled over my forearm.

She gazed up and I smiled at her and gestured to Benjamin. She turned her head to look at him and gave a frown.

"Please hurry." Benjamin placed a hand over her eyes. "It's best she doesn't look."

"And you," I said. "Turn away."

I leaned into her neck and kissed her milky, soft skin. Rachel shuddered. Flawless pleasure, the purest claret stolen from an innocent. Images so perfect that I hesitated to cease, indulging in the moment, aware enough that it wasn't mine.

Another bite into my wrist and blood flowed again, dropping onto her grey lips and trickling into her dry, plump mouth. Rachel's tongue greeted the bloody drops, her breasts rising and falling. A hint of lavender wafted. Rachel and I shared the lull. She quivered again as she swallowed, and death's scent dissipated. Her cheeks, once a dusky hue, now flushed.

The door flew open.

The silhouette of a large man loomed. With lightning speed, he neared us. A vampire *Status Regal*, a haunting, evocative face, transformed in his late forties, or so. He had a hooked nose and a heavy lidded gaze that bestowed a seductive quality. Dressed lavishly, he emanated wealth.

From Benjamin's expression, I assumed I'd just met Count Delacroix. He didn't blink as he traced Rachel's curves with a lustful stare and then his gaze fell onto Benjamin.

"Stay where you are, Benjamin." I shot him a look of insistence.

Benjamin prodded Rachel's arm.

With an iron-clad grip, Delacroix clutched my wrist. A strange hypnosis ensued. He still hadn't blinked. A familiar trance-like sensation filled me, one that Sunaria had tried on me once. I hadn't liked it then, hating the powerlessness it wrought. With all of my will, I fought his.

Rachel tugged on my trouser leg and broke the spell.

"The Manor, Belgravia," the count commanded. His voice had an unearthly resonance. "Bring her."

Rachel reached for me and I interlocked my fingers through hers.

"If I'm not mistaken," his crooked smile widened, "you'll see a fair exchange in Rachel for Sunaria."

Delacroix vanished.

"Who's Sunaria?" Benjamin said.

XXXVII

THE COUNT'S HOME WAS a sprawling gothic mansion of extraordinary character.

The striking facade rose out of the midst of the lesser homes surrounding it. The magnificent workmanship suggested French design. Blackfriars Manor was forged into the entry gate's cast-iron arch. With my hands formed into fists, I reconsidered. My time could be better spent.

I'd not brought the girl.

On my detour via The Fountain Hotel, I'd panicked at not finding Sunaria. No open book, her latest read, just the clothes she'd worn the previous night, neatly folded over the armchair. Everything was exactly where she'd left it, with no sign of a struggle.

Delacroix had a penchant for manipulation.

Sunaria hadn't lived this long without learning a thing or two about survival. She'd be too fast for this bully of a vampire, but a nagging doubt refused to let up. The fact that I still hadn't heard from her made me cautious.

The castle was a bedrock of power, a veritable vampire's lair. High florid railings encircled the property and served to deter. Anyone who visited would probably never find his way out.

I yanked open the gate. Gravel crunched beneath my feet as I neared the manor. It rose into the starlit sky, four floors up. Slender vertical columns and dramatic arches dominated the facade. Surprisingly, the structure had many windows, but these were shuttered. Stone hunting dogs sat halfway up huge towers with melodramatic carved details, threatening to pounce on an unsuspecting visitor. The edifice was easily out of place compared with the modern buildings that had sprung up around it. Unknowingly, mortals had nestled into a dangerous domain.

I tried to get a sense of what lay within.

Transforming Rachel had been remarkable. A wave of emotions flowed through me at her rebirth, as Rachel's beauty had intensified, if such a thing were possible, and afterward, within my arms slept titian haired perfection. She'd risen with an expression of wonder, as she took in the world with renewed senses. Benjamin asked that it be he who explained what had befallen her. He wanted to give her time to adjust. Memories of my own death and life again came flooding back.

There'd been awe in Rachel's gaze as those big green eyes of hers had fixed on her maker. A bond forged in blood. A token bride fit for a count. He'd plucked her out of a crowd of mortals for his very pleasure.

Caught off guard, an uncommon devotion for the girl whom I'd saved, as an extraordinary ardor captured me, prevailing a feeling that I'd always known her. I considered this was the reason vampires kept their young. Sunaria had obsessed over me and even now with my behavior as wayward as it had become, she still loved me. As only the bearer of a life can.

The oak doorway squeaked on its hinges. Candlelight threw shadows over the spacious foyer and up the sweeping staircase. Vampires were everywhere, just casually mingling. Their attire reflected wealth—the finest linens for the men and lavish velvets for the women. All leaning toward darker colors, they'd blend in with the night. This sophisticated crowd easily passed for aristocracy. I was regarded for a moment by them, then—much to my relief—ignored. Their conversations continued as their stares fell away.

No sign of Delacroix, and no detection of Sunaria, caused me to question the sanity of my decision to come here. Receiving an occasional glance, I continued on through. Lavish décor, though signs of wear and tear, and casting an eerie atmosphere were line upon line of weird looking characters represented in numerous paintings, strewn randomly upon the walls. I ascended the stairs and they creaked underfoot. A slight wobble of the banister proved my theory. This place had to be over one-hundred years old.

One had a sense that soon these nightwalkers would be out stalking. Unknowingly, I'd walked amongst them, naively unaware that I'd shared the city with so many.

I proceeded down the north corridor, passing a few lone characters, focusing on the way ahead. The vastness of the place caused a nagging futility. I pushed all thoughts of my son away. Sunaria, too.

Within one of the rooms hung a portrait of Delacroix above the fireplace. Dressed in Italian fashion, he held a carnival mask by his side. His wry smile revealed a knowing expression. Several other masked characters stood behind him. I didn't need to see their faces to know they were shady. At the end of the far wall, I tried to exit through a fake door that, when opened, revealed not an exit, but a brick wall. A clock on the mantelpiece ticked away, but the time was off. The dial lied that it was morning.

Delacroix' library appeared well stocked. For a split second, I wanted to linger, but with no time for such indulgence, I headed out and trekked down the corridor.

Two vampires were in the throes of passion on an overly embroidered couch. The female straddled the male, who controlled her pace. Her long raven hair was so similar to Sunaria's that it was alarming. She paused and turned to glance at me, then turned and resumed as though I weren't there. Her partner gestured for me to join them.

Heading back the way I came, I passed a sorry looking vampire, and at first considered whether to ask him if he'd seen Sunaria, but thought better of it. I peeked back down into the main foyer and caught a glimpse of Delacroix just before he disappeared.

Into the shadows, I followed him. He disappeared through a doorway and descended a dark stairwell. The lower I went, the lower the temperature. As I reached the end, I almost crashed into a towering, carved stone statue of a naked man. The six foot sculpture guarded the entrance, strangely out of place. I passed under the arched doorway and headed further on in. Three gaping tunnels lay just ahead.

A loud bang behind me made me jump.

I flew back toward the door and tried to turn the brass handle. It was locked. I yelled with anger. Something had been shoved up against the door. The stone sculpture by the sound of it.

I chose the east corridor, careful of my footing as I traced along the wet ground. A rat scurried over my foot. I broke into a sprint as the tunnel veered off to the right. The cold water deepened and the darkness wrapped itself tighter around me the further I went in. Waist deep, I waded on, nervous of what may be lurking.

Sunaria, can you hear me?

Swimming through murky water, the never ending tunnel narrowed, and brick work crumbled. When a bloated body floated by, face down. I turned around.

Dripping wet, I ran down the middle corridor. After ten minutes, I reached a dead end. Layers of clay had been heaped over the exit, shoddy workmanship, but effective. My wet clothes cleaved to my skin.

My last choice was the left tunnel, the ground patterned with dark stains and dead insects. With my handkerchief pressed up against my nose, I rallied my courage and continued on. A series of doors lined the way. I reached the last one, another dead end. If ever I met with Delacroix again, I'd thank him for his hospitality.

And then kill him.

I prized open a rusty hinged door and peered in. A lone chair with leather straps that hung from the armrests was positioned in the center. Beside it lay a small table, strewn with assorted instruments and strange contraptions, designed for the sole purpose of torture. My gaze hovered over the worn saw. From the sticky discolorations on the floor, it had been used recently. Lined along the far wall upon poorly constructed wooden shelves was a collection of oddities—stuffed dead animals, their fake eyes bulging. The skeletal remains of small creatures, impossible to make out what they'd once been, were ghoulishly preserved. Lined along the top shelf were large glass bottles filled to the brim with stained water.

I approached and peered into one of the jars.

Through the cloudiness, I made out a familiar shape. "Bloody hell!" A floating severed hand, pallid and wrinkled. For a split second, I thought that the middle finger twitched. On the small finger, a gold band with an ornate crest was embossed into the metal. I pressed my nose up against the jar.

The hand jerked.

"Fuck!" I leaped back.

The clang of the door echoed as I slammed it shut.

A sob startled me. Using caution, I followed the noise and peered into the end jail. Two young men and a girl, wearing rags, were shackled to the wall. Studying their faces, hoping for a sign that would indicate sanity, I stepped inside and tried to mouth breathe to avoid the stench.

"Take me," the redheaded man muttered. Tatty spectacles balanced on the bridge of his nose, his right lens smashed.

I shook my head.

"Did Evan send you?" the girl asked.

She looked about fifteen, but her dimpled cheeks, button nose, and pony tails were misleading. I wondered if it had been Evan's corpse that had floated past me.

"Have you seen a woman, twenty-ish," I asked, "raven hair, the bluest eyes?"

"She's gone missing, as well?" said the redheaded man.

"Others have gone missing?" I asked.

He answered with a nod. "Her brother and my sister."

"She has red hair, like you?" I stepped closer.

"Have you seen her?" He shuffled uncomfortably. "Her name's Rachel."

"She's with Benjamin." I peeked down the corridor.

"Who's Benjamin?" His voice was tinged with fear.

I hid my surprise and knelt beside him.

"She's safe," he said. "That's all I needed to hear."

I wondered if there could be another Rachel, but their similarities went beyond just their hair color.

"Who's this Benjamin?" he asked again.

"A friend of your sister's."

He squinted at me. "Where did you see her?"

"In the cathedral."

"She disappeared two nights ago." He sounded miserable.

I tried to take my thoughts off Benjamin and why he'd lied. Perhaps he'd tried to protect her.

"Did you talk with her?" he asked.

"Not really." I glanced at the sickly, young man in the corner.

Stress and sleep deprivation had aged them. The redheaded man looked thirty, but he could have been younger.

"What's your story?" I pointed to the chains.

"What's your name?" he asked.

"Daumia."

"You're not from around here, are you?"

"No," I replied, half-distracted.

"We thought the house was empty," he continued, weakly.

"You were trespassing?"

He held up the shackle's chain. "Our punishment."

"How long have you been down here?"

"About three days." He gestured to himself, "I'm Marcus," then pointed, "Lilly and Ted." He fiddled with his shackle. "Take off your jacket. You'll catch your death."

Though the cold didn't affect me, I removed it nonetheless. Lilly needed it more, so I laid it by her side. When it dried, it would provide some well needed warmth, but I hoped we'd be out of here by then.

"We promise we'll leave quietly," Ted's voice wavered.

"I'm not the one you need to convince." I gave a comforting smile.

"Can you reason with him?" Marcus asked.

"Delacroix?"

Marcus fidgeted. "Is that his name?"

I nodded. "I don't think that's an option."

Marcus slumped in despair.

Lilly leaned back against the brick and wrapped her arms around her legs and rocked.

"When did you last see your friend?" Marcus asked.

"Last night," I said.

"What makes you think she's here?"

"How can you even see out of those glasses?" I asked Marcus.

He nudged them up the bridge of his nose. "Well, do you know anywhere down here where I can purchase a new pair?"

"Will you talk to them for us?" Lilly asked.

I nodded, though knew it would be useless.

Marcus leaned. "Can you help us?"

"Evan must have made it," Lilly said. "I knew he would."

While examining Marcus' shackle, I marveled at my actions. I'd spent the last few months feeding off mortals, and here, now, as though compelled to heroism, I wanted to aid an escape. The thought of anyone in that torture chair motivated my valor. I grabbed Marcus' slim wrist and eased it through the shackle.

I followed his stare and peeled back his trouser leg. His calf was badly deformed, the skin mottled and bruised.

"I've lost weight so it was easy to pull my wrist out." Marcus gazed off. "Last night, I headed down the middle tunnel."

I cringed.

Marcus nodded.

"It's sealed with some kind of clay," I said.

"Wasn't last night. They must have done it after they snapped my leg."

"I'll carry you."

"You're going to have to carry him." Marcus nodded toward Ted.

I locked gazes with Marcus. "I'll come back for you."

"Why are you helping us?" Lilly mumbled.

"Why not?" I glanced at Ted. "What happened to him?"

"He thinks that one of them bit him," Marcus whispered. "He thinks the man drank his blood."

Ted stirred. "He *did* fucking drink my blood."

"He's been in and out all night." Lilly's voice was low.

Marcus gave me a pointed look. "You didn't answer her question."

"I'm a victim too," I said. "I'm not leaving you down here."

Lilly's brow furrowed. "You could be saving yourself."

"I fully intend to."

"Can you get us out?" she asked.

"Yes."

"Do you promise?" she said.

"Yes." I headed for the door.

Marcus grabbed my ankle and whispered, "Who are you really?"

"I told you." I pulled away.

Marcus ran his soiled fingers through his hair. "Why should we trust you?"

"Do you have another option?"

He swallowed hard. "What's your plan?"

"I'm going to prize open your shackles."

"We're as good as dead." Marcus slouched back against the wall.

"Thank you for saving us," Lilly said.

Ripping the shackles from the wall would be easy to explain away as corrosion, but the clanging of the chains would alert our enemy. They'd have to come off.

"These things are so rusty." I grabbed hold of Lilly's cuff.

Masonry sprayed, splattering me with dust, and the chain hung from Lilly's wrist. She gawped her surprise.

"Why look at that." I shook my head in fake amazement. "Turns out I'm stronger than I thought." I yanked open the metal cuff.

"How the hell did you do that?" Ted sat up.

With a snap, the metal gave on his cuff, too.

They rubbed their wrists. I considered Marcus' leg. A sip of blood would do the trick, but Lilly and Ted would probably freak out. Ted was so weak, I doubted he'd last long. He clambered to his feet, leaned on me, and I took his weight.

Marcus shook his head. "I'll slow you down. Just get them out."

"I'll come back," I said.

"If your chance comes, take it and don't look back."

"A promise is a promise." I flashed a smile, though it was out of place.

Lilly, Ted, and I headed down the corridor and soon made it to the door that was now open. We passed the statue that someone had pushed back into its original position, and ascended the stairs, then crept our way through the empty foyer. With a turn of the door handle came the cool breeze of freedom. I shoved Lilly and Ted out and slammed the door shut.

Delacroix came out of nowhere and threw me at the foot of the stairs. My head bashed against the banister. Not since I'd taken Felipe on had I felt such fury. Delacroix's servants reappeared, dragging Lilly and Ted in with them.

A wave of despair hit me hard.

Lilly and Ted cowered with fear. Fumbling hands behind me tied my wrists together with fine rope, so tight that my hands grew numb. I struggled to get free, but they overpowered me. Delacroix's iron-glad grip crushed my throat and his gaze bore into mine.

Lilly and Ted were hauled away.

I glanced up at the ceiling. Even with my hands bound, I believed I could rise, but if I escaped, it would seal their fate.

Delacroix struck my face and my jaw cracked. He leaned in and his tongue lapped at my neck.

I jolted when he bit hard.

He stormed on into my psyche. I struggled to stay conscious as he pillaged the farthest recesses. He was draining me.

I sank to my knees and my face struck the floor. Delacroix's shoes were the last thing I saw.

* * * *

I was back in the cell.

I'd been shackled to the wall. I resisted the weight of the chain and ran my fingers along my neck. My shirt was stained in blood. Marcus stared back. His shackle had been refitted around his left wrist. Lilly and Ted had also been re-secured.

"What happened?" Marcus appeared even more worn down.

Sunaria, where are you? I didn't even sense her, and hated the thought that she may be in danger. "I'm getting us out of here."

Marcus glanced uneasily at the others. "Yeah, we can see that."

I stretched out.

"So this is all part of your master plan?" Marcus asked.

"So far, so good." I ran my fingers through my matted hair and scratched my itchy scalp.

Marcus shook his head. "We're as good as dead."

I raised an eyebrow. "That's one option, yes." I lifted my shirt collar to hide Delacroix's fang marks, unsure if they'd dissipated.

Marcus leaned back. "What do they have over you?"

I shoveled into a more comfortable position.

"Perhaps I shouldn't ask." Marcus threw my jacket at me. "Here, you look like you need it."

I wrapped it around my shoulders.

"Where are you from?" Marcus' tone was laden with suspicion.

"Spain."

"Near Scotland?" Lilly said.

I laughed and then realized she wasn't joking.

"It's across the sea, Lilly," Marcus frowned. "He's a foreigner."

"What's it like?" Lilly asked.

Examining my metal cuff, I tracked the links up and along to where it met the brick.

"How far away is it?" Lilly asked.

I tugged the chain and dust sprayed as the bolts loosened. Somewhere within the house, a violin struck up.

"Like things can't get any creepier." Marcus stared at the wall.

"I run errands for Mr. Simons." Lilly sat up. "He owns the bakery."

With my fingers wrapped around the chain, I prepared to give it another tug.

"I deliver groceries," she continued. "One time, I went to the wrong door of the great house in Greenwich, not the servants', but the main one."

With an incredulous expression, I said. "What's your point, exactly?"

"Well, I got into trouble and Mr. Simons refused to read to me."

"Lilly loves books," Marcus explained. "Mr. Simons reads to her."

"It's just that you're a man of education," Lilly said.

I gazed off.

Lilly leaned forward."Perhaps you could read to me?"

"Sure."

"I'm sorry," Lilly sighed. "You're worried about your friend and I'm talking about—"

"Books are a good distraction." I rubbed my temples.

"What's a distraction?"

"Distraction," I corrected her. "Well, say you're trying to think that you're not in here, for example. You could read a good book and forget that you're . . ."

"In here." Lilly's tears streamed.

I hugged her. "I'll read to you, Lilly."

She softened into me.

I looked at each one of them. "I will get us out."

Lilly's mortal scent arose. I suppressed all desire and ignored the carnal drag. Lilly calmed, full of trust. I did for a moment feel like my old self again, the man who'd acted with integrity. I covered her with my half-dry jacket, providing some warmth. With a rusty, grinding clang, I opened my metal cuff and slowly rose to my feet.

A key turned in the lock and the door swung open. Delacroix greeted me with that crazed, half smile of his, and just behind him lingered three of his minions.

"I was promised a room with a view," I said.

Delacroix's servants dragged me out, pulling me along the corridor. I fought against them, digging my heels in. They forced me into the torture chamber and shoved me into the chair, strapping me in.

Delacroix loomed over me.

"Maybe it's just me," I said, "but I think I've pissed you off?"

The chair flew back, tilted in such a way that I now lay flat staring up at the ceiling. From an upside-down perspective, I viewed the jars on the back wall.

Benjamin stood quietly in the corner. Delacroix turned and walked out of the room, leaving us alone.

"I came here looking for you." Benjamin swallowed, hard.
"Untie me," I said.
Benjamin hesitated.
"I told you to wait for me." I tried to squirm free.
Benjamin shrugged.
"Does he have Rachel?" I asked.
"No."
"Why did you tell me that Rachel's your sister?"
"I didn't think you'd help us otherwise."
"Hurry up and get these straps untied."
He gazed at me.
"I'm not angry with you," I said. "You need to get out of here."
"Not without you." He loomed over me.
"I can look after myself." I tugged. "Famous last words."
Benjamin fiddled with my right strap.
"Have you seen Sunaria?" I asked.
"No."
"Stupid question." I shook my head. "You don't even know what she looks like. Has he hurt you?"
"He's been kind to me."
"I can imagine." I raised an eyebrow.
"What's in those jars?" Benjamin asked.
"It's probably best if you don't know."
He stared at me with hungry eyes.
"That's tighter," I suppressed my annoyance. "You've pulled it the wrong way."
Benjamin glanced at my neck and then checked the strap.
"Don't even think about it." I bit into my lower lip in frustration.
He licked his lips.
"I'm serious," I said.
With shocking speed, he flung himself at me and I felt the sharp sting of his fangs in my neck and his full weight on me. He let out a muffled groan, gulping loudly.

* * * *

Delacroix loomed over me.
My tongue cleaved to the roof of my mouth and I tried to hold my head up, looking for Benjamin. Delacroix held his wrist over me. He'd made a small incision there and blood promised to drip. My tongue gratefully received the red droplets. They stung my taste buds. I wanted more, needed more.
"What do you want?" I rasped.
The wrist straps were painfully tight, and I felt a surge of panic when I saw two men holding Lilly. She looked terrified. My sobs escaped through my clenched jaw. Delacroix waved the saw in my face and then rested the blades against my right wrist, sending blinding pain into my

hand and back up my arm, as the blades ran along. The warmth and stickiness of spurting blood caused my head to spin.

Lilly's screams were deafening.

"Shut your eyes, Lilly," I yelled as the saw gnawed back and forth.

Delacroix stopped and ran his fingertips over the bloody blades. Lilly was close to fainting. Her eyelids flickered.

The pain receded. "Let her go."

Delacroix studied the blades.

My left arm broke free but was quickly restrained. They shoved Lilly forward, leaned so close that her neck came within reach, her scent a mixture of fear and sweat. The blade came down upon my right wrist again and pressed into my flesh.

Delacroix pointed at Lilly.

"This is not who I am." Terror washed over me. "This is barbaric." I turned my head away.

Agony, the serrated edge sawed and scraped through muscle. I screamed again and again, sucking in air as the blades reached the bone and continued on through.

Morality dissipated.

Numbness now where my hand had been, and a phantom pain reached my fingertips. I dared not look. The blade rested against my left wrist now. A cruel tease as it sliced. I sprang forward and buried my fangs into Lilly's neck. *"Forgive me . . . forgive me . . ."*

She didn't even flinch, too terrified to move, as I absorbed her fears, unfolding memories stolen by the unworthy. This perfect child with her dimpled cheeks and button nose, her trust betrayed. I shared her thoughts as they faded.

My lips trembled as I felt her go. *"Don't forgive me."*

They carried her body out.

"No . . . no . . . no!" I sobbed.

Grasping onto thoughts of her, I buried them deep within, refusing to let her fade. I clutched at the remnants of her memory. Something inside snapped, a realization of the monstrosity of what I was. My excuses had no foundation and denial was impossible. Thrashing, unable to suppress my rage, I felt the right strap give.

Groping hands held me down and, with a shove, Delacroix pressed my severed hand back against my blood soaked stump. I surrendered to the vertigo caused by the excruciating sensation of nerve endings realigning.

* * * *

"Lilly, is she all right?" Marcus' lips quivered.

This time, they'd not chained me. The prison walls closed in. Relieved that my hands were still attached, I opened and closed my fingers instinctively. No evidence of what Delacroix had done to me, I massaged my wrists anyway.

"We heard screaming." Marcus shook.

Leaning with my back against the cold stone, I wrapped my arms around my legs.

"What did he do?" Marcus' gaze fixed on my shirt. "Where's Lilly?"

I looked down, ashamed.

"Whose blood is that?" he said.

I glanced at my soaked shirt, and then up at Ted. His shallow breaths signaled that he neared death.

"Can you help him?" Marcus asked.

"Let him die."

"What?"

"At least one of us will be at peace."

Marcus slumped against the wall.

"I want to find my son, find Sunaria, and go back to Spain," I murmured.

"You're our only hope of getting out of here."

I sobbed.

"Whatever happened in there," Marcus said, "it wasn't your fault. He's a monster."

"I'm the monster." My vision blurred with tears.

"No, Delacroix's a sadist. You, me, we're the victims here."

"I'll never forgive myself," I whispered.

"God will forgive you. He forgives those—"

"Don't spout religion at me," I snapped.

"I'm just trying to help."

"You're not."

"It's always comforted me."

"What? Like after you steal, you ask for forgiveness? How convenient."

"Don't you dare judge me. You don't know me."

Ted moaned.

"I just need quiet to think." I rubbed my wrists.

"Taxes forced us into the city." Marcus' nostrils flared. "But they hire children. It's cheaper. We work for virtually nothing, twelve hours a day, seven days a week, and all we get is scraps. So yes, when we heard this place was empty, we foraged. We trespassed." He held up his wrist and the chain dangled. "But I think I've served my time. Don't you?"

Ted coughed.

"Sunaria, that's the name of your friend?" Marcus asked.

I nodded.

"Well, she needs you."

"It's my fault she's in danger."

"Delacroix's the one to blame. Shit! Coming here was my idea," he said.

I climbed to my feet.

"When we get out of here," Marcus gestured his belief that we would, "I'm going to show you the London that I know. The street acts, poets, and playwrights, and the artists. Have you ever been to Covent Garden?"

I checked the door and found it locked. "No, I've been a little busy lately."

"Venetian's best painters have traveled to London and—"

"Sounds *lovely*!" It was impossible to suppress the sarcasm in my tone.

"I'm going to help you find your friend," Marcus vowed. "And then all three of us can visit artist's row."

A bang rattled on the other side of the door.

We shared a glance and I stepped back, ready to fight.

Benjamin entered.

I looked at Marcus. "Do you know him?"

Marcus shook his head.

"I'm sorry about earlier." Benjamin blinked several times. "He told me he'd kill me if I didn't do it."

"What did he do?" Marcus asked.

"Where's Delacroix?" I asked.

"He's gone out," Benjamin said.

"And he lets you just roam around?" I considered his shifty eyes. "I don't believe you."

"Have you seen Lilly?" Marcus asked.

Benjamin gave me a sorry look. "Perhaps you should, um . . ."

I hated Benjamin for suggesting it. I turned to Marcus. "I'll carry you."

"There's no time." Benjamin's expression hardened.

I hesitated. "I'm not leaving without him."

"Delacroix has Sunaria." Benjamin scratched his chin and looked away.

I stepped closer, wanting to believe him.

"I saw her." He nodded and glanced my way.

"Where?"

"Upstairs, in one of the bedrooms," Benjamin said. "I couldn't leave without telling you."

"How do you know it was her?" I asked.

"Kind of glimpsed her when I," Benjamin glanced at Marcus and then back at me, "you know."

"Is she guarded?" Marcus asked.

"No." Benjamin pulled at my shirt sleeve. "We don't have much time."

I knelt at Marcus' side. "I'll get Sunaria and then I'll come back for you," I whispered. "Your sister's at the River Thames Inn."

Marcus nodded. "If you see Delacroix, kill the bastard."

* * * *

I followed Benjamin up the steps and through the house, vigilant for any sign of a wayward vampire, and wary that this seemed too easy. We reached the landing and Benjamin pointed to an oak door, a few rooms down.

"In there?" I asked.

Benjamin nodded.

I didn't sense her as I approached.

"She's unconscious," Benjamin said, as though reading my mind, but closing his.

"Now get out of here." I turned the handle.

Benjamin strolled away, back down the corridor.

The room was pitch black. I sized up the shadows. In a corner chair sat Delacroix.

The panic hit me like a fist. "What is this?"

Delacroix's grin caused a chill. Benjamin sauntered in and sat on the floor next to Delacroix.

"So how old are you really?" I asked Benjamin.

"Fifty."

I scowled at him. "You snide little shit."

Benjamin shrugged. "Got a lot of stuff from that little drink I had."

My knuckles were white. "Sunaria was never here, was she?"

My filthy jacket lay on the end of the bed. Delacroix picked it up and offered it to me.

"I'm free to go?" I studied them, listening to my gut feeling that screamed danger. "Just like that?"

Delacroix wrapped my jacket around my shoulders and patted my back.

I tried not to cringe. "What about the others?"

He strolled over to the bed and lay upon it, placing his hands behind his head.

Benjamin folded his arms. "He wants you to go back and finish off your cell mates."

"Yeah, right." I headed for the door.

Delacroix's gaze fell on my jacket pocket and I reached in and pulled out a silver locket, immediately recognizing it as the one I'd given to Jacob. My legs felt weak.

Delacroix snapped his fingers and Benjamin jumped up like a well-trained dog and dropped to his knees beside Delacroix, who patted his head and scrunched his hair. Benjamin's eyelids flickered in pleasure.

"Do you want to see your son again?" Benjamin asked.

I glared at Delacroix. "Why doesn't the count ask me this himself?"

"The offer is about to be rescinded," the count mumbled.

* * * *

I entered the cell.

"Did you find her?" Marcus asked.

Kneeling beside Ted, I tilted his head and bit into his neck and he trembled beneath me. Lost in the drink, I followed the pathway of another life. Marcus screamed but his cries sounded distant, as flashes of images flooded my senses. Ted's breathing quickened and then became shallow.

And then ceased, proceeded by the slowing, and then stilling of his heart.

Marcus hacked through his wrist with a splinter of stone. Blood spurted. His spectacles tumbled off as he collapsed and I reached for his bleeding wrist and suckled, glimpsing his wavering thoughts.

I forgive you, he conveyed. *Now find your son.*

Jolted out of my trance, I slowed. With my fangs buried into my wrist, I drew blood and shoved my arm against his lips. Marcus gasped for air, unable to resist the supernatural snare. His hips pumped the air as he rode out the bliss, the perfect pleasure betraying him.

Marcus lay dead in my arms.

I jumped when he shuddered, his mouth wide in a silent scream.

Reborn.

Realizing what I'd done, I pushed him off me. Marcus reached for the stone again and I kicked it out of his reach. His hair was now a striking titian and his green eyes were piercing. He pulled up his trouser leg to see his injury healed, the bruises gone.

He flew at me. "What is this?"

I shoved him back.

Marcus slammed against the wall. "There is no Sunaria, is there?"

"What?"

"You work for him?"

"No."

"What have you done?" Marcus found his spectacles and with fumbling fingers, he picked them up and put them on.

I gasped. "He has my son."

Marcus fiddled with his glasses.

"If Delacroix finds out that you're alive," I leaned forward on my knees, "my son is dead."

* * * *

Delacroix met me halfway down the corridor.

I tried to control my rage. "It's done."

Benjamin loomed nearby. He glanced at the cell door.

"Now tell me where my son is." I said.

Delacroix held a wide grin.

"You have no intention of freeing me, do you?" I glanced at the prison. "They died for nothing." Out of the corner of my eye, I caught Benjamin's smug smile. "At least show me that loyalty is rewarded." I tilted my head, casually.

Benjamin's grin fell.

Delacroix's eyes flickered, and with that small gesture of permission, I strolled over to Benjamin and peeled back his shirt collar. Benjamin reflected excitement intermingled with frightful anticipation. He whimpered when I bit and, despite his struggle, I had him.

Swallowing both Benjamin's blood and his memories, I traced through his dark domain, the hidden images, suppressed by him, deep within. I stormed further on.

And then I found her.

It wasn't only Marcus who'd fled through the central tunnel last night, but hours later Sunaria had, too. Delacroix had entombed her in a coffin and then sealed off the exit with a wall of mud.

I let go of Benjamin and bolted down the middle tunnel.

* * * *

They flung me into the chair.

I assumed the stake sticking out of my side was the cause of my inability to move. Pain radiated down my right leg. I'd almost reached the end of the tunnel, but they'd gotten to me first. The torture chamber reeked of blood and fear—my own.

I realized that was how they forced Sunaria to remain in the coffin, using a similar stake. I cringed at the thought, and wondered if she, like me, couldn't even talk.

Delacroix loomed over me.

Feeling pure terror like I'd never known, taking small breaths, grateful for that at least, I thought of Sunaria being so close. My inability to rescue her was harrowing.

Delacroix's fingers lingered at the end of the spike and he muttered something, but made no sense. My gaze followed his over to a cabinet and I gulped my dread.

Get me out of this fucking chair!

He lifted out a large jar. A decapitated head—a grotesque sight—bobbed inside, the likeness to Delacroix uncanny. The same mop of black hair, pasty, mottled skin, eyelids closed, and a drooping mouth in a sorrowful expression. Delacroix peered into the jar.

The idea that Sunaria suffered provoked an inner force within me and stopped me from passing out. Delacroix placed the jar down on top of the cabinet and reached in. His maniacal gaze reflected affection. With all my strength, I strained to move my right hand, but a weak twitch of my middle finger was all I could muster.

Delacroix carried the wet, grisly head back to me.

You're insane.

He held it close and droplets of fluid plopped onto my trouser leg. Cold soaked through to my thigh. The walls closed in and my surroundings swirled.

"I was right," he mumbled. "You're the perfect build."

XXXVIII

FEAR LIKE I'D NEVER known gripped me.

Despite being paralyzed, my entire body trembled, so much so, that the chair squeaked beneath me. Delacroix pressed the jagged blades of the saw against my throat. I begged him with my eyes.

Time slowed.

Blinding pain as the blade punctured and then sawed, and bright, red blood squirted and spilled and warmth burst down my neck and chest as he cut deeper. Blood gurgled in my throat and my stomach readied to spew. I hoped madness would possess me and take my mind with it.

Dear God, save me, but more importantly, save her.

Outside, sudden chaos, strange sounds carried, alluding to an unearthly brawl. Delacroix rested the saw on the side table and left.

Silence.

I struggled to breathe as the gaping gash restored. The scarlet flow slowed and receded and the agonizing spasms dissipated. In the corner lay my discarded jacket. Jacob's locket was in one of those pockets.

Delacroix returned, dragging Marcus in with him. Marcus' spectacles poked out of his tattered shirt pocket.

Get me out of here!

"This is a nightmare," Marcus whispered.

"One that I control," Delacroix seemed to say.

Marcus scrambled to his feet and did a double take at the jar. Delacroix picked up the saw.

"He isn't tied down?" Marcus uttered, and then his wide stare shifted to the stake protruding from my side.

"Do you want to see your sister again?" Delacroix handed Marcus the saw.

A rasp escaped my lips.

Marcus swallowed a sob. "I want to know why."

I was caught between survival and the need for it to be over. In a trance-like gaze, Marcus traced the serrated edges along my neck. Delacroix loomed close behind him, clutching the head. His hands appeared to shake with excitement.

"You manipulated me." Marcus held my gaze.

I couldn't let your sister die, I conveyed.

"Manipulated us." Marcus swung round and sliced through Delacroix's throat.

Delacroix staggered back, aghast. Blood gushed from the gash, and the head he held landed with a thud. Marcus spun round to face me and reached for the stake in my side, grasped the wooden handle, and yanked it out.

Delacroix vanished, leaving a bloody trail. Marcus kicked the head across the room.

I flew out of the chair and we headed into the corridor.

"I owe you my life." I resisted the urge to touch him.

"You owe me more than that."

I pointed to his spectacles. "You won't need those anymore."

"I noticed."

"We'll talk."

"I've got to get to Rachel," he said. "The River Thames Inn was it?"

I nodded.

"I'm coming back for him." Marcus sped along the corridor.

"Don't take him on alone," I called after him. "Avoid the sun!" I cringed at my damp shirt, stained with residue from the glop, mixed in with my blood. I ran in the opposite direction, down the central tunnel.

Someone had carved their way through before me. I climbed into the muddy hole following in their tracks, and soon reached the other side. Benjamin sat beside a black coffin, its lid off. He rocked Sunaria in his arms, talking to her. She looked paralyzed.

"Let her go." I spoke the words slowly.

Benjamin clutched her close to him. "He wants me to bring her to him."

"You and I both know that's not going to happen," I said.

"I drank from him. I saw things."

"Saw what?"

"His power."

"He gave you up to me." I stepped closer.

"I did whatever he asked because I'm scared of him."

"It's me you should be scared of."

Sunaria slid out of his arms and I caught her. Grasping the end of the stake in her side, I eased it out. I'd never seen her so vulnerable. Her dress was filthy, evidence that she hadn't surrendered without a fight.

"I've got you now," I whispered.

I grabbed Benjamin's arm and, controlling his squirming, clutched the scruff of his jacket and held him over her. Even with Sunaria's face nuzzled into his neck, I could see her color returning.

I peered down the tunnel and wondered where it led, considering that it may very well be like the others and lead nowhere, though the faint sound of water hinted that it may lead to freedom.

When Sunaria pulled back, having had enough, I shoved Benjamin out of the way. A fine, scarlet line trickled from her mouth onto her chin.

I wiped away the bloody smear. "I'm never letting you out of my sight again." I kissed her, my tongue searching her mouth, tasting the tangy remnants of the blood.

Benjamin staggered off and dived through the clay hole.

Sunaria rubbed her dissipating wound. "That bastard stabbed me with silver." She stared at the state of my clothes. "What happened to you?"

"Later." I led her after Benjamin.

She pulled her hand out of mine. "Where are we going?"

I wrapped my arm around her waist and we trekked down the passageway. Sunaria covered her nose, the smell having reached us. I pushed open the door to the torture chamber and locked gazes with Benjamin. He held the head.

I glared at him, my patience fast fading. "Give it to me."

Sunaria looked disgusted.

"He'll let me live if I return it." He stepped back. "What are you going to do with it?"

"End it."

Benjamin wavered.

"We've all been through enough," I said, calmly.

Benjamin looked at Sunaria and then back at me. "And you'll let me go?"

"Sure. Take off your shirt."

"Why?"

"Just do it." I unbuttoned my shirt, removed it, and threw it.

Once Benjamin's shirt was off, I grabbed it from him and put it on. It was a snug fit, but clean at least. I reached for my jacket and withdrew the locket from the right pocket. "Delacroix had this." I showed it to her.

Sunaria looked puzzled. "He found it on me."

"What?"

"I found it in a jewelry store. Delacroix stole it from me before I could find you."

"He recognized me from the portrait." I cringed. "And Benjamin, you filled in the holes."

Benjamin sidled along the wall.

"He doesn't have Jacob." Sunaria's expression flickered with anger. "He just wants you to think that."

But we don't know that for sure." I tucked the locket into my trouser pocket and grabbed the head out of Benjamin's hands. It was truly nasty. I wrapped it in my jacket and grasped Benjamin's arm. With the head under my left arm, cringing with the feel of it, I dragged a bare-chested Benjamin out and back down the central corridor. With a shove, Benjamin climbed through the clay opening and I followed him out the other side. I offered the head to Sunaria for her to hold and she gave me one of her stares. I carefully placed it down.

I pulled Benjamin over to the casket and forced him in. I reached for the lid with my other hand, grasped the edge, and dragged it over. I rammed it into position and sealed it in place.

Benjamin banged on the lid. "You can't leave me in here."
The locks flicked easily into their catches.
"Why?" he cried. "Why did you lie?"
"Because, Ben, I'm all out of nice."

XXXIX

INSIDE ST. PAUL'S CATHEDRAL, a few parishioners were saying their late night prayers.

The gnarly, wet head had soaked through my jacket. I pulled Sunaria past the nave and down into the lower chambers. "This is where I first met Benjamin and Rachel."

The night of lies.

"When I found the locket," Sunaria explained, "I questioned the storekeeper. He didn't remember Jacob."

"He needs help remembering."

"Perhaps Jacob's living near the store?" She hesitated when she saw the crucifix hanging above the door to the chamber.

I lingered just inside, recalling how Benjamin had reeled me in.

Sunaria waited in the doorway. "Why the hell are we here?"

I strolled over to the farthest coffin and prized open the lid. A corpse lay within, freshly wrapped. There was just enough room for the head. I laid it inside and closed the lid.

"I never want to see that thing again," Sunaria said.

"I knew you never liked that jacket."

She gave me a wry look.

Easily disguised as two late night parishioners, if scruffy ones, we walked up and out, back down the aisle. I stopped when we reached the ornate stone font.

She looked irritated. "Now you're really pushing your luck."

I leaned over the edge of the fountain. "You once told me that holy water can harm us."

"That's what I was told."

"Where's your curiosity?"

"Can we go now?"

"When was the last time you saw your reflection?"

"An obvious question."

"You never told me my hair has a tendency to stick up."

"I'll be outside."

"Humor me."

Sunaria gave a sigh, and stepped closer to the font. She gasped her surprise, and stared into the still water.

"See how beautiful you are?" I said.

"How is it possible? I don't recognize myself."

I shrugged. "Your misguided belief prevented you from seeing yourself."

"How does it work?"

"I wish I knew."

"We can't see ourselves in mirrors, but we can in this?"

I gave an incredulous stare. "You're telling me this is the strangest thing you've ever seen?"

"I can't work out who's better looking." She arched an eyebrow.

"That'd be me." I grinned.

As she stared at herself in wonderment, I realized that there may be other things that she believed to be true that weren't. Like a cure.

Sunaria was still reeling when we strolled out under the archway of oak trees, their yellow leaves half bare. With London's nightscape as our backdrop, we moved as mysterious shadowy phantoms speeding over the roof tops.

* * * *

Midnight, and all seemed quiet in the courtyard of the River Thames Inn.

Buried in the heart of London, near St. Paul's Cathedral, this modest hotel was a perfect place to hide out for a night.

The skies opened and it poured, soaking our clothes.

"Rain." I tried to suppress my annoyance. "That's unusual."

"What the hell are we doing here?" she said.

"A little detour."

She gazed at the upper windows. "Benjamin overheard you, and he told Delacroix."

My fingers ran over my throat. My hand lingered.

"You turned the girl?" Sunaria snapped.

"Rachel, she's Marcus' sister."

"Why?"

"Now's not a good time."

Delacroix's silhouette lurked at the window.

She tossed her hair back over her shoulders. "Do you plan on turning everyone in London?"

"There must be some way of stopping him."

"He's a difficult vampire to kill."

"Daylight?"

Sunaria shook her head. "You'll have to weaken him first. Drain him completely. But . . ."

I leaned in, hanging on her last word.

"But it would mean . . ." Sunaria looked away.

"What?"

"He's an ancient. Such potency would affect you."

"How?"

Sunaria stared up at the window. "Daumia would no longer exist."

XL

FEAR HAS POWER OVER US when we cannot foresee a solution.

Standing in the rain, I knew that to enter that room could be my last mistake, but until I had my son in my arms, I had no other choice. Even if Delacroix didn't have Jacob, he'd become too much of a threat. And he now had Marcus and Rachel.

Sunaria's words resonated. I wondered if there might be any truth in them, if drinking from Delacroix might irrevocably change me. Another warped myth, perhaps, though I had to admit, I'd occasionally experienced an invisible essence radiating from my victims, though nothing definable.

Sunaria stayed in the courtyard and I flew up and onto the window sill and in. Delacroix sat in the corner. Marcus was hugging Rachel and I could see the similarity between them—their red hair, their English features, and the kindness in their faces, the innocence. The room was unbearably small, the décor bare—single bed, a chair, and a side table upon which lay a time-worn book with dog-eared pages.

Instead of reading to Lilly, I murdered her.

I swapped a glance with Marcus.

Delacroix smiled.

"Where's my son?" I asked.

He shrugged.

I wondered if I had the strength to tear his throat out. He read my mind and returned a stare that blazed with hatred and then he rose out of the chair and strolled past me. He gazed out of the window and his lips slid into a grin.

Despite everything he'd done, I had to suppress my anger and let nothing distract my focus. "What do you want with them?"

Delacroix shook his head in dismissal.

"So why are you here?" I neared him.

He smiled again.

"Because you knew I'd come." The realization hit me.

Marcus signaled to me that he wanted to attack him.

I gestured, *No.*

Delacroix's attention fell onto Rachel.

"Let them go." My tone remained calm, controlled.

I glanced at Marcus and then back at Delacroix. "What's going on?"

A gust of wind caught the curtain and it billowed.
"What have you done?" I felt a pit in my stomach.
Delacroix peered out again.
"Get out of my way." My voice broke.
He put his hand up, blocking me.
"I take it you want your head back," I said.
His eyelids flicked.
"You'll never see it again." I shook my head to make my point.
He glared at me.
"St. Paul's, tomorrow night," I said. "Witching hour."
"Sunaria's as good as dead," he rasped.
"I'll burn the thing," I yelled.
Delacroix's dark stare was a fierce warning. He was gone.

Marcus joined me by the window and stared down at the hooded figures surrounding Sunaria. "Who are they?" he whispered, and then stepped back, fearing he'd been seen.

* * * *

My feet left the ledge and I landed in the courtyard.

Sunaria's expression reflected her usual calmness, pride even. The Creda had tied her hands behind her back. The six shady looking vampires were huddled around her, all dressed in the garb of monks, their complexions ghostly white, their irises glistening in the moonlight. There was something vaguely familiar about one of them.

He moved languidly. "Orpheus is what she calls you," he said, "but that's not your real name."

"And you are?" I asked.

"Elijah."

"Do I know you?"

"No." He looked young, twenty-ish, at least he had been when turned. He smiled, but his eyes didn't. He'd never pass for normal. In fact, none of them would. That would explain why they dressed as friars, wearing long, brown robes, their hoods pulled all the way forward to disguise their freaky pallor.

"Go," Sunaria said to me. "Get far away from here."

"Laws have been broken," Elijah spoke softly. A lock of stark, white hair peeked out from under his hood. It contradicted his youth. His eyes moved under heavy lids and his pupils penetrated what he focused upon. He didn't blink, the mark of an ancient.

"Sunaria, his memory of you can be a good one," he said. "Come quietly."

She avoided my stare.

"I'll get you out of this," I whispered.

She gave a subtle shake of her head. "I'll find you."

"Will someone please tell me what's going on?" I demanded.

"They're punishing me because I turned too many." Sunaria looked back at Elijah.

Thoughts of turning Marcus and his sister came to mind. "What's the limit?"

Elijah gave me a wary stare. "It's not necessarily how many."

"Then *who*?" I asked.

"They hid my daughter from me," she said it quickly.

In a flash, Elijah was right next to her. "And why did we do that, Sunaria?"

I reeled with her words. "You have a daughter?"

"Did," she said.

"You never told me this, why?" I'd never seen her this distressed before. "Why did you take her daughter?"

His gaze shifted slowly to me. "Sunaria murdered her master."

"He tortured her." I took a deep breath.

"She broke our rules." Elijah gestured to the others that he was ready to go.

"And you've never broken them?" I asked.

"No, I have not." He neared me. "She wiped out our descendants."

Although Sunaria had revealed her capability for cruelty, I'd never imagined that the woman I loved could be this dangerous. "What happened to her daughter?"

"We don't know." Elijah waved off the question. "And we don't care."

"Let her go," I said.

"This doesn't concern you." He turned away from me, as though wishing I weren't there.

"Actually, it does."

"You can't contain her."

"I won't let you take her."

"Daumia," he spun round gracefully, "it's time for you to leave."

"I have information that could prevent your annihilation," I said.

Elijah's stare seemed hollow, unworldly.

"If you think Sunaria's out of control," I said, "you should take a closer look at Delacroix."

"And why is that?" Elijah asked.

"He has a penchant for body parts."

From Elijah's thoughts, I picked up images of two men, one was the count, and the other his brother, and I realized that the decapitated head had once been Delacroix's brother.

Elijah's snapped his attention back on me, aware that I'd been rummaging around his thoughts.

"The Delacroix brothers have formed an alliance with Lord Archer," I told him. "They plan to wipe you out."

Sunaria glanced up.

Elijah tried to access my thoughts but failed. He went on to say, "Roman would never betray his own."

"Apparently, he would." I nodded, surprised at how easily Elijah let slip Delacroix's brother's name. "Roman's desire for power matches his brother's." I nodded knowingly. Unless I'd seen it myself, I'd never have believed Delacroix was insane enough to try to attach his brother's head to me. I cringed and looked up.

Elijah was staring intently. "Why would the count arrange for us to be here?" Elijah grimaced, revealing stark, white teeth and a glint of the sharpest fangs. "It doesn't make sense."

"It's a ruse. He wanted to distract you while he takes another meeting with Archer."

"Archer will kill him."

"He's setting you up."

Elijah's expression showed emotion for a split second.

"They're selling you out," I said.

"Prove it." Elijah swapped stares with the others.

"I'll tell you when and where they'll be tomorrow night," I said, "and you'll give up Sunaria."

"Bring her." Elijah signaled to the others.

"At this very moment, Roman is spilling your secrets." I reached into my trouser pocket and withdrew his gold engraved ring. "Here."

Elijah took it from me and examined it. "How did you come to have this?"

"Roman invited me to join them."

Elijah turned to his men in silent conversation and then faced me again. "Why do you refuse me entry into your mind?"

"Did you ask the same of Delacroix?" I said.

"You'll say anything to get Sunaria back."

"Then you're on your own."

"You're playing a dangerous game."

"It's more of a war."

"Where no side wins," he said.

"You now have the advantage. Knowledge is power, after all."

"Where?"

"Tomorrow. St. Paul's. Midnight."

* * * *

As quickly as they had appeared, they'd gone.

I untied Sunaria. "Well, that was easy."

"What were you thinking?" she snapped.

"Did I miss something?"

"You're out of your mind." She shook her head, annoyed.

"'Why thank you for saving my life,' was more the response I expected."

"What happens when they realize that all that's left of Roman is his head?"

"I'll think of something."

"Like what?"

I shrugged. "Who did you transform that's made them so mad?"

"What does it matter now?"

I rubbed her wrists, soothing where they'd tied her. "It matters to me."

"Where did you get that ring?"

"You don't want to know."

She gave me that look.

"I removed it from Roman's hand. Delacroix keeps it in a jar."

Sunaria squirmed. "They won't go through with this."

"We'll see."

"They have no intention of just letting me go."

"You didn't fight them," I said, "didn't try to run away."

"They threatened to harm you."

"I can look after myself. Why did you never tell me about your daughter?"

Sunaria turned away.

"Are you ever going to open up to me?" I asked her.

"I've imbibed from each of their descendants. A great collection of information rests within me."

"There's something else though, I can feel it."

She wrapped her arms around me. "Let's get out of here."

"After this is over, you'll tell me everything and I won't take *no* for an answer."

She snuggled into me.

"So the Creda's descendants have really been wiped out?" I asked.

"Yes."

"I wouldn't want to cross you."

"After that performance, I'm not so sure I'd want to cross you, either."

I kissed the top of her head. "Fancy a trip to the country?"

"You've been reckless enough. Let's find a hotel."

"What's that new place on Bond Street?"

"The Cavendish?" she said.

"Now that's more us. Find somewhere for Marcus and Rachel to stay, will you?"

"Where are you going?"

"A quick change of clothes and then I have one final stop to make."

She read my mind. "That's suicide."

"Book us into The Cavendish and I'll catch up with you there."

"You're not going."

"I won't be long."

"Listen to me."

I rubbed my chin. "Right now, Delacroix, the Creda, and the Stone Masters all have an agenda."

Sunaria sighed. "And we're right in the middle of it."

XLI

THE STONE MASTERS WERE *RUTHLESS*.

Or so I read in the leather bound book I found while waiting in their library. This was the headquarters that Lady Bradbury had led us to. The secret society's townhouse enjoyed its desired privacy provided by the extensive land that surrounded the building. Verging dense woods provided even more cover.

Inside, a dying fire struggled to warm the room. Below the far window, a writing desk sat, and up against the three other walls were dark maple bookcases. Stacked along their shelves was book upon book on the supernatural. I pulled another off the shelf and turned to a random page of mishmashes of fact and fiction, distorted truths, documented by men who'd risked so much to gain so little. Through their investigations, they'd determined that vampires were evolving and mingling more and more with society. This was riveting reading.

Someone approached.

The door opened.

The grey-haired man, easily in his forties, had a weathered face, expressing a lifetime of worry, and his tall, self-assured bearing gave away his background of privilege. He oozed old money. His hand remained on the door handle.

"I'm admiring your collection," I said. "Particularly enjoying this book here." I held it up.

"*Vampire lore?*" He entered cautiously.

"It says here, and I quote, 'The art of mind reading is common in the elite.'"

He looked like he was considering leaving. "I find it intriguing that you'd come here."

"Stonehenge, what a way to go."

He glanced at the jimmied lock on the wall safe, its contents of papers now strewn over the desk.

"The lock kind of gave." I glanced back down at the book. "Captivating reading. Talking of secrets. 'Stone Masters,' which one of you came up with that?"

"Excuse me?" He took a step closer.

"Well, if I wanted to create a secret cult, I'd name it something a little more discreet."

"We're not a cult."

"So, Stone Master, what does it feel like to drink the blood of a vampire?"

"What makes you think that I'm *the* Stone Master?"

I peered down at the book again. "The art of mind reading is common in the elite."

"So you consider yourself elite?"

I smiled. "How does one become a Stone Master?"

"One earns the title."

"Inherits it?"

He shrugged.

"What a lovely gift to bestow to a son," I said. "I wonder, what does a Stone Master do when his wife bears him only daughters? Who inherits the title then? Which child has a lifetime of carnage to look forward to?"

His right eye flickered. "How did you get past my dogs?"

"I fed them."

"What do you want?"

"I have something that you may find of interest."

He gave a half smile. "We don't do business with your kind."

"Why ever not?"

He glanced at the door. "Your name?"

"Orpheus. And yours?"

He closed his eyes, a split second shift.

"It's an honor to meet with you, Lord Archer," I said. "So do tell, what gave me away?"

"You're pale. Your irises are enhanced in color. You move in a fashion that is, how does one say, elegant and . . ."

"And?"

"And you have the ability to seduce."

"I'm flattered."

"Why are you here?"

"I have information that could prevent the end of the Stone Masters."

"You have to do better than that." He smiled.

Our gazes locked and he closed his mind.

It was my turn to smile. "Impressive."

"Entering this house is a dangerous ploy. I hope you find it worth it."

"I'm not so different from you."

"How do you figure that?" Sweat settled on his upper lip.

"Well, you seek out the innocent and murder them."

He approached the desk and gathered the papers.

"Pretty interesting stuff." I raised my eyebrows.

"You had no right."

"I'll note it for next time."

"Unless this material is read in context, it will make no sense," he said.

"I found it easy to follow. Grasped what you chaps are up to. Let me see how to sum up . . . Capture vampire, drain their blood, weaken them, and then off to Stonehenge to get your fix. Kill the vampire and—"

"This is all conjecture."

I sucked on my forefinger and bit into it. His gaze followed the bloody trickle. In a flash, I leaned in and stroked my finger tip across his lips.

He pushed my hand away. A flicker of his tongue was instinctively drawn to the scarlet drop. His eyes rolled and then closed, and he rested against the table. "That was impolite."

Flames in the fireplace flickered. Wood in the hearth crackled and sparked.

He regained composure. "Was that," he sighed, "your attempt to keep me in the room?"

"It's addictive, isn't it? And as only the Master himself can drink it, only you know what it feels like. The older the vampire, the more potent the effect."

He loosened his shirt collar.

"Want some more?" I asked.

"No."

"Sure?"

He coughed. "How does your blood have that effect?" He reached back, his fingers fumbling and then finding the sharp letter opener.

"Put it down or I'll use it on you," I said, calmly.

He dropped it and it landed with a clang.

I kicked it out of his reach. "See, our blood can be pretty persuasive."

"You had a family once, yes?"

"Yes, so?"

"You know what it is to love, to care for someone. When you murder, you kill someone's loved one."

"You're breaking my heart."

He glanced at the door. "How do you sleep at night, knowing that you've done the unthinkable?"

"I sleep by day."

"Under this very roof, there are at least thirty Stone Lords. You'll never leave this place alive."

"I'm already dead. Or is that undead?"

He backed up. "One word from me and I'll bring down hell upon thee."

"Nice."

"You seem unafraid."

"That's because from where I'm standing, you and I will both benefit from my visit. Call in your hounds and you'll never know what that thing is."

"Go on."

"In every man's life, there comes a defining moment," I said. "This is yours."

He glanced at the door. "Start talking."

I stared at him for the longest time. "Creda."

His eyes widened.

"Their plot to wipe you out, it's masterful." I neared him.

"What's your agenda?"

"What do you mean?"

"How do you benefit from giving me this information?" He turned away and went for the door.

I shoved him backward over the desk and leaned against him, knocking items, flying papers scattering. "I'm not finished."

He glared at me.

"Being this close to me," I sighed dramatically, "it reminds you of that desire of yours."

He tried to push me off him.

I pressed up against him. "Don't you want more than a sip?"

Something passed between us and we both felt a connection crackle, igniting an unexpected intimacy.

I stepped back and Archer straightened his jacket, though it didn't need it.

"I don't frighten you, do I?" I said.

"I don't frighten easily."

"You *are* a Stone Master."

"Please leave."

"And risk not knowing?" I replied. "And let's be honest, now that you have me, I doubt you'll let me go."

"Orpheus, such aggression is unnecessary."

"Mine or yours?"

He regarded me with those idealistic eyes of his. "Despite evidence of your remaining humanity—"

"Don't demonize me."

"You're a hunter." He raised his eyebrows in a condescending fashion.

"As are you."

"This back and forward, are you trying to find some kind of approval from me?"

I folded my arms. "I don't believe so."

"How did this happen to you?"

"What does it matter?"

"I'm trying to understand you, that's all."

"That would be a first," I said. "I hardly understand myself."

"Your father, was he a good man?"

"Such questions, do you think the answers will make it easier to hunt me?"

"I find myself alone in a room with a vampire. There's no guideline on how one proceeds."

"My father was a good man. Was yours?"

"Yes."

I gestured. "And yet he chose this life for you."

"I accepted my fate."

"Your father, did he show you affection?"
"Why?"
I smiled. "Just trying to understand you. *That's all.*"
"Ridiculous."
"I take it that's a no."
He gave a look of disapproval. "Assuming anything would be foolish at best."
"Is that the philosophy on which you base your life?"
Archer glanced at the letter opener. "My life is not my own. I serve a greater purpose."
"But you hate this life, don't you?"
He softened and his thoughtful face reflected concern.
"A reluctant Stone Master." I folded my arms. "How's that working for you?"
Archer rubbed his eyes. "This conversation is over."
"You're tired. You hate what you do."
"Mistakes have been made."
"What kind of mistakes?" I asked.
"Please step back, give me some room."
"It's the killing, isn't it? You've been feeling this way for quite some time."
He shrugged. "What do you want me to say, that I enjoy the act of murder, even if it's meant for the ultimate good?"
"What path would you have chosen otherwise?"
"I can't believe I'm having this conversation, with *you*!"
"I could always extract it."
"Please don't."
"A priest, well that's original."
He turned away. "That was rude."
"But it's so easy to rummage around in there. Your thoughts are fascinating."
"You kill every night. How do you come to terms with murder?"
"They die because I want to live."
"Has any part of the old you survived?"
I leaned against the desk. "I think so."
"Which aspect?"
"Well, I feel the same for the most part."
"Can you still experience love?"
"Of course."
"What were you like as a mortal?"
"Not half as dashing as I am now."
He almost smiled. "What does it feel like never to age?"
"Untouched by the impact of time," I said wistfully.
"You find it romantic?"
"It is what it is. Eternity has its privileges."
All fear had gone from him. "How old are you?"
"You're stalling."

"It must seem that way."

"It does."

Silently, he invited me to read his mind.

And I did. "You're a man of philosophy?"

"What does it feel like to change?"

"So you've read the books but not actually spoken with any of your victims?"

"By the time they get to me," he said, "they're not really up for a conversation."

"A part of you dies inside. But you still have a sense of the old you."

"Can you control it?"

"Feeding?"

He nodded.

"Well, I'm not biting you, am I?"

He squinted into a smile.

"Not yet anyway." I grinned.

"Do you hunt alone or in packs?"

"Alone," I said. "Only your men hunt in packs."

"We must agree to disagree."

I smirked. "Our differences will bring us closer."

Archer chuckled.

"I dare to believe that, although I'm different," I said. "I'm no less deserving to share this world with you."

"Your species has evolved."

"It seems that it can go either way."

"Perhaps, but your kind has developed new skills."

"Tracking us has become harder?" I interrupted.

"You could say that."

"That's good." I stared at the far shelves and wished that I had more time to read the books stacked along them.

Archer followed my gaze. "What other gifts have you developed?"

"Do you have to take a lover?" I asked.

"Excuse me?"

"Hoping that she'll bear you a son?"

"And you were doing so well. I was rather enjoying our conversation."

"No, you weren't. But I do fascinate you."

"Perhaps we could come to some arrangement. You could teach me more."

"Visit again?"

He nodded. "I'd like that."

"This closing your mind thing, you only seem to be able to keep it up for about one minute. Then, it's full access."

"Ah."

"Your invite includes a trip to Salisbury."

He seemed concerned. "I've offended you."

"No more than most who'd like to slash my wrists and then burn me up."

"Now it's me being rude."
I burst into laughter.
Archer smiled. "You're not what I expected."
"Really?"
"You have a serene presence. I really am interested in learning more about you and—"
We both froze. Someone lingered outside the door.
"They'll be wondering where I am," he said.
"The Creda have turned the tables."
"In what way?"
"They have a secret rendezvous tomorrow night to discuss your downfall."
"Where?"
I frowned. "Perhaps *secret* wasn't the best word."
"What time?"
"First, you must swear that you'll not try to capture me."
"You know I can't do that."
"I offer you the elite vampires of London, where you can annihilate every last one, and you decline the offer?"
"When something sounds too good to be true, it very often is."
"I hear the Creda's plan includes the destruction of Stonehenge."
Despite his attempt to look disinterested, his voice broke. "Impossible."
"Apparently, in or around 2800 BC, the Welsh were hired to construct the monument."
He raised an eyebrow. "Is that so?"
"They plan to hire the Welsh to deconstruct it."
"What do you gain from betraying your own?"
"I have the freedom to find a way back without interference."
"The way back from?"
I gave a look of surprise. "This."
"And how do you plan to do that?"
I reached for his hand, prized it open, and slid a small object into his palm.
He closed his fingers around it. "What is it?"
"One more thing to document in your collection."
Archer opened his fingers and stared down at the small, black carved rook. "You play chess?"
"The Creda have found a cure but refuse to share it." Scrutinizing his thoughts, I confirmed he'd fallen for it.
Archer's brow furrowed deeper. "Where are they meeting?"

XLII

THE CAVENDISH WAS EASILY one of London's finest hotels.

Overlooking the Thames, its views were awe inspiring, though when the wind blew in the wrong direction, the smell sucked all joy out of the vista. Inside the room were the finest of furnishings, the long, thick drapes suited our taste perfectly. Sunaria had procured one of their larger suites. The chestnut, four-poster bed was preferable to any casket, and revealed the soft linen sheets I'd become accustomed to. We paid the staff well to stay away.

I awoke to see Sunaria huddled up in a corner chair, her legs tucked beneath her. I raised myself up onto my elbows. "Come back to bed."

"You have a death wish," she said.

I shrugged.

"You were having nightmares." She sighed.

"Can't imagine why."

"You ask me to share my secrets and then you keep yours from me."

I threw off the blankets and rested my legs over the side. My behavior had always been reckless, but last night, I'd outdone myself. In one of Archer's books, the ritual at Stonehenge had been described in detail. They'd unwittingly gathered the ashes of all the vampires they'd slaughtered in one place.

"Don't look at me like that." Sunaria gave me an uneasy glance.

"I was miles away."

"Where?"

"I meant miles away in my head."

She rose and approached me. "Darling, we've agreed we mustn't keep anything from each other anymore."

"You first."

Her fingers caressed my scalp and it felt good. She closed her mind to me. I pushed her away and reached for the clothes I'd thrown onto the floor that morning, and dressed.

"Where are you going now?" she said.

I pulled on my jacket.

"You're not going to St. Paul's," she continued. "It's too dangerous."

"I have to see it through."

"You went to that society's house?"

"I don't think it's their official base."

"And afterward, you visited Marcus." She slid between me and the door. "What did you talk about?" She glared. "You're not the only one who suffered. Delacroix trapped me in that awful coffin."

I nudged her. "Step aside."

"I know I should have told you everything. I didn't think you'd understand."

"Then you insult me."

"Try to see my side of things."

"When you don't let me in, I can't." I pulled away from her and strolled back over to the bed.

"And why are you bringing Marcus into this?"

"Sunaria, too many questions."

"You trust him. Why don't you trust me?"

"Get dressed."

"I'm not going with you."

"Meet me there."

"I refuse."

"I'm not asking you," I snapped, "I'm telling you."

She grabbed my sleeve. "You don't order me around like this."

I shoved her onto the bed.

She tried to get up. "Why are you being like this?"

I pushed her back down and held her there. "Because I don't trust you."

"You can't take the Creda on. As for Delacroix, we both know what he's capable of."

"I'm going to right your wrongs."

She slapped me.

My glare caused her to freeze. Unable to push me off, she turned her head away. I pressed my mouth against hers, kissing her leisurely, passionately.

"I forgive you," she whispered at last.

I wrapped my left arm under her waist and yanked her into me. "But the question is," I grazed my fangs along her neck, "do I forgive you?"

I stole her breath from her with another kiss.

Sunaria gave an insistent glare and I turned to see Rachel in the doorway.

"Well, hello there." I smiled.

"How long have you been standing there?" Sunaria said, annoyed.

"Please hurry." Rachel looked miserable. "Marcus is drunk."

I sat up. "He can't be drunk."

"Unless his victim was," Sunaria said.

Rachel bit her bottom lip. "He's drunk three bottles of wine."

Sunaria and I swapped a wary glance.

"Has he eaten food?" I asked.

Rachel nodded.

"That's just great." I sighed. "Bloody great."

* * * *

Rachel and I found Marcus lying in his own vomit.

They'd created a den of sorts in the lower rooms of a rundown East London shack. Paint peeled off the walls and broken windows gave a horrid sense of vulnerability. No thought had gone into choosing their temporary refuge. At least, I hoped they considered it temporary.

"Nice place," I said.

Despite my consideration that I'd take care of them, I'd let them down. Finding Marcus lying in this filth showed evidence of my abandonment.

"How do you bear it?" Marcus slurred.

"It gets easier." I said flatly. "Rachel, bring me a cloth."

She scurried off.

"I thought you were staying at the Old Towne Inn?" I held a tight smile.

"Rachel took a fancy to the innkeeper."

"She didn't—"

"Drank him dry." His eyes fluttered shut.

I shook him. "Did you finish the job I gave you?"

"Are you sure you want to go through with it?" Marcus asked.

"Yes. Though I didn't account for you getting shit-faced."

"I'm dying."

"You're pissed. You have a headache."

He retched and I dodged his vomit.

"My head's spinning," he mumbled. "We can't eat food. Does that not strike you as strange?"

"We've been over this."

Rachel returned and placed the bucket by my side. I dipped the old rag into the water and washed Marcus' face.

"She doesn't seem to mind drinking blood." He pointed to Rachel. "She almost looks like she's enjoying herself."

I found Rachel's guilty expression endearing. "You need mentoring."

"If you die tonight, we're done for," he sobbed.

"What's happening tonight?" Rachel asked.

"I'm a vampire!" Marcus cried.

"You're a sorry excuse for a vampire," I said.

He clutched my shirt sleeve. "Am I insane?"

"Help me get him undressed." I turned to Rachel. "He'll sleep off the booze. He'll be fine."

Marcus pulled me closer. "I've let you down."

I glanced out of the window and wondered how long it would be before he sobered up. "We have to be at St. Paul's in under an hour," I said.

Marcus fell asleep.

"Shall I throw the rest of the chicken away?" Rachel said.

I stared at her, hoping she was joking. She wasn't. "Get your things. You're both staying with me."

Marcus stirred and grabbed my shirt collar. "It seems so wrong."

"It's the only way." I watched Rachel wander out.

She hesitated and stared at me, smiling, and then went all coy and disappeared from sight.

"Think you can pull this off?" Marcus asked.

"*We* can pull it off."

"What about the others?"

"The Creda will free us from the Stone Masters."

"But does she have to die like that?" Marcus said.

I sat back and stared out of the window. Witching hour fast approached. "If I'm to be free from the Creda," I said, "it's the only way."

* * * *

A storm raged over London's skyline.

Thunder rolled, followed by flashes of lightning, and flooding rain, weaving through the city's lanes only to find its way back into the Thames.

I entered St. Paul's alone, just missing the worst of the downpour. A schism in the silence, whispers up near the nave. Hugging close to the walls, using the shadows for cover, I approached. Incense hung thick, bestowing a faint fragrance of rare spices.

Count Delacroix murmured to a man who was hunched over in the front pew. Trying to get a better view, I drew closer. I bit down hard on my hand to suppress a gasp.

It was Roman and he was talking. The very head that I'd stuck in the coffin the previous night, down in the catacombs, was now frighteningly animated and attached to someone else's torso. His head was easily out of proportion to the slender body and his features moved sluggishly. Along his neck ran shoddy sutures all the way around, and his flesh bubbled up in between the thick stitches. A macabre rush job, stitched with a callous hand. It was Roman's head, but Benjamin's body.

Despite all that Benjamin had done, I felt awful. I'd trapped him in the casket, making it easy for the count to catch him and perform his sick work. Delacroix nodded in response to the morbid head's utterances. Roman, or what was left of him, was struggling to be understood.

No Creda yet, but the Stone Masters were here. They hid somewhere far back in the west cloister and they were also watching the spectacle. I tried to count how many of them were here, got to twenty men and then movement pulled my attention back onto Delacroix.

Grasping the handle of an axe, he raised it high above his head, and then swung the blade wide, slicing through Roman's neck sending his head flying off his shoulders. The body shuddered, slumped, and then slid to the floor and stilled.

I stepped out from the shadows. "Even your brother isn't immune to your madness."

Delacroix's hands shook with anger.

"You can't blame that on me." I tried to keep my eyes off the decapitated head.

Delacroix gazed down at Roman. I wondered if he'd been mad as a mortal. I dashed away from the nave and down into the lower chambers. He followed me, closing in, and soon passed me, almost colliding with the far wall.

"Dead end!" He spun round and headed back the way we'd come, passing me again.

I rammed the silver stake into his back, straight through his heart and he stumbled and fell.

I knelt beside him.

He lay conscious, but incapacitated.

I buried my fangs into his neck and closed my eyes. A wave of images flashed before me, dragging me with them and carrying me down. Macabre visions of Delacroix's life unfolded with each mouthful, revealing a million fragments of moments, experienced over centuries. A continuous revolving nightmare sucked me in. Slipping away, the present was no longer perceptible as my mind struggled to grab hold of something solid, something real. Drowning in him, I lost my way and had to pull back.

He picked up on my reluctance and his mouth slid into a smile. Pressing my lips against where I'd bitten him and bruising them, I gulped the scarlet flow again, impossible to subdue the turmoil. As if peering into the blackest mirror, my authentic nature was realized. I barged past his resistance. Tortured faces, each human life I'd taken and he'd taken appeared, only to be replaced by another, the madness of murder entangled. I was unable to ignore the visage. It was impossible to turn away. I faced my own atrocities as they intermingled with his.

The count didn't have my son.

I tried to pull away, but something held me at his neck, an invisible force. It wasn't Delacroix, it was something supernatural that kept me drinking, and it came from within. No turning back. Secrets passed over, information unraveled, and all sinuous links disintegrated.

Crawling on my hands and knees, with his blood mixed with my saliva dripping from my gaping mouth, I scrambled away, eager to put distance between me and him.

Remnants of my essence were listlessly evanescing, and I was powerless to stop it.

* * * *

"Breathe, Daumia . . . breathe." Marcus' voice was distant. "Breathe . . ."

Lost somewhere within my deepest recesses, I had an out of body experience and a glorious feeling of empowerment, one with the sublime. *Breath, so simple and yet so unnecessary.*

"My name's Orpheus." A tingling all over that settled in my groin, the rush caused me to shudder, an experience unlike anything I'd ever known. My body pulsated and I quivered in response to the sensations, enshrined within these invisible pleasures.

Marcus' breath felt warm on my ear. "I thought I'd lost you," he whispered.

"Glad you could make it." I rose up.

Marcus looked confused. "You kind of look . . ."

"What?"

"Different."

Everything felt different. My movement seemed effortless, spectral even, and I took my time to adjust.

I heard the sound of footsteps descending the stairwell, heading fast our way.

I yanked at the stone door of the passageway and it scraped opened. I turned to Marcus. "Go."

"Not without you."

I shoved him through it.

Stone grated against stone as I secured it shut. I sensed Elijah before I saw him. With my back against the clandestine wall, I waited. Elijah flew around the corner. Underneath his arm, he carried Roman's head.

"I was hoping I'd never have to see that again," I said.

Elijah glanced at the count.

I gestured to Roman's head. "Was he always that glum?"

"Whatever you tried here tonight didn't work," Elijah shot back. "Where's Sunaria?"

"I have no idea."

"We saw her enter."

"You have Roman, or what's left of him."

He glanced at the head. "You told me he was alive."

"He was, kind of, a few minutes ago."

"What is this?"

"Ask him." I pointed to Delacroix.

"Seems you impressed Lord Archer," Elijah said. "But you don't impress me."

I shrugged.

"Out of all our descendants your lover murdered," Elijah lowered his chin and locked his stare on mine, "you were the last."

The truth had been glaring at me all this time and yet I'd not seen it. Elijah's familiarity, a faint likeness distorted by time. The feeling that I knew him even though we'd never met.

"She planned to start with your brother, Ricardo," he said, "but his friends took care of him. You were next. That night in the mausoleum, she couldn't go through with killing a boy. She waited for you to age."

I showed no reaction.

"Why do you think she left you in that house with Roelle?" He looked smug.

My gut twisted. "Give me one minute with her."

"Then you'll hand her over?"

"She'll be in the tower."

"We'll be outside."

* * * *

The aroma of iron flooded the nave, the scent of blood. There, scattered along the aisle and amongst the pews were men, some dead, others dying. The Creda had taken on the Stone Masters and won. I searched each man's face. Glass and broken artifacts crunched beneath my feet. I found Lord Archer on the floor taking small breaths, leaning up against the font. I knelt beside him.

Archer's complexion was morbidly pale. "We weren't prepared." He gasped.

"They're ancients." I offered him my wrist.

He turned away.

I ran my fingers up his blood-soaked sleeve. "Your right arm's broken."

He glanced at the deformity. "If I had any strength in that arm, I'd strangle you with it."

"You want me to speed your death? That's why you're provoking me?"

"I want to die with honor, not discussing the finer points of life with the very creature I've dedicated," he cringed with the pain, "my life to tracking down."

I applied pressure to his wound. "Something's different with me."

"You look the same." He pushed himself up and looked around. "My men?"

I bit into my wrist and held it over the gash on his arm, splashing my blood into the laceration. Archer flinched and his wound leaked serous fluid, as our blood intermingled, bubbling up and then reabsorbing. The cut healed.

I lifted my wrist to his lips. He pushed it away.

"How's that pain?" I asked softly.

"Bastard, your filthy blood's in me."

"That arm either heals or you lose it. Or worse."

"At least it would be an honorable death."

"Death is death."

"What do you want, Orpheus?"

"You must live."

"Why?"

"Two reasons."

Archer's breathing was calmer. "Go on."

"Firstly, because I find myself rather fond of you."

"Ridiculous. And the second?"

"Deep down, you desire to truly understand what we are."

"Get out of London." Archer closed his mind.

"One minute and I'll have what I need," I whispered.

Archer's fingers affectionately traced my cheek. "You don't have that much time." His eyes flickered to the right.

Several Stone Lords headed straight for us.

* * * *

The lid to the coffin where I'd placed Roman's head was back in place. Candlelight threw shadows over the dark walls of the burial chamber. In here, there was nothing but stillness, a complete contrast to the mayhem above.

Sunaria loomed in the shadows. "Are they all dead?"

I looked her up and down. "Not exactly."

"Elijah? Archer?" She studied my expression.

"This time, you behaved yourself and stayed put."

She looked serene, beautiful even. I tried to shake off the effect she always had on me, considering whether to fuck her, or worse.

I stared at my hands. "You didn't try to stop me?" Blood surged through them like never before. "You knew this would happen if I drank from him."

Sunaria rested back on the middle casket. "You went through with it?"

"But you knew that when I entered, I saw it in your eyes." A timeless essence rippled. A supernatural wellspring threatened to spill over into this moment and force my carnal hand. I quivered.

"Anyone who consumed him entirely and survived . . ." her gaze seemed to take in my new form with nervous excitement. "You are *Status Regal*, the most feared among us." She slid off the coffin. "You're magnificent."

Stronger now, my muscles were taut, my physique sinewy.

Sunaria read my mind. "Elijah lied to you."

"Did he?"

"I would never have gone through with it." Her lips quivered.

"You were in my home town to kill Ricardo. To kill me?"

"Please listen—"

"Elijah was pretty persuasive in his argument." I stepped toward her. "I read his thoughts."

"That night in the mausoleum was meant to be my last. When I came across Ricardo, your brother, he was so brave and so sweet that I couldn't go through with it."

"So you admit that's why you were there?"

"Yes."

"Why didn't you tell me?"

"I didn't think you'd believe me." More tears. "When I first saw you, saw Aaron holding that cudgel over you, I had to stop him."

"Why didn't you warn Ricardo?"

"Daylight robbed me of the chance."

"Why should I believe you?"

"Because I love you."

I raised a hand, gesturing for her to keep her distance.

She looked lost. "Let me explain."

I nodded my permission.

"You're not the last descendant of the Creda to be turned. Jacob is. This proves my innocence."

I stared at her.

"I couldn't let you die in Felipe's courtyard," she said. "Not after the night we spent together, after I rescued you in the carriage."

"You know I still can't remember it."

"I gave you a small taste of me and then you reacted . . ." She sighed. "You took me." Her eyelids flickered. "It was a dark promise of what it would be like if we became lovers."

"Great, the best sex of my life and I don't remember it."

"Their ancestry endures through Jacob."

"Are they searching for him?"

"I don't know. I made sure they weren't following you. I never once saw them."

"You'd better be right."

"You wanted to hear the truth, but I was terrified you'd leave."

"Tell me how this all started," I asked her.

"Mara, my three-year-old daughter, was taken from me by my master. He told me he sold her."

"Why did you wait so long to kill him?"

"He warned me that if anything happened to him—"

"That's what he had over you?"

"Yes."

"But you killed him anyway." I added coldly.

"Eventually, yes."

"And the Creda?"

"They seduced me with the promise of helping me find my daughter."

"They lied?"

"I would never have harmed you." She tilted her head and stared off. "Some part of me hopes Mara's still alive. Some part of me hates myself for even thinking it."

"That she's one of us?"

She nodded. "After you went to live with Roelle, I returned to Rome to continue my search for her."

"When will the whole truth come out?"

"You won't give me up to them?" she whispered.

My rage ignited and I bared my fangs, stomped my foot, and roared at her.

She cowered away from me.

My gaze wondered over her curves, her breasts rising and falling with each nervous breath.

"What does it feel like?" Her voice was low, husky.

"The view, let's just say it's different." I pushed Sunaria back against the casket. Grabbing her dark locks, pulling her lips to mine, kissing her, I utterly possessed her. Sunaria's hands shook. I pulled back, losing myself for a moment in her reverent gaze.

I wrapped her legs around me. "It's like being drunk on the finest wine." I thrust up against her and ripped at her dress, dragging it off over her shoulders, exposing her.

She shuddered.

I yanked the material down further, restraining her arms. "Or intoxicated by the purest opiate." I offered her another kiss.

She closed her eyes and parted her lips, ready. I enjoyed seeing her vulnerable. My tongue found her nipple, encircling it, and then suckling, eliciting a moan from her.

My strength was such that I knew I'd surpassed hers, a rapid evolution that served only to strengthen my authority. *Status Regal*, the very title imbued power. I let her go and she glided off the casket. I yanked down her red dress, easing it over her hips, letting it fall to the floor, pooling around her feet.

"All vampires will bow before you," she said in awe.

I directed her onto her knees. "Let's start with you, shall we?"

* * * *

I opened up the secret passageway, making it ready.

Clutching Sunaria's red dress, I flew back into the heart of the cathedral, up and into the nave. A row of candles resting on their brass holder burned brightly. I kicked them over and flames spilled out along the central aisle.

I flew up into the cathedral's tower. It looked smaller on the inside than it had looked from the outside. Marcus had gone through with it. He'd coaxed one of Delacroix's raven-haired vampires out of Blackfriars, and, once seduced, he'd tied her up in here. She looked familiar. I'd caught her making out back at Blackfriars. Her lover had gestured for me to join them.

I pushed her dark locks out of her face and dressed her in Sunaria's red gown, which fitted her fairly well. I tried to ignore her crazed stare. Marcus had drunk from her, leaving her weak, but she still had a fight left in her. From a distance, it would be hard to discern that she wasn't Sunaria. By the time the flames reached the tower and burned through her rope bindings, it would be too late. Ablaze, our maiden would fling herself out of the window. I doubted she'd make the ground.

I kissed her forehead.

XLIII

WITH A RESTLESS SPIRIT, I lingered outside the jewelry store where Sunaria had found Jacob's locket.

A distant memory of who I'd once been barely remained. Fragments of my old life drifted in and out, but nothing that I could hold onto. Ancient blood refined my features, dissipating previous character traits. The promise I'd shown could never have foreshadowed such a transformation. Had I known that the elders possessed such preternatural power, I dare say I'd have pursued it, nevertheless, fate delivered.

Sunaria reassured me that this feeling was merely transitional, that my past would again catch up with me and I'd remember everything with even more clarity than before.

I hoped she was wrong.

With no sign of the Creda, it seemed we'd shaken them off. The decimation of the Stone Lords, with the only apparent survivors, Lord Archer and a handful of his men, lessened the fear of their return. The year 1497 promised to come to an end. A new year would be better than the last.

And Jacob would be another year older.

Using all my will to stroll with a somewhat natural gait, I entered the store. The owner couldn't remember where he'd acquired the piece. I did what I could, even going as far as sucking out his last drop of blood to nudge his memory.

I left with no answers.

* * * *

I found Sunaria with Marcus, standing outside the gates of Blackfriars Manor. Gothic towers loomed before us, a terrible reminder of all that had transpired. The blaze that raged through the building would leave no evidence.

"I thought you'd be long gone by now," I said at last to Marcus.

"And miss this? Never. Where did you start the fire?"

"I went back to the painting of Delacroix in Venice," I replied, "and started with that."

He peered through the brass railings. "Locals will think it's the great fire of London all over again, what with the cathedral and now this."

"It'll burn itself out," I said. "As long as the properties don't encroach on the buildings around them, the fire won't spread."

The inferno lit up the London skyline.

"Nothing wipes out the past like fire." I gave a long sigh.

"When will you go back to Spain?" Marcus asked.

"When I'm ready. What are your plans?"

"I'm not sure. Still trying to . . ." Marcus shoveled his feet. "How do we justify the things that we do?"

"We take the criminals off the streets," I faced him, "one man at a time, but it all adds up."

"Look." Sunaria pointed. "There are still vampires in there."

"When the flames lick at their heels, the rest will leave," I said.

The structure imploded and clouds of dust billowed, sending puffs of smoke around us. These dying vampires were Delacroix's servants who'd assisted him, others had merely done nothing.

A rush of fiendish pleasure made me shudder. "Or maybe not."

Orange fire reflected in Sunaria's eyes, dancing flames mirrored in her irises. She caught me staring at her and gave a subtle smile, a gesture of regard. Thunder roared above us and more clouds gathered. An imminent storm threatened.

"Typical," I said.

"What do you think the Creda will do to the count?" Marcus asked.

"They'll bury him in a casket," Sunaria said. "Deep underground."

"Still alive?" Marcus sounded anxious.

"Yes." She gave him a look. "That's what they do."

"And Roman's head?" he asked.

"It will probably be placed in the same coffin." She sighed.

"Bloody hell." He nudged up against me.

"You're safe with me." I smiled.

Sudden rain struck the ground and splashed around us, and yet we remained stock still, watching, waiting. Gradually, the rain suppressed the fire. "Delacroix," I shouted, "you were weighed in the balances and found wanting." I pushed open the gates.

"Now it's you quoting the Bible." Marcus followed close behind me. "That's from the book of Daniel, isn't it?"

All three of us were drenched, but we didn't care. With my arms outstretched, open mouthed, I stared up at the grey sky, enjoying the sensation of the fine rain drops striking my tongue. I spun round and round. I faced them both. "Welcome to Belshazzar's."

* * * *

Sunaria and I remained as guests in The Cavendish Hotel.

Marcus needed to learn to hunt and establish his independence. I'd arranged to meet with him in the old Woodgrange cemetery, known more for its exclusive clientele, the once wealthy, and now deceased, resting soundly beneath finely crafted, ornate tombstones. This graveyard provided a safe place of rest for those who could afford it. Though, whenever I'd previously visited, the night watchman had fallen asleep. Scent from the eucalyptus trees permeated the air. The gravestones were all well tended. Some of the time-honored monuments were watched over by carved angels, and their stone gazes followed me as I ambled through. Oak trees lined the winding pathway, providing much needed shelter during the summer months and, for us, privacy. City life had for a moment been suspended in here.

Marcus rested on one of the older tombstones, deep in thought and very nervous. I lingered behind him for a moment, enjoying reading his thoughts. His ruminations were of me.

I chuckled. "I'm flattered."

Marcus jolted and spun round to face me. "You scared me half to death!"

I laughed. "You need to be more cautious."

"Let's get it over with."

"You make it sound unpalatable."

"Please tell me you're joking."

I leaned against the tombstone next to his. "To survive, you're going to have to look at it differently."

Marcus paced.

I sighed. "You can't go on like this."

He rubbed his hands together. "Is there any other way?"

"No."

"So you just bite, suck, and run?"

"One does not gulp a fine wine, or scoff a delicious meal."

"You mean you enjoy it?"

"Pleasure like no other."

"You really find that when you do it?"

"Marcus, calm down."

"Look, I'm bloody terrified."

"And you're starving too, right?"

He nodded. "After I took that girl in the tower . . . not sure I can do it again."

"I'll walk you through it."

"What if it goes wrong?"

"It never does," I said. "We're designed to be the perfect predator."

"Dear God."

"Yes, by all accounts, he is." I rested my fingertips on my temples. "If your sister can do it . . ."

"That's women for you, natural born killers."

"Rachel's so sweet, they don't even see her coming."

"What if they beg for mercy?"

I grabbed his arm and guided him along the pathway. "The art is to have them begging for more." I stopped before a tomb. "See that."

"The gravestone?" He sighed. "I'll never have one."

"Exactly. Something good comes out of every situation, and for us that's one hell of a benefit."

* * * *

Within the hour, we'd taken a corner table in a noisy, public house, The Baker's Dozen. The beer flowed and the finest food was offered. This place attracted the more discerning customers. Apparently, it had once been a bakery, but had soon become a meeting place for locals. Next, warm ale became available and its popularity had grown.

Marcus stared at a young man who leaned on the bar, sipping his ale.
I nudged Marcus. "I hope you're not eyeing him up?"
"I thought you'd be pleased."
"He's rolling his wedding ring."
"So?"
"He's not used to wearing it."
"He's a newlywed?"
"Are you really considering separating young love?"
"Oh, God."
"Try again."
Marcus shrugged.
I discreetly pointed to a rotund gentleman in the corner. The man, easily in his fifties, snuggled next to a well-dressed, middle-aged woman.
"Him?" Marcus cringed.
My gaze fell on his escort.
"His wife?" Marcus said in surprise.
"Not his wife."
A ruckus in the corner caught our attention. Two men argued and all eyes were on them. Taking advantage of the distraction, the woman pickpocketed the rotund man and then headed out of the door with her prize.
I gestured to the barmaid. "I'd like to pay for our drinks."
"You're not eating then?" she asked, raising her voice over the din.
"Prior dinner engagement." I winked at Marcus.
We left a handful of coins to pay for our untouched drinks and tracked the woman, waiting for the opportune moment when she disappeared down a dark alley or, as she did now, headed fast into Manor Park.
Facing her, we strolled through the well-tended gardens, the epitome of two gentlemen taking the night air.
"Excuse me?" Her voice beckoned.
We stopped and offered her a polite bow.
"You're out late." She pushed her breasts up and gave a seductive smile, revealing a mouth full of rotten teeth. To our right, the bushes rustled and out jumped a twenty-year-old, pointing his pistol at us. I recognized her accomplice, one of the men who'd caused a ruckus, just minutes ago in the pub. His broken nose and cauliflower ears revealed his penchant for boxing.
"Sometimes, they make it easy for you." I gave Marcus a sideways

glance.

"I can see that," he said.

"Hand your money over. All of it," the man snapped.

"Which one would you like?" I asked Marcus.

"You choose," Marcus whispered.

I turned to him. "This is not about what I want."

The woman scowled. "Shut up and give us your money."

"Or I'll shoot your ruddy head off." The man jabbed his gun barrel closer to my chin.

I winked at Marcus. "Looks like the decision's been made for us."

XLIV

BELSHAZZAR'S ROSE UP out of the debris.

The stately manor's exterior, with its classic architecture, was a modest property compared to what it had once been. As such, it would draw less attention, though I had a suspicion that with Sunaria's expensive tastes, the interior would be decadent. Neither of us felt sentimental about living in a home erected upon what had once been Blackfriars. In fact, we looked upon it as a victory. The bohemian lifestyle of the city enabled us to blend in.

Delacroix's disappearance sent shock waves through the underworld. The rumor spread about a new *Status Regal* in town. We were left alone.

With my recent transformation came a soaring confidence. Intuition came easily, though despite insight, I'd become painfully unforgiving. I felt as though I'd personally traveled through centuries, earning every last drop of knowledge, instead of having stolen it from Delacroix that night.

My desire to spend more time alone heightened. I wandered the streets like a dark phantom, a threat to anyone who crossed my path. Hunting took on a heightened pleasure. I refused to question these feelings, fearing that, should I examine them, I'd lose the ability to muster an exquisite sense of dominion at any given moment.

My new obsession was myself.

* * * *

As predicted, Sunaria became engrossed in the new interior designs. When she wasn't out helping me look for Jacob, she spent money like water. We shipped in marble from Italy, furnishings from Madrid, and artwork from the country. We installed the grandest of chandeliers, their candlelight reflecting exquisitely off the luxurious, homey furnishings. The mahogany staircase swept up and along, leading to both the east and west of the manor.

We moved into our new home. Luxury and ensured privacy aided our transition. Despite the guard dogs we acquired, ironically the breed known as bloodhounds, we were still cautious. The animals soon got used to us and at times Sunaria could be seen wandering around the manor with several of them in tow. Very often, I'd hear their paws on the marble floor before I saw them.

We hired servants, maids to take care of the day to day running of the house, and gardeners for the grounds. With constant mindfulness, we passed for normal.

Our bedroom on the upper floor had no windows, a genius design that Sunaria came up with. Although the architect had at first resisted implementing such an eccentric plan, the money we paid convinced him it would do just fine. After a month, I settled in, no longer wondering where the hell I was when I woke up. Stability was a welcome change.

The one thing that I had not accounted for was nature's most frightening bestowal, a woman's jealousy, that formidable sting that comes without warning. Had I had any inclination that inviting Marcus and Rachel to live with us would have incited the worst in Sunaria, I'd have reconsidered. Having awoken from a restless sleep, I sat back against the headboard. A pouting Sunaria dressed. I admired her curves as she moved about the room, though considered staying quiet, hoping that her mood would improve before I spoke. She sat before the vanity dresser and brushed her long dark locks. Despite the lack of her mirrored reflection, Sunaria behaved as though she had one.

"You look beautiful," I said, breaking the silence.

She expertly applied rouge to her pale cheeks and rubbed lipstick over already pink lips.

"This place is huge, there's more than enough room for all of us," I told her.

"How long will your friend and his slut of a sister be staying?"

"Indefinitely."

"And what say did I have in that decision?"

"Is it the fact that I've shagged her?"

Sunaria glared. "*Not* funny."

I smiled. "You know you're the only one for me."

"*And* you're beginning to sound like a Londoner."

I howled with laughter.

She turned, twisting on her seat to look at me. "You find this amusing?"

I rose and approached her. "Sunaria, how can you have any insecurities?"

"Rachel flaunts herself. I see the way she looks at you."

"I read books to her, that's all."

"Well don't."

"There's no harm in it." I assisted Sunaria, pulling the silk straps of her scarlet, fine-boned bodice and weaving them through the minute holes on the back and tightening them. My hands rested around her small waist. Aroused, I considered untying her.

She rested her hands on her hips. "I want them gone."

"Do you now?"

"Why are you being so difficult?"

"Marcus is helping me find Jacob, so I let him stay here."
She turned to face me.
"Look, this is my first night not scouring the streets like a madman." I shook my head in frustration. "I need just one night to take a breath."
"What about what I need?"
"I know what you need. Tomorrow night, I'm going to give it to you."
"What is it?"
"And ruin the surprise?"
"Make them leave."
"If you don't shut up, it will be you that leaves."
She frowned.
"You've had decades to come to terms with what you are," I said. "They've had weeks."
"The old ways dictate that those of us who survive their first steps alone, may just prove that they have what it takes to face eternity."
"And where's the sense in that?"
"You were always so persuadable before."
"I kind of like the new me." I smiled. "Always being right has its privileges." I leaned in and kissed her. "Take Rachel out and teach her."
"Where are you going?"
"Marcus and I are going out."
"Perhaps it's Marcus I should be jealous of."
I spun Sunaria round and spanked her. "I'm watching you."

XLV

I ENTERED MARCUS' BEDROOM and he turned to face me.

I climbed onto his four poster bed and lay beside him. "I'm considering purchasing several more properties," I said. "Safe houses around the city."

Marcus nodded, half-distracted.

I lay on my side. "Perhaps you could help me find appropriate residences?"

"I'm ready."

"Are you?"

"If I'm going to help you find Jacob."

I moved closer to him and pressed my wrist against his mouth. "This is what he looks like."

Marcus' bite felt gentle, lapping, he took just enough to envision Jacob, the purest images passed on through my blood. He fell back and gazed up at the ceiling.

"Are you all right?" I asked softly.

He looked shaken but blissful. I sucked on my wrist, licking the remaining drops as the fang bites dissipated and my taste buds tingled. I glanced over, but Marcus avoided making eye contact.

I studied him. "Did you see enough?"

He nodded and sat up, having not only glimpsed my son, but also experienced me. Disquieted, his desire for more left him blushing, aroused. He shifted away from me.

Trying to make it easier for him, I subdued a smile, all the while listening to him stumble over his thoughts. An endearing crush, cravings ignited. I'd stirred a vampire's nature. I offered him my wrist again.

"I should be going." He let out a deep sigh.

"What's wrong?"

"Your blood, it makes me feel . . ." He pressed his hand against his chest.

"Makes you feel . . . ?"

He climbed off the bed and stared back at me, full of desire.

I arched an eyebrow. "As good as that?"

Marcus quick footed it out the door.

* * * *

Waiting for Sunaria, I sat in the living room, warming myself before the roaring fireplace, though it had no effect.

Despite the fact that Marcus had taken my place tonight, making good on his promise, I couldn't help but feel that I should also be out there scouring the city streets. Melancholy lingered like an unwelcome guest.

Sunaria entered. She'd dressed in a gentleman's attire, handsome, but masculine.

I rose to greet her. "I'm taking you out for a romantic night and you dress like that?"

"I thought you'd like it." Hands on her hips, she studied me. "You won't tell me where we're going."

"Your blue dress, wear that."

"It's safer to dress as a man."

"You're a vampire for God's sake. It doesn't get any safer."

"If we're going to be flying over roofs!"

"We're not. Change, now."

"I saw Marcus before he left," she said sharply. "What went on between you?"

"I know I'm a flirt but that's ridiculous."

"Is it?"

"Yes. Come here."

She stood her ground.

"Look, I just showed him Jacob, that's all. Marcus is out there searching for him so that I can be with you tonight." I approached her. "Come here." I wrapped my arms around her.

"Why do you close your mind to me?" She stiffened. "I should be able to probe the secret out of you, but no, you're keeping all sorts of things from me."

"One of the benefits of sucking a *Status Regal* dry is that you learn new tricks. Now get changed."

"Not until you tell me the surprise."

"That's why it's called a bloody surprise, woman."

Sunaria stormed out.

I shouted after her, "You have ten minutes."

* * * *

Sunaria reappeared wearing her blue empire line gown, with elegant sweeping floor-length sleeves. Her seamstress had designed the dress to complement her small waist and emphasize her breasts. A European twist on the English fashion, enhanced by the deep bordeaux lined cape, bestowing a classic style. I'd donned my dark trousers and luxurious velvet jacket. Black on a man provides an air of mystery, but also ensures ease in mingling with the crowd and disappearing into it if needed. London's streets were at times so choked with shadows that if I stepped back into a doorway, I'd become invisible.

At night, Fleet Street teemed with well-dressed pedestrians, and along the newly constructed roads rumbled fine-looking carriages, taking their wealthy passengers home after a day of wheeling and dealing, or for the lucky few, after an afternoon of frivolous entertainment.

Sunaria and I strolled hand in hand, taking in the fresher air found in this part of town. We experienced many lingering stares from passersby, though we proceeded on regardless with our heads down, ignoring them all.

I resisted pulling Sunaria down a dark alley, wanting nothing more than to pleasure her. Aware of my long strides, I slowed my pace. She enjoyed me taking the lead, as only a strong woman can. Our lessening arguments were a sign she'd stopped vying for dominance.

We turned down Bouverie Street, heading in the direction of Temple Avenue, and the breeze from the Thames reached us. We stopped before an English townhouse. The exterior brickwork was interlaced with wooden beams, and upon the roof rested the tallest chimney. Judging by the dark windows, the residents were not at home. Just a little way back from the house on the estate stood a smaller structure, a white-washed, one-room building to the side of the property, that looked over the Thames.

I guided Sunaria around to the side entrance and shoved her up against it. "Don't move," I whispered.

I withdrew a small strip of black velvet material from my inner coat pocket and used it as a blindfold on her. I spun her round to face me, savoring the excitement I'd stirred in her, delighted by her quickening. Sunaria was breathing fast, her bosom rising and falling with arousal.

"Stay here," I ordered her.

She nodded.

The room was pitch black. At the center of the farthest wall was the only window. I approached and drew back the curtain to let in the moonlight. I found a box of matches and lit the first of twelve candles, trying not to be drawn in by the striking display.

Sunaria was where I'd left her, and she'd obediently kept the velvet strip over her eyes. Taking her hand, I led her into the center of the room and then waited, feeling her excitement building.

I nuzzled close, and then loosened the blindfold, and it fell.

Sunaria let out a sigh.

We were surrounded by thirty or so paintings of sunsets and sunrises. Sunaria stepped forward, awestruck, admiring the large canvas before us, a rendering of daybreak over the Thames, with its lush yellows, oranges, and deepest golds, an exuberant mixture of colors and textures, a glorious array, a magnificent depiction.

She suppressed a sob.

The painting shimmered, reflecting light from the quivering candles.

"I don't know anything about art," I spoke quietly. "But this is like seeing it for real."

Sunaria's fingertips hovered near the canvas, respectfully not touching, but lingering close. We marveled at the way the artist had duplicated the finest details, and we both sighed in wonder.

"Let's commission him," I said. "His name's Alberto Ceravassio."

"He's Venetian?"

"I believe so."

Sunaria was joyful.

Sharing this moment with her made me burn with pride. "I knew you'd like it."

"The family in that house provides this studio for him?" she asked.

I nodded. "In return, he paints."

"They sell his paintings?"

"Yes, and I imagine he gets hardly anything for them."

"That's a shame." Sunaria sighed. "Still, the high paying aristocracy probably double what the Vatican offers."

"The Church considers painting for them a privilege, therefore they pay little."

"How did you find him?"

"Marcus visited artist's row near the Strand. He met the painter and admired his work. Cervassio told him about his studio here."

"I *love* my surprise." Sunaria reached up and planted kisses on my cheek.

I smiled at her. "And I love you."

"Even after everything?"

"Lucky for you I'm obsessed with you." I squeezed her into me. "Can't get enough of you."

"I promise that I'll never disappoint you again."

"I don't doubt it."

She snuggled into my neck and then leaned up and kissed my lips. "I'm rather enjoying London."

"If you're willing to brave the unknown," I added, "it's certainly not boring."

XLVI

THE FULL MOON LIT UP the night sky, making up for the few low lying clouds. A storm threatened to break at any moment.

The carriage lumbered along London's well-worn streets, providing its passengers, Marcus and I, with a dramatic view of the shifting landscapes as we both gazed out of the window, deep in thought.

My mind was on Jacob. I hoped that my son had found somewhere warm and safe to shelter. It was still difficult for me to think of him somewhere out there, alone. The sprawling city was an impossible place to find a small boy.

Marcus sensed my melancholy, and broke the silence. "I've always wondered what it felt like to be in one of these."

With his hair tied back and his new attire, he'd completely transformed his appearance and, like me, he now passed for a wealthy gentleman.

"Do you think we'll ever see the Creda again?" he asked.

"I'm more concerned about Archer."

"Why?"

"He warned me to get out of London."

"That's strange." Marcus' eyes narrowed. "I thought they wanted us all dead."

"Must have impressed him with my charm." I sighed. "What if Jacob doesn't recognize me?"

"A son always knows his father."

The homes had gone from small shacks to luxurious residences in a matter of minutes. The tower of London loomed large in the distance.

"Sunaria's not happy that we're living with you, is she?" Marcus watched my response.

"She'll get over it." I avoided his gaze.

Our carriage swerved to miss a small, black dog. The animal yelped and bolted down a back alley, and the horseman quickly regained control of our spooked horses.

"You didn't even flinch." Marcus still clutched the seat.

"What's the worst that can happen?"

"Do you really believe we're immortal?" he asked. "Come on." He laughed. "I mean really?"

"Yes."

"So how old are you?"

"Thirty."

"How long have you been . . . thirty?"

"About six years."

"I'm not half as impressed now." He smiled.

I focused on the pedestrians, and tried to extract a thought, or some sense of who they were before they disappeared from sight. My mind braved revisiting a disturbing memory, one that I'd buried deep, but now felt compelled to reveal to Marcus. A monstrous recollection that I hoped he could cope with as I now disclosed it to him.

Marcus' smile faded as he picked up on my ruminations. "You drank from Lilly and . . ." He sank back in his seat, devastated.

"I assumed if I told you in a speeding carriage, you wouldn't jump out, and you'd have no choice but to hear my side."

"Delacroix forced you to do it?"

I nodded. "Still, I deserve your hate."

He reached forward and rested his hand on my knee, and in that moment, we shared something unexpected, a mutual understanding that went beyond the physical.

He looked away, embarrassed that he'd revealed such affection. "I still can't quite believe that we can avoid . . ."

"Death's sting." I tilted my head and smiled at him. "The Stone Masters believe that we can reform from ash."

"Really?"

"Outlandish, I know."

Marcus stared out of the window again.

I followed his gaze. "The self-discovery seems unending."

"Will God ever forgive us?"

"Probably you more than me."

"You didn't choose this life?"

"No, but I revel in the dark."

"You like being this?" He looked surprised.

I shrugged. "I find that I do."

"How old is Sunaria?"

"You better ask her."

He chuckled to himself.

"I want to open an orphanage," I said.

"Where did that come from?" Marcus leaned back. "And why?"

"For all the right reasons."

"And the money?"

"Not an issue."

"I'd like to help in any way I can."

"Good."

"We'll have fun tonight, eh?" Marcus said. "Are you going to tell me where we're going now?"

I rested my feet on the seat opposite. "You look good."

"This shaving three times a day thing is bothersome, though."

"As you've discovered, when we're turned, we keep the same look, and as stubble is considered passé . . ."

"I'm feeling awfully dapper." He pulled at his shirt collar. "You still haven't told me where we're going."

"King's court."

Marcus' jaw dropped.

I slid down in the seat and closed my eyes.

"*The* king's court?" He sounded utterly amazed.

I opened an eyelid. "Blue blood, I hear, is a delicacy."

XLVII

Circa 1500

I AWOKE TO THE most awful noise.

An unearthly screeching resonated throughout the manor. Half-dressed, I flew out of bed, closely followed by Sunaria.

We found Rachel in the living room with a violin positioned under her chin. "Hello." She grinned, seemingly unaware of the terrible sound she had made.

I raised my eyebrows. "Hello."

"Look what Marcus bought me." She raised the instrument triumphantly into the air.

"Remind me to thank him." I suppressed the sarcasm.

Sunaria stifled a laugh.

"Perhaps you could find somewhere else to practice?" I said, "Like France?"

Rachel dropped the violin to her side. "You don't like it?"

"Let's get you an instructor." I winked at Sunaria. "I'm sure we'll find one across town."

Sunaria strolled over to the window and peeked out the side of the curtain. "It's dark already, but it's still so early."

"It gets darker earlier in winter," Rachel said.

I joined Sunaria by the window. "So England does have its benefits." Outside was the usual hustle and bustle of Belgravia—carriages rolling by, children playing catch and annoying the street merchants. I turned my attention back to Rachel. There was something familiar about her instrument. I gestured for her violin.

Clutching the neck, I tweaked the peg box, strumming the strings to check the pitch, and breathed in the woody fragrance. I admired the walnut form and ran my fingers along the delicate shape. Music vibrated through me. I rested my chin on the black rest and the fingers of my left hand positioned naturally on the fingerboard. With my right hand, I slid the bow.

The violin rejoiced, responding to my touch, a violinist's interpretation as music flowed with the perfect sequence, moving past what I'd heard and straying from the familiar, articulating timbre and texture, composing notes, and conveying emotions, a voice beyond words, a cadence of extraordinary intimacy. Swaying now, I disappeared inside the melody and became the music.

Savoring the final note, I came back.

An eerie quiet descended on the room.

"Will you teach me to play like that?" Rachel eventually whispered.

Sunaria frowned. "I didn't know you could play the violin."

I held the instrument at arm's length, trying to ascertain what had just happened. "I can't."

"*He* played the violin, didn't he?" Sunaria's tone was edgy.

The bow slipped from my fingers.

An awful memory stirred of being shackled to the wall, deep within the dungeons of Blackfriars, below where we stood now, haunted by the music of this very instrument, awaiting my next torture, and full of fear that it would never end.

"Delacroix." His name caught in my throat. I swung the violin and smashed it against the wall, sending splinters flying.

Rachel's face fell and her tears welled. I stared down at the scattered pieces. Sunaria stared back at me incredulously.

I cleared my throat, and tried to reclaim some decorum. "I'll um, get you another one, Rachel. This one appears to have a flaw."

Rachel gathered the walnut fragments and Sunaria assisted her. The tip of my shoe tapped the discarded bow and Sunaria pulled it out of my reach.

I was dazed.

Marcus crashed through the door and stared at me wide-eyed. He gazed down at what had once been a violin.

"I'll get her another one," I said.

Marcus neared me. "I've found him."

"What?"

"Jacob." Marcus nodded. "I know where he is."

* * * *

If I could have willed Marcus to go faster, I would have done so. We flew over the rooftops, quickly arriving at Number 12, Petherton Road, nestled in the hamlet of Newington Green.

Marcus and Sunaria waited for me across the street, shielded in a shadowy alley. Using darkness as my cover, I approached the townhouse, and peered into the half open window. Meager candlelight vacillated within the sparse room.

I'd found Jacob.

I bit into my hand, stifling a sob. I wanted to burst in and grab him. Jacob, now nine-years-old, appeared well. He sat before a wooden bench, pummeling into the base of a small basin. Close by sat a man in his fifties, studying the contents of several books that he'd balanced on his lap. He had a wise, kind face and a serene demeanor.

I turned back to see Sunaria staring at me, her eyes full of hope. When she saw my expression, her face lit up.

With pride, I studied Jacob, reassured that he'd found a safe haven. He appeared content. Jacob resembled his mother even more now, an uncanny reminder of Annabelle and a painful reminder of his elder brother. He'd grown in height, evidence of being well cared for, and his modest attire was smart. His warm clothes were perfect for another harsh English winter. I felt thankful to the gentleman for taking such good care of him.

Jacob jumped off his chair, approached his mentor, and topped up his cup. His reward was a warm smile. They both resumed their activities.

Fearful that I'd start sobbing with joy, I rejoined Marcus and Sunaria in the alleyway. With my hand on my chest, I tried to steady my nerves. The relief was immense. In a moment, I'd burst into that house and grab him, but first I had to think it through, work out how I'd explain myself to the fresh faced boy who may have forgotten me. Didn't want to frighten him and push him away.

"Jacob's the physician's assistant," Marcus explained. "His name is Doctor Potts."

"How did you find him?" I asked.

"The old man made a late night call to a patient," Marcus continued. "Jacob was with him."

Sunaria looked harried. "Marcus doesn't think you should remove him."

"What? Why?" Disconcerted, I stared back up at the window. "We have servants that can watch over him when I can't."

"He's settled here," Marcus said.

"This is none of your business," Sunaria snapped.

"I've been searching for him, as well," Marcus said, sulkily.

Sunaria folded her arms. "Then you know the best place for him is with his father."

"Wait, wait," I interrupted. "What's brought this on?"

"What if the Creda come back?" Marcus asked.

"Get Jacob and let's go," Sunaria insisted.

"Jacob is getting an education," Marcus said.

"He doesn't need to work. We can take care of him," Sunaria's tone rose with her impatience.

I leaned against the wall. "Does the physician have a wife?"

"I haven't seen anyone other than them," Marcus said.

"We've waited this long," Sunaria said, panicked. "We're not leaving him here."

I tried to shake off the procrastination. My inability to watch over him before had put him in danger and I'd lost him. The thought of making the wrong decision again scared me. Running my fingers through my hair, trying to suppress the nagging doubt, I paced. Enemies of ours, known or unknown, could threaten him. My inability to protect my son during the day would leave him exposed.

There was movement at the window. The curtain was drawn closed.

"He's right." I felt panic as I spoke those words, trying to find the truth in them.

"I don't believe what I'm hearing," Sunaria sucked in her breath. "You think that this place is safe? Being dragged to sick people's homes? What if he catches something?"

I hesitated, searching for the right words. "She does have a point."

"He's living with a physician," Marcus said. "He won't put the boy in harm's way."

"How do you know that?" Sunaria asked annoyed. "What if he beats the boy?"

"He looks well cared for." I glanced back up at the window.

"The old man does appear to have reached a good age," Marcus said.

"What has that got to do with anything?" Sunaria snapped.

"Well, I was just answering your concern about disease," he replied. "When he's old enough for you to explain, he may want to live with you."

"He will live with me," I said abruptly.

"I don't believe we're even having this discussion." Sunaria gestured in frustration.

"This day should be glorious . . ." I rubbed my temples, "instead, it's tortuous."

"Look, we know where he is now." Marcus squeezed my shoulder. "Let's just give this decision some thought."

I pushed Marcus' hand off.

"Jacob has found stability," Marcus continued. "I'm not saying don't see him. He's just safer here."

"If he's seen at the manor, he could be at risk." I sighed.

"You're seriously considering leaving him here?" Sunaria asked me.

My throat tightened, restricting my breathing. I felt sick.

Marcus shoveled his feet.

"We're leaving him here." I turned away from them. "It's decided."

"Why?" Sunaria said.

"Because this is home." My voice sounded strange to me. "I want him to have everything that I can't give him."

"What can that old man give him that you can't?" Sunaria's lips trembled.

"Daylight," I said.

* * * *

Despite having made my decision, I lingered, staring up at the house.

I couldn't bear the thought of leaving him. Not even getting the opportunity to hold him was torture. It would be an easy thing to break in, seize Jacob, and whisk him off, go through the motions I'd been planning since I'd first stepped foot in London. Leaving him in the place where I'd found him had not even been an option. Marcus had planted doubt and I hated him for it.

Unaffected by the morning chill, though slightly distracted by a nagging hunger, it dawned on me that I didn't want to expose Jacob to this life. True love, I realized, was about letting go, freeing those whom we cared most about.

Sunaria had left hours before, too upset to argue anymore, and Marcus had withdrawn soon after, giving me time to think.

Far off, a cockerel announced the morning. If I'd have had the time to find it, I'd have done so, and then rung the bird's neck. I strolled away, along the winding street, glancing back several times before leaping up onto one of the rooftops. The night seemed blacker and the cold reached into my bones. London's nightscape was a mass of grey buildings in disarray, the bleakest city. Longing for Spain, I reassured myself that soon I'd return with Jacob. Heavy-hearted, I made my way home.

The house was deserted, the servants having gone home hours earlier. I found Sunaria in the lower chambers. She wore a transparent gown, and a plumage of fine, black feathers at the neck and cuffs. Two coffins were pushed up into the corner.

"When did we acquire those?" My uneasiness persisted.

She'd placed candles around the den. Plush blue and gold colored pillows were scattered here and there.

My gaze hovered at eye level. "You're not planning on sleeping down here, are you?"

"I feel safer down here." She glanced at the coffin. "And in there."

"Why?"

"I don't trust him."

"Marcus has our best interests at heart."

Sunaria sat down on the coffin lid.

"What's gotten into you?" I said.

"He hates you for turning him."

I frowned. "He understands that I had no choice."

"He hates me, too."

"No, he doesn't."

"He won't accept what he is."

"As I recall, I needed time when you turned me."

"That's not the point."

I struggled to suppress my frustration.

"You understood what it is to be a vampire." Her tone was brusque.

"You left me buried for days," I said. "That helped to persuade me."

Sunaria rose and approached me. "You deserved that."

I bit my lip and didn't respond.

She stared off at nothing. "It was my right to do what I wanted to you, and when."

"It's 1500, time to realize that progress means change."

"And what is that supposed to mean?"

"That your old ways . . . No, that your ancient ways are redundant." I gestured my exasperation. "Your ridiculous obsession with myth, for example."

"What myth?"

"Superstition."

Sunaria wouldn't look at me. "You're angry because you know you should have brought your son home."

I glanced at the coffin. "You're not sleeping in there."

Sunaria pouted.

"What is this really about?" I asked.

"It's you who hinders us by exposing us to outsiders. You should never have allowed Marcus here."

"Marcus risked his life for us."

Her turquoise stare fixed on me. "Ever since you brought him into our home, I've been unable to sleep."

"Be straight with me."

"You left Jacob in that house."

"He's safer there."

"You must get him tonight," she demanded. "Start preparing him."

"For what?"

"Don't tell me you haven't considered it?"

"I don't believe we're having this conversation."

"We are superior beings."

"Are you deliberately provoking me?"

"I'm not ashamed of what I am," she screamed.

"Neither am I." My voice was calm, concealing my alarm.

"Do you want me to transform him?"

I grabbed her wrist. "Stay away from my son."

"Immortality is his birthright." She dug her nails into me.

"Never speak of this again," I warned her. "Do you understand?"

"You're hurting me."

I loosened my grip. "Sometimes, I don't think I know you."

"You're too caught up in yourself to know anything about me."

A feather from her cuff came loose and spiraled, and I watched it float to the floor. It appeared as though it had always belonged to the sleeve of that long, black chemise, and had never been ripped from the small body of a dead bird.

"Marcus and I, we're not like that." I tried to believe it myself.

"He's in love with you and so is his sister."

I wrapped my fingers firmly around her throat. "I love you."

"He's obsessed with you, but you don't see it. Drink from him and you'll know the truth."

"I don't need to."

She broke away.

I grabbed her. "You and me, this is different."

"How?" She leaned away.

I spun her around and grasped her arms. "You need me more than I need you."

Her gown slipped off her left shoulder, exposing her breast.

"I'll not tolerate this." I shoved her against the wall. "If you think that burying me in the earth was a fair punishment, then you have no imagination. Your dark soul needs to be restrained."

"Your soul is blacker."

"I don't doubt it, but that too, I'm able to control."

"You have no power over me."

I pulled away. "If you want to stay in this house, you'll obey me."

Sunaria softened, relenting. "Marcus is upstairs."

* * * *

Rachel turned the corner and stopped, giving me a questioning look. I was, after all, lingering before her brother's bedroom door. "What?" I snapped.

"Would you like to join me tonight?" she said softly.

"No." My hand hesitated on the door handle.

"I'm going to the opera."

"Why in God's name would I want to go with you?"

Her face fell.

"Don't you have something better to do?" I turned the handle and then paused, waiting for her to walk away.

"Are you visiting Marcus?"

I ignored her.

Marcus stirred when I entered. Red stubble was speckled over his jaw and his English complexion was pale. He'd obviously not fed. His appetite, like mine, had dulled with tonight's events back on Petherton Road.

I ignored his questioning expression, as well as his resistance, and nuzzled into his neck. He tried to shove me away, but I restrained him, pinning his hands down on either side of his head, his strength no match for mine. Marcus jolted when I bit. There was no turning back.

His life flashed before me—*Marcus as a simple farm boy, the death of his parents at age fourteen, his inability to maintain their farm, the property being taken away, the loss of his livelihood, Marcus and Rachel's journey to London, them scouring for food, striving to survive. As though I were there with them, I followed Rachel, Marcus, Lilly, and Ted as they trespassed into Blackfriars.*

Beneath me, Marcus relented, softening and letting me in, exposing it all, offering himself as an open book. I rocked against him, exchanging intimacy for knowledge. Swallowing, I continued on, wanting to know every part of him, memorizing his wants, his fears, and devouring his lifelong yearnings, his innermost secrets.

Another visage now of Blackfriars, Marcus' hope when I'd turned up at their cell door. The rush he'd experienced but suppressed when I'd transformed him.

And I wanted to know more.

I tapped into Marcus' streaming thoughts, and witnessed him scouring London's streets, no matter the weather. His passion in looking for Jacob and exultation at finding him, and then taking special care to remember the doctor's house. Marcus flying across London, wanting to share the news with me, and his troubled ruminations of how we'd keep Jacob safe, and how best to protect him. His fear of the others, as dark eyes stared back at him from the shadows outside Belshazzar's, wayward vampires new to London. And, finally, his fear of disappointing me, his loyalty and an infatuation with me that verged on obsession.

His fingernails dug into my forearms, holding me against him.

Placing my fingers over the bite, I stemmed the trickle.

"Did you find what you were looking for?" he asked breathlessly.

I wiped my mouth.

"Stay with me tonight." He clutched my sleeve.

I pulled away and sauntered out.

* * * *

The following night, I returned to Petherton Road.

I wanted my son.

Standing across the street from the doctor's house, lingering in the alleyway, it felt good to be close to Jacob again. After an hour of just staring, waiting for the opportune moment, the door opened and Jacob appeared, dressed in a woolen coat. The doctor followed him out. Hand in hand, they headed down Petherton Road and took a sharp turn on Flower Avenue. I wanted to sweep Jacob up into my arms.

Savoring every second, I followed them across town, now and again pulling back so as not to arouse suspicion. Jacob's English accent was flawless. There remained no evidence of his Spanish drawl. I wondered if he had any memory of me. Envious of the doctor, I wanted my son's hand in mine instead of his.

His mentor showed kindness, slowing his pace so that Jacob could keep up with his master's strides. After half an hour of walking, they reached a shack, and the doctor disappeared inside. Jacob paused for a moment, and then turned and stared in my direction. Although out of his line of sight, he did appear to detect me, peering in my direction before going inside.

Torn with what to do, I wavered. The sky opened and it poured. Perhaps I'd imagined it—my need for my son to know me so great that my mind believed that he'd sensed me. I turned on my heels and strolled in the opposite way, unable to go through with it. Strange that we can be right next to the ones we love, and yet they still seem like a million miles away.

I headed home.

Although long gone from my own life, I wanted normalcy for Jacob. Putting my own needs aside, I concentrated on his.

My arms ached for him.

Back in Belshazzar's, standing in the lounge before a roaring fireplace, I lost myself in the orange glow. My clothes were soaked through and clung to my wet skin, making me feel even more miserable. I wasn't sure how long Sunaria had been standing behind me.

"I'm going to start a trust fund for him," I said at last.

In silence, Sunaria undressed me, starting with my drenched shirt. A log slipped in the hearth and sparks sprayed around it.

Naked now, the warmth of the fire reached my bones. She guided me into the drawing room where a hot bath had been prepared and I climbed in.

The water rose high, trickling over the edges. With a glazed stare, I traced the marble mantelpiece. Upon it rested a maple clock, the tick tock of time so sure, so perfect, and so irrevocable.

The only noise in the room harassed me with its relentless progression.

Sunaria climbed in with me, lying between my legs, her fine, red negligee floating to the surface and billowing. I rested my head back onto the edge of the tub, staring up at the ceiling.

"You have nothing to forgive yourself for," Sunaria whispered.

I burst into tears.

XLVIII

SNOW FELL, BLANKETING the London skyline in a perfect powdery white.

It felt good to be indoors. The fireplace, pre-lit, warmed the study. An array of books lined the shelves and I stood back to admire them. I'd selected the finest publications, covering many diverse subjects. Such a collection would make any scholar ecstatic. I held on to the hope that Jacob would soon be whiling away the hours in here, and I'd have him all to myself. Thinking back to my own childhood, I remembered my father and the tales he'd tell.

When the right time came, I'd bring Jacob in here. With a deep sigh, I strolled into the adjacent study, this room above all, easily my favorite. I hoped it would become Jacob's. I'd procured a large oak writing table for him and placed it in the center, taking great pleasure in organizing paper, ink, and a feathered fountain pen, essential items to make him feel at home. Finding one of my ornate letter openers, I placed it near the other items.

Long, sweeping black drapes hung from the tall window. Looking out past them, I viewed the muggy, grey nightscape of London's skyline. Running my fingers over the mahogany mantelpiece and along the engraved design, I admired the ornate carving that was the room's focal point, chiseled by one of the city's finest carpenters.

Although I'd not played the violin in months, the notes struck up inside my imagination. Not fighting the flow, I allowed the music to carry me away. Indulging in my imagination, haunted by the promise of spending time with Jacob, my mind drifted.

I left the room and descended the sweeping staircase. The vastness of Belshazzar's meant that I could go for days and not see anyone. I seemed to be the only one who enjoyed the vastness of the manor. On many an evening, I strolled along the pitch-black corridors, my cloak sweeping behind me, lost in memories and captured by possibilities.

Sunaria enjoyed the more visceral of pleasures. To subdue her, I'd agreed to join her on a visit to one of her more bohemian vampire friends—a promise I had no intention of keeping.

Marcus had also searched out new acquaintances, widening his social circle within London's underworld. I declined his frequent offers to join him, preferring my own company, when I wasn't in that of my son's, albeit from a distance.

Culture and class beckoned nightwalkers from afar. Regardless of my desire to hold back time, it unraveled, senselessly betraying me.

Despite the Christmas evening, Sunaria and Rachel braved the elements. Not even a harsh English winter could deter Sunaria from the erotic spoils of city life.

I took a seat in the corner of our lavishly decorated lounge and opened *Sir Gawain and the Green Knight*, resting the book on my knees.

A bloodhound sluggishly settled at my feet. This was the first room Sunaria had furnished and she'd gone all out. We were immersed in decadent colors, lush textures, and sweeping curtains. The far wall was painted a deep red, enhancing the semblance. Despite my initial reservations, the color actually complemented the décor and went well with the candelabras positioned here and there, providing a soft yellow illumination.

I barely looked up from my well-worn novel to greet Marcus. Quietly judging my mood, he joined me, taking the seat opposite. I glanced up at the bookcase, now half-stocked. Sunaria enjoyed assisting Rachel with her collection, and I'd granted permission for her to shelve it here. Though I preferred a more modest setting, this room had become the center of activity in the house, and tonight I desired company, if only for a while. A robin hopped along the window ledge and pecked at the frame.

I broke the silence. "The doctor accepted the money?"

"It wasn't easy," Marcus said. "He's a man of integrity, which is—"

"A good thing."

The robin flew off.

"He needed some gentle persuading," Marcus added.

I gestured for him to elaborate.

"I just told him the money came from a grateful custodian," Marcus explained. "And as you're always calling Jacob your rock, I told him the gentleman's name was *Roch*."

"You must have intrigued him."

Marcus opened his mouth to reply, though cautious of my mood he chose not to. I saved my page and closed the book.

"The money will be used for Jacob's education," Marcus said.

"And Jacob?"

"He looked well. He has your eyes."

Unable to be that close to my son and not be able to embrace him, I'd sent Marcus. "He has his mother's eyes." I looked up. "And that other matter?" I pulled at the frill beneath my white ruffled sleeve.

"Our third orphanage has just been purchased and the children are being schooled," he said. "Do come and visit."

"No."

Marcus' knuckles were white as he clutched the armrests.

Not that I cared. "Sunaria tells me that there's a place in London where mortals and our kind mingle?"

Marcus smiled. "Madam Rouge's. Where the wine flows like water and so does the blood."

His words faded into the background. Entranced, my thoughts wandered, hypnotized by the snow. A robin jumped onto the sill again and pecked at the window.

"Do you think that's the same bird?" I asked wistfully.

Marcus frowned. "What *are* you talking about?"

I breathed in the scent of burning oak. Oranges and yellows lapped in the grate, the log almost turned to ash, and, as though striving for life, fresh flames burst up around it and smoke rose into the chimney.

XLIX

TWELVE YEARS PASSED before I considered setting foot in Madam Rouge's illustrious home.

Despite its reputation, I found myself reluctant to pursue any kind of personal pleasure in her private East London house. For an hour, I'd lingered outside, trying to coax myself to enter. Eventually, with hope that my depression would lift, I headed in. Such a spontaneous visit would be a nice surprise for Sunaria and I wondered if Marcus would be enjoying another evening here.

Wall to wall guests mingled in every room. Admittance wasn't something to be taken for granted. It took a notable recommendation and a great deal of money. Endless decadence, although not reflected by the unassuming exterior, once inside, one discovered an exotic den. Large couches were positioned here and there, with love seats scattered amongst them. Dark colors painted upon the arched walls and minimal candles threw mysterious shadows, enhancing the sultry mood.

Socializing here were the forward thinkers, holding late night discussions into the early hours, and when conversations became tedious, guests were encouraged to roam the upper chambers and search out amusements that would keep them coming back for more. Wine flowed.

This sumptuous home, nestled in the heart of London, welcomed those who desired to forget, a promise of feeling human again, if only for a night. Or for the mortal, the chance to embrace what it is to be bohemian. Although many of the mortal visitors had no idea with whom they mingled, there were a few who did, and the chance to taste our blood was the motivator for their risk taking. Just as Archer's documents had suggested, we were integrating more with society and disappearing into its very heart.

If I could appear normal to them, then perhaps I could find the confidence to finally reveal myself to my son. Jacob was now twenty-one years old, and had made a life for himself, having realized his dream, following in Dr. Potts' footsteps and becoming a physician. Although I'd never have chosen such a life for him, I did have a sense of pride that, despite everything, he'd prevailed. I resigned myself to remaining in England for the duration of his life.

He still did not know me.

I'd gone to great lengths to discover the classic nuances within the city, forcing myself to find captivating elements, searching for a pathway that would not lead to sadness. Within me was the desire to grasp the last trace of whom I'd once been, and find the answers to the questions I'd once been afraid to ask. To let go would be self-betrayal.

Although we'd invested in property, it wasn't out of a fondness for the city, but rather to secure several safe houses. Marcus often joked that if we lived for over one hundred years, taking inflation into consideration, our net worth would be substantial. Although as a young man, I'd strived to obtain wealth, my motivation had been that it brought with it freedom.

Sunaria and Marcus had taken over the day to day dealings of our business. Marcus also discussed the importance of creating wills, so that by the time we were meant to be dead, we'd inherit our property back. He always looked to the future. I, however, preferred living in the present. As I now found myself in the most erotic of places, I wanted to explore and shake off this moodiness and rekindle the old Daumia.

Holding my tall glass of red, a house special, I strolled on, following the trail of rose petals that crushed beneath my feet as it led through the house. The fragrance still sparked a visceral response.

This place enabled people watching at its best. Music struck up from somewhere in the house. I recognized the violin and another instrument with a deeper base, one that I was unfamiliar with. The dark melody enhanced the already risqué atmosphere.

Out of the corner of my eye, I caught a young blond woman staring at me.

She nudged the man next to her and mouthed, "Déjà vu."

Trying to work out why she'd uttered it, I followed her gaze. It settled on a man ascending the staircase. To my astonishment, he not only appeared to have the same haircut as me, but also a similar physique. He reached the top step and headed along the balcony. I quick-footed it after him, down the dusky corridor, hugging the walls. I backed into an alcove, transfixed, watching him.

His age and height equaled mine. Astonished, I realized that his jacket, white shirt, and black trousers had actually come from my own wardrobe. Now that *was* creepy. His hair, a contrast to my unruly mop of black, lay where he'd combed it.

He knocked on a door and then disappeared inside.

From within, I heard two men talking. A young couple passed by me, and shared a suspicious laugh.

With them out of sight, I turned the handle.

Marcus, wearing a blue robe, stood by the edge of the bed, talking intently with my double. The man sunk to the floor, kneeling before him. I took in the vision as the intimacy between them unfolded. He ran his fingers through my counterpart's hair, ruffling his dark locks so that they resembled mine. Marcus swooned.

I slid in and lingered just inside. The woman downstairs had looked at me and mouthed, 'déjà vu.' She was right. This situation brought back memories of observing Salvador with his lover. Regrets of all that could have been, came back. Salvador's kind eyes, his dashing smile, the way he'd held me and what I'd missed, and I longed for him even now.

Marcus was staring at me.

I sipped my drink, savoring the awkward moment. Marcus gestured for the man to stop and the stranger stared up at me with equal fascination. He also saw the resemblance. I placed my glass down on a cherry side cabinet and approached them. Marcus' cheeks flushed. I lifted the kneeling man's chin, studying his features, an uncanny likeness, both pleasing and yet disturbing.

"Forgive me?" Marcus barely whispered.

I rested my thumb on Marcus' trembling lips and then kissed his tears, tasting their wetness, and then pressed my mouth against his with such firmness that he almost lost his balance. With my hands on either side of his face, I held him in an ironclad grip.

This was the kiss I should have given Salvador, stealing precious time with him, holding him like this in my arms again, perchance to trust where the moment might take us. My heart still ached for him. He'd been stolen from me, but here now the opportunity had arisen for me to show my true affection to another friend, and prove that my love for Marcus endured.

Marcus rocked, our mouths ever widening, our fangs grazing each others, our tongues brushing together, increasing to a brutal roughness. Marcus' entire body shuddered. He verged over the edge.

I pulled back.

Glancing down at the man at our feet, I threw him a smile. "Nice jacket." I stepped back, turned, and headed for the door.

* * * *

I followed the pathway of petals, crushing them underfoot, and strolled out the back door into the garden.

In the corner was an ornate fountain, a stone angel pointing a bow and arrow right at me, out of which water poured. Nearby, under the low lying leaves of a maple tree, lay Sunaria. She reclined upon a burgundy chaise lounge, surrounded by several admirers.

She smiled when she saw me. With my subtle gesture, she knew to remain seated. I needed some cooling off time. Marcus wasn't the only one left breathless. Thoughts returned to our kiss and I gave a wry smile, wondering how much longer he'd lasted after I'd left.

Breathing in the exquisite scent from the many exotic trees and flowers within the garden, I wanted to get a feel for the place. A feel for the people, and find a commonality that would help me to believe I belonged.

These open-minded individuals had been invited into our private world, one of London's most exclusive parties. Madam Rouge had established what could be best described as a gentleman's club, offering its guests a rich assortment of erotic entertainment. Words flowed along with the liquor. Controversial conversations were encouraged and guests sworn to an oath of secrecy. Delicious foods, tasty delights were offered up in abundance, rich delicacies that satisfied the palate and stirred one's passions, setting the mood for what followed.

Taking a seat in the corner enabled a discreet vantage point. Sunaria held court, arguing with a young fop who failed miserably to impress her. It amused me that we'd both developed flawless English accents, two iconoclasts living it up, the ultimate aristocrats, easily mingling with mortals, and often receiving frequent glances of respect from our fellow immortals.

London continued to flourish.

We were witnesses to the city's growth. Increasing political stability brought an increase in business and a thriving economy. Architecture had advanced in both common structures and the homes around us. London had become the center for European trade, introducing the newest fashions, entertainment, and both modern and ancient art. Westminster became established as the seat of the royal court and here too, England's political office grew in power.

Urban crime, such as that of street gangs, London's mafia of sorts, became more discreet, with the threat of hanging as a form of punishment for commoners. As their activities became subversive, it transformed into a feeding ground like no other.

An argument pulled me back into the garden. Two men were fighting over a young brunette. Madam Rouge stepped in to intervene, and with aplomb offered the woman to both of them. Several mortals strolled by, gawking.

A servant topped up my cup.

Sunaria approached and flopped onto my lap. "Well," she said, "what do you think?"

I wrapped my arms around her waist. "This is a den of iniquity."

"I know. Isn't it wonderful?"

I sighed.

"You used to like this sort of thing," she said.

"My tastes have changed."

Sunaria whispered into my ear, "Do you see anything you like?"

Glancing up at the bedroom windows, I wondered what kind of guilty pleasures Marcus might be enjoying.

Sunaria followed my gaze. "Let's throw a party like this at Belshazzar's."

"Let's not."

Just as I started to explain that I didn't want strangers strolling all over our home, Madam Rouge appeared.

"It's time to leave." She looked frantic.

Sunaria pouted. "What, why?"

"One of my staff just let in a new guest." Madam Rouge gestured to the house.

Despite the long, dark cloak and heavy hood over his pale face, I recognized those piercing eyes. I jumped up and almost knocked Sunaria to the floor.

"What's going on?" Sunaria easily regained her balance.

"Out the back now," I snapped. "Elijah's here." I headed for the side of the house.

"Where are you going?" Sunaria asked, panicked.

"I'm not leaving without Marcus." I headed for him.

* * * *

Pacing the lounge back in Belshazzar's, I subdued my anger. "How long?" I asked Sunaria again.

"Six months, maybe more," she said.

Marcus stepped forward in an attempt to intervene.

I raised my hand to stop him. "Madam Rouge's letters have been delivered here, yours sent to her?"

"Yes." Sunaria couldn't meet my gaze.

I balled my hands into fists. "Missives using servants?"

Sunaria nodded.

"How much did you tell her?"

"Hardly anything."

"Don't lie to me."

"I'm not."

"And yet when Elijah turns up at her door, she warns you," I said.

"She knows about the Creda," Sunaria blurted.

"Do you have any understanding of what you've done?" I snapped. "Keep a low profile. No one must know our address. I was specific."

Marcus stepped closer. "Calm down."

I turned to him. "They may have been watching us, watching me. Following where I go."

"You don't know that," Marcus said.

"Then how did he find us at Madam Rouge's?"

"It's a hot spot for vampires." Marcus shrugged.

"Great, you invited me into a death trap." I glared at Sunaria.

She covered her face with her hands.

Marcus looked horrified. "*No.*"

I shut my eyes for a moment, trying to stay calm. "You told Madam Rouge about Jacob?"

Sunaria waved a pointed finger at me in defiance. "She's my friend. I trust her."

I headed for the door.

"Where are you going?" Marcus asked.

"To get him."

"Bring Jacob here?" Marcus said. "Is that wise?"

Clutching the door handle, I turned to face him. "What choice do I have?"

****

Waiting outside St. Theresa's infirmary, I searched the many faces in the crowd. Minutes turned into an hour. I flew from the roof and went in search of him.

It was the usual hustle and bustle of Burberry's Sunday fair. On foot now, I pushed through the shoppers on either side of me while market owners tried to grab their attention. My gut wrenched in fear that Elijah was amongst them. I neared the hospital's main entrance and walked under the stone entranceway. I slowed my pace in an attempt to appear normal, but was hit with another wave of fear, and rushed around the corner, bumping straight into Jacob.

He dropped his leather medical bag. "Whoa, steady on." He gave a smile.

Trying to avoid his stare by lowering mine, I picked up his bag and handed it back.

Words failed me.

With my head down, I continued on, not wanting him to recognize any familiarity. Taking the longest strides, I headed along the corridor. The institution's scent carried and made me even edgier. I turned to see Jacob standing at the end of the corridor. He stared back at me.

I procrastinated, then strolled back in his direction.

Jacob turned and headed out.

Back on the tin roofs, tracing along the London skyline, I continued on after him. Jacob's long strides led him through alleyways that were fast becoming slums.

Panic struck when I saw a shadowy figure looming a few roofs down. Elijah's stare caught mine.

In my anger, I'd not thought it through. I blamed Sunaria for what I'd now done, unwittingly led him to my son. Jacob was oblivious to the drama unfolding above him and trekked on. Four children trailed behind him, and he threw several pennies in their direction.

Elijah shot across the alleyway that Jacob had just passed. He was closing in. I darted between the rickety shacks and landed in a puddle in the courtyard, near where the children were busy counting their coins.

"The physician, which way did he go?" I asked.

The pale faced children peered up. I reached into my pocket and threw the few coins that I had on me at them. They pointed east. With a painfully normal gait, I strolled in that direction, away from them.

Within the cul-de-sac, the homes were smaller and closer together. A few doors down, Jacob disappeared inside a rundown cottage. Out of nowhere, Elijah dashed into the house right behind him.

The scent of death caught my nostrils as I set foot inside. Whoever my son had arranged to visit had died. A black cat scampered over my foot and hissed. Several more steps in and I entered the largest room, everything in disarray. There, in the corner, clutching his medical bag, stood Jacob.

Elijah turned to me.

"*Get out,*" I signaled to him.

"I'm sorry for your loss." Jacob looked puzzled. "Didn't I just see you back at the hospital?"

Words failed me.

"Did you come to give the last rites?" Jacob turned to Elijah, trying to get a better look beneath his hood.

Well-dressed, I looked out of place, and by Jacob's expression, he thought so too. But even stranger than me was the monk-like figure, Elijah.

Elijah's pale lips quivered. "Sunaria, it appears she's not dead."

I turned to see Sunaria lingering in the doorway.

"Where do I know you from?" Jacob asked Sunaria, his frown deepening.

Elijah neared him.

"I should be going." Jacob started for the exit.

Elijah's gaze slid my way. "Jacob, meet your father."

I bit my lip, holding back my rage.

Jacob glanced at me, and then at Elijah, and then stared back at me as his bag slipped from his hands and landed with a thud.

"What do you want?" I asked Elijah.

His mouth slid into a grin.

"If it's my attention, you have it," I said through gritted teeth.

Sunaria stepped into the room. "Elijah, I'll go with you."

"No, you won't." I gestured for her to stay put.

"You're not my father, *are* you?" Jacob asked.

"I'll answer every question," I replied. "But you are no longer needed here."

"My father's dead," Jacob muttered.

"Now." I threw a glance at Sunaria.

I hated Elijah for forcing my hand. I'd planned and re-planned my first rendezvous with my son, and this wasn't it.

Sunaria guided Jacob out. My insides turned as my son disappeared from sight.

"I will find him." Elijah's voice was void of emotion.

"This obsession with your descendants is annoying."

Elijah reached out and gestured. "Return with me and everything will be explained."

"Talk here or not at all."

Elijah sighed. "When I'd heard that Sunaria had turned you, I wept for days."

"As you can see, I'm over it."

"You have a forgiving nature."

"Not so much now." I folded my arms.

"Your son inherited your recklessness."

"By reckless, you mean tending to the sick?"

"The woman he came to visit, do you know what she died of?"

"Old age? How would I know?"

"The Black Death." Elijah almost blinked.

"I'll send my condolences to the family."

"Perhaps Jacob has your sense of immortality?"

"I'm leaving." I headed for the door.

"There are some who believe that there is only one way to rid the city of the Black Death."

"Why are you telling me this?"

"I'm telling you why I'm here," he said. "Generations ago, *they* started a fire. It swept through London, and gutted the city."

"Disease got out of hand?" My voice was barely a whisper, as I realized where this was going. "They tried to suppress it with fire?"

He nodded. "This plague is even worse than before, imagine how they'll handle it now."

"That was Roman's secret?" I took a step back.

Elijah's eyelid's flickered. "Decay leaves a bad taste in one's mouth."

"Keep talking."

"During the time that Roman spent amongst the Stone Masters, he gathered information that hinted that they planned a repeat of 1212."

"Are you saying that Archer plans to burn down the city, again?"

"I am."

"Delacroix told you this?" I said.

"Yes."

"And you believe him?"

Elijah dismissed my remark with a wave of his hand, and shot me an uneasy glance. "Archer found out that Roman spied on him."

"Roman was betrayed."

"He was, and when Delacroix discovered who'd double-crossed his brother, he seduced him, luring the boy vampire with the promise that he would one day rule at his side."

"Benjamin?"

He nodded. "Roman's assistant. The Stone Masters captured Benjamin and only let him go because he swore to deliver his master to them. An ancient's blood is worth more. Benjamin had no idea about Roman's secret."

I leaned against the wall.

Elijah stared with that empty expression of his. "Delacroix brought Roman back to life."

"Well, if you call having your head attached to someone else's body being brought back," I said.

"Delacroix was desperate to discover the Stone Masters' plan."

"So he's not mad after all." I let out a laugh. "Perhaps I should rephrase that."

An awful flashback of being strapped into Delacroix's torture chair. Jitters slithered down my spine.

"Your inability to stay in the shadows has caused rumors to circulate." Elijah frowned. "If people needed proof of our kind, you've given it to them."

"I don't believe that."

"But of course you don't."

"Why didn't Roman just leave the city?" I asked.

"The Stone Masters are growing exponentially."

I realized that if another fire swept through the capital, Jacob would be caught in the middle of it.

"I'm here to get Jacob out of London," Elijah said, having infringed upon my thoughts.

I secured my mind from any further breach. "You have no right to go anywhere near him."

"I disagree."

"You're insane."

"You always were arrogant." He sighed. "When you drank from Delacroix . . ." Elijah's cheeks blushed. "You have within you information that can stop Archer."

"Ask Delacroix."

"He's not talking."

"That may have something to do with the fact that you've buried him."

Elijah flinched.

"If Roman was right," I said, "and the Stone Masters intend to burn down the city, why haven't they done it yet?"

"Only Roman knew that secret." Elijah neared me. "And he passed it on to Delacroix."

I cringed at the thought of his pale lips going anywhere near my neck.

His pale tongue flicked. "Let me drink from you."

My stare gave my answer.

"Why are you being so difficult?" He rose to his full height.

"You made a mistake coming here."

"In the bigger picture, Jacob's unimportant. Sunaria has tainted your view of us. We are the elite."

"You punish her for threatening your descendants, and yet you're guilty of what you accuse her of."

"This is different."

"No, it's not."

Elijah's face was calm, but underneath his cool exterior, I sensed his aggression.

His attack sent me hurtling. My head struck the wall and, when I opened my eyes again, Elijah glared down at me.

He sighed. "Your history runs in my veins."

I tried to break from his grasp. "I've never been one for holding onto the past."

Elijah's sting went deep. His strength almost overcame mine, but with a quick yank, I pulled one arm free and reached for the dagger tucked inside my jacket lining, withdrew it, and swung it up, thrusting it into his chest. His face contorted, his mouth gaping in horror. Using all my force, I plunged it in further. A rasping rattle escaped his throat and his eyes bulged. He was paralyzed. With a shove, I spun him onto his back, and attacked his neck.

Drinking, taking it in, I exulted in the potency rippling through him, and now through me, an exquisite elixir fermented over centuries. Gorging, I tumbled back in time and went to a place where nothing existed, *and yet everything did.*

I stayed sharp, maintaining a steady course, as a legacy faded.

L

BELSHAZZAR'S FELT DIFFERENT.

Jacob waited in the lounge. His presence brought a tangible serenity. I carried his medical bag, retrieved from the cottage.

A lifetime of waiting had finally come to a close.

Surging through me was power, but also our history. If Elijah's words held any truth, wedding them with how I felt, my mind tried to grasp the concept of what I now possessed, centuries of knowledge. Though this buzz provided an interesting, if not arousing sensation, the fact that Jacob stood on the other side of the door was easily more compelling.

Despite what I'd done within this very hour, I felt calm. Elijah's heritage was not lost, but absorbed, his memories stolen, perchance to be liberated some other day. Willing to do anything to protect my son, I'd brought down the most ancient of legacies and felt no regret.

Having fed, my pallor would at least grant me a few hours. Trying to find the right words, searching for a way to convey feelings unaffected by time, I traced the door with my fingertips and then gave it a shove.

Jacob's smile greeted me.

I laid his leather bag onto the side table. It was a familiar item in an unfamiliar setting. I needed to pass for a man in his late forties, despite my thirty-year-old appearance. Mindful of the way I moved, I stepped closer. "You look well."

He looked lost amongst the lavish décor. Despite his youth, work had taken a toll. Even at such a young age, he looked older than twenty-one.

"Jacob." I approached him.

"Are you really my father?"

"I am."

"You look so young."

"I live well." I strolled with the air of a gentleman. A manner with which I hoped to convey I had indeed reached middle-age.

"What were you doing in that house?" he asked.

"I came looking for you."

"And the monk?"

"He couldn't stay."

Jacob gave the deepest sigh. "I wasn't born in London?"

"No."

His stare wandered the room. "You're Spanish? I'm Spanish?"
"Yes."
"Tell me then."
"My nephew sold you." Stupid way to start. I paused for a moment and rested my hand over my heart, gesturing that it was good to be near him. I searched for the right words.

Teary-eyed, Jacob seemed lost.

From within my trouser pocket, I withdrew the locket. "This is yours." I handed it over to him.

As he took the piece from me, his hand brushed against mine, and I felt an inner tremor, relieved that he was here with me after all this time.

Jacob prized open the clasp and gazed at the renderings inside. "How did you find this?"

"Sunaria found it."

Jacob studied the locket. "I sold it for food. Two days later, Dr. Potts saw me begging and took me in."

Arms out, unable to hold back anymore, I gestured to him. Jacob neared me and wrapped his arms around me. I held him tight and everything that had once seemed important slipped away. Here, now, in this moment, I found truth like no other, and despite this foreign land, this foreign place, we were home.

He broke away. "How did you find me?"

Taking a moment, I considered my answer, unsure whether to reveal that I'd watched over him all these years, and been part of his life, when all the while he'd not even been aware of mine. His uncanny likeness to Annabelle threw me for a second. "My friend found you. I'd . . . described you to him."

"I'm glad."

With my hand on my chest, I conveyed the same.

"Aunt Alicia?" As he spoke her name, his face lit up.

Being here with each other stirred memories.

I smiled, remembering her. "She's still in Spain."

"You write to her?"

"I do but . . ." *I never send the letters.*

"Do I have a brother?"

"You did."

"What happened to him?"

"He died."

Jacob's face flushed. "And mother?"

"I'm so sorry."

"How?"

I shrugged, reluctant to discuss it.

"That monk, back at the house?" Jacob began.

"He won't be coming back."

"He knew that you were my father, though."

"We had a disagreement." I looked away. "But we came to an arrangement."

Jacob raised an eyebrow at the décor. "This is your house?"

"Yes."

"It's huge."

"I'd like to think that you'll consider living here."

"How long have you been here?"

"A while." Feeling unsteady on my feet, I gestured to Jacob to sit. "You'd settled into a new life. It was wrong to pull you out of it."

Jacob sat in the chair opposite and seemed to be holding back tears. My own reasons for suppressing mine were far from human, more of a supernatural centering. *I'm sorry I failed you.* But couldn't say it out loud, couldn't express my shame of not being there for him.

"So much to say, not sure where to start." He shook his head.

"You sound so English." I smiled.

"So do you." He chuckled. "My Spanish father is now an English gentleman. Although I still detect a slight accent."

"Are you hungry? Can I get you anything?" With those words came the realization that there would be little food in the house, though there may be something left over from the staff's meals.

He gestured that he needed nothing.

"Dr. Potts, he took good care of you?" I said.

Jacob nodded.

Over the years, the question had been answered.

"Where has all this money come from?" Jacob asked.

"Business, property dealings."

"You're established here in London?"

"I came here to find you. I plan to take you home."

"Spain?" Jacob gave an uneasy smile.

"Yes."

"London's my home now."

"You don't remember your birth place?"

He gazed at the chess table. "You play?"

The game with Marcus had been abandoned a week ago. He'd been too distracted to be a worthy opponent. I'd been winning. "Do you?"

"No, but I'd like to learn." He looked around at the sumptuous furnishings. "Business must be good."

"Why were you visiting that home today?"

"I still make house calls to Dr. Potts' old patients." Jacob saw my wariness. "I'm careful."

I wanted to pinch myself, amazed that he really sat opposite me—a man in every respect, a fine gentleman, his presence demure. Even his thoughts reflected integrity. A sense that with him, through him, I might find some inner peace, and dared to hope I'd rediscover our lost years.

"My memories are a little hazy," he said thoughtfully.

"Do you remember your mother?"

"I have memories of being told about her."

"Her name was Annabelle."

"She died when I was very young?"

Too young to recall the attack, his age had protected him from the atrocity.

"Soldiers killed her," I said.

"Why?"

"They were ordered to by a senator who hated me," I explained. "He murdered my brother years before that. The fact that I knew this threatened his political career."

"Why didn't he kill you?"

He did.

I shrugged and my mind wandered back to a perfect summer—*a Sunday afternoon, and the coolest breeze, Miguel leaning against the paddock gate, the man with the smiling eyes. Annabelle calling to me from the steps of the house, begging me to take Eduardo off the pony, after all he'd just turned four.*

"Did they suffer?" Jacob said.

Breathing in the scent of blood, seeing Miguel splayed out upon the floor and, upon the bed, Annabelle, still clutching our son.

I cleared my throat. "I don't believe so."

"And the senator?"

I loosened my neck tie. "Dead."

"How did he die?"

The blood of my enemies not spilt but imbibed.

Jacob's stare was persistent.

My beloved Spain's darkest hours.

"I finished it," I said, wistfully.

"Father?"

I liked that he called me that. "Power can turn in on itself, blinding one to reason." I gave a smile, remembering. "When I met your mother, she was a dancer. She was so beautiful. You take after her."

"How did the senator die?"

The door flew open.

Sunaria entered, carrying a bottle of wine. "Time for a toast." She raised it high. "Tonight, we celebrate."

Sunaria's timing was perfect. She poured white wine into three cups resting on the chestnut sideboard.

Violin music struck up from somewhere in the house.

"We have a lifetime of catching up to do," I said.

Jacob accepted the cup from Sunaria and nodded. "I remember you."

"She's impossible to forget." I raised my drink. "To Jacob."

Jacob lifted his cup high. "To my father. Our reunion."

I feigned a sip, trying not to stare, nervous that my gaze would hold too long and he'd see more than I was ready to show him. Jacob gulped his drink and stared off, hypnotized by the beautiful notes. Sunaria and I swapped a wary glance.

"That's beautiful," he said. "Who's playing?"

"Rachel," Sunaria answered. "Both she and her brother live here."

I gave Sunaria a knowing glance. "She's come a long way with that instrument."

Jacob's cheeks blushed. "Is she as bewitching as her music?"

LI

I SAT OPPOSITE JACOB, the inlaid chess table with its elaborate border between us.

Even after a month, I still reveled in his company.

Jacob peered over the ivory carved pieces and then slid his bishop. I raised an eyebrow and he beamed at me. Staring down, considering my next move, I allowed myself to smile, but it wasn't due to the fact that I was letting him win.

It had all been worth it—every second of scouring the city, sacrificing my needs for his, spending years watching and waiting for this moment when we'd be reunited. Jacob was perfect in every way. I savored being near him. He'd inherited my bone structure, but he also had his mother's eyes, her dark olive skin. He exuded an exotic aura from his Middle Eastern descent and faint laughter lines gave away his penchant for smiling. He'd drawn on his faith to cope with all that he'd seen in his young life. The fact that I'd stopped aging at thirty could still be concealed, just.

Enjoying the game, wanting it to last, I searched for something less aggressive. Chess was not the only game being played here. My gestures were slow and deliberate, as I advanced a pawn.

I hadn't found the right moment to show Jacob the private study I'd designed for him, anxious not to overwhelm him. More serious than that, the matter of my immortality was never discussed. I feared more than just losing the admiration of a son's love. Our rekindled relationship breathed new life into Belshazzars, and this sprawling manor no longer seemed lonely. This once solitary house had become a home because of him.

Jacob positioned his knight, taking a pawn and threatening my bishop.

"Do you remember how to ride?" I said.

"I remember you forcing me to get on one of those huge horses. I was terrified."

"You had the time of your life."

"Is that what you call it?"

"You never complained."

"Too scared to talk, no doubt." He pulled a face.

"Your brother loved to ride." As the words faded, I sucked in air. The pain of losing him had been unbearable, and until now I'd pushed out all thoughts of my child's death. Jacob's presence brought great joy, but also stirred memories that I'd once suppressed.

"Tell me about him." Jacob gestured for me to continue.

"Eduardo? He was a headstrong boy." I smiled and then it faded. "He died before you learned to walk."

"Did we look alike?"

I nodded. "Do you remember running away?"

"I ran away?"

"Well, you ran out of your Aunt Alicia's house and hid in the barn."

"Why?"

"I can't even remember now. I found you asleep in one of the stalls."

"How long did you search for me?"

"Hours." A wave of melancholy, the story of losing him had been repeated on a grander scale.

"I'm sorry I caused you so much grief," Jacob said.

"You brought nothing but joy to us." I paused and smiled. "Still do."

Jacob's eyes crinkled into a smile and he sat back. "You still haven't introduced me to your house guests."

"Marcus is looking forward to meeting you."

Much to my relief, Marcus had seen the wisdom of keeping Rachel and Jacob apart. She'd been forbidden to play her violin.

"Tomorrow night, I have to visit an old acquaintance," I said.

"May I come with you?"

"It's rather a delicate matter."

"What kind of business?"

"I'm severing ties with an old fraternity." I picked up one of my knights and feigned interest in moving the piece. "Their purpose is obsolete."

* * * *

I donned a disguise.

With a gentleman's attire of hat, a well-tailored suit, and over that my finest long, black jacket, I bestowed an air of confidence. Wearing tinted, horn-rimmed glasses, eager to obscure my eyes, I strolled with an assured step.

During the short time in Archer's study, I'd rummaged through his papers, leaving the notebook in his walled safe so that it appeared undisturbed. And yet I'd studied the contents, reading the accountant's notations, revealing what they spent their money on, and discovering the locations where the Stone Masters liked to stay.

The Manor Grand, famous for being one of London's better hotels, provided a discreet meeting place for lawyers, businessmen, and politicians alike. It was popular amongst those who desired to stay in the heart of the city.

Just inside the lobby, an elderly night porter snoozed in his high-backed chair. Reading upside down, I checked the guest book. Archer had signed in under the name of Salisbury. Had we been better acquainted, I'd have offered advice on keeping a low profile.

Taking three stairs at a time, I made my way up to the third floor. Strolling along the corridor, I wondered how many of the other rooms had been taken by Archer's men.

Listening at the door, checking for the presence of Archer, I made sure the room was empty. Upon the bed rested a well-traveled suitcase, already packed. This didn't appear to be one of the hotel's better suites. With its virtually bare décor and poor view, it reflected how business took precedence over luxury. Against the left wall was a writing bureau, upon which rested a letter that Archer had begun. He must have become distracted, leaving the missive unfinished. Within the hearth, cinders faded.

A creak in the floorboards out in the corridor gave away the person fast heading my way.

The door opened and my gaze connected with a well-dressed, burly looking, bearded man. He went for me and I stepped back, ready for the second punch he threw. I dodged the strike and my spectacles fell off.

"I have an appointment with Lord Archer." I tipped my hat.

He picked up my glasses.

"I'm completely blind without them." I reached for them and wrapped my fingers around his wrist and thrust him back, cracking his head against the brick. I could smell his fear.

Archer glared at me from the doorway. I let go of the man, tilted my head, and gave a roguish smile. Archer gestured for his colleague to leave.

The bearded man was clearly shaken. "Sir, I'm not leaving you alone with it." He rubbed the back of his head.

Archer patted his friend's arm. "Five minutes."

"I'll come back with the others." He handed Archer the spectacles and left.

"He referred to me as an 'it'" I tut-tutted. "Most rude."

"My men are well trained."

"It's good to see you."

"Wish I could say the same."

"How's that arm of yours?" I gestured for my glasses.

"This disguise doesn't work." Archer dropped them.

"Nice."

He sighed. "I'm done pretending that any interaction with you is acceptable."

"Good thing I'm not easily offended."

He approached the writing desk and peeked at the letter, checking to see he hadn't left anything important out.

My mind raced with the idea that he wanted to slay me. I neared him. "1212, a good year for the Stone Masters?"

He raised an eyebrow and turned away. "I have no idea what you're referring to."

"The fire wiped out one-fifth of the city's population."

Archer strolled over to the window. "I may have misjudged you."

"Let me clear that up for you. Yes, you have." I joined him and stared out at the bleak view. "I'm the son you never had."

Archer glared. "Careful."

"I intrigue you. My world offers mysteries that yours lacks. A freedom from the weight on your shoulders that's so heavy, you find yourself daydreaming about alternatives."

"You obviously have a death wish."

I gave a smile. "I find myself rather enamored with you. The feeling is of course mutual."

"My men are outside waiting for my order." Archer's glare traced my face.

I picked up my spectacles, the frames smashed and the glass splintered. Archer turned to me, his fists clenched.

I shot him a wry look. "Yet your thoughts say otherwise."

"Take a good look at the stars. It's your last."

I nudged Archer and he frowned. I beamed at him, and he sighed in response, running his long fingers through his silvery-grey locks.

"What part did the Stone Masters play in the massacre?" I asked.

Archer's expression changed.

"Your ancestors started the fire, didn't they?" I said. "They believed the fire would destroy disease-ridden London."

"People were convinced that it was the cats and dogs in the city, the animals believed to be spreading the sickness. They slaughtered them immediately." Archer's voice was grim. "It was rats carrying the virus. They'd wiped out their natural enemy. Disease became rampant."

"That's what you were told?"

"And I believed it."

"Too young to be trusted with the entire truth?" I shook my head. "Not yet initiated into the old man's club?"

"The disease spread at an alarming rate, and yet your kind was unaffected."

"That's how they justified it?" I said. "What is the age that a son is initiated into your order?"

"Don't go there."

"Do you remember that first taste?"

Our gazes locked. A knock at the door, and then it opened.

"I'm all right." Archer raised his hand insistently.

The door shut.

He turned to me again. "What do you know?"

"That you're planning on repeating history."

"Who told you this?" His right eye twitched.

I remembered Felipe twitching like that. His expression had been still, like Archer's, but fear had shown in that reflex. And yet something about Archer drew me to him, making the risk of coming here all the more worth it.

He reached inside his inner jacket pocket for the wooden stake he had hidden there.

"Now that's impolite." I raised an eyebrow.

Archer withdrew his empty hand and glanced at the door.

"You will not start this fire," I said.

"London is awash with rodents and the disease continues to spread."

"Again, you use this excuse to take more life?"

"We will extinguish the disease."

"Thousands of innocents will die."

Archer grabbed my shirt. "And your kind will die with them." He let go and wiped off the droplets of sweat from his upper lip.

My stare lingered on his mouth, and then rose to his deep, brown irises.

He turned away. "*No.*" His breathing increased, his chest rising and falling, and he gazed at me with those soulful eyes, seemingly affected by that familiar pull, the promise of what my blood bestowed. His lips formed words, but he didn't speak them. Archer's grip on his desires weakened, and I sensed him yielding. If I had wanted to, I could have seduced him merely with the power of my presence, and entrance him to the point of bondage.

And he knew it.

Retracting my supernatural hold, I gave Archer's arm a squeeze. He straightened up and tried to conceal his arousal.

I rested my hand on his shoulder. "London must be rescued. This is wrong."

"Wrong, like taking a life night after night. Wrong, like saving thousands of lives by sacrificing a few."

"So glad we got that cleared up."

"Immortality has affected your brain," he snapped.

"So I take it there's no invitation into the old boy's club?" I handed him back the wooden stake that I'd just pick-pocketed.

"All your exits are blocked." Archer clutched the end of the stake. His knuckles were white.

"You personally plan on starting another fire, don't you?" I asked.

Archer's face flushed with misery.

"No one would suspect." I sighed.

"You once asked me about my father."

I gave a nod.

"He inspired me," he whispered, staring off. "He served the cause. Gave his life for it."

"What happened to him?"

He tried to close his mind.

I rifled through his thoughts. "You won't neglect your own son."

Archer looked fazed. "I can't let you go this time."

"Do this thing and you'll bring down the wrath of our kind on your family."

"Perhaps if you agree to share your knowledge, they won't torture you."

I gave an incredulous smile.

"You are a vampire, after all." Archer pulled out a handkerchief and mopped his brow. "The chess piece that you gave me, the rook, it has a meaning?"

I studied my shattered spectacles, symbolic perhaps for everything that I touched, though here, now, I did something good. My desire to save London was evidence that I still had the ability to care, and still possessed sensibility.

Archer was staring at me.

"You'll make a fine father to your son," I said.

He let out a long sigh.

I held his gaze. "Don't do this thing."

"You really are arrogant, aren't you?"

"That's part of my charm."

He smiled, but it quickly faded. "I'll make sure that your death is quick."

Archer turned away in response to the insistent rapping on the door. By the time the echo of the knock had faded, I was gone.

LII

MY DESIRE TO PUT mayhem behind me felt achievable.

Bored with the smoke and mirrors of secret societies and ancient cults, I wanted to leave it all behind, relax and enjoy time with my son. Sunaria and I also needed to spend more time together. I missed her.

Belshazzar's offered up its quiet familiarity.

Halfway up the stairway, the patter of paws came first, then four bloodhounds appeared on the balcony. Barking, they scampered around my feet, acting as though I'd been away for days, not hours. Patting each one, I tried to extricate myself from their unending need for attention.

Violin music struck up. Taking three steps at a time, I flew along the east wing and the dogs bolted alongside me. Rachel was silhouetted at the window, caressing the strings with her bow. She stopped abruptly.

Jacob sat in the corner. "Isn't she talented?" He rose out of his chair to greet me.

Rachel lowered her bow.

"Where's your brother?" I tried to keep the anger out of my tone.

"Don't know," she said.

"Doesn't she play beautifully?" Jacob beamed a smile.

I gave a nod, and Rachel, still clutching her violin, headed for the door.

"Thank you for playing for me," Jacob called after her.

When her gaze caught mine, she quick footed it out.

"The music's morose," I muttered, "the last thing you need to hear."

"She plays like an angel."

I suppressed a cringe. "What did you two talk about?"

"You mostly."

"Really?"

"Turns out you've been keeping a secret from me."

I tried to discern whether the trepidation was mine or his.

He pointed to the violin. "Play for me."

"Perhaps later." Unable to look at him, I strolled over to the window. I had just violated his privacy and stolen his thoughts.

Jacob approached me and wrapped his arm around my shoulder. "What other talents are you keeping from me?"

Rachel had merely told him that I also played the violin. Across the street, a woman was shouting at a man, standing on the street corner. He was either deaf or ignoring her.

I craved peace, a drama-free life. My nights had more than enough excitement. My son's happiness and safety took precedence.

"Penny for your thoughts," he said.

Yet his were free. I would not read them again. A vow I intended to keep. "Have you ever taken a boat down the River Thames?" I asked.

"Are you changing the subject?"

"Apparently, the view from the Thames is extraordinary."

"You are changing the subject."

"Wear something warm."

* * * *

The river boat swept along.

The broad strokes of the oarsman guided us down the River Thames, and Jacob, Marcus, and I viewed the ever changing vista. England had recently endured some harsh weather, but spring had morphed into summer. Having endured the bitter winter, we were grateful for the warmth. Despite the sun having set an hour ago, the heat lingered.

Marcus seemed comfortable to look me in the eyes again and hold my gaze. After that evening back at Madam Rouge's, when I'd kissed him, he had for a while tripped over his words. I'd done what I could to allay his reticence, trying to talk about it, clear the air. But he'd refused to discuss it.

Marcus' fixed stare eventually fell away. It seemed as though he hoped for the promise of something more. He appeared to struggle with his feelings and wavered when I smiled his way.

As I did now.

Our boat rocked in the wake of larger vessels that passed by and smaller boats too nudged past. We were not the only ones taking advantage of the warmer climate.

With all my will, I tried to resist the urge to trespass on Jacob's thoughts. Now and again, I caught a wisp of his ponderings. Leaning back against the side of the boat, I tried to avert my gaze.

"How did you meet?" Jacob asked.

I felt Marcus' silent insistence that I should answer.

"We were introduced," I said.

"Where did you meet?" Jacob asked.

"Here in London," I replied.

Jacob gave an incredulous look. "Why do I always feel you're avoiding my questions?"

"We met at Belshazzar's," Marcus added. "Just before your father bought the property. Of course it wasn't called that when we met there."

"What was it called?" Jacob asked.

"Blackfriars." I was unsure whether the chill that ran down my spine came from the river breeze. The oarsman's stare locked on me. It dawned on me that anything we discussed could very well wind up circulating around the city. The oarsman visibly shivered.

Jacob caught our interaction and gave me a baffled look. "Where's Rachel tonight?" he asked. "I'm sure she would have enjoyed this."

Marcus shrugged.

"Rachel plays the violin beautifully," Jacob said.

Marcus smiled. "You should have been around for rehearsals in the early days." He laughed. "That takes brotherly love to a whole new level."

"Is anyone else getting sea sick or is it just me?" I pressed my hand over my mouth.

"On the Thames?" Jacob said.

"Take us in," I ordered the oarsman.

"Already?" Jacob looked at Marcus and then back at me.

I'd dropped many a body into these waters and my imagination ran wild as I envisioned that one of the corpses might spring out of the dark depths and scream at me.

That would take some explaining.

Jacob looked up at Marcus. "Is he like this with you?"

Marcus smiled.

Jacob studied me. "You need to get more sun." He looked at Marcus. "In fact, you both do."

I wondered if the oarsman could swim.

* * * *

Jacob insisted that we visit an old favorite inn of his. With his enthusiasm to show us his old haunt so great, it had been impossible to refuse him.

All three of us sat on the hard, wooden benches, right in the middle of the rowdy pub, awaiting our order of drinks. I regretted agreeing to dinner. The tavern was small and dark, atmospheric even. Marcus' ability to make light conversation softened what could have been an uncomfortable soiree.

"So, Jacob, have you made a decision yet?" I asked.

"About moving into Belshazzar's?"

I nodded.

"Perhaps."

Doing my best to hide my disappointment, I leaned back against the bench and folded my arms.

"So do tell." Jacob turned to Marcus. "What can you tell me about my father?"

Marcus raised an eyebrow. "Oh, where to begin?"

I lifted my cup and pretended to sip.

"Your father searched for you relentlessly," Marcus offered.

I found myself gripping the table, aware of the tension I let go.

"Every night, he scoured London for you," Marcus continued. "He never gave up."

I was relieved when the waitress interrupted and yet disconcerted when she plopped down bowls of soup and the smell hit me. More food arrived, freshly baked rabbit and a full plate of vegetables.

Conscious of being watched, I seriously contemplated eating, but with the memory of Marcus vomiting on me, I decided against it.

"Tell me more about your business." Jacob offered me some bread.

I accepted a piece and rested it on the side of my plate. "We buy land."

Jacob offered some to Marcus.

Marcus declined with a wave. "We purchase old homes and tear them down."

"And then we rebuild," I said.

"How many homes around Belshazzar's do you own?" Jacob asked.

"Almost all of them," I answered.

"What, like the whole street?" Jacob joked.

"Yes." Marcus gave up pushing his food around his plate and put his fork down.

Jacob glanced at me and then at Marcus.

"Those reluctant to sell are offered double for their property," Marcus said. "Within three years of moving into Belshazzar's, we owned the majority of land surrounding the manor."

"We rent them out." I poked my food.

Jacob turned to Marcus. "Not hungry either?"

Marcus sighed. "That boat left me feeling a little queasy."

"I would like your permission to take Rachel to the park tomorrow." Jacob dipped a chunk of bread into his soup.

Marcus glanced at me. "My sister's heading out of town."

Jacob's face fell.

Marcus coughed. "This trip has been planned for quite some time."

"Where's she going?" Jacob ate the damp morsel.

"Cornwall," I blurted.

Jacob swallowed. "Who does she know in Cornwall?"

"Our aunt," Marcus said. "She's taken a turn for the worse."

I feigned concern. "Nothing quite like sea air."

"Rachel mentioned nothing," Jacob said.

I pulled at the cuffs of my sleeves.

"Rachel's very private," Marcus offered.

Jacob folded his arms. "She's not the only one."

"And what about you?" I asked Jacob. "What are your plans?"

"I hope to continue with my studies, keep Dr. Pott's old practice running, just as he intended it. Medicine for the poor. A few of my clients are wealthy and, as such, I'm able to take care of those less fortunate. I've had a private benefactor who's supplemented my income." Jacob's face reddened, his expression one of realization.

I gestured to the waitress for the bill. I wanted out of here.

"That money, it came from you, didn't it?" Jacob's face was flushed.

"Well I—"

"Of course." He shook his head.

I pushed the bowl of soup away. "Sometime in the near future, I imagine you'll want to join the business."

"My vocation is medicine." Jacob shook his head. "I have no head for business and no interest in it."

"But still."

"I take great pride in what I do." Jacob thrust his chin upward. "Any other kind of life is superficial."

"Why thank you." I sighed.

"Life isn't all about decadence." Jacob glowered. "You've pushed your food around with your nose in the air. That would have fed a starving child, of which London has many."

I sighed.

"You too." Jacob turned to Marcus.

"We get it, Jacob," I said, frustrated.

"No, you don't," he snapped.

"Being wealthy enables us to give to the poor," I said.

Several of the other guests stared in our direction.

Marcus quickly inclined toward Jacob. "Rachel would love to go to the park with you."

Jacob's face showed a subtle change.

"She leaves for Cornwall Wednesday," Marcus said, "so why not take her to the park tomorrow?"

Jacob flinched. "You're trying to placate me?"

"I'm offering you an olive branch," Marcus said. "Look, your father and I came from those lowly origins you talk of. We dressed in rags and ate bread and water."

I gave Marcus an incredulous stare.

"But," Marcus continued, "we survived. Crawled our way up out of the gutter. And yes, we do enjoy the finer things in life, but it's not like we don't work for them."

Jacob looked at me. "Why don't you tell me these things? When I try to find out more about you, you change the subject."

"Some things, I choose to forget." I reached into my jacket pocket.

"But I've missed out on all of it."

I placed several coins on the table. "We should go."

Jacob frowned. "I'd very much like to take Rachel out tomorrow. That is, of course, if my father approves?"

With a nod, I rose from the table.

Jacob stared up at me, again with that frown.

* * * *

Here in the study, one could find assured privacy.

Tonight though was an exception. Sunaria, Marcus, and Rachel stared me down.

"This is not open for discussion." I turned away from them and faced the fireplace.

Rachel sniveled. "But I don't want to go to Cornwall."

"You don't actually have to go to Cornwall." I spun round to face her. "Just tell him you are."

Sunaria glared.

"He's infatuated with her," I said.

Sunaria sighed. "I don't see the harm."

"Rachel," I feigned compassion. "Pack your things."

Marcus wrapped his arm around her waist. "Sweetheart, what he's trying to say is that Jacob is not ready to learn about who we are."

"But Sunaria's shown me how to mingle," she sobbed. "I know how to act normal."

"Define being normal, Rachel." Dealing with her was making me weary.

She suppressed a sob.

"Jacob's a man of science," I explained, annoyed that I had to. "He'll detect you're different."

"Don't say it." Sunaria gestured insistently to me.

"He'll meet a nice girl, marry her, and then you can come back," I said.

"You bastard," Sunaria muttered.

Rachel burst into tears.

"Can't you see her heart's breaking?" Sunaria snapped.

I waved off her statement. "Don't be ridiculous."

"Rachel, go to your room," Sunaria rubbed Rachel's arm with affection. "I'll join you in a minute."

"Go on, love," Marcus said.

We waited for Rachel to exit.

"What the hell are you doing encouraging her?" I snapped.

Marcus shut the door and turned. "At least be a little more patient with her."

"Don't play your violin in the house," I continued. "Could I have been any clearer?"

"I've spent years helping her confidence flourish," Sunaria said.

"Yes, but you didn't always feel this way about her, did you?" I neared her.

Sunaria looked furious. "That's unfair." She glanced at Marcus, uncomfortable with where this was going, and then grabbed my arm. "She's like a sister to me."

I pulled away from her.

"In one night, you undermine all my work." Sunaria rested her hands on her hips. "And you refuse to consider the future."

"Not now." Marcus gave her a stern glare.

"What, you'll just let him grow old and die?" Sunaria said.

"Sunaria." Marcus shot her a wary glance.

"Or worse, catch something from one of his patients," she continued.

"If either of you touch my son," I said bitterly. "I *will* kill you."

The room fell quiet.

****

Strolling through the graveyard, it felt refreshing to be outside.

Fog hung just above the ground, layering the cemetery with an eerie white, an exquisite haze. Taking a seat on one of the older mausoleums, I tried to think, considering Sunaria's words.

Turn him.

With my son growing older, nearing my age with each passing year, I failed to see the advantage. At some point, I would either have to tell him or withdraw. Jacob would turn twenty-two in August. Two choices and I liked neither of them—both threatened unhappiness.

I regretted my earlier outburst.

Sunaria's perfume caught in the air and she stepped out of the haze dressed in a black laced bodice and a flowing skirt.

"Why do things never turn out the way they're supposed to?" I sighed.

She snuggled against me and brushed her fingers through my hair.

"I've missed you," I whispered.

The fog swam around us.

Leaning back on my elbows, I admired the view and she pushed me back onto the mausoleum. I imagined that whoever lay entombed beneath exulted with that which unfolded above.

Savoring the moment, I gazed up at the obscured stars, our bright witnesses of the night. I reached out to the side, my hand sweeping through the mist, disappearing into the blanket of white.

I flinched with the sharp sting of her bite. The sensation of her drawing the finest claret sent a thrill, our perfect scarlet sustenance. The sensations mingled pleasure with pain.

"I love you." I conveyed that I needed this, needed her. "You're mine eternal," I whispered and disappeared within to that place, *within the perfect place* . . .

LIII

HEADING UP THE STAIRWAY, I hoped Marcus hadn't left.

I couldn't wait to find Sunaria and reciprocate her affection. She had a knack for knowing just how to deal with me and soothe my angst. A bark signaled the dogs would appear at any moment.

Hairs on the back of my neck stood up. I spun round and peered down into the foyer and saw Jacob standing at the base of the stairs, resting one hand on the banister. I had a mental recap on how quickly I'd flown in through the front door, and at the same time threw what I hoped was a convincing smile.

"I've come to apologize," he said.

Descending, I neared him. "For what?"

"My behavior at dinner."

"Actually, I feel I owe you the apology," I said.

The patter of paws sounded as the hounds ran to greet us. They barked when they saw Jacob. I ordered them to remain at the top of the balcony. My tone stopped them in their tracks.

I turned to Jacob again. "The work you do, it's magnificent. I just want you to have the life that I never had at your age."

"I spoke out of hand last night." Jacob sighed. "Will you forgive me?"

"Already forgotten."

My skin tingled. Dawn lingered close.

"You seem distracted." He looked puzzled. "Would you like to talk about it?"

With a wave of my hand, I dismissed the idea. My fingers fumbled for the banister and I turned away.

"Perhaps we could spend more time together?" he said. "I've got a few things on my mind I'd like to—"

"Sure."

"You have to be somewhere?"

I nodded.

He looked disappointed. "I let myself in."

"That's fine."

"That's not my point." Jacob's tone changed. "You don't have any staff?"

"They'll be in shortly."

"But no housekeeper?"

"As I was saying—"

Jacob's face changed. "I'm sorry, I shouldn't be so touchy."

"We've been apart for so long. We're just getting to know each other, that's all."

"You're right. of course."

Jacob rose up onto the first step. "Your business . . . perhaps you can introduce me to some of the finer points. I'm interested in what you do."

"Don't want to push it on you." Ascending the stairs backward, I tried to look natural. and hated the sun for its selfish act of rising.

"I know it's early," he said. "I thought you might like to stroll with me. We can catch the sunrise in the park. I thought you might like that." He took another step. "Have I disappointed you?"

"Of course not. I'll see you tonight."

A shimmer of daylight leaked beneath the front door and threatened its approach.

"First in the tavern you couldn't wait to get out of there, and now here, I feel like I'm being avoided."

The shimmer crept along.

The doorbell rang.

Jacob turned.

* * * *

The fire roared in the hearth warming the study.

I watched Jacob's expression as he took in the central table, dark leather, and oak furnishings.

"This room has the best view of the house." I studied his reaction.

Jacob seemed nervous. "You move fast."

I feigned pleasure from the fire's warmth. "Sorry about that."

"And when I say fast . . ."

I nodded. "Sunaria tells me I need to slow down."

"Where did you go?"

Behind that bookcase lies a clandestine doorway. One of several in this house that leads to a chamber, where safety goes hand in hand with a good day's sleep. "Had an appointment and couldn't miss it."

"I see."

"What do you think?" I gestured.

"You designed this room for me?"

"Yes."

"You went all out." He stretched up and eased one of the books off the shelf. He opened it and leafed through it. "You chose these for me?"

"I did."

"I'm speechless."

"Look here." I pointed to the hearth.

Jacob approached the mahogany fireplace and ran his fingers over the engraved fleur-de-lis. "It's beautiful."

As his fingers traced the design, I sensed his anxiety.

"You approve?" I tried to read his expression and stay out of his thoughts.

Jacob reached into his inner coat and removed a dispatch. Impossible to tell if he'd opened it. "This came for you." He rubbed his fingers over the red seal. "Just after you . . . disappeared."

Studying the envelope, I tried to make out the handwriting.

"I'm looking forward to playing chess again." He gave an unconvincing smile. "I'm beginning to understand that it's more than a game to you."

"You're a quick learner."

"Not fast enough."

I faked disinterest in the letter that he still held. My gaze fell on the portrait above the fireplace, a sunrise over the River Thames. We'd commissioned Alberto Ceravassio to paint it and paid him well.

"You've won the last three games," Jacob said. "Occasionally, you let me win in order not to sabotage my morale."

"Ah."

"I'm getting to know you." He handed me the envelope. "Understanding you helps me have a better understanding of myself."

"And what do you see?"

He smiled. "Who's it from?"

Ascertaining whether the seal had been compromised, I opened it and recognized the handwriting.

Jacob seemed distracted, but then his focus fell back on me.

I peeled open the cream paper. "Did you read this?"

"Why would I read your private letter?"

Had I really been stupid enough to teach Rachel to read and write?

"Daumia,

I fell in love with you the moment you rescued me in the cathedral. You made me with your blood, therefore, our connection is great. I believe it's your love for me that prevents you from allowing Jacob to become my lover. After all, you turned me, brought me over. To have your approval is all that I desire."

I couldn't read anymore.

Jacob's expression changed. "A problem?"

"Nothing that can't be sorted."

I'd nurtured Rachel and gone to great lengths to smooth her transformation, be there for her, and it had backfired. I'd selfishly enjoyed the way she'd stared at me, her admiring smile, and her coy blush. I'd encouraged her. I looked up at Jacob. "You read the letter?"

"I did."

Sounds from the streets carried—carriages rumbling along, someone calling a name—but I didn't catch it. I tried to maintain my composure.

Jacob approached the mantel and turned to face me. "It all makes sense now."

"I've never been romantically involved with her."

"I'm sorry."

"For what?"

"Doubting you."

I gestured for him to continue.

He shot me a wary glance. "Rachel is clearly unsound."

Rachel had always acted a little scatterbrained, but crazy? "I didn't know how to tell you." I shrugged.

"May I visit her?"

"It's best if you don't."

"Your idea of her taking the sea air, it's the best thing for her."

"Yes."

"The blood thing?" Jacob ran his fingers through his hair. "Where do you think she gets her ideas from?"

The painting's dramatic reds and oranges were lit up by the firelight.

Jacob followed my gaze. "Very often, it's a stressful event that triggers such an episode."

A stark visual of Rachel sucking from those whom she'd seduced, rocking with pleasure as her once willing consort had quickly become an unwilling victim, fading in her arms, and I'd been the one to teach her, Rachel's bloody smile after her first kill, like a child who'd learned a new trick.

A knock at the door made me jump.

Marcus appeared and stuck his head in. "Can I have a word?"

I approached him. "Not a good time."

"I've searched everywhere," Marcus whispered. "Rachel's gone and so are all her belongings."

"Find her," I said. "And make it quick."

"Something wrong?" Jacob asked.

I closed the door. "Everything's just fine."

"From her letter, she appears to believe she may be a vampire," Jacob said calmly.

The room felt horribly stuffy, the air thick. I loosened my shirt collar.

Jacob's stare met mine and he nodded, revealing more than just his suspicion. "She told me everything."

Outside, a dog barked.

"You don't go out during the day," his voice changed ever so slightly. "I've never seen you eat anything."

As his words continued, I felt myself unraveling, my worst nightmare unfolding. I placed my pale hands behind my back.

"So I can see where she gets her wild ideas from." He neared me.

"Quite an imagination, that girl."

"Living with an eccentric can rub off." Jacob nodded my way.

I forced a smile, self-conscious that the stress may cause an elongation of my fangs.

Great, give yourself away, for fear of giving yourself away.

"Any thoughts?" he said.

"On what?"

"Is there something you're not telling me?"

"How do you mean?"

Jacob rifled through his jacket pocket and withdrew a small bottle, inside which a small amount of liquid swooshed. He flicked the contents onto the back of my hand.

I wiped off the moisture, unsure whether to be shocked or annoyed. "And I thought you were a man of science."

"I am."

"Then why not study your subject objectively?"

You've lost him, again.

"You make it sound so cold," he said.

"You just threw Holy Water on me. I assume that's what it is?"

"You look so incredibly young. I mean, we could pass for brothers."

"I'm flattered."

"You find this funny?"

"Not so much."

"You've never eaten in front of me. I've never spent a day with you. And the way you move . . ." Jacob reached into his coat pocket.

"Please don't tell me that's a cross."

Jacob spun round and held up a mirror. His gasp grated. "I didn't believe her." He held up the mirror again.

"I could never muster the courage to tell you."

"I deserve the truth."

"I reasoned that if you got to know me first . . ."

"Why did you come back into my life?"

"Because I love you."

"Are you even capable of such an emotion?"

"Yes."

"I wished you'd stayed away."

My heart felt like something had punctured it. I pressed my hand against my chest, trying to ease it.

"Deny it." He sucked in his breath.

"You want me to tell you that I'm not what I am?"

"Yes."

"I'm not a vampire."

"How long have you been one?"

"Twenty years."

His face paled even more.

I ran my fingers through my hair. "I wanted to be the one to tell you."

"You should have."

I turned away.

"But it's meant to be a myth, folklore," he said.

"People are comforted by that."

"I have to sit down." Jacob took the seat near the fireplace. He stood up again, fidgeting. "Are you really my father?"

The question stunned me.

Jacob's face softened. "And I thought I'd seen everything."

"I never asked for this."

"Someone did this to you?"

"I chose this life so that I could save yours."

"What?"

"Hanging by a thread, literally seconds from death, I had to make a choice."

"You were given a choice?"

"Had I not taken it, they would have killed you."

"Don't blame me for what you are."

"I don't."

"How is it done?"

The courtyard. My arms pulled back in their bindings. A scarlet flow that seeped from my wound. Sunaria's voice, her scent mingling with her taste. Death summoning me and then that dark decision . . .

Outside, a crow squawked, shattering the silence.

"Rachel cut her wrist." Jacob gulped. "And it healed instantly."

"She wanted to prove to you what she is?"

"Yes."

"Where is she now?"

"I don't know." Jacob's voice almost broke. "Do you drink blood?"

I avoided his gaze.

His eyes widened. "Have you murdered?"

I picked up a lit candle and approached the bookcase, then yanked at an obscured handle and the shelves swung open, revealing a doorway.

"Where does that lead?" he asked.

"Like to find out?"

"You don't expect me to go in there?"

I headed on through, paused for a moment, and waited for him to join me.

Jacob sighed deeply, and then took his first step into my world.

* * * *

Jacob leaned back against the door with his hands wrapped around his legs, while I rested atop the long, black coffin.

Jacob's pupils adjusted to the dark. The fluorescent glare of mine spooked him for a moment, but then he settled. The candlelight helped.

My philosophy had come up short. I refused to accept my lot in the great scheme of things, but rather to strive for a glorious life, to be authentic, true to myself and learn to live with the consequences. But now my relationship with Jacob felt threatened.

Having not fed, the slight shake in my hands increased, though my appetite had dulled. Within the small chamber, the drama of a troubled past unfolded, evolving over decades, a fantastical story that stirred the same emotions as it left my lips.

Jacob listened.

Yet again breaking my own rule, I trespassed into his thoughts, needing reassurance that this would not be the last time I'd see him. Jacob's flushed face and fresh tears caused frequent pauses in my dark monologue, but his insistence for me to continue forced me to do so.

As I recounted my past, it revealed a new perspective and other possibilities arose, highlighting better choices that could have been made. Decisions of my youth were just that. I fought off the regret. Years ago, I'd mourned briefly and then moved on, hoping that my future would make up for the past. Taking full responsibility for what I'd become, it had been easier to accept. Trying to explain this to my fresh-faced son, who stared up, riveted, offered a new challenge. I gauged Jacob's reaction.

He wiped away another tear. "If there's a way back for you, I'll find it."

I allowed him solace in believing that.

Jacob stood up. "So light is your enemy?"

I subtly checked, watching for any sign that would indicate he'd test the theory and inadvertently put me at risk.

Jacob's hand brushed over the door and then he pointed to the coffin. "What's it like sleeping in that?"

"You get used to it."

"How have you not been driven mad?"

"Does the mad man know that he's even mad?"

Jacob squinted. "All those times I thought you were working and you were actually asleep."

And while you slept . . .

"Your whole life is a lie," he muttered.

"Smoke and mirrors, that's all."

"This is how you justify what you do?"

"You're not my judge."

"But God is."

"I could be pedantic and say that God stood by and watched this being done to me."

"He doesn't interfere."

"How convenient."

"Do you not fear hell?"

"You and Marcus can have this discussion," I said. "It bores me."

"But what of your soul?"

I sighed. "What of it?"

Anxiety in his expression, his mind surely raced. "Are you damned?"

"Perhaps."

"Aren't you frightened of dying?"

"No more than you."

"But are you not excluded from heaven?"

"Me and half of London, if you believe what you read."

"You're destined to walk the earth for eternity?"

His words echoed. Not for the first time had I considered the idea—immortalized in this body, being more than I'd been as a mere man, with God-like abilities.

"I will find a cure for you." He broke the silence.

My fingers traced my jaw line. I was deep in thought.

"What did it feel like when you actually changed into this?"

Death's drag... "I lost all sense of time and place and then blacked out. When I reopened my eyes, it felt as though I'd awoken from the deepest sleep." *Sunaria's voice luring me, the thrill of her blood surging through mine, reanimating every nerve, sinew, muscle, and bone...* "When my eyes took in the world again, shapes were more distinctive and colors vibrant. Your senses are so sharp, it takes a while to adjust to the sensory overload."

"Is there pain?" Jacob's voice seemed far off.

A difficult question to answer, having been impaled by a child's sword, the agony of that bled into what followed. I shrugged.

"And now what does it feel like?" Jacob asked.

The ability to feel pleasure so intense that you lose yourself.

So acclimated to my new physicality, I tried to compare it. "We move with great agility."

"But what does it actually feel like?"

I turned over my hands, studying them. "As though you've taken on a new body, one that is made out of something other than flesh, and yet it passes for it."

"When you died, what did you see?" he asked.

"A blinding white light. A beautiful angel beckoned."

"Really?"

"No. Just blackness. Nothing. An awful feeling of being awoken from the deepest sleep, and then being dragged backwards over hot coals."

Jacob was riveted.

"Then the agony subsides into euphoria." I sighed. "I suppose it's what entices you to come back into your body."

The candle flickered.

"What other benefits are there?" He glanced at the fading flame.

"My ability to detect the slightest sound."

"You can read minds?"

"Rachel told you that?"

He nodded. "Do you read mine?"

"I try not to."

"But you can. I mean right now you can hear every thought?"

"Yes."

"Bloody hell."

"It's not what it's cracked up to be," I said.

"How do you mean?"

"The chatter's overwhelming. And when someone thinks a bad thought about you, it feels shitty."

"But you get used to it?"

"You get to control it."

Jacob removed his jacket. "What did you think I'd say when I learned the truth?"

"That you hated me."

"You underestimate me."

"Actually, I don't."

"The drawbacks, what are those?"

"Well, you've seen one, no reflection."

"That explains your hair."

I ran my fingers through my dark locks.

"Just joking," Jacob said.

I gave a wry smile.

"Actually, I'm always impressed with how dapper you look." He almost smiled.

"Can't say the same for you." I winked.

"Ouch."

"My tailor can remedy that."

"Thanks, I think."

I gestured to the door. "No sunsets."

"That explains your artwork."

"Dining takes on a whole new meaning."

"You can't eat at all?"

I shook my head no.

"What else?" he pushed.

"I can seduce anyone."

"Is that how you trap them?"

I sensed where this was going and didn't like it.

"You have to kill to survive?" he asked.

"The alternative is to take just a sip. But it results in several victims instead of one."

"What if they see you again?"

"It doesn't work like that."

"What do you mean?"

"We return the favor with providing a taste of us."

"How do you persuade them?"

"Eyes closed."

"That's not what I meant."

"I know. One sip and their arousal is their reward. Then they forget everything."

"Are you suggesting that, for us, your blood is some kind of elixir?"

I stared down at my shoes.

"You're talking of an erotic experience?" Jacob said amazed.

"Now you understand why Rachel going anywhere near you made me nervous."

"Your blood also affects memory?"

"Yes."

"Please don't try that on me."

"Now that would be interesting."

"I mean it."

"You have my word."

"How do you find your victims?"

"Take a walk down any back alley and you soon find yourself threatened. I turn the tables."

"What do you do with the body?"

I gave the deepest sigh.

He couldn't hide his horror. "You throw them in the Thames?"

"We're all faced with complex decisions." I rose off the coffin. "This is not how I want you to see me."

He disappeared inside his thoughts. "There are some physicians that bleed their patients. Although I don't practice this technique, perhaps we could give you the blood that they draw?"

The thought of drinking clotted blood caused a wave of nausea. Drinking for me was so much more than survival, a sublime sensuous ritual. "Please don't see me as one of your patients."

"How would you prefer me to see you?"

"As your father."

"You look more like my brother."

I shrugged.

He was suddenly anxious. "What happens when I age and you stay the same?"

The sense of evening looming brought little relief. We still had a few hours or so to go before we could welcome the fresh air of outside.

"Have you given any thought to that?" Jacob asked.

"I have."

"Well?"

"We'll just have to work through it."

"This is surreal."

"You have my word that you will never find yourself in my predicament."

Jacob shifted uncomfortably. "That's good to hear. But I'd assumed it was a given."

"If there's one benefit to being what I am, it's that I have the ability to protect you."

"I don't need—"

"Trust me, we all need someone to watch over us."

"I have God."

"He doesn't like to interfere, remember? I have no problem with the concept."

"Some things are best left alone."

"Like what exactly?"

He was taken aback.

"Jacob, you have my blessing to continue with your vocation, but not to spend any time worrying about me."

"I'd like to study you."

With a cringe, I gave my answer.

"I've offended you?" he said softly.

With a gesture, I dispelled the idea.

He bit into his lower lip, aware that he'd over stepped. "Perhaps I could follow you one night?"

"Or perhaps you could just stay home."

"Well, that's no fun." Jacob stretched.

"You're beginning to sound like me." I smiled.

He stared off at nothing. "Wait a minute."

"What?"

"All those times we were playing chess?"

I gestured sincerely. "You're quite adept now. I actually have to pay attention."

"I really have to go out with you and watch what you do."

I gave a smile. "Over my dead body."

Jacob gave a brief, nervous laugh.

"I'm going back to Spain," I said. "I want you to come with me."

He looked crestfallen. "I've made a life for myself here."

"Consider it."

"I don't even speak Spanish."

"London is not the city it once was. It's so dangerous."

"In what way?"

"Spain has so much more to offer."

He shrugged.

"I'll always love you," I whispered. "You do know that, don't you?"

His gaze fell onto the quivering candle flame. "This city may have some questionable provinces, but for me it's still home."

With his words came the realization that I'd have to face Archer one final time.

LIV

WHEN WE'RE PUSHED to the limit, we discover ours.

With speed so fast that my ears rang and my head spun, I flew out of Belshazzar's, heading southwest for Archer's country estate, my feet barely skimming the roof tops, following the main road out of London.

Landing near the great house, I arrived just in time to find the Stone Masters loading the last of four carriages parked outside the front. Deciding to head them off, I started down their pathway and waited.

And paced.

Within the hour, the first carriage rolled in my direction. The horseman's expression changed to one of horror as he caught sight of me.

I glimpsed a flash of black as the carriage veered off to the right. The driver had tried and failed to navigate around me, and the left two wheels lifted off the ground. Tipping onto its side, scraping along at speed, the carriage crashed into the dense trees, spraying up leaves, dirt, and dust.

The other carriages came to a stop. Lord Archer stepped out of the last carriage, saw me, and recoiled.

Several Stone Lords closed in. Archer held up his hand and they yielded, swords readied. Archer gestured to his men, ordering them to assist those injured. His gaze turned back on me.

"You know why I'm here," I said.

"I can't stop it." Archer lowered his voice. "I tried to find another way, but they overruled me."

"I'm not here to negotiate."

"Neither am I."

"Why now?" I asked.

But despite his refusal to answer, I perused his mind and took what I needed. The Stone Masters had taken years to comprise a list of those whom they deemed savable: London's beloved artists, scholars, politicians, and a few well chosen aristocrats. Missives had been sent, warning them all to leave the city. On this, the eve of the impending disaster, the Stone Masters moved out and headed back to Salisbury.

"How can burning down one city solve an issue that affects the world?" I said.

"Just because you have the facts, doesn't mean you know the story," Archer replied. "In the heart of London resides a threat like no other."

"What threat?"

His mind closed to me.

Slicing through the air, I heard the sword before I saw it. The thud struck my chest, the tip leading the weapon through. Staggering, I fell onto my back.

Numbness in my legs and I couldn't move them. The blinding pain burned like fire.

The fireplace, the carved symbol of a Fleur-de-lis engraved in the center, representing the Holy Trinity, having come to respect Jacob's faith, the emblem had been a gesture of that.

I should have told my son why I'd chosen it for him.

Running my fingers over the design, admiring the workmanship.

Heavy eyelids closed, and then strained to open. I gazed up at the twisting tree branches stretching out, reaching for the stars, the bright full moon visible through winding, wooden limbs.

The flawless emblem of an iris, the symbol of perfection.

I watched through bleary eyes as Archer stepped back, his hand covering his mouth, a gesture to hide his angst. Straining my hand across my chest, I reached for the weapon's handle.

"Bind him." Archer's voice was far off.

I clutched the hilt and yanked. So deeply imbedded, the blade resisted. I pulled again. A terrible feeling that it had severed something, I squeezed my eyes shut.

The oscillating vision of Jacob's face lingering, his faith inspiring mine . . .

Another yank and I had the sword out, and I sprang to my feet, and flew past Archer, close enough to touch him.

Archer's voice came from somewhere behind me. "Find him. Make it fast."

Out of sight, I collapsed behind one of the larger oak trees, willing the pain to recede, and the wound to heal while ascertaining how much blood I'd lost. Lifting my shirt, I was relieved to see my wound closing.

The faint whiff of vampires carried in the night air, emanating from the last carriage parked about twenty feet away. Flying through the woods, making a wide sweep so as not to bump into any of Archer's men, I stalked the two men guarding the carriage.

I froze, momentarily startled.

Rachel was incarcerated with two other sorry looking vampires. I snapped the neck of the first guard and threw the other high into the air. He lay still where he landed. Rachel sobbed pitifully when she saw me. The other two prisoners appeared so weak that I feared they wouldn't make it very far. One of them, a virtual child, sucked on the back of his hand with a lost look in his eyes. Rachel's fear was palpable. After ripping off her gag, I untied her. Feeling her trembling in my arms, I lifted her out.

When I turned around, I found us surrounded by Archer's men. Rachel burrowed her face into my chest. I clutched her to me.

"It's over," Archer said.

"It's over when I say it is." Remembering the verbal sparring we'd done before, the remarkable connection, the mutual respect shared for our differences as well as our similarities, I felt regret.

Out of the corner of my eye, I caught sight of Marcus standing near the overturned carriage. He'd followed me here.

Archer reached into his left coat pocket and withdrew the chess piece I'd given him, and threw the carved rook at my feet. "Was this not meant to represent that your best is yet to come?"

"That's one meaning, yes." I glanced to the right of his jacket.

Archer frowned and his hand disappeared into his right pocket, and he pulled out another black rook. I'd slipped it in, moved with a wisp-like speed just seconds before finding Rachel.

"That one means you've left your king exposed," I said.

Archer's face reddened.

His men fell, attacked so fast that to the human eye, Marcus' assault went unseen.

After securing Rachel deep within the woods, I returned to Marcus' side, and together we finished off Archer's men.

The air was stark still, the forest now quiet.

Archer appeared bewildered as leaves fluttered to the ground around him, gathering at his feet.

I picked up the black rook. "Now tell me it's over."

Archer, staring blankly at nothing, gave a slight nod, and then slumped to his knees.

LV

I GLANCED DOWN AT the two tickets for the best seats in the theatre.

The Royal Playhouse, situated on the south bank of the River Thames, had attracted the city's best playwrights. Over the last eight years, Jacob and I had enjoyed many an evening here, whiling away the hours watching the performances. Tonight, I'd arranged to meet with him but he was late, which was uncharacteristic.

I was being watched.

Although I didn't make eye contact with the young man in his twenties, staring at me from across the street, I did take in his well-educated demeanor. I strolled away from the theatre and turned down an alley, and then ascended to the roof, waiting for him to pass beneath me.

I landed behind him, and he spun round, his face full of fear, and backed up against the wall.

I pressed him against the cold brick. "Archer sent a boy to do a man's work."

"I don't know what you're talking about," he mumbled.

"I can read your mind, boy."

He squealed like a girl, and I laughed and stepped back.

He trembled. "Are you going to kill me?"

"Where's Archer?"

"Like I'd tell you." He surreptitiously gave me the answer.

"Tell him that if he isn't out of London by morning . . ."

He looked distraught and his hand disappeared inside his jacket lining, and he withdrew a small wooden cross, and waved it in my face.

"That's a lovely thirteenth century artifact." I wrapped my fingers around his throat. "Whatever they told you, it wasn't adequate. I'd reconsider this vocation if I were you."

"You're going to let me go?" His lips quivered.

I leaned into him again. "You're a pretty thing," I revealed my fangs. "I imagine if I were to turn you, you'd be even more so?"

A tell-tale patch of wetness at his groin spread down his trousers. So scared, he'd wet himself.

I laughed. "You just sucked all the fun out."

Marcus appeared out of nowhere. *"You have to go home,"* he said, his expression fraught. He glanced at the young man, and gave me a wary stare. *"It's Jacob."*

"What?"

"He has it." Marcus sounded panicked.

The ground beneath my feet became unsteady.

"Go." Marcus glanced at the boy. "I'll take care of him."

* * * *

The Black Death.

Anger struck me that Jacob had caught it, probably while tending to a patient. My most awful fear realized.

"Which room?" I asked Sunaria as I headed up the stairway.

"Ours." She grasped my arm.

I pulled away and my eyes roamed the door, dreading what I'd find on the other side. Sorrowfully, trying to keep my emotions in check, I entered.

Jacob was in a fevered sleep, lying beneath a sweat-soaked bed sheet on our four poster bed. His pallor was eerily grey. A sob left my lips as I settled beside him, trying to steady my hands.

He shuddered, caught in the terrible grip of a nightmare. Peeling back the sheet, I saw that his chest was covered with dark pustules and his lymph nodes were swollen on his neck. Lumps appeared under his armpits. He mumbled something.

I wiped away a few stray hairs from out of his eyes. My tears streamed onto him, moistening his arm. I grasped his hand, pressing it against my lips, as though the very action may save him.

Sunaria gave my shoulder a squeeze.

"How long has he been like this?" I asked her.

"He came soon after you left," she said. "Marcus was right behind you."

"Jacob was meant to meet me at the theatre." I pulled out the two theatre tickets and stared at them.

"He's been asking for you."

Resting my hand on his cheek, it burnt fiercely. "We have to cool him down."

Sunaria's stare was insistent. "At least give him some of your blood."

"I promised him."

"He's dying."

I shot her a look. "I need you to be strong for me."

She stepped back and turned away, frustrated.

A rasp escaped Jacob's lips. I pulled him to me and hugged him, rocking with him in my arms.

Turn him. Save him.

Jacob pushed himself back in a moment of lucidity.

What if there is no heaven?

"Do it." Sunaria's hushed voice willed me on.

Not ready to let him go, my teeth pierced my wrist and bright red droplets appeared. Jacob's eyes met mine.

I lowered my arm. "I've bought more books for you." I tried to comfort him, comfort me. "I'll show them to you."

The candlelight vacillated, as though with its very wavering it foreshadowed the unthinkable.

"Don't leave me," I mouthed. "I can't go on without you."

Jacob's eyelids fluttered and then closed. I clutched him to me, my sight bleary from tears, the terrible anguish unbearable. "I love you." The words barely left my lips.

Jacob stopped breathing.

Finding no air in the room, I ran from it.

* * * *

Standing on the bridge of sanity, I felt it giving beneath my feet.

A flash of lightning struck nearby and rain drenched everything in its wake, including me. Archer headed out of the house that had once served as his headquarters, and he caught sight of me.

I glared back at him full of rage.

"Don't turn me!" Archer backed away. His eyes shone with terror. "I'd rather die."

He lay in my arms on the forest ground, fading with me in his thoughts, stripping away any chance of him taking comfort in a vision of his loved ones. As I drank, all unfolded, images revealing secrets passed on from one generation to another and, as an ancient legacy dissolved, I grasped a few of them. Others slipped by, taken to the grave, like the underhanded remark Archer had made about a threat in the heart of London, which I could find no evidence of within him, and therefore didn't believe.

Surrounded by the darkest, densest woods, I cried out, my screams shaking the trees, causing the birds to scatter and the animals to burrow deeper. An eerie silence followed, as though nature itself feared to make a sound, aware that what stood in its midst was not of this earth.

Holding on, I felt myself scrambling for the last remnants of humanity, fighting the drag into the very center of the unknown. Entranced, I flew through the forest, as it transformed into an urban landscape, an array of habitation.

Just inside the front door of Belshazzar's, I took a moment to gather my thoughts. With a renewed fascination, I considered my ability to move with lightning speed. The more I resigned myself to my authentic nature, the more my supernatural adroitness increased. Having fought it, I'd stunted my potential. I welcomed in the shadows and surrendered.

I collapsed on the first step of the staircase and slid down, rolling onto my back, gazing up at the ceiling. The low-hung central chandelier, heavy with crystal prisms refracted candlelight in every direction.

But not the light that really mattered.

This place was no longer a home.

With a flash of thought, I now lingered at the top of the stairs, my hand resting on the thickly carved, rosewood banister that swept up and around to both east and west corridors. An illustrious setting, a gothic place of extraordinary character that reflected the decadent lifestyle we'd once enjoyed. Just as Sunaria had predicted, Belshazzar's could one day become a sanctuary.

The bloodhounds kept their distance, watching me from the end of the corridor.

I entered Jacob's study, desperate to hold on to memories that already threatened to fade.

Before the bridge completely gave way.

I picked up the letter opener from the desk and attacked the mahogany mantelpiece, scratching the design, gouging the fleur-de-lis, with confused thoughts that it had somehow betrayed me, betrayed Jacob. Failing to completely deface it, I withdrew.

Finding one of our discarded coffins in Belshazzar's' lower chambers, I lay down in it.

Sunaria caught me before I lowered the lid. She wavered and ran her fingertips over the edge of the casket. She appeared distracted, and searched but failed to find the right words.

I yanked at the lid, trying to shut it.

Sunaria prevented it from closing. "Orpheus." She looked fraught.

I stared blankly at the ceiling, waiting.

She climbed in beside me, softening against me, and I closed the lid on us.

Sleep edged closer, its somber promise of oblivion beckoning.

PART FOUR

LVI

Circa 1745

"DO WHAT NEEDS to be done," I demanded.

Marcus glanced at Sunaria and then back at me and then stared at his shoes, avoiding my glare. "But he's a harmless old man."

I scoffed. "Since when have you become so sensitive?"

Marcus flopped down into the seat on the other side of my desk. Turning the pages of the leather bound book, I took my time reading what Marcus had presented, our business records, and leisurely assessing the contents.

When a room remains the same, it provides the impression that time has not passed. The study was unchanged from when I'd commissioned the finishing touches—the central oak writing desk still in mint condition, the arched window overlooking London with its ever changing view, and the large fireplace framed by its imperfect mahogany mantelpiece.

They knew well enough not to question me on that.

Despite my hatred of London, I'd continued to reside within Belshazzar's. Our business affairs had taken off and kept me distracted. Commerce had been the reason Marcus had entered my private chambers tonight.

He crossed his legs. "We own every piece of land within a mile."

"But not that one," I said. "And you've done everything in your power to persuade Mr. Lewis to sell?"

"Offered triple."

I shrugged. "Then we have no choice."

Marcus looked crestfallen. "You want me to . . . ?"

"Yes." I closed the book.

"Why kill him?" he said. "He's already so old."

"From this little performance, you'd never know you were vampires." I pushed the book across the desk. "His children will sell the property to the government, or worse, the Church."

"There must be some other way."

"And risk having some religious monument encroaching," I said.

Sunaria neared Marcus' chair. "Then we buy the land from them."

"Do I have to take care of it myself?" I shook my head.

Marcus leaned back and stared up at Sunaria.

Recently, I'd noticed that I blinked less, the subtle response that broke the intensity of one's stare. With my gaze locked on Sunaria now, I saw the reaction evoked by such a stare. "Darling, how about you? Fancy a trip out?"

Sunaria turned away and Marcus studied his fingernails.

"Turns out being seduced by three whores *is* considered an affair." I found myself smiling.

"You need some fresh air." Her gaze flitted from me to Marcus.

"What do you think, Marcus?" I smiled.

He reached for the book, but I grabbed it and dragged it to the edge of the desk and it fell, landing with a thud.

"Perhaps we should discuss this another time," Marcus suggested.

"Why not invite Mr. Lewis here?" I said. "Sunaria can be very persuadable."

Marcus rose. "I should be going."

"Sit down," I snapped.

Marcus did so, rubbing his hands together. "I don't like seeing you like this."

My stare forced him to look away.

"Sunaria, pay the old man a visit."

She glared at me. Purposely, my expression blank, I replied with silence, and she headed for the door.

"I expect you back by ten." I squinted her way. "With the deeds to his house."

Sunaria's hand rested on the doorknob, her back to the room. "And if I'm not?"

"I've seen your dark side. I know what you're capable of." I reached into my jacket and withdrew my pocket watch. "And I know you like it." I flipped open the hunter-case to check the time.

She twisted the handle, slowly. "I won't do it."

"I'm not asking you to."

From Marcus' expression, he'd picked up that the quiet was due to my berating Sunaria with unspoken words.

She spun round and in a flash grabbed the book off the floor and threw it at me. My laughter followed her out.

* * * *

So engrossed in reading, I hardly noticed Sunaria standing before me with the folded parchment in her hand. She'd just returned from her visit to Mr. Lewis'.

"Put it there." I pointed to the desk.

She'd donned her favorite dress, a red silk gown. I liked her in it, the daring color a refreshing change from her usual black.

"Aren't you going to ask me what happened?" Her eyes widened.

"Did he sign it?"

"He did."

I shrugged.

She dropped the paper onto the desk and I slid it beside the others. Her lips quivered, a welcome sign that she neared breaking. Taking my time, I admired her low neckline, the curve of her bodice, the taut luster of the material, the silk clinging to her small waist, emphasizing her litheness.

Pushing back my chair, I joined Sunaria on the other side of the desk. Standing close I traced her spine, running my fingers up and down it and then nestled into her nape, kissing her tenderly.

Sunaria responded.

My left arm wrapped around her waist, my right pushed her forward, bending her over the desk. She used her hands to support herself, though I had her. Sunaria's dark locks cascaded over her bare shoulders and face.

She sighed.

I let go and grabbed her dark locks and pulled her up and toward me, whispering, "How did you get him to sign it?"

"I've always been loyal to you."

"That's not what I asked."

"I told him that another orphanage would be built on his land and that something wonderful would come of him selling his property," she said.

"And then you paid him one hundred pounds?"

Sunaria spun round. "You now own more property than any other businessman in London."

"That wasn't the sum we discussed."

"Long term, it was worth it."

"Orphanage? That'll be the fifth."

"The only good thing you've ever done," she snapped.

My mind drifted to the work houses, and their undernourished children, with dark circled, wide-eyed stares that had stayed on us as we'd trekked through, searching for Jacob. I'd promised myself that I'd come back for them. Years later, when the hours I'd spent searching for Jacob were mine again, I'd made that pledge a reality. Though those children had long grown up, we saved the ones who'd replaced them. A perpetual cycle, society's darkest side, rarely spoken of.

Perhaps this endeavor also helped me to hold onto my essential goodness. The sweetest lie that I kept telling myself.

Sunaria tried to pull away.

"Why don't you leave me?" I drew in a sharp breath.

"What?"

"All these years you've stayed, but I'm not the man I was."

"I love you."

"That tells me nothing."

"For the first time in decades, I like myself again."

"What are you talking about?" I said.

"Time changes everything. Our hearts harden as we try to cope with all that life brings. But a fresh perspective . . ."

"Fresh blood." I smirked.

Her attention shifted for a moment, then settled back on me.

"I'm not that man anymore." I sighed.

"I see such good in you."

Deep in thought, I tried to tap into those old feelings and with my outstretched hand, I traced an invisible line. "It's this close."

"What is?"

"It brushes against me, luring me."

"Orpheus?"

Staring at her, a real sense that she might be the only thing holding me back from this looming faceless entity, tempted me to walk the path of least resistance, and surrender.

"To what?" Sunaria uttered nervously, having read my thoughts.

The weather had turned. Rain pelted the tin rooftops, soaking the street sellers and their miserable customers.

Strange how alone I felt.

I turned Sunaria around and leaned her forward over the desk again. I felt her push back, a moan escaping her, as she clutched the edge of the desk tighter.

Whispering into her ear, "I lied about the whores."

She let out a deep sigh.

"I'll make it up to you." I raised the hem of her dress. "You're the only good thing about me," I confided, or perhaps I thought it.

I remembered the time she'd offered me eternity, the darkest gift.

Quietness loomed in the deserted courtyard. No sense of balance. Intoxicating . . . soothing, a woman's scent. "Do you choose life?"

My mind drifted back into the room. "*I chose you.*"

Sunaria, my supernatural maker, imperious mistress and flawless lover. The exquisite pleasure she brought was the finest escape. This one truth we shared, unraveling within timelessness itself as I promised her not with words but with affection that I'd never leave her and that I'd always love her.

* * * *

"You're the only thing holding me back." I gazed at her.

"Back from where?" she asked, her voice low.

My eyes glazed over as I considered whether to concede to its pull, seemingly full of promise. I raised my hand, declining the affection she offered.

"But you've felt that way before," she uttered.

She wasn't getting it.

I approached the window and stared out over the soaked roof tops. Drenched people below scurried along, unaware that on the very edge of their world lay ours. Sunaria joined me and peered out.

I gave a crooked smile. "I've been thinking of going to Salisbury."

Her aversion was instant. She slapped me.

A flash of pain on my left cheek, a residual stinging, and it felt good. She'd left a mark. I smiled and rubbed my jaw. "Did I say Salisbury? I meant Spain."

Sunaria let out a sob. "Don't."

I ran my fingers affectionately through her silky locks. "I've been considering your idea."

"Converting Belshazzar's into a private club?" Her eyelids flickered in response to my touch.

"We can lure in affluent businessmen and politicians."

She fell against me, wrapping her arms around my waist. "Please tell me this isn't another one of your games?"

"Marcus can run it. He's expressed an interest in managing a gentleman's club. He believes we can establish a prestigious bedrock."

Sunaria nuzzled in further. "Keep our enemies close."

"We'll be at the very center of society's advances."

Turning this place over to Marcus would be the final step in letting Jacob go, though I was not sure that such a thing was even possible. The idea of lessening the anguish was comforting, but the notion of this inner pain dissipating brought with it guilt that I was betraying him.

"We can refurbish." Sunaria tried to calm my rambling thoughts by changing the subject.

"Not this wing. It mustn't be touched."

"You're not planning on staying to see your plan through, are you?"

"I'm done with London." I pushed her away and sauntered over to the desk.

"Orpheus?" Wary of me, her tone was timid.

"We leave tomorrow." I waved her out of the room. "Tell Marcus I want to see him."

LVII

SPAIN HAD NOT FORSAKEN ME.

She greeted us with glorious, vibrant landscapes, the freshest breeze, and the friendliest Latin faces. I had to hold back my tears of relief at returning to my homeland, for fear of drawing attention.

My feelings were soured. Having long ago dreamed that I'd one day return with Jacob, I had a real sense that we'd both been robbed. My chest wrenched with grief. Sunaria squeezed my hand, aware of my anguish, and with a nod, I acknowledged my appreciation.

Marcus had argued with me when I'd told him my plans. He'd been heartbroken. I'd stood before him silent, stone-faced, waiting for him to finish beseeching me to stay. He'd eventually agreed to remain behind and continue to take care of all our business dealings. Marcus' expression that evening never wavered from memory, his words still resonated. "Promise you'll come back to me," he'd begged.

I vowed that I would, though even as I spoke those very words, I wasn't sure such a promise would ever be realized. London offered nothing but the saddest of memories, the deepest pain.

The future beckoned.

With no business dealings to keep me occupied, having left Marcus to initiate the transformation of Belshazzar's, my time became wrapped up in Sunaria and she loved the attention.

Settling into a modestly decorated, desolate château overlooking the ocean, we took our time to acclimatize. Before we ventured into the heart of the country, we wanted to get a feel for the societal changes that had unfolded since our departure. Taking our time, we gauged the mood of the people, researching how far they'd advanced with their knowledge of the undead. Catholics were known to burn the accused, whether they'd actually sinned or not. With our affected accents, we'd stand out. A foreigner with a strange inflection could alarm even the most passive of villagers. Not that the thought of a man chasing me with a burning torch made me nervous. The disruption to my evening would be more of an annoyance. Not so for Sunaria, who insisted that we sleep in coffins again for the first three weeks upon our arrival, until I persuaded her otherwise.

Discreetly, we tried to ascertain how many night walkers were in the province, those who slept by day and withdrew at sunset, eager to play all night. We wanted to keep a low profile.

After an entire night of seeking out new pleasures with Sunaria, we returned to the château. Sunaria had teased me all evening. We made it home with an hour to spare before sunrise.

I had my revenge before the fireplace in the great hall.

After wrestling with each other, each vying for control, I managed to restrain her, binding both her hands behind her with a silk sash that I'd found. She lay prone, perfectly vulnerable on the silken rug.

Starting at her ankles, I planted kisses there and then moved upward, driving her into a frenzy, her well deserved punishment, giving her no choice but to submit. I left her lying there, unsated and desperate for me to finish, her hands still secured, her movement restricted.

I withdrew from the house, strolling along the neglected pathway, hoping to free my mind while all the time imprisoning hers.

The sea air stung my nostrils and the cool air cleared my mind. Over the grassy bank, waves buffeted the golden shoreline. The swell of the sea was a continuous rhythm, inducing a soporific sensation. Foam sprayed up onto the beach and several birds flew along the horizon.

Coming home to Spain was one of my better decisions.

I liked it here.

After several minutes, I returned to the house.

Sunaria's turquoise stare begged me to resume. I wondered how long I could just stand over her, full of desire. Pleasure before the pleasure . . .

* * * *

Outside the wind howled as though jealous of the lovers inside who tumbled daringly close to the hearth. Sunaria's head fell back and her tussled locks cascaded over her flushed face.

Daylight loomed.

"You're my everything," I whispered.

The fire crackled in the hearth and an oak aroma lingered. The lapping of the ocean lulled us.

This was the longest that I'd ever held her gaze. "Do you miss London?"

"What does London have that Spain doesn't?" She sighed.

"Endless rain."

Sunaria's laughter rippled.

"How do you remember it all?" she asked.

I shrugged.

Her inquisitive stare pierced me. "Why do you refuse to talk about the past?"

"Some memories, I choose to forget."

"The pain fades," she whispered.

"What if I don't want it to?"

A soft smile curled her lips. "So you hold onto the pain and forget the cause?"

"Whatever it takes."
"To survive eternity?"
"To exist." Now I smiled.

Sunaria rose and pulled my black cloak around her shoulders. "I don't have your sense of danger." She pointed at the window and headed for the door.

Leaning up on both elbows, I glimpsed the ocean. The sun threatened to cast its colors upon it. I jumped up and dressed.

I froze.

An envelope lay on the maple table. I ripped open the seal. We'd been summoned to a local vampire's coven.

Apparently, Sunaria and I resided in the very center of a lair.

* * * *

We ignored the dubious invitation, enjoying our own company instead, preferring to visit old haunts, and finally put old ghosts to rest.

We traveled to Nuevo Portil by carriage. Years had changed the city, and the population had increased. Having ridden along this pathway several times, we now saw new home after new home. The Ocean View Manor was no longer there.

Close by, we found a well tended churchyard. It took us very little time to find Alicia's grave. Ricardo, her son, had been buried next to her. Their tombstones were the only mark of their lives, and a dragging regret for leaving her came out of nowhere. We found no grave with Miranda's name on it. I gave a smile, considering that she'd probably searched out another nightwalker and persuaded him, or her, to transform her.

Sunaria left me kneeling before Alicia's tombstone, and I tried to convey feelings that I no longer felt, honoring my sister with my fondest memories of her. Alicia would have wondered what had happened to us. I'd written to her, but had never gone through with actually sending the missives I'd penned. I hoped the rest of her life had been easier.

Shaking off the melancholy, I rejoined Sunaria. She was lounging upon an old grey mausoleum, and with her black locks dangling over the side, she appeared like a dark goddess, here to guide the newly deceased, not into heaven and not even to hell, but somewhere else, somewhere forbidden.

Leisurely, she lifted her head and raised an eyebrow.

She slid off the monument and together we strolled through the graveyard. I looked forward to sharing new luscious delights with her, an array of thrills.

She stared up at me with a glint of something indeterminable in her expression and her hand took mine. I felt her slide something onto my ring finger. I gazed down at the gold band.

"The mark of ownership." Her voice was low, sultry.

I went to respond, and then felt that familiar craving capturing me, as her words lingered. Only in silence could the sensations be best appreciated.

LVIII

1789

DECADES UNFOLD AS EASILY as ripples on a pond and just as fleeting.

Eternity, the perfect promise.

As though in a warped time zone, people and places transform. We, however, remain unaffected. Time advanced, though for us stasis was a given.

To ease my adjustment, Sunaria encouraged frequent moves to new provinces, her belief being that such would provide the subtle illusion that one had merely changed to a more progressive town, though the world evolved.

Falling back into the leisurely pace of life had been easy. Removing myself from the tediousness of residing in a frenetic city, immersing myself in solitude, rediscovering old pleasures found in literature, music, language, and art, and finally allowing what little was left of the man within to reawaken.

A personal renaissance.

Preferring coastal life, taking solace in long walks barefoot along golden sandy beaches, beneath starlit skies, I stilled that inner, unquiet voice. Evoking the delusion that I wasn't really alone, and that somehow, God might find a way to forgive me, and I him.

Even at night, midsummer's warmth lingered, and a gentle breeze carried that sweet, salty scent of the blue-green ocean.

Standing precariously close to the edge of the cliff, admiring the rocky shoreline, the crescent moon reflected sunlight off its grey-silver orb. I'd never been one for sunsets, at least that's what I told myself.

Remembering Señor Machon, my first tutor, I smiled fondly recalling his lessons, which enlightened me at such a young age, feeding me knowledge that I'd actually used. And later, my relationship with Miguel, his lessons not from books but drawn from life itself, his wisdom that only now I appreciated.

The voices in my head had almost gone. Here I'd managed to suppress many of the old inner ghosts, subdue the angst that disallowed any sense of calm, searching for self-forgiveness or even insight as a poor second. Striving to keep at arm's length that awful feeling of being overtaken by the unseen, and fearing I'd be unable to prevent it.

The hairs pricked on the back of my neck. With a quick check of my surroundings, I confirmed that I was alone.

Holding Marcus' letter, I re-read the missive: London was even more avant-garde than when I'd left, Rachel flourished, and Belshazzar's thrived.

"Come back to me," his final words written in a steady hand.

Out of the corner of my eye, I caught Sunaria approaching. "How long have you been watching me?"

She looked surprised. "I just got here."

I knew that expression. "What's wrong?"

She gave me a wary nod, uncomfortable with me being so near the edge. Her dress billowed.

"The clouds broke an hour ago." I flashed her a smile. "I love this view."

"How many times do you have to see it?" Sunaria grumbled. "I yearn for something else, something different."

I turned away. "We're not going to Madrid."

"I wasn't thinking of Madrid."

"I'm not ready to go back yet."

"But I am."

I pointed to the small fishing boat off in the distance. "Now that's a hard life."

"I can't stay here."

"What's brought this on?"

"Boredom."

"Why so desperate to return to London?"

"Cornwall."

"Seek out your ancestors?" Reluctant to bring up an old argument, I looked away.

"Why not?"

"Because there's risk and no gain."

"I'll gain joy in seeing how my descendants have fared."

"You're not going."

She pouted. "I hate this place."

"But it's so peaceful."

"Too much time to think."

"That's what I like about it, less chaos."

"I'll only be gone for a few months."

"You've made up your mind then?"

"This is important to me."

"You're being reckless." I sighed.

"Please try to understand."

"Your relatives are dead. Their ancestors are a diluted version of them."

"You think that this is living? This is stagnation. Marcus and Rachel are living the high life, mingling with society's finest, and I'm here. Sand is in my hair, under my fingernails, and in my knickers!"

I burst out laughing.

She also saw the funny side, her laughter rippling, as she snuggled into me. "The same view is driving me crazy. I need variety."

"You're the one who suggested this place." I squeezed her into me.

"Not for forever."

"My mind's getting close to some kind of resolution."

"Finding you will be easy. You'll still be here." Her lips met mine.

With the deepest kiss, I tried to persuade her to stay.

Sunaria strolled back along the cliff and then she turned and a gust of wind blew strands of hair across her face. She smiled.

I considered going with her.

Far off, where the ocean met the sky, a melding of dusky blue hues, a glorious array, bestowing a familiar, restless mood, a precursor to a night of hunting, when I'd search out new ways to amuse myself. A large seagull swooped low over my head and I ducked, losing my footing. I quickly regained my balance.

Sunaria had gone.

LIX

SUNARIA'S SCREAMS SHATTERED the silence.
 I flew out of bed, feeling abject fear, finding myself alone in the small chateau. Sunaria, now a continent away, was calling out to me. Paralyzed with terror, an awful realization hit me that she was in the utmost danger, and I was powerless to save her. Unable to get to her, I used the mind gift to relay that she must stay calm. *Escape.*
 She'd only been in Cornwall a few weeks.
 "*Stone Masters,*" her voice drifted in and out.
 They had her.
 I'd slaughtered Lord Archer along with many of his men, but the Stone Masters had reestablished.
 I'd failed her.
 Within that dark prison, I shared her misery.
 The agony unfolded as sounds, sensations, and feelings were relayed by her. I refused to leave the château, refused to abandon her. As the hours unfolded, everything unraveled. Sharing Sunaria's suffering was unbearable, but I wouldn't let her go, or let her down, staying with her in thought and trying to comfort her.
 I'd never known her so afraid. *Or me.*
 She lay blindfolded, gagged, and bound. From what she conveyed, I gathered that she was held in a dungeon.
 They bled her.
 In the process of moving locations, they lost their grip. She'd bolted and her blindfold fell. The faces of two small boys stared back at her aghast, seen also by me and imprinted into memory.
 The men overpowered her.
 Lord Archer's study. His books referencing Stonehenge. The ritual. The separating of the ashes, pouring them into the fissures of the stones.

* * * *

Madness promised the greatest escape.
 What followed when one found oneself immersed in the alternate reality of insanity, those of us who manage to hold on will never know. Pacing the house, I struck the furniture and threw it against the walls that

confined me, rousing a once dormant fury, and sending me into a diabolic frenzy. I decimated the place.

When Sunaria's screams were eventually silenced, there came a moment of relief that her suffering was over. Falling to my knees, my cries were unceasing. My maker, my lover, my beloved, was dead.

I nuzzled my nose into one of her soft gowns that she'd left behind, finding no easement from her scent.

I want her back. I want her back. I want . . .

The anger raged on and took me over. My blood lust disrupted my ability to think straight.

When I reached the edge of the cliff, I hesitated. The sheer drop was enticing. For the first time since Sunaria had given me the gold ring, I eased it off to read the words inscribed along the inside of the band, "*Orpheus, I'm yours eternal.*"

With a trembling hand, I slid the ring back on.

Far off, twinges of crystal-like orange flickered along the horizon, promising sweet relief.

The kind that's permanent.

With my back facing the cliff, I stretched out my arms, and fell . . .

LX

May 1805

I GAVE MYSELF OVER TO IT.

Inside the mausoleum, the same one that I'd been trapped in as a boy, Sunaria's resting place, I found some solace replaying my time with her, pretending she was near. I'd returned to Santiago de Compostela, hoping to remember in detail that first vision when she'd appeared to me. Holy ground, the one reason the tombs were not torn down, and as though God had taken pity on me, I remained undisturbed.

And so I slept for sixteen long years, on and off. Unconsciousness, my only respite, freed me from the harsh, glaring grief. On the rare occasion when I roused, I'd consider with fascination that I could survive without frequent feeding. It did result in exhaustion and a loss of will, but as such the drag of sleep came easier.

As society encroached, the noise outside my self-imposed prison increased. For the most part, I blocked it out, but as time and the elements wore away at the boundaries of my sacred resting ground, the time came for me to rise.

The faces of the two boys were mentally preserved, though they'd have grown in years. Still, such a lead offered me hope that if I found them, I'd find Sunaria's murderers.

I made my way to Palos.

Stopping off at a private residence, I found a change of clothes, grateful for the opportunity to freshen up. And feed.

The journey to the port provided proof of my longevity. I'd not changed like the landscapes around me, society ever enduring, ever evolving.

Upon my arrival, I arranged for my oak chest to be delivered to the largest sea-going vessel in the harbor, and placed in my private cabin.

That feeling of being watched again stirred a familiar feeling, but I shook it off.

Returning to England possessed my thoughts, and I ruminated on what I'd find. Unfinished business beckoned.

Strolling along, I was captivated by the way fashions had changed, though the people seemed the same. They still went on with their miserable lives, working and playing as though completely unaware that within them time ticked away, ever threatening to cease. With nothing in common, the reality that I was an outsider rippled through my veins.

Even at this late hour, the place was crowded, and I pushed through the horde. Thick fog lay heavy, reaching out amongst the docked ships, swirling around them.

A tall, slim figure loomed at the entrance to the pier. The man stepped out of the shadows; moonlight dancing upon his face, illuminating his features.

"Hello, Father." Jacob cocked his head.

Almost three hundred years since his death and he stood there. His complexion was pale. His translucent brown eyes held my gaze. A young face, but irises that reflected an era, evidence of his transformation, and proof that he'd not died that night in my arms.

And yet I failed to react.

"When I left the room?" I made it a question.

Jacob nodded.

This time upon our reunion, there were no open arms, no words to convey the relief I felt in seeing him.

I felt nothing.

"It's taken me all these years." He sighed. "This takes some getting used to."

I rubbed my eyes as though they needed it.

All this time, I'd grieved for the son I thought I'd lost.

"I was searching for answers," he responded to my silent ruminations.

"You took your time."

"Forgive me."

I looked away. "I didn't want this for you."

"Sunaria?"

"I told her not to go." My mind drifted.

"Father, Sunaria may not be lost to you."

"It's unlike you to be cruel." I narrowed my gaze. "How long have you been in Spain?"

"Years. But it's all relative, right?" He glanced at the boat. "You do realize the fashion in England includes the wearing of wigs."

"The women?"

"The men."

"Who started that craze?"

"Louise XIII."

"Of course," I said, "a French aristocrat."

He smiled for the first time. "Stay here with me."

The thick evening air was stifling.

"How have you been?" he asked.

"Fine, and you?"

He followed my gaze. "Don't get on that ship, Father."

A bell pierced the quiet.

"It's over," he said.

"It's the only way I'll have peace."

"Let her go."

"Never."

He looked away, breaking my stare. "What will you do?"

I smiled.

"Don't follow that path. It's an empty one." He stepped nearer. "Come with me. We can make a new life together."

With conflicting emotions, betrayal being one of them, I tried but failed to empathize with him. Sunaria had deceived me, breaking the promise that I'd kept, and I hated her for it.

Jacob sighed.

Sunaria had tried to tell me on the very evening I thought he'd passed away, as I climbed into my coffin deep within the depths of Belshazzar's.

And yet I still loved her.

"Come with me," I said.

He offered his hand to me. "Stay here."

Sunaria's ashes were buried within the pillars of Stonehenge, and I was going to retrieve her.

Retrieve all of them, every last vampire and then revive them.

"Things are never what they seem." He held my gaze. "You know that."

"I don't know who to believe anymore. Who to trust."

From the ship's deck came a last call for passengers. My life had been a series of regrets, and here now, I had to make another choice, either follow through on a promise, or come to terms with my darkest side.

"You're heading for its very center." Jacob read my thoughts.

Two last-minute passengers scurried up the ramp to board.

"Where have you been all this time?" I needed to know.

"Searching for the truth."

"Is this conversation veering off?"

"True spirituality has nothing to do with religion."

I shrugged.

"There are secrets about our kind, truths that will dazzle you." He opened his lips to say more and then stopped himself.

"Go on then, what are they?"

"Not here, not like this."

I'm dead inside.

He held out his hand to me again.

"Her face haunts me," I said, wistfully.

A lone sailor stood port side with both his hands on the wooden drawbridge, ready to pull it in.

"I'll always love you," he whispered.

The ship swayed and creaked in the dock.

"Jacob, you were my rock, you know that, don't you?" I turned back to face him.

A chilling breeze billowed my jacket.

I was alone, dazed, but strangely calm.

Strolling along the pier, heading for the *Blue Rose*, I hoped that the weather would hold, at least until I reached Cornwall.